THE
ILLUSION
KILLER

J. V. RUTZ

First paperback edition 2018
ISBN 978-1-7329385-0-2

Second paperback edition 2020
ISBN 978-1-7329385-6-4

eBook edition 2020
ISBN 978-1-7329385-7-1

Published and printed in the U.S.A.

To my mother, father, and brother, for their unwavering belief in me, to Rob, without whom this story would not be possible, to my family and friends of old and new, and to my readers "preparing for the ascent".

TABLE OF CONTENTS

PROLOGUE 9

A PRAYER IN THE DARK 12

THE DEGLIN BROTHERS 29

RETURNING FROM FIRE 40

GENTLE FIGURES 53

THE DECREE OF VALOR 77

OF GREAT DURESS 96

THE GENTLE CHILD 107

THE ROUGH CHILD 118

THE JAGGED LETTERS 138

A LESSON IN TRAUMA 150

THE KILLER MADE OF AIR.......................169

THE NIGHT OF SAFE PASSAGE................... 194

THE HILLOCK 218

DEADLY KNOWLEDGE 229

SHADES OF WRONG 242

A Deal with a Demon 255

Tears of a Sentinel 276

Roland Unwanted 294

The Path to Rebellion 306

The Assault 317

The Battle of Visitant's Forest 335

Aurascape 346

His Right Hand 360

A Beginning and an End 370

Acknowledgements 381

About the Author 382

PROLOGUE

A beginning and an end, there is one to any story. For every being, city, and nation that had ever graced creation had forged themselves a path of existence.

In the wake of this path was the concept of history, a story of sorts. Pinnacle, the Defiant City, was of exception. If every city had a tale to tell, then the ashen swathes that crept upon the verdant valley, had to be Pinnacle's ending. The Fog of War, the folk there had come to call it.

With the help of brilliant minds using powerful and desperate magic, the city stifled the spectral force's advancement, but only temporarily. For you see, like cutting off diseased fingers to save the hand, the city slowly cut itself off from the last hospitable parts of the valley as their old efforts of stemming the Fog had failed. In time there would be no hand left to heal and no world left to toil in. As if compelled by an irresistible divine fate, the valley folk embraced the Fog as an inevitable demise. For this reason, births were discouraged and sanctioned only to fill quotas of the recently deceased. The final generations of children were reared with the ghastly reminder ever-present—something that beseeched them to cope with the grim reality.

Most curiously, many of these children catered to the dead here, tending to the well-reputed corpses made presentable to the passersby from within their glass-plated caskets. A cursory glance would suggest these elaborate displays were made to hold the remains of magnificent, extinct beasts as a part of some macabre exhibition. Inside, however, one would find bodies strung with luminescent wires allowing them to evoke their former lives, be it a man of academia holding a treatise and snifter, or a patrician woman resting a lace-trimmed umbrella delicately upon her shoulder—dreadful things like that.

Donning their medic masks, the small bodies made rounds beneath the edifices carrying with them their opaque cosmetics, aspirators, and trocars. Each presentable corpse within the case was inspected; flushed tones were dappled onto cheeks and chins daily to ensure the picturesque memory of the living was well maintained. Like the Fog, time was but another enemy; another foe even a corpse could still succumb to. When they were no longer proper for public eyes, only then would they be placed with the common rabble beneath the earth.

To keep more memories of the past from fading, old stories were shared with every child reared here about the world before this divine punishment was unleashed. Yet the dreadful part of history was that the very fabric of its being was becoming its own demise: time.

Slowly, the vast written accounts of Man's humble beginnings, tribulations, and tumults that seemingly led to the advent of the Fog's scourge were distorted and twisted with each passing moment, each retelling, and by every ear listening. In Pinnacle, there were always truths and falsehoods, but isolation and fear made it difficult to distinguish the two. The city became blind to its history, solely focused on what was lurking on its threshold and the hellish creatures within.

These black swathes floating amongst the churning mists were a herald of a battle for most, a final and desperate defeat. So worried about the pending doomsday, did the people forget all but the last shreds of their heritage that survived time's scrutiny. These words were branded as an evil manifestation of the Fog's influence, the Heretic's Dictum.

Pinnacle was nearing the maw of the unknown; the end was nigh. The ever-encroaching Fog was to be the conclusion of its story. Many thought the end meant nothing more, but a few feared skeptics, branded as heretics, clung to the sliver of hope the end meant something entirely different. Their only path to a new future, it seemed, fell within the ambiguity of the Heretic's Dictum but not knowing if salvation or slaughter was to be at the path's end. It seemed their only chance for a new beginning relied upon bringing about the end.

CHAPTER ONE

A PRAYER IN THE DARK

Confinement shall be punishment inside worlds
born of deceit;
Woe unto the wayward souls that treads
within these realms;
Sundry monsters lie in wait, but the greatest
beast is Man…

- THE HERETIC'S DICTUM

A cool waft accompanied the light of another precious dawn that seeped its way through the chamber window, fluttering the curtains, and caressing a sweaty brow.

Roland Deglin, formerly of the Elder family, awoke to this gentle sensation. It was most certainly not to be mistaken that he was not a boy, but a young man, seventeen as it were. There were far too many instances that he felt compelled to correct any who failed to see it. After all, there was proof of it pinned to his wall, a diploma from the Pinnacle Academy making him an official citizen, no longer some silly schoolboy.

Each morning seemed to bring a crisp fragrance that enticed him to scoot closer to the window. The uninterrupted silence was appeasing, not just in his room, but through the entire barracks he had grown to call home. An overwhelming sense of relief added to his comfort upon the first breath he noticed he had drawn. He was still alive; doomsday hadn't arrived yet. Though the way folks prattled on, each morrow was bound to be the one where they snuff it.

Another great comfort of the morning was discovering no one was standing over him with raised eyebrows which meant no one had heard his so-called "violent dreaming". He had discovered, in embarrassing fashion, that dreaming aloud often imposed someone shaking him aggressively to awaken as if he were in danger. Though one would suppose that constantly thinking of monsters in the hills beyond would bring about that sort of thing.

Nestled near the far wall of the shadowy room was a glossy writing desk. There were no stacks of papers and nothing else to cover its smooth surface, exactly how he liked it. He had no use for candles to light the room when needed; they had a tendency lately to be difficult to procure. To compensate for this hindrance, he memorized the arrangement of his living space. It bore a striking resemblance to a jail cell than a bedroom, as it was decorated plainly with only the things the masons had left, the quarried stone surrounding him. Roland found most possessions to be a pointless commodity to collect beyond the basic needs of survival when his life could be culled any day.

"Can't take it with you," he had often reminded his visitors.

He stole out of bed and passed seventeen crude streaks carved into the wall the bedroom door had concealed when left open. With some effort, this wooden slab opened with an awful squeal that most certainly disrupted the serenity of dawn. Quickly, he glanced down one side of the hall, then the other. It was quite empty, nothing to keep the wall sconces and side tables company.

Carefully shutting his door, he crept over to his desk to sit. A tattered letter was pulled out from one of its several drawers. He began reading it greedily as if its words were meeting his eyes for the first time. Countless days had come and gone since he first discovered it, marking countless times he read it. Each morning he sat alone to study it by the waxing light of the magical pinnacle lamps outside, his ritual.

Roe, the name he preferred, felt alone. It was a letter from his brother that completely severed him of the Elder name.

Roland,

Try to remember me as your brother, not the disreputable malcontent they'll try to convince you of. No one wants to see it, the walls of Pinnacle are closing in on not just me, but the city itself. The city's honor is decaying and with it a crumbling empathy. The "Settlement of Humanity" has a way of changing people. It may be the only world we know, but it's no longer welcoming. It's time you see that tales of Pinnacle, usually end with fire, like the heretics they have a knack for finding out of thin air.

Mother and Father had made me promise to do what they couldn't, love you. I tried my hardest to stay with you, but my hatred for these people has grown unbearable. By this time, I will have crossed into the Fog to await my ultimate fate. You will never see me again. Don't ask for help to look for my body. It will not come. You are a far better person than those wretched people you share breath with. Don't let them take your share of it.

Armin

The words evoked the same question in his mind: Why would running away from Pinnacle solve anything?

There was nowhere else to live other than the woods on the fringes. Even there, Armin would surely meet the occasional hunter or axman getting their bounty for the day. There was nowhere to relocate and certainly nowhere to avoid those that dared to insult him by their mere presence. Was death that appealing?

Roe tried to understand what drove him to leave ever since finding the letter. Although he deemed it a futile task at times, he couldn't let go of any question left unanswered in his short life.

With Armin's disappearance, any potentially plausible answer simply forked its way into more questions. There had been fleeting instances where he thought Armin simply up and left, having grown tired of his little brother. The young man's brow furrowed knowing Armin had created a unique form of suicide for others weary of living.

Before, no one had ever dreamed of careening into that wretched hellscape, the Fog of War. Despite constant attempts to ignore the conversations in the streets, Roe discovered the slang of the streets called it "huffing mist", inhaling the fatal vapors within. Some tried to go so far by saying Armin was a pioneer as a morbid way of lifting the mood. Roe couldn't find it in himself to take pride in this so-called "accomplishment" of his brother's, however.

Whenever someone decided to huff mist, the state never bothered to mount a search. Bodies were never recovered and deemed forfeit to the Fog. Scholars made lame attempts to explain the rise of such occurrences recently, but many lost interest with time. The most prominent theory was that Armin, like the rest of the Elder family, was considered a malcontent, trying to disrupt the fragile peace. The other deaths that followed seemed to be chalked up as oddities that didn't seem to belong in the city.

Roe sat in silence letting the letter's words crawl into his mind and stew. Each day his understanding of why the people so disliked the Elder name grew stronger.

And why not? he mused to himself.

Pinnacle was agreeable enough. Surrounded by the mountains and a river flowing from an untainted aquifer deep within their bellies, there was nothing left of the world to know. The valley was completely reliant on this source of water to irrigate and consume. The people knew not of what rain or snow was, only read about in dusty books.

The thick ribbons from the Fog eclipsed the sun and stars of the old world—if they still existed. In their place were the white pinnacles—tall structures resembling lighthouses—that surrounded the small swathe of land left. The glow of the lamps atop the structures changed from blue, signaling the end of the night, to the vibrant yellow glow to mimic that of morning. This simulation of celestial bodies bathed the valley with colors that were missed and provided an artificial sense of time.

In fact, the very concept of time had been reborn by the watchmakers that set their pocket watches and made their clocks in accordance with the perpetual flux of colors. The advent of a new calendar was established early in Pinnacle's history from this display.

Among the city's intellectual circles, there existed certain truths regarding these supernatural structures. Firstly, was that the pinnacles' role was highly debated within the city's guilds of education. A majority of the scholars and citizens viewed them as guardians for humanity. Their presence demonstrating man's valiant attempt to buffering the malevolent mists from collapsing down on the city, allowing for more time to find a permanent solution. A brave minority viewed them as captors telling the people when to rise and sleep, and what to be afraid of. This left the cynic to argue that humanity being in control was merely a convenient delusion.

The second terrifying absolute was that each spire was slowly failing, and mathematical formulae were constantly derived and revised to determine when the doomsday might occur. Many postulated it was only a matter of a few years, or cycles, as timekeepers called them. Despite all of this, every effort was made to shore up the coffers of researchers and learned folk alike in a vain attempt to save the tatters of mankind. Sadly, there was no room within the city's infrastructure to build another perimeter of pinnacles to retreat behind.

The last part was straightforward enough: the structures served as Pinnacle's comfort and limit. No one dared to pass them. If they did, as Roe found out, they wouldn't last long. Thinking of that made Armin's decision more perplexing.

Roe shook his head slowly.

There had been a hint of contempt in his voice when he muttered, "Suicide…but why, Armin?" Feeling helpless, it had been the only thing he could say.

Torchlights flickered away in the distance. The procession's dull, indistinguishable laughter allowed the two figures to emerge from hiding. Slowly, their forms appeared, one towering over the other, to walk among the blackened shambles of what were five pyres set ablaze.

Looking up and all around, the taller one gained a better appreciation of the situation, the urgency, and the disbelief that a city could exist in this awful limbo of haze. It was a fine miracle that they could see any of it at all. The mysterious words penned on the parchment in his pocket hadn't made sense until their arrival. They were told those words made up what the city branded as the Heretic's Dictum. They were told the mission's success would hinge on its words being used as a weapon.

Time was short.

Neither one spoke at the horror in front of them. The number of victims alone told of the tumults happening within the spired city beyond. Tired of the silence, the wee figure finally spoke up.

"Who"—the boy looked up wide-eyed—"who were they?" His eyes were fixed on the woeful shapes immersed in smoke.

"Turn away, boy," the other grunted, as he looked around for any epitaph or sign of ceremony, but only found footprints and the jagged black heads of used torches. The man knew an explanation now would prove to be an extraordinary effort to explain to such a naïve mind.

"Don't see nothin'," the boy continued, walking gingerly around the debris.

"S'pose that's the point," the man coughed. He stepped closer; a cloth dampened with a pungent, spicy fragrance pressed against his nose. "They don't honor the dead this way"—he prodded the wood for a bit— "no, it's to punish dissent, little one. Those they brand as heretics."

Heretics, the man thought, *hell, could be anyone that sneezed the wrong way.*

The city wanted its citizens to forget them, not hold them to martyrdom, he had speculated. It had been years since the last time he saw a pyre set ablaze, though the man refused to admit he had still been counting the days it had been. Something suddenly welled in his mind, and he clenched his fists wishing a certain face was at the receiving end of them.

Again, he gazed at the sky and to the horizon, shaking his head in disbelief. A fine miracle, but a disgusting one at that. It resembled nothing but a dirty gray smudge stretching all around like being caught in a forest fire without flames dancing about. He knew this world was slowly dying, but by what means had still been rendered to wild theories, and no probable one nailed to the wall.

The boy's trembling eyes betrayed his seemingly calm demeanor, suggesting one of the bodies present was who they were sent to find. His fears were allayed after being shown the characteristic features of the adult form at the base of every single pillar of smoke. From the large size of the craniums alone, one could see no adolescent was among them. Though the lad was warned they couldn't dally.

Time was short.

Looking down on the lonesome city in the valley, the man spoke suddenly, "This world, *their* world is going to end one way or another. Though as loathsome as it may be, they can at least choose how they end it…with our help, that is. Problem is *that* boy we are tasked to find must be the one to make it as was decided."

"So…it's true?! But…but does it have to end all willy-nilly like that?" the boy asked rubbing his eyes reddened from the smoke.

The man remained silent for a while, but the young one knew better than to urge him on.

"Come on, Tobias!"

The boy named Tobias found himself in a solid run, frantically trying to keep up with his companion's longer strides.

As he led the child down the gentle slopes to the teaming lights creeping up before them, the mission was the only thing the man could think of. There was no room for haunted memories the pyres stoked up…at least not yet. Revenge would have to wait its turn. But he also knew better than to keep Tobias—or any child for that matter—dangling on the end of a question and tried to find the best way to answer it without instilling fear. After all, this boy was his only lifeline and companion, without him…well, he didn't want to think what would happen.

Finally finding the right words, his expression changed suddenly, as if hopeful, "Maybe it can end better, that is *if* we don't dally!"

Beckoning Tobias down a narrow alleyway sheltered by the tall buildings, the man scanned the area. As they stole closer to their arranged destination, the boy's trembled breathing became prominent with every exhale. Like small birds building a nest with the bounty of anything scrounged nearby, so did the two construct an adequate hiding place among pallets, crates, and tarps behind the commissary.

"You know what to do, right?" the man asked as they looked up at the tower standing forebodingly above them. He remembered it being called *Aura*-something; the man wanted to forget as much of the city as possible when he made his miraculous escape from it but the familiar imagery made the task quite difficult.

The boy nodded quickly and winced a bit as he slid on a burnished metallic bracelet. A small trickle of blood escaped from beneath his skin, then suddenly ceased as he brought out a detailed portrait of a woman from his satchel. He studied it for a few moments then spoke, a trace of fear in his voice.

"I-I'm ready. I can picture her in my mind. She's supposed to be in trouble…right?"

"Yes—yes. Remember, it must be convincing. Now bring her out…"

A shrill call in the distance cut the silence of the morning. It echoed for a moment and disappeared. Roe's eyebrows furrowed again when he gazed through the window to find the murky sky was still dark, but the lamps beyond were in transition, glowing more sun-like, causing brighter spectrums to cover the paved streets below. Columnar swaths of black crept over the streets, the glow seemed to crash into the steeples and chimneys of the architecture with shadows being the result of this affair. This noise matched that of a woman in distress, seemed like a nightly occurrence, another unanswered plea for help.

Once more it happened, though the scream was cut off abruptly as if from the work of a hand or a knife. The all too familiar sound caused Roe to quiver and cover his mouth in horror. Images from his childhood. Of a calloused hand striking his mother, and her squealing in a similar fashion gripped his mind as if seeing it unfold before his eyes. Looking at his pike in the corner for comfort, he fell to his knees and began to feverishly whisper over and over asking for the strength of a soldier.

Alone in the dark, he tried to summon words for a prayer to help the troubled voice lost in the hewn streets below. Though, "strength of a soldier…. strength of a soldier…" was all he could muster. Courage gripped him for but a moment as he tore himself from the floor out into the hall.

"Guard? Guard?!" he cried into the gloomy corridor. The rapid footfalls grew louder as a heavily armored man approached, a grunt being his only response.

"Did you hear that?" Roe asked, frantically. "That scream? Someone's in trouble! You must do something."

"Where'd you hear it?" he asked, clearly annoyed by the intrusion from an unsanctioned nap if his drooping eyes had anything to say in the matter.

Roe flushed terribly knowing he had not bothered to gather any information, no notion of who she was.

The guard looked at him wrapping his knuckles tightly around his pike, "So you've no idea of who, what, or *even* where? And what am I to do about it? You're more than welcome to play hero rapping on every door in town for something you know nothin' about."

He pivoted away, leaving Roe to fume back into the darkness of his room.

The guard was right. Not a single soul knew the minutiae of every occurrence in Pinnacle. What could he do to help her? What could Roe do? There was no way of rendering aid without the *where* and its dim echo seemingly placed it anywhere within the teeming streets below; Roe was rendered useless in the matter.

Knowing the moans in the night seemed to go unheeded, he understood very few souls appeared to care about the problems of others, especially with the omnipotent visage of the Fog present. Laws and rules seemed almost trivial. The truth was never so unbearable for him, not that he was left embarrassed for being wrong, but that he surrendered to the futility of the issue.

The thought of frightened victims at night disheartened him, but he had to shake the bad thoughts, hoping someone would be in a better position to find and, gods forbid, help the victim beyond. He had to focus, he had to forget the troubles outside.

To do this, he took out another piece of paper that rested with Armin's letter that read:

Roland Elder born 4-237-253
Parents: Cyrus Elder (formally executed) and
Theda Elder (formally executed)
Adopted on this, the date of 12-97-267 as the son
of Priority Augustine Eamon Deglin

This serial translated to read as the fourth hour of the two hundred and thirty-seventh day of the two hundred fifty-third cycle of the Pinnacle Calendar as his birthday, but 12-97-267, merely three cycles ago, felt like his second birth, a new life for him. A fresh start. It was a proud declaration, indeed. The city's leader, called the Priority, had it announced in the *Pinnacle Word*, the sole publication in the valley that printed only when enough scuttlebutt was known to burn through resources. He came to know the words by heart as if they were lines from his favorite writer.

A loud thumping tore him from his small internal reverie. The heavy wooden slab-of-a-door made its ghastly noise more as it opened slowly to an old delicate face appearing by candlelight. The boy stuffed the papers back into the drawer like he had been caught with contraband.

"Whelp!" she huffed, "The Priority wanted me to make sure you were up for the start of the formal week." Taking a deep breath, she let it out with such a rare enthusiasm, as if the Fog of War had existed only in the confines of a fantasy book, "Ahh, it's the start of a special week truly!"

The sweet delicate voice belonged to Ophelia, Priority Deglin's personal servant and maid of the barracks.

"Keep pushing that slab open like that and you'll be in shape to wear armor and be a brute like the captain!" Roe teased.

Even though he hated being tested on his ability to dress himself properly, Roe salvaged some joy out of it when Ophelia was the proctor. She was one of the closest people in his life, as he had known her dating back to his earliest memory of childhood. She knew his family, watched him grow up, and painfully witnessed his family's slow disintegration.

Despite his being the first of many rooms to scour and sanitize, the maid was determined to never utter a word of disdain about it. She considered it a small victory each grueling day, despite the complaint issued from her stiff back. Above anything else, her endless duties well in mind, were ensuring her hair was in an orderly bun and maintaining her practiced demeanor. Being one of the more compassionate people he had grown to meet, Roe made her an unsanctioned grandmother of sorts.

"Aye," she laughed placing a steaming platter of breakfast in front of him, "I'd put the whole lot of 'em through their paces if I wasn't stuck cleanin' up after those armored babies. I'm surprised that I don't have to feed them-"

"-or change them," Roe added throwing specks of food from his mouth. "You could drop hints."

Intrigued, she stopped in her tracks.

"Like what?"

"Just an example"— he leaned forward to whisper— "but you *could*...I don't know… misplace Berl's House of Sentinels badge somewhere in the mess of his room. He'll have to recognize how badly he keeps it knowing he can't find anything he sets down in there."

"Roland! I'm certainly not clever, nor sneaky enough to rummage through another's things to purposely and properly 'misplace' 'em just to teach 'em how to not live in filth. Seems like more work than what I'm puttin' in."

"Easy now, just an idea! I guess I can lead by example. Maybe the others will feel bad about being slobs and take after me." Roe couldn't help but grin at the unlikelihood of that ever happening.

The maid maneuvered closer to the small patch of light he sat beside as to see his exuberant face eating away. Her auburn hair was slowly losing its battle against age, now showing fewer of its original color within the gray woven spiral kept on top of her head. Small creases of a tired face were only found when she smiled. Gazing into her small, brown eyes made him wonder how such an honorable and kind-hearted woman could end up with such a miserable and unfulfilling job. It made him sad to think of it, but Roe knew she would not accept any sort of pity. All he could do was issue a helpless sigh.

More futility at work.

"Don't understand why you like to keep these like this." She walked briskly across the room to open the curtains properly tousling bits of dust into the air. "I can't see a thing in here and the dark can't make you none too productive."

"I prefer it dark"—Roe rubbed the back of his neck nervously—"I guess I feel more secure this way, makes me feel like I'm hidden from the world. Sometimes I just want to be left outside the eyes of the public. Away from it all. Them I mean."

He soon found his words tripping over themselves as he tried to defend his living arrangements. The maid constantly brought up his isolation so much that he was convinced she was beginning to lose sleep worrying about the matter. She must have heard the horrible things people had said the day he was adopted, how they were absolutely sure he was only after the power behind the Deglin name. If so, those horrible lies would certainly keep her sleep disturbed.

For Roe, fitting in was never a desire or a problem. It was constantly finding ways to maintain his elusiveness that was becoming the issue.

"The public? Huh! Whelp, you're one of the few the public *should* know."

"Not me."

"Boy"—the maid gently sat on the bed next to him— "I know this is hard to get used to, after you've been so accustomed to bein' alone out there fendin' for yourself after…well…your family n' all. Open your eyes, and you'll see most folk here are interested solely in ascendin' through the ranks, willing to do anythin' they can to make their status known to this small world with what little time they have left in it. Folk don't seem to care what befalls another. You're different…like you're on a path to somethin' great in your life."

His head drooped as if speaking to his knees. "One problem. What happens when I get to the inevitable fork in the road? Go left? Or is it right? How will I know if I make the right choice? How is anyone to know?"

She stared blankly for a moment before she smiled as if speaking from experience.

"My dear, Roland. In life, reaching the fork in the road won't matter if you lack the freedom to choose a path to begin with. It is a great tragedy to exist and yet have that wonderful burden stripped from you. But know this, so long as you still hold the power to choose for yourself, you are always headin' in the right direction. Remember that."

"It'll be hard. You've had me commit so many damn things to memory already!"

"Language," she warned, "anymore of that and you'll be helpin' me retrieve the keep's dirty unmentionables! I know 'bout them filthy words the others try and teach you. Anyway, they'll be plenty more memorizin' where that came from. You see, kids today…" That phrase was Roe's cue to tune out for a bit as a rather passionate rant was underway.

It was always intriguing for Roe to see her so willing to rant. He was never sure why, but he noticed how the old codgers especially loved to let the youth know their opinion on anything remotely related to anything. But unlike most that had fallen victim to it, Roe relished in it. On occasions, he played into their passion like a game of sorts, acting more intrigued than any normal adolescent would while seeing how long he could keep them talking. When they grew red in the face and out of breath, he knew he'd won.

He sat there at his desk grinning a bit at her when she ended with, "You'd better get goin'. Don't be late or I might get the sack!"

"Keep dreaming. Doubt the Priority will let you off that easy," he smirked.

She huffed from the entry as Roe tried to scuttle to his dresser in the still dimly lit nook when he stubbed a toe on the leg of his chair that had been displaced by the maid. His complacency in walking about a rearranged space sent Roe reeling to the floor. This was yet another reason he rarely entertained visitors.

Fingers clutched at his toes like they were bleeding. *Of all the pain,* he thought, *I'll never understand why this hurts the worst!*

After he finished picking himself up, he hobbled over to the dresser to grab the pressed uniform resting on top of it, making an attempt at looking professional. Checking for placement, flattening it against his lap, Roe delicately sewed his identity badge back on the breast, something Ophelia taught him from a punishment another time past.

Any official guard of the city possessed the Badge of Pinnacle, a necessity of the entire get-up. It designated rank as well as work detail. Guards fell under one of two branches of Pinnacle's military forces. First, there was the more benign, white-clad Pinnacle Guard, charged with more basic functions like keeping the general peace and settling disputes that would inevitably arise before they got too violent. Second, there existed the lethal, black-clad collective christened as elite soldiers of the House of Sentinels, that dealt with…more escalated issues. Men and women were allowed to join either branch of duty, but sentinels were far more disciplined, selective, and considered lifers— in it until death came to claim them. House sentinels were privileged with guarding the sacred and important locales of the valley as well.

Again, a coarse wail interrupted his preparations, louder and fainter than the first occurrence of the morn. He paused a moment listening, but quickly found his palms pressed against his ears to shutter it all out. Frustrations had mounted inside as he tried convincing himself that somebody was bound to investigate, someone was bound to hear it and help so he pressed on. As much as he hated to acknowledge it, he didn't have time to worry about someone else's problem at the moment. He still had one of his own to pick at. With his short brown hair slicked away from his brow, he grabbed his pike and closed the heavy door behind him.

There was no time for small talk or pleasantries when he came across familiar faces of the other barracks inhabitants.

Priority Deglin was waiting for his answer.

"Don't disappoint me, boy."

Roe shook his head to rid it of the dreadful memory away. The words of the past echoed in his mind as he got closer to his destination. The quick, shallow breaths he developed grew more apparent to him as he pictured the angry face that he knew he would be confronting soon.

Chapter Two

The Deglin Brothers

"Ever since I was little, Father always told me I needed to be tougher. But being tough never comes easy for me, at least before Roe became my brother. With someone like him, I feel I can learn what it means to be tough."

- Excerpt from Berl Deglin's journal

Cycles ago, Roe caught wind of a scholar from The Learner's Guild of Pinnacle who made a daring proclamation to his colleagues that rekindled the debate of the towering pinnacles' role.

It stated: "Man is a slave to the world. He is but a lowly prisoner to the mountains that tower over him, an indentured slave to the plains he toils in, and a coward to the mists that are all-encompassing."

Though the investigations that followed had been kept quiet, rumors ran rampant. The scraps of his inquiries left behind on smeared canvas clued the state on his clandestine activities and his exceedingly dangerous thoughts. These notes revealed that this man of academia had a dedication revolving around some sort of mystery many didn't observe. To him, the world had been asking him a question and he was supposed to find the answer. The world's lips were sealed to him, yet the clues manifested all around for him to piece together. The troubling question ultimately rendered him frustrated, asking himself - *What is the answer?* - as evidenced by the many times it was scrawled on the pages.

When he heard about this sensationalist, Roe could only find himself intrigued by this controversy. Though his identity remained a mystery to almost everyone, Roe felt more in common with a stranger than any friend, acquaintance, or colleague. Little did he know, how common that sentiment was to others who came across the scholar's inner machinations.

To some of these state-sanctioned heretics, the words of the Dictum and the inquiries of the mad scholar were a shared experience, or connection only they could identify with. There was an affinity to an awareness that many either had forgotten or perhaps, through generations of learned ignorance, no longer possessed the ability to see the answer to Pinnacle's problems.

However, this all-important answer was not going to help Roe's current predicament. A life-altering choice was forthcoming. Here was that annoying fork and despite Ophelia's puzzling words of encouragement, the freedom to make a choice was certainly not comforting.

He scurried down spiraling steps into the main atrium where the bright white tapestry and banners glistened from the influence of the torches and lamplight outside. Roe walked briskly across the polished flagstones under the pretense of examining a painting on the other side of the room to avoid speaking with anyone, as it was time for much-needed concentration. With considerable trepidation, he stopped and laid his hands on an end table. Realizing his legs were shaking just so, he stiffened them to cease their annoyance.

"Come on", he whispered to himself, "Roe, you just have to say 'no'. People say it all the time. All you have to do is-"

Suddenly, he gasped as a pair of hands seized his shoulders in such a quick and tight fashion, that he half-thought he must have committed a heinous crime.

"You're under arrest for loitering," the unnaturally low voice quivered. He turned to gaze at his stepbrother, Berl, being his typical slapdash self. This boy's face was peculiar in that it always seemed to hide a mischievous smile in the corners of his lips as if all his thoughts revolved around scheming yet another juvenile prank.

"Dammit, Berl, way to scare a guy deep in thought! I swear you do it on purpose."

"Course I do! You're so easy. I know you don't like it, so… naturally I do it more! Simply irresistible! Besides, I can easily sneak up on a man while in thought *or* on his guard."

Berl's unfounded boasting happened to be one of many bad tendencies developed.

"A man in thought is easy to sneak up on, nothing to brag about," Roe said coolly, trying to smooth out the wrinkles in his uniform. "And as far as I'm concerned, I've never seen you able to sneak up on someone reading a book let alone someone on their guard."

"Don't question my skill as a spy just because I caught you with your pants down."

"Yeah," Roe mumbled, "that's about the only way you can get a jump on anyone. I knew it was bound to happen today eventually, as it seems to be a part of some sick ritual of yours."

"If you know I'm going to do it, why do you set yourself up for it?"

"I hold out hope one day you'll age beyond six, but I set myself up for disappointment each day I find myself shrieking."

"What can I say? Being a child's more fun."

"So, I've been told. But you know something? I was thinking-"

"-you do that way too much-" Berl interjected with a smirk.

"-I was thinking that I must feel bad for you and let you do it"—Roe stroked his chin with intrigue— "now that I think of it, you couldn't even sneak up on me while deep in thought. You might have to try on a corpse for starters and work your way up from there, perhaps a baby when you get *real* good!"

Berl shifted his weight and looked down to his feet to gather himself.

"Boy, you sure know how to cut me down. I suspect that's all you think of locked away in that pathetic prison you call a room. Your self-pity is why no one will ever love you and why you'll die alone!"

"Yeah? Seeing your ugly mug skulking about is what actually keeps the Fog at a distance."

"You slag!"

"Shove it, you stupid chafe!"

His eyes pierced back at Berl's. They stared each other down for a few moments, but both had wavering scowls as one's lips began to break upward, while the other began shaking his head trying to deny any amusement.

"Until death, dear brother, I've got your back!" they chorused as they smacked each other on the back. This creed was more than adolescent play but rooted from a basic mutual need of survival similar to that of shelter and food—kinship, belonging. The connection they sought was laced into those words. Both had troubled upbringings—for different reasons—yet found unparalleled companionship in each other as time marched onward.

Unbeknownst to Roe, his stepbrother had developed a habit of being the last to break the handshake, not desiring to forget the euphoria of feeling wanted.

"Hey, Roe, I was just kidding about you…dying alone, you know that right?"

"Like most people, I don't take anything coming out of your mouth too seriously."

"Hey now."

"Anyway," Roe said, his voice lowered to a hush, "think we should check in with fath-I mean the Priority for our new duties?"

"Nah. He wants us to report to the commissary to see if the commodities are ready for the upcoming festivities. Nothing noble or remotely close to the risk of being valiantly decapitated, if that's what you're hoping for."

Roe was relieved about delaying his inevitable meeting with the Priority but also distraught that this humdrum task hadn't been dealt with already.

"I'm not complaining. I just think we should make things look, uh, official. Don't want the others to think we get special treatment, especially with this easy work assignment for someone like you"—Roe leaned in looking around cautiously—"a sentinel."

"Relax! Father's good about making sure we're treated the same in the eyes of the guard and the public. And if he does treat us better, well, not to worry. We always have the mean old captain to break us down after he's worked *so-o-o-o* hard to build us up into *real* guardsmen," Berl gesticulated wildly.

"S'there a problem with how I train you, Deglin?" a hardened voice asked from behind.

Roe's lips pursed, and he stopped laughing on the spot when he saw the roughened, stern face of Captain Raleigh standing behind the unsuspecting Berl. His militarized, brown-streaked gray hair coupled with his poisonous green eyes made for a formidable countenance indeed. Cycles of an arduous and brutish military life chiseled his jaw to a handsome but back-alley thuggish finish. But the crown jewel of it all was that devilishly naughty grin he showed as if waiting for someone to ridicule him just to gain the license to utterly thrash them senseless.

"N-No, sir!" Berl's voice cracked horribly causing Roe to stifle a laugh despite the tension.

"No? Funny, I could have sworn you were flailin' your scrawny arms like an idiot to your comrade here, questionin' my methods. That'd be the biggest blunder you've made to date, and I could fill the commissary to the brim with 'em. You gotta' problem? Have the stones to look me in the eye when you say it! At least then I might have a small chance of findin' some respect for a waste of food like you."

As the man stepped closer, Berl could see his scared reflection in the dark pits of the captain's eyes. His knees gave out and he collapsed to the floor continuing to listen to this particularly nasty diatribe. The captain's hands were opening and closing as if he were trying desperately to restrain himself from choking his subordinate.

"Boy," Raleigh gritted his teeth, "if it weren't for your father's orders for no extra drilling this week, I'd make you climb rope to the top of Aurascape and light a fire under your ass for a bit of encouragement!"

Upon promotion, the captain wasted no time developing a reputation of being a forbidding man who wouldn't tolerate such buffoonery. In fact, there were very few in town that even talked to him without fear of being verbally chased off. Raleigh wasn't showing the full extent of his anger, but he had Berl shaking, though many found this a simple enough feat. The Priority's son was at his mercy and begging to be spared from the public embarrassment based on the way he held up an arm to shield himself from the flecks of saliva being rained upon him.

"N-no, sir. I-I mean y-y-yes, sir!" Berl squeaked.

"I expected more from a sentinel than a walking joke like you. Watch yourself. Your father's power only gets you so far," the captain said prodding the boy's chest after he mustered enough courage to get back to his feet.

The abrupt turn he made caused the black cape on the man's back to snap at them like a serpent giving notice. He thundered through the entrance of the keep darting his head to and fro, ready to belittle the next poor soul dispensing an invite.

Berl had turned away but not fast enough to hide the rosy shade forming in his cheeks. When he finally decided to face the world once more, he saw Roe with widened eyes silently mouth the word "ouch". His stepbrother shook his head motioning toward the door the captain had stormed out of. Public humiliation was nothing new for Roe when he was with the young sentinel and learned long ago that this was something inescapable when in his presence.

By getting embarrassed by their superior officer, the day was already starting to turn typical. The churning misted ceiling of the Fog was still above them and stuck to the horizon just beyond the towering structures. The glow issuing from the pinnacle lamps tried to break through the haze but could only cast an ambiguous, but even light around the city.

Up above, Roe tilted his head up to marvel at the city banners hanging at their daring height. Trying to catch a glimpse of their sheer length way above was enough to make Roe weak in the knees as they hung from poles jutting from Aurascape—the highest pinnacle tower in the valley. There was purpose to their structure, he remembered his teachers telling him incessantly. The sheer size of it and its towering brethren beyond were built to intimidate, to issue an air of permanence and defiance or so he had remembered from his school days.

Every time he saw it, Roe had feverishly hoped its formidable height was scaring off any creatures lurking beyond in the misty hills. Below, at its base were the barracks and the Priority's chambers. Another wing was built on the opposite side which served as the jail.

The first steps the boys took out of the barracks were made on the Hardscape's immense cobblestoned sprawl. The area was a vast terraced square built upon a small escarpment that jutted above the city proper. It was large enough to house the city's amphitheater, within which many heralded events and spectacles took place. Several shops and upscale housing—Pinnacle's regency mostly—had found their way onto this sprawling platform.

The city below from where the boys stood was teeming with citizens bustling their way down the flagged stone avenues that extended off Carriage Lane, the main thoroughfare lined with vigorous trees whose bark emitted pleasant spicy scents along the banks of the river. Alongside this thoroughfare, were the well-maintained streets that led to the walled district gates. Dirt walkways entrenched with sloppy ruts were restricted toward the more undesirable locales of Pinnacle, specifically, the perimeter that gave way to the plains.

Stone spires, domed towers, and gaunt steeples from the houses, government buildings, stores, and warehouses climbed toward the murky sky. Each building's creation seemed like an attempt to pierce the heart of safety the lamps provided from above. As a young boy, Roe would gaze up at them and wonder if the people who had designed them, were trying to find ways to reach out and touch the ceiling above.

As they ambled their way down the many steps toward the squat building, among the chatter and hubbub of a waking city, Roe heard the poor squeal of an animal in distress which reminded him of why he didn't want to go to the commissary. He turned to his companion.

"Berl? You didn't hear anything awful this morning, did you?"

"Hmm…come to think of it, I heard the butcher snuff out some poor animal that made one helluva sound. I always shudder thinking about doing that kind of work. I couldn't kill something and eat it like that, especially if I had gotten to know it…probably give it a name like Lil' Bleater…Why I was-"

"No, no!" Roe waved his hands about. "I heard a woman moaning like she was in trouble."

"You think some poor gal got axed, do ya?" he grinned, giving Roe a playful nudge in the ribs.

"Fills me with such confidence knowing your job's to keep us safe."

"Hey, we've heard people in distress before. It's nothing new and Pinnacle is sort of large if you haven't bothered to look. Besides, we've got our assignment."

Roe's pace hastened to clue his stepbrother in on what he thought of this response.

Racing to catch up, Berl grabbed him by the arm pleadingly, "This city has its problems, but what's the alternative? The Fog? You think just running away into it is gonna"—Berl choked on his words knowing he accidentally trudged into territory deemed taboo: Armin's death. "Sorry, I didn't mean to bring that up."

"That was his choice, but I just can't stand to hear someone distressed like that. Same story every night. Someone crying out for help, yet no one seems to care. Look! No one else is even acting like anything happened."

"We can check it out, but it's probably nothing. You haven't heard anything since, right?"

"Right."

"Well then shut your pretty face and let the guards on patrol worry about it. We hafta go to the commissary as that is our official order. When we know everything's on the up and up, we'll go satisfy this whim of yours."

"Fine, let's hurry and get this over with," Roe huffed, shoving his hands in his pockets.

"Say, Roe?"

"What?"

"You's just a spoiled wittle brat, aren't ya?" he cooed, pinching Roe's cheek.

"Shove it."

They shared a laugh before Roe dared to ask the leader of Pinnacle's son one burning question that had been nagging him since he came to work with Berl.

"Our jobs are easy – well – certainly compared to what you *should* be doing. Do you think we earn our pay, or do you feel like we just steal from the city?"

The answer seemed obvious enough that Berl replied almost immediately, "Oh, we're a couple of dirty thieves."

Roe nodded. "Ahh, so it's not just me. I didn't want us to be deceiving ourselves."

There was a crumb of relief to know that they could agree on something for a change. Looking to start another dull day of work, he stopped before entering the commissary shrugging, "Suppose it's time for us to go steal some more. Shall we then?"

CHAPTER THREE

RETURNING FROM FIRE

"And to my only daughter, Tessa Serene Emlan, I hereby bequeath the deed to my commissary in the event of my death, untimely or otherwise. It is my hope, my strong and proud daughter will keep it from the corrupted hands of the state, if nothing else purely out of spite and out of Rufus Warrick's cold and limp hands."

- EXCERPT FROM LEOPOLD EMLAN'S
LAST WILL AND TESTAMENT

The woman standing in the doorway briskly shut the door behind her, practically slamming it. Panic had gripped her so that she found her tense arms clutching themselves across her chest. She spoke in hushed tones all the while.

"That sounds like dissent, to me, Warrick. The way you speak, you might as well ask me to fetch the wood and cook the flesh from your bones."

The old man with the spare wisp of white hair perched atop his otherwise bald head simply continued to write in his business ledger ambivalent to her concern. Regent Rufus Warrick gave a sigh of frustration—it was not to be mistaken that the numbers enclosed within the columns brought poor tidings to his business. No—far from it. He possessed a veritable monopoly manufacturing weapons that no one else could replicate.

Trauma gloves.

From the beginning of his entrepreneurial career, he struggled to vault his way above the rising tides of the common rabble, often fruitless, through dozens of cycles. From the beginning, he felt, no, *knew* everyone was against him; from his foes leveraging competition against him by undercutting their prices or secretly paying workers he had unknowingly hired to produce shoddy blades that would crumble at the first strike. The blows made against him were countless, some successful, though many were not. He thought back to their most recent attempt to drive him to the streets begging for alms; it was the day those...*things* slogged their way from the wretched Fog seeking shelter.

He smiled again, his quill dancing away beneath his chin.

Those damn fools trying to pawn the mist-suckers on me thinking their feeble minds and withered bodies would serve only to do my business in. I ought to pay my enemies as thanks for unknowingly gifting me such a windfall.

The woman interrupted again.

"Are you listening to me, Warrick? This is *serious business.*"

"Of course, it is. You are standing in my office after all," he said, gesturing to the numerous safes that surely housed most of the circulating coinage in town. The woman, however, was not pleased with his attempt at humor but listened.

"Magda, is it being heretical to question what is best for Pinnacle? I merely want to ensure that our current leader is equipped to take on the role. Don't you find it…disturbing that he was so willfully selected to rule, despite our experience?"

His eyes never left the margins as he spoke. No, he would continue to scratch at the pages laid out waiting for her response, toying with her frantic emotions at the present. Arranging this meeting was merely gauging her loyalty to the man who beat out what was rightfully his.

The woman gave her own personal decorum's proper amount of time to answer such a question, though she probably knew it immediately. Everyone among the regents understood it was a vexation of hers for anyone to blurt out a response without at least airing the perception that proper diligence had been made upon the subject. Regent Magda was of like mind with Warrick on most things: the equal disdain shown to the mist-suckers that leached on their hospitality, the eternal pursuit to the apex of power, and her disapproval of Priority Deglin. Her response reflected this. She locked the door of the office and strode over to fondle the metallic armored glove resting on a display plinth. She paid close attention to each articulation, even if some flaws were present. It was the prototype that made Warrick powerful through wealth—the trauma glove. As she did this, her movements stopped.

"You must be wondering what I have planned?"

"You can say that, but how did you know?"

"Just a natural course of the conversation, being among lawmakers you should be well-versed at anticipating rebuttals and the like."

"I see. Go on then."

"That man has been playing favorites," Warrick barked, all the while sending specks of ink across his desk. "That lickspittle son being the benefactor of such nepotism. It's misappropriation of a sentinel, I tell you! Shouldn't even sniff the uniform, let alone wear one. Folk won't like it one bit when they know their leader plays favorites. It would be only natural to see how far it extends."

Magda nodded in agreement, still rubbing her fingers in the carved sockets near the apex of the glove's index finger.

"But what help can I provide you?"

Warrick didn't have to think hard to arrive at an answer. This plan was in the making since the day the other regents spurned him for the youthful and charismatic Deglin. What better way to know the enemy than to keep a close watch on them?

"Magda, my dear…who's the boy that you speak with that guards the senate? You told me he is friends with Deglin's screw-up?"

"Yes…Ivan Fern's his name—but wait! I work with politicians daily…I know all the lies they tell and how their loyalties extend only to whose coin purse weighs the most," she said, stepping away abruptly. "This Ivan would fit in far too well with those fiends. I don't think-"

"-He's perfect. Fortune smiles kindly on us both as I happen to have the heaviest coin purse in town, excuse me the world as it were, and he's so eager to sniff it," he said, casting a wicked grin. "Fetch him for me as soon as you can, would you?"

"Of course, but can I say-"

Unfortunately, there was no time for Regent Magda to voice her concern about the task at hand. The office door rattled from someone trying to get through the lock. A brisk rapping accompanied soon after.

"What is it?" Warrick yelled through the door, not wanting to disturb the aching bones in his feet. The urgent voice on the other side of the door was muffled and difficult to register.

"Sir, it's one of the mist-suckers. She hasn't reported in."

Warrick sat up alarmed, "Which one?"

Immediately, Warrick stabbed his scrawny finger onto the ledger, resting on the name shouted at him, Little Hex the Tenth. This gray-skinned girl happened to be the one that he favored the least as she was known for this sort of breach in protocol. Cussing under his breath, Warrick tried to reason with himself the only reason he hadn't strangulated the child was that she was by far the most productive when it came to carving and setting the glyphs properly into the grooved fingertips similar to the set his colleague had been admiring.

Regent Warrick then asked the question that was burning in his mind since the meeting had started.

"Magda, I heard a rather scandalous rumor the other day that you have begun to dye your hair. Any grain of truth to it?"

This, being a vindictive ploy at diverting attention away from his own foreseeable predicaments, was a joyous hobby of his.

Clearly bothered by the question, Magda casually ran her fingers through her renewed brown plait and scoffed as she tersely left his office.

"Petty gossip from those gutter village bitches again."

The Deglin brothers cut through a wall of warm, dry air as they stepped over the planked threshold of the smoky warehouse. It being so arid here was a mere byproduct of the furious industry housed within. As they crossed into the atrium of the commissary, the sconces on the walls lit the way for the boys who were searching for their mark. The clangor of metal striking metal echoed through the foyer. Scents of cooked meats, freshly sawed wood, and crushed verbena became enticing to the nose despite their anomalous mixture. The persistent chatter and small talk made it harder for them to focus on anything. High above, beautiful adorned exotic birds and furred beasts fluttered and flapped in and out of the woven canopy above the trading floor where keepers dangled from ropes tossing anything from larvae to raw chunks of meat. Irritated bellows of restless animals from the pens outside only added to the commotion.

"Berl, I'm gonna wait outside," Roe coughed, fanning at the air to be rid of the smoke assaulting his eyes. Immediately, he was overcome with the sense of hundreds of eyes dissecting his every move and intention.

"Oh, c'mon! Our duties don't get much easier than this, enjoy it while it lasts. Besides, what did you expect from the place?"— Berl placed his hands on his hips frowning—"Well, if I were in charge, I'd be running a tighter operation."

Roe shot his companion a look of displeasure. "That is *not* fair. You know her father up and left like what Armin did! I think she's doing the best she can… given what's happened. Tessa helped manage the place during an apprenticeship back in school and hasn't stopped since." He gestured over to the enormous mound of straw trapped within a cage that appeared as though it housed a beast at one time and warned, "You might want to line the seat of your pants with some of that if she catches you criticizing her operation. Ass kickings are the only thing in the commissary that are given freely you know."

Though not completely purposeful, Berl was a natural at embarrassing the people around him, usually Roe being the most frequent victim. Sometimes it involved putting his feet on the table at dinners while regaling guests of his heroic deeds that weren't really that heroic; other times it was sitting on a proprietor's market stand while haggling in such a poor manner that a greenhorn would laugh at.

This time, he grabbed a handful of seeds from a wicker basket and shoved them into his mouth. Almost instantly, his head lurched forward and a muffled cry escaped his lips as he gagged on the seeds and his saliva. Roe wiped both from his face and saw the sentinel already on the floor with a dirt-speckled fruit resting next to his head. As people gathered, he was found swaying back and forth in pain.

With blanched cheeks, Roe subtly kicked him with his boot urging him to get up. For the second time in the short morning, Berl had embarrassed him in public.

"Deglin! Do I have to report you to the captain?" A voice emerged from the crowd. "Because I can say I won't hesitate to make your life miserable for trying to do the same to mine!"

Luckily for them, the irritated voice belonged to the person they were looking for. Tessa Emlan had a fiery look in her eyes—as per usual—and wore a smug grin on her face. Her black hair was tightly woven into a single braid that swayed on her back like a pendulum, as it always had since Roe first met her at the Pinnacle Academy many cycles ago. Her ebony skin looked as though she took diligent care of it despite the dirt and soot she stirred up during her work in the commissary.

"Berl, you try to steal from me again and I'll just have to hit you with something harder until you get the hint," she growled. Then she fixed her gaze at Roe, "I'm sorry to embarrass you like this."

"When I'm with him, I've come to accept that as a certainty," he chuckled.

"Berl, one day I might have to tell your father why you had to die by high velocity produce but keep it up and it'll happen with my trusty girl at my side!" She began swinging the sling she kept at her waist until it cut the air with a whistle.

"Come on, Tess!" Pretending as if nothing happened, the sentinel scampered to his feet. "What's a little bit of food between lovers? I hadn't had a lot to eat this morning bein's how I had to see you on this assignment."

"*Your* problem! Besides, just because we're 'courting'—as your father puts it—doesn't mean you can take, take, take! My father entrusted this place for me to run when I became old enough..."

And there it was again. A cold grip seized Roe's innards. Tessa looked down at her soiled leather apron pressed against her figure. He had noticed it the moment the straps fell from her shoulders, making the task look as though she was shedding a burden she could no longer bear. The cracking leather was being stroked delicately between her soot-coated fingers. Her eyes fell upon it, garnering far too much attention than a timeworn apron would normally warrant. Clearly, from the fraying edges, its ties were knotted through innumerable amounts since inheriting the daunting task of running the outfit from her father.

"Grown attached to that thing, have you?" Roe had carelessly joked a time back when he found himself to be rather humorous. This proved to be a phase that he quickly dropped soon after. "You hold it like it were your blankey, Tess."

"Shove it, Roe!" she snapped at once. He could vividly remember the glossy sheen of tears rippling over her eyes. The onslaught did not stop.

"This was my father's you insensitive dunce! I'd expect someone in your shoes would understand how stupid little things like this start to feel like precious gold when you desperately cling on to someone you'd die to have back. Someone you'd almost feel like you could kill for. I could think of a fair few that would do while we're on the subject."

It had frightened him to see this side of her, to see what Pinnacle was doing to her to make her speak in such a manner. They had taken him from her and Tampson. Just as they stole his mother from him. But why? Was compassion that dangerous?

"From where I stand, Armin's letter could look like a bunch of ink scribbled on the backside of used stationary, but to you I can see they must make you feel like you can still hear him, see him desperately enough to keep it the way that you do." She gestured to the leather bunched up in her hands, "This is my goodbye letter."

The flagstones were smattered with even more teardrops as Roe had been beset with a sickly feel over how stupid he had been. In time, she grew to regain trust in him, but only after seeing his contrition unfold in front of her as throngs of people gawked at the commotion, at the tears on the floor. Then she opened up more, to allow him inside the wound she could never manage to heal. She explained all this as Roe's head hung low.

Donning it conjured —like it was a sort of unconscious response—the unbidden memories of her brother holding her on the floor in the parlor of their old house had surfaced. She understood the grief Roe must have felt knowing she would never see her parents again.

There wasn't a time when its rough texture forced her to hiss at some point in the day to herself, "My parents? Branded heretics? For what? Thinking? Breathing? Might as well set the whole damn valley to flame."

To see her now, still holding it close, wearing that loathsome heart-rending smile, Roe felt the same as if it happened all over again. It was the all too familiar dreadful punch of ice-cold embarrassment plunging into his gut and cascading into his flimsy legs. How desperately he wanted to rush over and embrace her as nothing more than to show his presence and how he would never allow her to feel alone so long as he drew breath. But here in the hurried commissary where she practically spent every waking hour? Or in the temporary privacy of her flat hoping Berl wouldn't burst through the door at any moment? But really when did Pinnacle or the Fog of War provide proper time to expose one's vulnerability? Even so, the last thing he wanted was to ever hurt someone like that, even if it meant withholding his good intentions that had the potential to backfire.

She drew a deep breath, seeming to acknowledge the feeling of annoyance she had been harboring, and continued to the here and now.

"Why are you here anyway? I'm busy if you can't tell already. Everyone's placing orders and I'm having a hard time finding the labor to fill them *and* ensuring we don't starve ourselves in the process!"

"Sorry, we just wanted to make sure that the commissary had the Priority's orders," Roe squeaked knowing Miss Emlan was not in the mood for any answer he could give her.

She drew a hand to her mouth.

"My goodness! What a daunting task he's asked of you two. Can't imagine how hard a decision it was for him to throw his two best guards into such a dangerous mission. Tell me something,"—she smacked the back of Roe's head— "when did you two get demoted?"

"Ask your *lover* over there! I wanted to do what most consider as *real* work, but somehow this is more important. Since we are here…are you ready for this week?"

Acting as calmly as she could, the young proprietor drew in yet another a slow, calming breath, "I always make sure that we're prepared for the Night of Safe Passage. It's only the biggest event our defiant city can put together. Five nights of rowdy and elaborate celebration of life and distractor of death.

"It's these nights that can make a common beggar feel wanted and appreciated. A night the poor grayclan can use the hope they carry to find their way to a new home beyond. Everyone knows they aren't welcome here. A shame really." The tension in her voice picked up once more. "That's completely beside the point! I'm insulted that you have to check in on me!"

"Yeah, I suppose our work is done now that the shopkeeper here is about ready to throw us out." Berl nudged his companion, who rolled his eyes growing more suspicious of the validity of this visit. Was this just another excuse Berl made to visit his sweetheart?

"Tessa, can I count on you to be at my father's dinner tonight? It'll be a while before I can get some time with you. You're expected tonight as well," he said turning to Roe.

"I look forward to it…for the potential business and associations, of course," Tessa nodded, having corrected herself.

"That it?" Berl threw his hands in the air.

She slowly walked toward him and cooed, "I suppose you can be my… very distant third reason to come."

As if addressing the entire commissary, he laughed, "HA! Did you hear that? I used to be—what—fourth or fifth in her life. Now I'm THIRD behind back-breaking work and strangers! I'm moving up the ladder one rung at a time folks!"

With his attention drawn away from them momentarily, Roe realized they weren't paying any attention to him when he turned back to speak about taking his leave. Unfortunately, he found them hard at work kissing and doing their best to make him feel even more uncomfortable—he was sure of it—so he walked away.

Behind him, Roe could hear people shouting their leers at the couple, but they weren't listening. When their lips locked, their brains shut off, as Roe inferred. The area he found himself in was something he was unfamiliar with, so he used that as a reason to leave and explore, but at that moment, an uneasy feeling crept over him. The farther he was from his friends, he experienced the sensation someone was watching him, or perhaps worse, following him.

He surveyed the stacks of crates.

When he saw nothing to verify his suspicions, he kept walking—lighter this time—to hear any pursuer. Frustrations mounted when he heard "Roland" being whispered and yet saw no one. The whispering grew louder as he neared the rear of the large trading floor where the crates were kept. He waited for the voice to give him more direction, but he no longer needed any.

For a moment in the back of the room, Roe could see her, a woman's face looking down at her feet. She sat in a white frock wringing her hands as if she were in agony. Her head was covered with a hood and her long golden hair was draped over her face. She motioned for him to come closer. And so, he took cautious steps forward. She wanted to say something but seemed to struggle to summon forth the words.

Roe looked away. He couldn't bear to see her, to see anyone like that. The sight caused him to immediately recall the same fear he experienced when he heard the poor woman in distress earlier. When he mustered the courage to look again, she vanished. Instead of sitting on the bench in front of him, she reappeared at the door clear on the other side of the warehouse. The darkness of the hood covered all but her mouth. A trail of tears seeped down to her quivering lips.

Slowly, she lowered her hood as she began to leave. At that moment, Roe was struck down with shock. It was a familiar face, a familiar sorrow that caused him to shake. Every sound around him turned hollow and the world around him ceased to be. It seemed as though time itself had arrested. He tried with all his being to step forward. She shook her head slowly.

Roe disobeyed.

She stepped back and managed to whisper, "Roland…there still is agony abound. A mother has lost her child. I know you wish to help others, here is your chance. In Visitant's Forest, death stalks her there. You will begin there."

They stared at each other for a moment longer. He had just enough time to see her dull eyes before she vanished among the walking patrons. Once again, the woman he recognized abruptly vanished from his life. Again, she left without saying goodbye. The familiar face, that familiar sorrow belonged to that of his mother, a woman many remembered to have burned on a pyre many cycles ago.

Chapter Four

Gentle Figures

"As this is a guide meant to be catered toward all levels of knowledge, the *Imbecilic Guide* must therefore assume that you are in fact an imbecile for liability purposes and until further reading dictates otherwise. As such, one must first understand the long whip-like appendage is the tail, the end with the sharp teeth is the mouth. Refrain from sticking appendages in their lest it be gnawed off!"

- Excerpt from Bellows at Dawn:
The Imbecilic Guide to Blazebeast Training

Roe felt he had withdrawn to the safety of his bed and drifted to sleep. He had dreamt all of it, or so he thought. His figure had been transfixed to focus solely on the vacant doorway for a considerable time now, because only persistent, confused echoes of his name brought him back to the reality of the present. Tessa and Berl stood flanking him, but their amorous kissing had long since stopped. The whole scene slowly returned back to the familiar for him, where exactly he was and what he was supposed to be doing.

"If you can't live without us, you will fail," he whispered to no one in particular.

Those words were from his father, Cyrus, who habitually told him that each night before he tried to sleep. Roe would express his love to him and his mother, but his father would brush his affection off with that remark. His mother, Theda, was different. She'd always secretly follow the cruel remark—outside of earshot—with something different. Instead of more cruelty, she would provide a warm, secretive kiss on the cheek and whisper gently, "You can never fail if you have love."

Naturally, Roe had preferred her saying goodnight when sleep was calling. Regardless of what his intentions were, Cyrus would try to quell her attempts of showing her sons any compassion. He was convinced her mother's melancholy reclusiveness changed because of the man, becoming reserved and empty as the days passed until their untimely deaths. As such, Roe no longer associated himself with his birth name, Elder, as it would be a way of acknowledging his father in a positive light. He inherited it from him and the name clung to him like some sort of hideous birth defect.

Each day was a personal challenge to distance himself from his former identity to the small world. Despite feeling hatred toward him, Roe desperately tried to scrap together any semblance that his father did indeed love him, or at least tried to.

As far back as he could recall, Cyrus always made each day a learning experience by showing his boys some new form of cruelty the world had to offer. Everything was a lesson to be learned. Within each tragedy lay an explanation, each hardship presented a test to pass. Getting lost in the Visitant's Forest as a child made him learn how callous the man was capable of being.

It was a day Roe let his curiosity allow him to wander off from a home where no one was paying attention to him. Following a gentle hum emitted from a nearby pinnacle lamp, he reached the edge of the forest near the mountains. For him, it was fun to explore at first until he began to recognize he had no mother to comfort him. Quickly, he became cold and frightened.

Everything the boy saw became an enemy to him, brittle branches that made snaps in the darkness or coarse bushes that would scrape at his skin. He can remember crying "I'm sorry!" to the forest repetitively, as if it had the capacity for clemency, asking for forgiveness toward his trespassing, but it wasn't the forest that spared him that day.

It took the efforts of a search party of Pinnacle Guard, to find him. And when he was brought home, Roe didn't receive a hug, a kiss, or even an expectant beating from Cyrus. Instead, his father barraged him with questions about the experience.

"Where did you go? If you walked out there, surely you could have found your way back?! Did you not pay attention?"

"Was there edible vegetation?"

"Did you at least hide, or just sit out there in the open like a half-wit?!"

The overly critical questions made the boy feel like his actions were another failure to Cyrus and another subject snared into his experiments of existence. His father must have thought the truest measurement of successful fatherhood was to rely on the experiences Roe encountered. How he reacted to hardship, and what, if anything he learned from those experiences.

These striking recalls of his father nearly made Roe forget that he had just seen his mother return from the grave. A ghost it seemed. He couldn't touch it because he couldn't go near it. He couldn't go near it because it wouldn't allow him to. Suddenly, a clammy hand uncannily resembling a chicken's foot clasped his arm as another fouler voice barged in his head.

"Excuse me! You're on duty, right? A guard? I need help and if you can't give that to me do not waste my time!"

A glance to his left revealed the puffy, wrinkled eyes and scrawny beak-like nose of an old man looking flustered and inpatient. The thin wisps of white hair on his nearly bald scalp gave more the appearance of a bad hairpiece than his own locks. He was a regent based on the heavy maroon robes he wore. Very elegant and made of precious materials, a garment like that didn't deserve to be wrapped around someone as unpleasant and wretched as he.

"And what exactly is your problem?! Deaf? A bit slow?" he snapped.

Roe chirped back with a dressed-up malaise that he was on duty and ready to help, but in his mind added on, "...*you ungrateful old toad.*"

"You haven't seen a little mist-sucker around, have you? She was supposed to be reporting for work. Her house clan hasn't seen her. I was sure they've been keeping her home with some feigned illness. If my quarter is lacking because I can't get my workers to do their job, I won't be in good standing to be the next Priority. My name will suffer! Her absence has me worried."

"Worried for the girl or your namesake?" Tessa snapped, stepping up to flank Roe. "Don't bother answering. Amidst the sniveling selfish complaints of it, I already know."

"How dare you! I will not stand such talk! Who are you? Anybody even worth knowing?"

"I happen to be the proprietor of this enormous building you're standing in, the *same* one that procures the goods that supplies your precious celebrations, those exclusionary parties, and boring sit-downs. I…am…the lifeblood of your social life!"

Berl found himself having to hold her back at the shoulders to keep her at bay.

"Tessa," Berl whispered tersely, "this is Regent Warrick. Regent Warrick!" It didn't appear Warrick had paid any attention as he sauntered forward sizing her up and down like he had found himself a new adversary.

"Ahh yes, Leopold Emlan's only daughter. I expected you to act a bit more… mature. Shame what happened to him, but one can't be too cautious when it comes to sedition now can we?" He paused for a moment; his hardboiled countenance softened suddenly. "Now see here, I can't afford to face such attrition from my workshop. I do have a business to care for. I figured a fellow entrepreneur like you could understand, Tessa."

"Miss Emlan to you, but what does it matter? I am sure when you leave this place you will forget it all the same," she hissed.

"Tess,"—Berl leaned into her ear— "you don't need to make more enemies now."

She backed away allowing Roe to take over.

"What's her name?"

"Little Hex…the Tenth" replied Warrick.

"What kind of a name is that?" Berl roared with laughter. "Surely, they can do better naming their own, sir."

"Of course, it's not our kind's name, half-wit. We won't allow it. They aren't like us. It would be grossly inappropriate to give them a name that is more suitable for a citizen of Pinnacle. They are of a filthy breed."

"But why Little Hex the Tenth?" Roe asked. "How did she come about the name? I suppose I have never known one to have asked them."

"We give their parents a pre-approved list of names to give their offspring upon birth. Such names encourage them to foster… certain identities and proclivities. They're labeled for what jobs they have shown to be adept at, or in special cases, jobs we *need* them to be adept at.

"Though we are starting to run out of jobs they can perform for us, so we have been relegated to add numbers at the ends of the duplicates. She happens to be the tenth Little Hex. They haven't shown any objection, and rightfully so. When we found them, they had no sense of being at all, no recollection of who they were," he said, rubbing his scrawny fingers through the sparse silver threads of hair.

"Don't worry, sir. I'm sure we can find her. There's been nothing too exciting in this little world of ours for quite a while," Berl said.

"Yes, well, aside from that grim ever-present gray visage closing in on us! By the way, my name is not 'Sir'. I'm Regent Rufus Warrick! If you weren't so damned ignorant, you'd know better." The very site of Berl seemed to rekindle the old man's fiery expression he struggled to suppress.

With one problem loaded onto someone else, the old man rubbed Roe's head like a child and smiled as he walked briskly out the door muttering something about Magda's progression.

"So, shall we?" Berl asked.

"I suppose your father's errand can wait 'til we get back. Seems he won't be complaining too much if he knows why we're late." Roe smiled. "Tess, see you later then?"

"You know where to find me." She smiled walking back to the glutted trading floor.

"So, where do we start?" Berl asked. "Little Hex could be just about anywhere. Should we try their enclave?"

Roe was genuinely puzzled. Perhaps he was wrong, but he was sure the enclave would be the last place she would be. Just as he was about to change his mind, he saw the empty bench beyond and thought about his mother and her instructions. He was certain the girl couldn't be tangled up in this predicament with her—the prospect was simply preposterous.

"Berl...I think we should try Visitant's Forest."

"What? Why?"

"Just a guess. I mean for a little girl, human or grayclan, I think the forest would be an ideal place to exercise an imagination. I got lost there once."

Berl turned to him eagerly, "Really? When?"

"It was before I knew you. I was trying to escape the house. Long story."

His reasoning had validity to it, as he did get lost there, but now he had regrets about telling Berl that much. He was bound to pry and beg for more though Roe was steadfast in hiding the experience back in the warehouse. Any normal person would dismiss it and suggest he was crazy. It wasted less time using a little sound logic to convince his friend, rather than attempting a drawn-out explanation.

Berl shrugged.

"Can't argue with that. But I'm not walking out there like you were dumb enough to. We need fresh legs..."

An uncomfortable silence hung in the air.

Priority Augustine Deglin apparently had his suspicions; the question he asked was inappropriate, but eventually, this sort of issue would be aired in a manner much more…openly. This way, he might find a way to deal with his problem inconspicuously, at least that is what the captain thought. True, the matter must have started off as a fleeting thought planted into Deglin's subconscious many cycles back, but over time, and with close observation, this seed soon gave life to an obsession. Their numerous conversations proved as much.

The Priority feigned a cough, secretly prodding his confidant to summon a response before some other duty of state could arise and take precedent. It was a typical ploy he had come to expect like a predictable tell an armed opponent would give just before a swing of his sword.

Captain Raleigh perched a leg over the armrest of his chair and brought the rim of a small glassware cup to his lips. The man pacing across from him looked more of a guilt-ridden banker awaiting the moment his unscrupulous deeds of client funds would be uncovered than the firm and confident leader his citizens knew him to be. This was a trap, Raleigh thought as he rolled the question around in his mind, breaking it down, allowing his emotions and reasoning to digest it into simpler parts.

Is Berl a liability to Deglin's leadership?

Through decades of cycles, the captain had made it his personal mission to derive an abrasive aesthetic about him so that people would refrain from asking these types of horrid questions where no pleasant answer could exist. The sheer rotten nature of this world didn't help nurture a Raleigh who was patient and understanding either. His eyes narrowed as he gazed at the fire licking against the stone hearth in the handsome-looking study.

Which road would he take? Take the high road and answer tactfully lacing the response to conform with what Deglin would want to hear? Or would he seek umbrage and permit his cold and painful version of the truth, allowing his personal disdain for Berl Deglin to burst forth? There had never been room for a third method for Captain Raleigh. It only allowed room for more fickle thoughts. The predicament filled him with a festering annoyance. The free drinks could only quell the feeling for so long.

Had Priority Deglin asked a question comparing Berl and Roe—that would be easier. Had it been a more carnal question regarding which alleyway fetched the best streetwalker—why, his subordinates would supply detailed descriptions of their favorite locales. But this…

"Captain, speak to me! There are no secrets between us, you know that! This is strictly off the record," Deglin pleaded, pacing the study somewhat faster.

Raleigh knew what this was about. The other regents were making a play at power—grasping at any low-hanging fruit they could, unfortunately, there might be fine harvests from the Deglin family tree judging from this clandestine meeting. If not, the rampant swipes taken at the numerous shortcomings of Berl could be their only weapon. There might be nothing for him to fear. The captain had no love for the regency…just more people to try and press him under their thumbs.

Anything I can do to undermine that old harlot's brood Warrick.

His thoughts fragmented by the sudden snap of fingers near his ear. The captain knew the beleaguered man had to know the truth. Raleigh clenched his teeth at once and flung himself into the foray of discomfort ahead.

"Yes," he said slamming the cup down on the side table, "in every way you feared." The Priority heaved a sigh of anguish but continued to pace soaking in each horrible piece of truth. "You had been toeing the line when you demanded his entrance in the Settlement Guard without so much as a field test to see his abilities, but *you really* pissed on it when you insisted his rightful place was actually in the House of Sentinels. You exposed him, nothin' I can do. He is who he is."

"That would be acceptable if his father was some meager lout working the fields," Priority Deglin grimaced.

After yet another moment of disquiet, the captain could see the Priority thinking to himself in what looked to be a hopeless manner, that his reality shouldn't be the way it is. There existed inklings that Berl couldn't be his own flesh and blood—clearly, he had not inherited any of his father's qualities. Everyone in town thought it. Looking back, however, the captain knew this was impossible, and dwelling in the bored gossiping of malcontents would not address the problem at the forefront. Saffron Deglin had to be the poor dunce's mother.

Still, Deglin rubbed through his smoothly combed hair thoroughly, pacing about contemplating under his breath.

"What if we demoted him?" the man snapped his fingers.

Raleigh frowned.

"Would only show you were too stubborn to see the obvious. The regents would pounce on you like rabid animals. Any idiot could see that, respectfully."

Priority Deglin poured more contents into the captain's glass, making his company a bit more enticing for him to stay.

"There is a charm hidden in your abrasive veracity. So let us test its confines further."

"Lay it on me," Raleigh grunted, suddenly wishing he had been born an imbecile when it came to conversation-making.

"What of Roland, captain?"

The captain's response was much brisker this time around.

"What of him? He's capable...survived the dark alleys and has a composure I haven't seen in a while,"—he shot out of his chair to brandish a brawny finger at the man—"don't tell him I said that!"

At least this candor gave Deglin something to smile about.

"If Roland is capable, Captain, then it seems he would be capable in helping his brother out. You know, show him how it's done."

"Not as a Settlement Guard he won't," the captain warned.

"Of course, of course."

Deglin turned away. The grandfather clock in the parlor tolled several times and it gave him one more reason to be concerned. "The boys aren't back yet from their patrol at the commissary."

Like bad habituations, the captain's thoughts lingered toward the worst outcome—at least when Berl was involved.

Deglin turned around to thank him for his confidence and company and explained he needed a sudden departure. Before he did, Raleigh stopped him at the threshold with a sort of trap of his own.

"There are no secrets between us, correct?"

"Correct? What is it, Captain?"

"The day you adopted Roe...why'd you do it? You might find the answer reveals what you make of Berl's capabilities...or lack thereof," he said beating the Priority out the door. "C'mon, you knew all along. Or did you just need someone to relieve you of this fine hooch?"

Deglin turned to find the glass decanter had vanished with him.

It wasn't hard for anyone to see that Tessa and Tampson were related, looks were enough but it was how they both carried themselves in eerily similar ways. Both were the type that looked ready for any challenge given to them, manning a look of quiet bravado. The Emlan family was renowned for their confident, yet stoic mannerisms. It was such an admirable trait in Roe's eyes. He resigned himself knowing Tampson was both taller, stronger, and certainly more capable of a fighter. In fact, he possessed more of what little the Deglin boys had amassed together. He even had a rugged beard that caused Roe to stroke his bare face with great envy.

When the elder Emlan saw their approach, he took a pause from his work and greeted them with what felt like an incapacitating military grip of a handshake.

"Hey, soldiers!"

"Geez! With that grip, how in the hell are you *not* in the House?" Berl squealed as he painfully waved his hand in the air. "You'd be one of the most qualified. Strength, intelligence, and a grip to make someone nearly piss themselves!"

"Hmph! I tend the pens and keep these beasts behind me under control. Not too many others can, nor want to. Besides, wouldn't you want the caretaker of your beloved Haddy to be all of those things you mentioned?"

"Wouldn't want her to wet herself every time she saw you but point taken."

Haddy was the animal that became Berl's pride and joy, the blazebeast inherited from his father after his ascension. Each guard, upon being initiated, was issued one for use on the job and for leisure, a fringe benefit. In almost all occurrences, the beasts had to be shared with at least one other guard. The fact that Berl and Roe were exempt was one of the rare exceptions.

Chief belonged to Roe and of course, was busy bellowing at the other creatures in his pen. He began to bump bodies and nip at the haunches of the others causing more dust to waft about. Roe could only smile at the spurts of dirt gushing through the thatched walls. The blazebeasts were anxious; the animals weren't meant to be caged. They needed a break from captivity, which is what the boys had intended to do…for two lucky beasts anyway.

Tampson caught Roe admiring the creatures.

"I assume that's why you're here?"

"Duty calls, the forest awaits, and we'd prefer to get there before a week passes by," Roe grinned.

"What? Don't want to walk out there and taken in another gloomy-misted doomsday ceiling?"

"Not really, no. I've seen the same old clouded mess every day since birth. It hasn't changed," Berl gestured above their heads.

Tampson smiled, patting Chief on the side. "I'm messing with you, kid. Anyway, they're ready. Give them a nice run. Makes them easier to handle when you get 'em back to me!"

Although riding Chief wasn't a daily occurrence, it was the high point of his day when Roe did get the chance. Even though he had owned the creature for a couple of cycles, each time he rode Chief felt like the first. It was the excitement, the anticipation, the thrill of riding such a fast and powerful creature. It sent shivers down his spine just thinking about the breeze kicked up in his face and hearing the turf underneath him torn by powerful claws.

The pen's latch lifted just enough to allow a thundering blur of bronze to explode from the pen. It lunged for Roe, who became winded, the brunt force pinning him against the ground. He gasped for air and discovered he was staring into Chief's yellow eyes. The small black pupils were trembling in place. His head cocked side to side, thoroughly sniffing under Roe's chin, around his neck, finally finishing at his now disheveled hair. The creature's warm breath brushed through his scalp like a bellows. Chief sent a deep chur at his owner as if to say, "I know you."

Chief's long serpentine tail could be heard whipping back and forth eagerly through the air, sometimes against the thatched wall or thwacking a wondering scaly snout that got too close. The hollow spikes creeping down his spine from his head were all intact except for a few in the middle, which were filed down for the rider to fit—a practice made easier the moment they hatch. The crown of the head held a taut membranous fan and Chief's was fanning up and down quickly at first but slowed down as he calmed. His bulky head sat on a short thick neck, with a color that had gradually faded from a dark brown hue back to a light bronze as the blood was shunted back to his core.

The boy patted the side where his ribs were and felt the warm scales against his skin. Rubbing the creature brought Roe a sense of security and confidence he wished he had always possessed.

Chief's four-clawed feet were tousling dirt in the air, then a vicious tongue bath followed. Roe was slathered with saliva as the slippery organ soaked his face and neck. It was disgusting for him not knowing the potential gambit of revolting things he allowed in his maw, but Roe knew a foul tongue on his face was better than razored teeth in his throat.

With Chief included, Roe could count all his friends on one hand and still have fingers to spare. Although he knew the animal couldn't possibly understand the many facets and subtleties of human emotion, Roe counted Chief as a good friend regardless.

"Same greeting, different day!" Tampson chuckled as helped the rider up. Roe looked over to find Berl had already mounted and quickly jumped up into the bare space just behind the head holding onto one of Chief's spikes for stability.

"I guess were off ah-." Roe was too slow in saying goodbye and ended up being abducted by Chief's impatience. The beasts wouldn't wait for pleasantries. They craved the dirt and grass being torn up beneath their feet.

Grayclan and humans alike were finding themselves in the path of these thundering animals while the two riders had to give them warning by any means the mere seconds would provide. They galloped through the great stone arch, which served as the entrance to Pinnacle. Up above, a replica of Aurascape jutted skyward, with the real one towering in the distance directly behind it.

Roe looked over and saw that Berl was trying to tell him something. His mouth was moving, but the words were indistinguishable. Instead, he made a gesture common to the House of Sentinels that meant to hurry.

A palm patted Chief twice on his side as the rider shouted, "Let's go, Chief!"

He tightened his grip around the spike knowing what was coming. Suddenly, Chief ducked his head down in front of his body and the membranous fan collapsed flush against the skull. The novice rider would think they've already reached full speed at this point, but the blazebeast would bolt like a gale instead, surprising the rider right before they tasted dirt.

The boys continued their dash through the plains that issued from the grayclan's enclave outside the city gate through crop fields and scattered houses. The farther they moved from the city, the scarcer the signs of settlement life became. In the distance, the forest crept over the horizon, and beyond that was the Fog, which looked more animated as swathes of the forest had succumbed to it over time. The mist churned within every now and then as something stirred.

Both beasts started to slow ahead of the tree line until finally, the two came to a small coppice. Upon dismounting, the riders tasked themselves with securing Chief and Haddy to at least a couple of brawny trees before the creatures could be lured away by some enticing scent filling their nostrils. In the past, Roe learned a hard lesson, as he thought one tree would be sufficient enough to keep Chief in place. An errant bird pecking at the animal had encouraged Chief to uproot it, causing him to tear through the market district of Pinnacle leaving branches and angry merchants in the wake. Not going to happen this time.

Berl sighed.

"Well, we're here. Now let's go look for this girl that may not even be inside of a forest… neither of us is familiar with…the very same one you got lost in."

"Less yacking, more tracking."

They tried their best to tread lightly in the forest as it grew denser and the ability for danger to hide was becoming easier. From the tree line, it was all uphill, gradually rising to meet the foothills that were the borderlands of the decaying pinnacles.

Roe placed a finger up to his mouth signaling Berl. They walked slowly on the rocks and avoided the shriveled leaves and twigs that broke easily. After a while, they skulked further in, stopped, and lowered to a squatting position.

His companion looked over, about a dozen paces to his right behind a bush, shaking his head. Roe did the same and joined up with him.

"Well, if anyone is here, they're being awfully quiet. I hope this wasn't a mistake."

"It just means she's somewhere else."

"Even so, if she's in trouble, we've taken too much time looking for her. We need to know if she's here, but I want to be subtle in case of danger."

Looking around dumbfounded, Berl asked, "Wait, you want to know if she's here or not? Why didn't you day so?"

Roe nodded heatedly.

"Hmm…let's call her name. What a novel idea!" Berl cupped his hands over his mouth yelling, "Little Hex! Is the tenth Little Hex in existence somewhere in this giant forest?"

Roe ducked behind a bush, alarmed at the broken silence. "Shhhh!" he whispered, "I…wanted…to…be…subtle!"

"C'mon, Roe! You want to find her, don't you? We scoped out a patch of territory and look how long it took. If she came in here, she could have done it on her own. Take a chance."

"Fine, but I'm not calling her that, sounds awful."

Roe still didn't like to call aloud like that, but he assumed no one lived out here. Any building would have been required to be documented with Pinnacle, as were all settlements and housing. A growing fear of the Fog's presence outside their backdoor also seemed to be a detriment to building in the remote wilderness.

As he cupped his hands to his mouth, he ceased his lips and caught a humming creeping on the breeze toward them. The sweet melody and chants that accompanied it were simple and chipper. Roe motioned to Berl to follow as he walked gently toward its source.

It grew stronger and the voice matched the sound of a little girl, but they were treading closer to a portion of the forest where the ominous opaque had encroached. They stopped and looked all around but couldn't see anybody. All the while, the sweet ditty became clearer:

With the breeze in the trees where the grayclan play;
follow me, worry-free, we can stay all day.
Where the clouds touch the trees and embrace the ground;
walk the mist, hand in hand, please don't make a sound.
Farther in, come and see, there's a big surprise;
gentle figures walk past you with big bright eyes!

At that moment, a rumbling of branches, and a shower of leaves scattered between the two of them followed by a carefree giggle. The flurry of leaves and the impending branches bound to follow made Roe's arms bolt to protect his head. Before he could raise them any higher, he saw the girl falling and instinctively clutched her to his chest. It was her. The one they had desperately searched for was indeed in the forest and was now in Roe's arms.

She looked at him as though he was a bit creepy in appearance. Little did he know it was because he was staring at her for an uncomfortably long time.

"I'm sorry. I just… thought I would comment on how…*shiny* your eyes are," he said.

"Oh"—she gave a giddy squeal— "You're too nice, really. I've never had a human say such a nice thing to me. A compliment is…strange to hear. 'Shiny eyes', I like the sound of it. I like the colors your kind has too," she replied.

"Brown, green, blue?" Berl said incredulously.

"Yeah. Your eyes have much more color to them, so exciting! For us, girls have gold, boys have gray. Boring," she huffed. "Good catch by the way."

Her wide, staring eyes, along with her lanky slender face had not been hindered by the shade of the dense forest; in fact, she seemed to shimmer gently. Her ears were flat against her head and – yes, the gray skin was there but gritty like sandpaper. Roe noticed that his hands had some abrasions on the palms where her rough, gritty skin had slid against.

Although she looked alien and peculiar to him, he warmed up quickly to how innocent she was and how similar they were. Same child-like spontaneity, the same sense of adventure that Roe himself could claim.

"You…can let me go now if you want," she said nervously.

Roe got embarrassed and lowered his arms quickly, nearly dropping her, but she landed on her feet without concern. When she touched the ground, she began to laugh and clap which was followed by brushing off the foliage that stuck to her long snowy hair.

As Little Hex settled down, Roe had a chance to look at her as a whole. As she stood, her head met them at their chins, but she acted so much younger than her appearance had suggested.

"Well, you found me!" she said.

"You were hiding from us?" Roe asked.

"Well…no. But you found me, didn't you?"

"Yeah, suppose we did. You know, you seem pretty brave traveling out here all by yourself."

"Yeah, not like Roe at all! When he was younger, he practically-" Berl ceased speaking from an elbow to his gut.

Walking away from them, she stretched out her fingertips to touch the different surfaces of the forest, the smooth bark on some trees and the jagged ridges on others.

"I wasn't here by myself. Besides, this forest is friendly enough," she said walking closer toward the mist.

"How ya figure?" Berl asked incredulously.

"Well, we're not dead yet," she shouted over her shoulder.

In their pursuit of her, Roe asked his companion if he knew of grayclan development. Apparently, they had dozed through that lesson during their Academy days. He thought if they aged like humans then she looked to be no younger than they were. Their curiosity was distracting them, however, as Little Hex was straying farther from them. Roe tried asking her more questions, any for that matter, in hopes that she would linger. She stopped for a minute when he made a noise of inquiry. When a bewildered Roe failed to ask anything, she shrugged.

Slowly, the girl disappeared as the forest became hazier; her clothes and skin began to blend in with the mist.

"We've come to bring you back to the city. Your regent's worried!" Roe shouted.

"Can't say I blame him. Never told him I left."

The boys' pace hastened as she began to disappear into the murk.

"Little Hex, Little Hex the Tenth we need to go, now!" Berl demanded.

"Ugh, don't call me that! I hate that name. Besides, that's not..." she paused.

"What?" Roe asked.

"Nothin'. If you're going to follow me, use your *toes*!" The boys shot each other a confused look. She continued annoyed, "Tip-toe! I want to see something before we go back. Who knows when I'll be here again?"

Before he could respond, Roe realized the sudden danger they found themselves in. He was so caught up in the splendor of meeting this peculiar girl, that their environment had made a sharp change. Ghostly tendrils slipped their way passed and began to consume them.

"Oh no," Roe whispered.

The trees in the area grew sparser and had long since lost their leaves. Their long and gnarled branches stretched up in an unnatural way like being twisted from supernatural winds. Some of the branches that sprawled away from the trunk, appeared nearly three times as long. The grass had long since left the ground that looked more like scorched earth flaking ash upward beneath their feet. The Fog grew thick and emitted an almost imperceptibly small hiss. Immediately, Roe began to search the area wondering if he would see Armin's body.

Berl found himself clinging to Roe's shoulder from behind. Visibility deteriorated as far as only a dozen paces or so of sight. The terrain leveled out as they reached the apex of the rolling hills where the mist grew stronger. They staggered beneath a half-decayed tower. Judging by the shoddy masonry and crumbling plaster, it was a faultier prototype from generations before that had failed the city, causing the citizens to retreat inward to the valley. They quickly sought refuge within it after spotting an immense hulking outline that appeared and disappeared just as suddenly.

"Berl - you breathing funny?" Roe asked, gulping the air like a liquid.

"Yeah, it's hard…to breathe this…stuff…feels like…air's heavy, I…gotta work to suck any…in…can't stand anymore."

"If something…happens…get her out. Don't wait…for me…go…okay?"

He nodded. They tried not to talk much knowing it made catching their breath harder. Looking at the girl's fluid movements and calm demeanor, the shrouds didn't appear to affect her breathing much.

Roe saw her silhouette crouching on all four slender limbs, crawling like an animal, creeping ever so slightly. Occasionally she stopped to giggle and then hummed her melody again softly in opposition to the ominous hiss of their purgatory.

Was she truly courageous? Or simply still young enough to bear contempt for fear. Little Hex's pursuers were left trembling in her wake. Without her, they couldn't go back home, though, with a glance over his shoulder at the emptiness, Roe could no longer tell where home even was.

Every noise from the forest, the chirping, the rustling of leaves, and the crunch of twigs under their feet were gone. It was deathly calm, and everything was still except the gentle hissing trickling in their ears and the echoes of a girl humming a haunting tone. The boys mimicked her movements, but it was Roe that started crawling quicker trying to mask the noise. Whatever monsters or horrors crept nearby, he wanted to keep them undisturbed, but the sounds grew, nonetheless. There were gurgled breaths in the echoing distance. A shudder from behind.

Again, Roe's thoughts immediately returned to the letter in his room. All the while, he couldn't shake the image of Armin's body lying in the mist somewhere alone. He became misty-eyed at the thought, but he came back to his senses knowing he was in the same predicament.

With a few more careful steps the girl was within reach at last. Roe collapsed next to her, shoulder to shoulder. They perched over a small ledge looking down into a cloudy basin. Although he had found her, he groaned realizing Berl had now vanished.

Turning to the girl he whispered a plea for them to turn back.

"No," she hissed, "I need to see something. If you're afraid, leave. I'll go back in a while, I promise." She waved her hand at him, shooing him away like he was a pest. With her chin on the ground, she was shifting her eyes down the slope.

"I can't find Berl!" Roe was nearly shouting clearly angry now.

"If you wanna see him again, you should probably keep quiet. Who knows what bad things are out here?"

"In a place like this, I can only imagine," he coughed. His eyes quickly scanned for any sign of life.

"There!" she said. "I see something. Its him!"

Roe saw a figure in black, standing in the distance behind them. Berl had been wearing his black sentinel uniform. It certainly didn't blend as well as Roe's white Settlement Guard outfit did.

"He's just standing there. He doesn't see us, Roe."

"Let's go."

Little Hex seemed to register his concern as she obeyed this time. Drawing closer, Roe began to whisper out to his friend. The black silhouette began moving away.

"Berl? Berl?! It's us." But it was no use, as he walked inward and was overtaken by the mist. Roe's heart sunk at the sight. He lost him again.

No! How am I going to explain this to his father?

Another problem was that he had no idea how to get the girl out of the Fog. Everything looked the same. They were trapped in a sightless gray.

"Let's try and find our way out, maybe he was smart and high-tailed it out of here," Roe said. "Let's retrace our steps."

A rustling from the rocks and soil behind them made Roe grab his pike. Whatever it was, it knew where they were. It came closer; rattling metal was heard against the ground.

"R-Roe? That you?" Berl's reddened face slowly crept into view, and he was still gasping.

"Berl, follow my voice."

The metal buckle from his bootstrap had come undone and was dragging against the ground.

"Didn't you hear us?" Roe asked bewildered. "We were calling you just a minute ago."

"No. I fell…behind. Crawling…made my…bootstrap unfasten. The thing is useless. I couldn't stop…otherwise I'd lose you two," he said, struggling to catch his breath.

"Oooh"—the girl turned giddy hopping up and down—"maybe *that* was the gentle figure! That's what I've been looking for."

"What *gentle* figure?" Berl asked.

"From the rhyme I learned. I was singing it when you found me. You know…*Gentle figures walk past with big bright eyes!*"

The boys looked at one another, startled. Roe felt his guts twist at the horror.

She continued, "I was told this is where they will come find you. I wanted to be the first person to meet one!"

"Well, I think you just did, so let's go before we see it again," Roe said with haste.

They staggered back from the ledge and saw the path in the earth carved by Berl. Long ruts bore into the soil like an injured animal dragging a broken leg. Roe let out a sigh and could hear a rattled breath below the ledge. The three peeked and spotted another figure walking among the sparse trees. It was slumped over, staggering about. Crouching down, it was sifting through the dirt with bloody fingers.

"Aaaaaah!"

The eerie calm of limbo shattered when Little Hex screamed. Without warning, another creature jutted its head from below the ledge and grabbed for her. Berl whipped off his fours and kicked it in the head sending it flying in an awful manner below. Another whirled around and glowered, making a horrific shriek that caused the mist to ripple like a wave. He couldn't tell exactly what it looked like, but Roe could make out its big bright eyes from the rhyme, which gave him no comfort; because it was certainly not gentle, and it was careening toward them with gnashing claws.

It was giving chase and wasn't alone.

Chapter Five

The Decree of Valor

"And whosoever performing an act of selflessness in the face of great peril and risk may be requisitioned into service of the Pinnacle armed forces by the acting Priority."

- Article Number 75, Section 1, Clause 4:
Decree of Valor

Everything stirred. The trees shuddered and swayed to the creatures' cries like stocks of wheat in a torrent of wind. The one drawn to Roe was hurdling with such a murderous fervor that it reached the rim of the ledge in no time. Roe grabbed Little Hex and hurled her backward, his pike jutting outward.

Frantically looking for a retreat, Roe could tell only where they came from by looking for the topsoil they had disrupted earlier. He looked behind long enough to see those shrieks hurdle the ledge with ease, another tried to head them off and flank. With each step they took, the safety of the forest was drawing closer. Not by the sight of foliage or healthy boughs, but by sounds and smells. But unaware of where anything was, Roe was merely guided by wild hunches when it came to direction. The rattled breathing grew heavier and faster. He was jerking the girl's arm so hard he worried the impetus would dislodge her shoulder, but she kept running.

"I can't make it!" she screamed. "I'm gonna die!"

A black figure lunged out. The second shriek. Roe dived forward taking in a mouth full of soot and could see Little Hex fly over him. Berl paused to turn around realizing what had happened, disobeying Roe's command to flee.

The shriek landed over them and whipped around lashing out with its gangly arms. Roe jabbed back at it attempting to match the creature's intensity. Standing his ground, Berl flanked his comrade ready to fend off the other still in pursuit, though this wouldn't last long. Roe's legs began to quiver, and his lungs began to burn and writhe. Berl wasn't fairing any better as he was bracing himself on one leg trying to spin around in all directions to protect them.

The creature jerked toward the noise Roe made from the shuffling of his feet against the loose earth. Its shrouded head sunk toward the ground, he shifted to the left and it shifted with him.

It swung with its left arm and Roe dodged, piercing through its arm with the point of his staff. Both hands were clinging to the spear lodged in the flesh. Suddenly, his mouth rattled, and a pain radiated to the back of his head. He nearly fell to the ground with the girl rendered defenseless. With one arm still pushing the spear, Roe yelled and braced his legs into the pike. The spearhead broke off in the creature leaving Roe with the useless shaft. It backed off as the gaping wound began to spew forth sludge-colored fumes that wafted up like a smoldering campfire.

"Berl! Switch!" Roe gasped.

He rotated making a half-turn toward Berl's left side behind Little Hex. Berl in turn executed a tight pirouette to fill the spot almost as soon Roe had left it. It was a maneuver Roe never thought him capable of.

"It's hurt!" Roe cried. "Just fend it off! Lower your spear a bit, I need it close! Drop when I tell you!"

"What are you going to do?"

"Just do it!"

Roe marched toward the pursuing shriek's direction. He started to bang the shaft on the ground and shuffled his feet making as much noise as he could. The mist began to churn ahead; the shriek burst through the curtain of fog forcing him to backpedal. The hair on his neck stood and his eyes widened at its unnerving approach.

When it was within range, Roe retreated and bumped into Little Hex where he fell to the ground shielding her. The sentinel had been signaled.

Roe's body felt the rush of air from the creature's force as it leaped over them and crashed into the injured beast ahead. They whimpered in place, stunned. The intruders used these precious few seconds to continue their course toward the distant chirping and scent of fertile soil.

"Berl, get her out. I'll hold 'em off!"

"I'm not leaving."

"It does her no good if we both die. Just go! Give me your pike. You still have your blade!"

With a frown, Berl turned to him and tossed the pike to him midstride. Within seconds their forms were swallowed up and Roe was left alone, though the mist started to dissipate, his line of sight had improved. Here the trees were showing life, but he began to wretch as his throat spasmed, and wet coughs followed. He felt his airway tighten, his throat feeling raw and damp. Panic soon gripped him, until he finally collapsed at the base of a large tree where the mist was not as thick.

He feverishly tried to wave it off to clear some breathable air. Slowly, he inhaled and the burning in his throat had ceased for a moment. The two pursuers stopped in the silence. Their exaggerated breaths were loud and brisk.

When he heard Berl's echoed voice announce they cleared the mist, Roe knew he had to act. Gathering a breath, he stood and urged his legs to defy their limits, knowing the denser trees gave him a better shot at evasion.

A sudden grip sunk into the flesh of his shoulder as he used his last bit of strength to dive for the descent of the hill he had climbed. Claws dug punched through the leather and it wrapped itself around the young man. Everything after that was a blur, as he saw only distorted blurs and heard only scattered noises the moment he collapsed from its weight.

Roe screamed as he hit a tree and tumbled with the two beasts swarming around him causing his body to go limp. Sharp twigs and thistles scraped against his skin and a gradual pain in his arm radiated inward. His pursuers didn't fare much better if the pained ethereal grunts they made were any indication. Audible thuds and cries from them continued as the branches pummeled them down the steep slope.

It seemed as if it was a never-ending fall to doom. The world was spinning in the darkness of his sealed eyes as he lay at the base of the foothill coughing. Upon opening them, Roe nearly forgot why he was staring at a canopy of trees rather than the masoned ceiling of his room. He thought he was dreaming, still in bed. But those thoughts betrayed him as a small gritty hand caressed his face, and he startled upon finding the girl staring at him with her vibrant and concerned eyes.

Shouting over to Berl, he asked, "Are you okay?"

Among the noise of rattling leaves, he heard the fast tempo: *tha-thump...tha-thump.* Berl was beating his chest with his palm. An old sentinel gesture. A heartbeat. Still alive.

"Are we out?" Roe closed his eyes when his head met the ground once more.

"Yes, thanks to you. And to you," Delphine said turning to Berl.

"Couldn't go back to the city without you…" Roe said gingerly. Then shifting his head to his comrade added, "Looks like you weren't completely skiving off Raleigh's instructions after all."

"See here. I-"

A groan in the dense vegetation alarmed them as the bushes came to life, two battered black figures arising from them. Their ragged black clothes barely clung to their skin, both possessed large, vacant eyes that were stained red on the fringes. The shrieks tried to step toward the threesome but began to choke and retch in the foreign atmosphere. Their bodies began to emit the same black smoke that the injured one had produced until their bodies were enveloped with the black stuff and disintegrated like the ashes from a scorched-out tree.

"Little Hex, did you get to see your kindly critters up close and personal?" Berl asked, with a languid air.

"Oh, it's *gentle figures*. And they didn't appear too kindly to me," she said looking confused. Then she gave pause.

"I need to tell you something. Little Hex…is the settlement name I was given. It was assigned to me by your Regent Warrick."

"We know. He told us when he reported you lost," Berl said.

"He didn't tell you my true name is Delphine… my birth name. But please, no one can know! No one!"

"Why? What difference does it make?" Berl asked.

Roe could plainly see his companion's patience with the girl had already reached its limitation. He never had a soft spot for the Visitants, grayclan, as normal folk called them. Was that from spending so much time around the regents and his father, he wondered.

She began to glare at Berl. "If you're meant to know, then you will!"

"Oh-ho-ho! Then why tell us anything at all?" he asked, crossing his arms.

"You saved my life. If I hid something to someone I owe a debt to, like my savior, it's dishonest and ungrateful. It is a greater shame to be viewed as ungrateful rather than exposing our secrets. Even my house clan would understand that"—she shook a fist at Berl—"but don't think you'll ever know why we hide it!"

Clearly, there was a palpable undercurrent of friction between the two. A fight was inevitable, but Roe was in no hurry to break it up. He was far too busy nursing a shoulder that was throbbing and a jaw that had stiffened up. Again, he closed his eyes in search of solace. His intentions were to rest, but the bickering between Delphine and Berl was wearing his patience paper-thin.

"WOULD YOU TWO KINDLY SHUT UP?! We need to get home. If you wish to rip each other's heads off, by all means, do it then."

"What's the hurry? Don't you like the forest?" she asked.

"I love the forest, but you're still missing as far as Warrick's concerned. Plus, I'm not exactly feeling great," he winced, pointing to his reddened jaw.

They both nodded as Berl said, "C'mon let's get you up hero."

Still hidden in the steep shadows of their new nook on the outskirts of Pinnacle, Tobias was heaving with a fit of tears. His companion's face was hidden, turned away from the solitary lamp glow of the cellar.

Between the sobs, they could hear the noises of a raucous city nearby. He was amazed to find that the hatch within the crumbled hearth had not been discovered. What luck. True, his childhood home was no more having been razed to the ground, a night whose memories were still raw and fresh. At least the dirty and cramped cellar was intact.

Despite its underwhelming appearance, the dusty, dank space, remarkably, was the proud headquarters of a movement that sought to uncover the deeply suspected state secrets of Pinnacle's leadership. Upon its discovery that horrible night, the captives were simply locked inside and burned alive or suffocated. The story seemed to vary depending on who told it. But it was a perfect trap.

Why go to the trouble of fetching the wood for a heretic's pyre when their headquarters would suffice? He had mused to himself the moment he saw the charred foundations once more.

Someone close must have snitched but after so long it proved pointless to dwell on who, it wouldn't change a lick.

Though his mother was not an official member of this movement, her presence in a kitchen —that doubled as her home— was enough to brand her one as well. The only solace he could claim was that he hadn't been unfortunate to be there to witness any of it. Of course, had he managed to make that fateful meeting, his story would have ceased cycles ago and the mission would be nullified. And speaking of the mission...

He turned back to the sobs of the curly-haired boy hidden in the corner. Amidst the noise and numerous insults, the man heard the most egregious thing he could hear: his own name.

"Do not *ever* call me that while we are in this valley, d'ya understand me?"

The boy tore his bracelet off his angrily red wrist and flung it inside his small travel bag, "C-can I c-call y-you the Ugly One, to match not only your attitude but your face t-too?"

The man tried to stifle a smile at this clever jab, wondering how such a sweet boy managed such a cruel remark. It must have been from the harsh streets' tutelage, him being an orphan. Bound to pick up that sort of thing hanging around all manners of filth in the world. Perhaps it was a ruse and he didn't know his young comrade as well as he thought.

"Call me a harlot's brood, Tobias—anything—if it means you will remember not to call me that particular one, not now anyway," he came to sit down next to the boy who began to draw nonsensically into the earth with his finger. "You did well, Tobes. I suspect he heard the scream and the act in the commissary was brilliant."

"It was my first manifestation outside of training," he said feebly.

"And a damn fine one!"

As the Ugly One brought the lamp closer to the boy, he could see he was a sickly, pale color. Tobias fell sideways against the earthy wall and into the arms of his companion.

Looking at the parasitic bracelet, the man sat holding the small boy with one arm while attempting to fish out a small vial from his larger satchel.

Spent too much blood, poor thing. Wretched bracelet'll kill 'em if he uses it for much longer, he thought.

With the cork popped off in his teeth, the Ugly One brought the bitter-smelling lip of the bottle to the tiny mouth who lamely tried resisting.

"Lemme be," he whispered lamely.

"What is it with you brats…you enjoy making manifestations with those damned leeches drinking your blood 'til you're at the cusp of death—no problem! But you can't choke down a mouthful of this tonic to restore you so you can do it more?"

The only thing to satisfy these little magicians was through acts of blackmail it seemed. Tobias had been quick to imbibe the mouthfuls of the swill when it meant his bracelet being snapped into pieces. Within a few minutes, he began to sit up only to give another scowl of betrayal on his face.

"I only did it to save you, little one. I don't like to see you like that,"—he scooted closer to cup the boy's chin with his fingers—"I can't afford to lose you, understand?"

Tobias nodded holding the bracelet firmly against his chest.

What a wondrous and equally dangerous bit of magic that is, the Ugly One thought to himself. A puncture…a bit of blood… the right glyph as the catalyst and the vivid imagination of a child to conjure a material form. Ingenious and yet despicable to use children like this. The man coughed from the stale air and began to feel that his namesake was spot-on. He was using the child as an instrument, but for what? The mission? Or something more personal?

It seemed like the only thing in the world—what was left of it anyway—was the boy in his arms. To ensure no more harm came to him, he had to prod the boy, always placing him under duress. The gravity of his circumstances must never be forgotten. That cruel reality was necessary to ensure the boy's survival.

The Ugly One looked at the smeared missive in his pocket which only bore a few ambiguous sentences for Tobias' benefit regarding the mission. The real grit was committed to his memory. If they were caught, at least they wouldn't be easily implicated for what they were attempting.

"Tobias," he said to the figured huddled in on himself, "what's our next step? Do you remember the plan?"

But he didn't respond. The boy was fast asleep.

"Alright. I'll give you a bit more time," he replied, taking a curious sniff of the foul-smelling tonic before taking a rapturous spit to the ground.

As Roe emerged from the tree line, Chief was found vigorously scratching the bark off his captor tree so hard it had nearly uprooted. It was obvious the animals were itching to move again. Unfortunately for Chief, his rider had to disappoint him, for he was in no condition to cling on to his back dashing carelessly about the plains home. The beast made his displeasure known with a few low-pitched murmurs. Berl offered to ride ahead to give everyone the news and to dispatch a healer for Roe, who didn't argue with the proposition. Delphine squeezed behind him while they rode at a crawling pace. The gate to Pinnacle was in sight when she finally spoke up.

"How are you feeling, Roe?"

"Hmm? Oh, I think my jaw's better since I can still talk, but my shoulder still hurts from that stupid shriek."

"I saw that! You and the—shriek, what you called it—came out of nowhere! It was really scary knowing they could pursue us beyond the mist like that."

"Agreed," He sighed worriedly about his next choice of words. "Do you mind if I ask you a question?"

"Depends on the question."

"You don't seem to be in a big hurry to go home. Am I wrong?" He gripped the spine in front of him hard, wondering if the question was too bold.

"I had to leave. The forest was a place that I could get away from people, a place where I could just sit in the treetops and forget. I enjoy the silence. I can think."

Roe chuckled as he began to appreciate the girl's need for solitude.

"You sound a lot like me, except I hide out in my room. The forest seems much nicer."

She, in turn, made a sound of approval. During the slow trip to the city, he learned that she was just a little bit younger than him but carried herself in ways a cursory glance would suggest she would be much younger. Berl nearly turned sixteen. Tessa and Roe counted seventeen cycles, seventeen Night celebrations that have passed by. Each cycle ended on the Night of Safe Passage when the lamps grew dim and weak due to the Fog's persistent advancement against their barriers. Delphine's parents told her she had lived for sixteen cycles.

By that time, they had passed under the gate near the enclave. It was close to evening, and the Visitants were being relieved from work. Roe could see many of them stopped to look at their approach. They weren't alone, as Berl was waiting alongside his father, both flanked by several regents and their retinue. Priority Deglin himself was smiling with his palms tucked away behind his back.

Tampson stepped up to meet Chief and rode him back to his pen. Roe gave his ride a good pat on the side, who unleashed a bellow in return. As they rode past, the beast trainer gave a rather hard whack on the back.

"I'll assume that means good job," Roe grimaced.

The two Visitants that set themselves apart from the group caressed Delphine's long snowy hair. It was her mother, who knelt to kiss her daughter and caress her face. Then she looked up to Delphine's hero with the same golden eyes as her daughter. Her hair was braided in tight patterned braids and nearly swept the ground with each step. As she stood up, she offered her hand to Roe and bowed her head. He awkwardly grabbed it and shook it gingerly not knowing what proper grayclan protocol was.

"My eternal thanks to you, sir. My daughter's intrepid nature gets the best of her. She lets her bold soul do the thinking for her," she said gracefully.

"It happens to the best of us," Roe said shyly.

The hulking figure that stepped forward, grabbed his hand and tugged Roe so close to him he could smell his bitter breath. The gray man who must have been her father was smiling fiendishly and finally released his grip before stepping aside.

The Priority, who had been eagerly standing by, gestured for Roe to come close. Normally, this was a welcome site until now. Roe never wanted his stepfather to be dissatisfied with him, being the closest thing to an ideal father figure left for him. After all, the man uplifted him from the streets. How could he disappoint him like that? How could he refuse his recommendation that Roe become a sentinel?

Deglin embraced his two sons gleefully. "There are *my* boys! I just knew you would come through."

That embrace always felt good for Roe, although he could never admit it to anyone. Many in Pinnacle cruelly reminded him that he *truly* wasn't Deglin's own, but Roe discovered the man was great at making him forget this painful truth. The Priority took it upon himself to care for the boy and provide him with many luxuries and advantages most would never have the opportunity to experience. Roe was so grateful for what the Deglin family had done, that he adopted their surname. It was his greatest fear that Roe would—knowingly or otherwise—do something that would make Deglin regret the adoption.

"Thank you, sir," Roe said as if addressing his superior officer.

"What have I told you? My workers call me 'sir', not my sons." Deglin smiled.

Roe knew that. He knew the proper name was "Father" or "Dad", but Roe still felt this simply didn't do him justice. "Sir" was a word of respect in its very meaning. People still had the capacity to hate their fathers as was Roe's reasoning.

"Sorry... Father."

Augustine Eamon Deglin was not new to his appointment of the city's Priority, it had been nearly twelve cycles. The other regents elected him, with majority, from his former position as chairman of the Learner's Guild. City records would indicate he was the youngest ever elected to serve, and his tenure would last until his death or if the regents viewed him as unworthy and voted to oust him.

Notwithstanding, if the lineage proved to be as capable, the regents were given the power to allow the heir to continue rule, which had yet to happen. A new leader was always voted in from within the regents to discourage nepotism, but none had ever been...ousted.

Staring at an uneasy Berl, who was slowly backing away from the congratulatory rabble, Roe couldn't help but wonder if he was staring at the Priority's demise. Warrick could be seen whispering something furiously into Regent Magda's ear—something seditious no doubt. Could it be he found out about the boys' commissary detail?

The Priority knelt to meet Delphine's gaze, who was standing behind her mother and spoke, "I am so pleased you weren't harmed, my dear. I trust you had an enjoyable time in the forest?"

She nodded slowly.

"I rarely have a chance to tread out there. Next time you go for a trip like that, you will have to bring me back something special! Would you do that for me?"

"Yes," she whispered.

There was nothing but bewilderment flooding Roe's mind. Delphine didn't seem like herself. She was cowering, whereas a few moments ago, she was willing to stand face to face with a shriek in the Fog. What did she have to fear? The Priority wasn't angry, and if he was, he didn't show it. Her regent was right next to him and this had Roe convinced it was because of Warrick's presence. He was looking rather furious, noted by the vein bulging on the side of his head.

"But, sir," piped up Warrick, "she ran off from work detail and didn't bother telling anyone. That is insubordination *by law*. How am I supposed to keep my quarter in order if my workers keep running off?"

The Priority smiled, but no one else knew it was that of a hunter finding something caught in his snare.

"Now, now, Warrick. There is no harm done here. May I remind you that she's but a child. You were one once if I'm not mistaken. As far as I can tell, you haven't lost any productivity from her absence, have you?" Warrick shook his head but frowned as Deglin continued. "The girl isn't hurt, and your quarter hasn't suffered from her absence. Are you still not satisfied?"

"Suppose I am, but if this happens again?"

Delphine's mother stepped forward with a nervous smile, "Oh, sir, it will not. I speak for both myself and my daughter that it will not happen again."

"Make damn sure!" Warrick spat at the trembling gray-skins. "The Priority may be forgiving, but I don't think that will last if she makes a habit of it!"

The man didn't depart with a farewell or anything of the sort; instead, he turned his crooked nose up and stormed in the direction of his quarter grabbing an unsuspecting guard by the chest ordering, him to serve as escort.

Rubbing his eyes, Deglin looked relieved at the sight of the departure.

"He means well, though quite terrible at showing it. I'm disappointed to admit the man places priority in his reputation, not the well-being of his workers. Sadly, I've reached my limit of disappointment today."

Roe's stomach lurched unpleasantly once more at those words.

"Are you feeling alright?" Deglin asked.

"Oh...I-I jammed my shoulder good, but I don't think it's anything serious. No need to fuss."

"If you insist. Berl made it sound more serious than what you let on. Regardless, I just wanted to let you know how proud I am of you both. And it appears Captain Raleigh should be commended as well for his exceptional tutelage that you've benefited from. Had I known you two were out there, I would have been considerably more worried than I was. I sent you on a simple task, and it turns out that I have myself a new sentinel to promote," Deglin said jovially.

Roe nodded but then found himself struggling to speak, as Deglin's words finally had time to sink in properly.

"But I haven't said 'yes' to your proposition to join the House of Sentinels. I thought I still had time to make a decision. I didn't think I just made it."

Deglin sighed with an awkward smile. "My dear boy, you did so with your actions. We need more outstanding guards to join the exclusive ranks of the House to prepare for that dreadful day the lamps fail, and we lay our lives in your hands."

The boy discovered that within Pinnacle's laws, there existed something called the Decree of Valor. It was deemed a necessary piece of legislation that allowed qualified citizens to be conscripted to the House without consent. Roe found himself staring back in time, trying to remember school. He knew it was a relic lost to obsoletion and that Deglin would have known its existence based on his high station alone. It was a remnant law meant to conscript citizens when soldiering an army of only volunteers fell short. But Pinnacle was certainly not, however short of volunteers, as the military paid fairly.

Why would he do this? Roe thought, rubbing at the throbbing in his shoulder.

"I wouldn't force you into anything if I thought you couldn't handle it. I've total confidence in you," Deglin finished.

"I know, sir. It's not that I'm ungrateful it's just…I'm used to my life the way it is. I'm afraid of change."

"I understand all too well. Change is inescapable, but good for us all. After your induction into the guards, I will have the captain give you your new gifts—made just for you—as well as some advice that I think you will find reassuring. How does that sound?"

How could he argue? How could he refuse such a thing from the man who saved him from death in the gutter?

Especially now after all that fuss Deglin made to make him feel comfortable with the idea. Roe knew that Pinnacle's past leaders weren't as accommodating, and most of them joined without persuasion. It seemed the Decree of Valor was his best-kept secret weapon, knowing Roe might decline on his own.

All Roe could do was comply.

"When should I expect this induction?" he asked listlessly.

"I wanted to wait until after the Night of Safe Passage, but that would be too long off. That only leaves me with this evening I'm afraid, before dinner. I know it's sudden, but you will be just fine. I'll have Ophelia fetch you when it's time and after you get some much-needed rest." He gave a dreadful eye at Roe's white attire which, after the day's events, could use retirement. "And it's time to toss that worn-out garb and get you into something that suits you better."

With that, he headed back up the main thoroughfare as everyone else who had gathered around began to fall in tow as well.

"Aren't you coming, Roe?" Berl asked.

"Go on. Not sure if you heard, but I'm being forced to take a job I don't want. I'm going to rest up a bit. I'm sure you want to tell your father what happened out there."

"H'oh no! I'm not saying anything! He wants you to talk about it to an audience at dinner tonight. That way you make us *both* look good." He waved goodbye as he tried to catch up to his father, leaving Roe and Delphine alone beneath the gate's archway.

"Oooh, that sounds pretty exciting," she said. "You get an induction and even dinner after that!"

"You don't get dinner?" Roe laughed incredulously.

"Of course—well sometimes—but yours is different. Where you're at, it's much more special than what we're used to. It'll be exciting to see you." She gasped at the dreadful thought she had. "Wait! Am I allowed to see you?"

"I don't see why not. After all, you did see my heroics firsthand." He sounded reluctant to admit his courageous actions, but she smiled wide and began to dance around humming her song again. Roe took this as a sign she was pleased and asked her about its origin.

"Someone taught it to me, while I was in the forest. I wasn't there alone. I didn't want to say anything with…Berl there." She turned her gaze away having seen Roe's puzzled brow but continued.

"There's something about him and his father that I don't trust. I can't explain it, but they hold something back, as if their real thoughts are elsewhere, like hidden behind their back like a knife."

"What? Don't worry about them. You and Berl just had a bad first meeting. They're both good people."

She stared blankly at him and looked around making sure no one could hear.

"I met this nice lady while I was on my way to the quarter for work. She seemed so sweet and caring, but she was sad too. Such a beautiful lady shouldn't have a reason to be sad, but she was. She told me how lonely she was and asked if I wanted to go to the forest to play with her."

Roe tried explaining to her that he had never seen this woman out there.

"We were talking, and she said that she was going away for a moment, but that she'd bring a friend. Until then, I was to practice the song she had taught me. I climbed the trees where no one would find me, and she went back to the city to look for someone."

The way she described the white frock made him say with great reluctance, "I think I saw her too. She told me to come find you."

Her jewel-colored eyes widened, "So you're the one she was going to get?! Do you know her?"

Roe couldn't tell her they were very much acquainted. There would be too much controversy if word got out and that was the last thing the Deglins needed. Delphine was not stupid, but he remained convinced she couldn't keep a secret like most eager kids if it meant the end of the world. He wanted to tell someone, but it didn't feel right, not yet at least.

"I should go, but I'll be there for your big induction, okay?"

Roe smiled and waved goodbye, but soon found her arms bound tightly around his waist insisting that he visit the enclave instead.

With such an eager face staring up at him, Roe couldn't refuse. She ran off toward the thatched huts where home was, most likely informing everyone about the trespasser they'd be scowling at.

"Damn," he whispered. "Don't think I'm allowed in there."

He was alone now underneath the city gate on a special day that was meant to celebrate him, but he wasn't in the mood to partake in any revelry. For he found himself conscripted and now it seemed his dead mother had resurfaced from death's clutches. He had many questions to ask, but none he could provide an answer for.

This was all before he discovered the many unfamiliar eyes glaring back at him through the fence.

CHAPTER SIX

OF GREAT DURESS

"And there came shadows. Dozens through the dead air. We all remember the account. We thought the Fog of War was so hellish that even the ghosts of the dead tried to escape it. But these were no ghosts we found. They were Pinnacle's Visitants. Living, breathing, creatures...barely. They spoke of a far-off land they came from but could tell us no more of where it was or why they left. They were spent, all of them."

- AN EXTRACT FROM THE FOG OF WAR
AND OTHER INTRIGUES PROLOGUE

The past few hours had kept Regent Warrick the busiest he could recall since the day the grayclan were abruptly thrust upon his enterprise like an unwelcomed relative demanding his precious time. The Priority's defense of the little mist-sucker earlier today was deftly executed with so many on the scene, but the regent knew other shop owners in town took notice. The gears in their heads would gradually begin to squeak to life. They too would begin to wonder when their workers would start to grow bold.

Yes...little does Deglin know his soft stance today will only show the citizens that they are less-than. Those mist-suckers can do no wrong in his eyes...

The door to his office closed just moments before, with Ivan Fern having trotted into the slow gloom of the artificial twilight cast by the lamps' murky tint of dusk. The muffled clank of a heavy lock setting in place allowed the man to finally acknowledge the most difficult part of the task had been overcome.

Yes, the captain raised a skeptical eyebrow when Ivan's name met his ears for the first time. But really, that drunkard Raleigh had no grounds to turn down a nomination from a regent so long as the candidate's record was clean and had military experience. Ultimately, it was the collective regents that made the decision. A boy with Ivan's character must have already run afoul of something, but to Warrick's astonishment, there had been none.

The rest would be up to the greedy little brute—after his coronation into the House of Sentinels that is.

The jangle of coins could be heard as the greedy little brute in question investigated his palm in earnest, "That's a good start."

"Fern, there will be more where that came from, assuming you do as your told," Warrick said fiendishly.

Magda had mentioned the boy loved his coin but never bothered to say how eager he was to do his bidding for such a pittance, a small jangle of coins rattling within a pitiful purse no more than a small apple in size. Warrick had absolved himself from giving a large sum upfront to the boy; such has always been his way in business transactions. The fact that he didn't have to part way with any more eased his concerns.

Whether or not he could rely on a boy whose loyalty was only to who paid the most, didn't matter. Ivan was entranced now, seduced. The old man was more worried about Ivan's ability to gather information without raising suspicions; he was only eighteen after all, and none too bright looking at that. Oh well, if nothing else, he would find someone else only after he cut ties with the dead weight. There was always someone out there eager for payment in this miserable city.

For now, it was only a matter of waiting for this evening's pompous event to slog through and then the celebratory dinner in which he and his nominee would be able to dine with Augustine Deglin and his son starving for affection.

Then the house of Deglin would begin to crumble…

Walking among the grayclan had always made Roe uncomfortable but the reason was unlike most in Pinnacle for he possessed no animosity toward the race. It was simply their ghostly visages that made them quite eerie in his eyes. This time the hair on the back of his neck prickled as if being pulled by an invisible force. Now he was in *their* territory.

Campfires were scattered but numerous. Many were sitting in a circle rejoicing and singing about the end of another laborious day. As he walked by them following Delphine, he heard the wild beats and antiquated rhythm of percussions in the background; a fast and beautiful sound. They seemed to be adept at making up rhythms because when one would start a tune, another would join in and supplement it with another. Hands, sticks, eating utensils, and anything that could be hit seemed to be used.

Even their dancing appeared strange to him, but Roe nonetheless watched with fascination at the limber techniques in motion. Their limbs were not stiff and stationary like those of the humans attending Pinnacle's balls and formals. Quite the contrary. They were light on their feet, some hopping from stools to barrels while others soared over the kids who were engrossed with dances dictated by nothing more than their own creativity.

Delphine huffed.

"This is the only time we have to dance, at night in the enclave, we aren't allowed to anywhere else…Warrick's rules."

Over her shoulder, Roe could see the grayclan dancing even when doing chores, whether it'd be cleaning their domains or dusting off clothes that were blanketed with the loose soil kicked up by citizens walking by. Sometimes it was done intentionally, which made Roe feel embarrassed on behalf of his own people. The children were very notorious for doing this, knowing first-hand as he occasionally traveled to view their misdeeds. Though he never was an active participant, he did nothing to stop them, either. Roe knew his inaction made him just as guilty and it sickened him to recall his own cowardice.

"Have you ever been here before?" Delphine asked tugging at Roe's dirtied sleeve.

"Never," he lied. "I've passed by it, but I've never been inside."

That untruth felt terrible too.

"Well, I'm glad you decided to. It means a lot to me. You're the only friend I have…er…that's not a mist-sucker anyway."

As the conversation progressed, he took notice that she was asking such strange questions. Delphine agreed and said she only asked because the humans gave her people their monikers, the proper name Visitant, the more informal grayclan, and the derogatory mist-sucker. It was a simple hierarchy of nomenclature to tell how a citizen truly felt about their neighbor's mysterious presence. The latter was a term Roe refused to say, and its utterance sent unpleasant pangs in his body as if he were the recipient of the slur. The Visitants considered the humans as their master race, the species that repurposed them, and gave them life those many cycles ago when they were found feebly trying to escape the reign of the Fog. So, curiosity was strong due to their separation from the day-to-day drag.

"We don't talk about you, we aren't allowed to." Puffing out her chest and wagging her finger at him, she grunted, "'Any time spent thinking about the nature of a human is time wasted not working!' Least, that's what Regent Warrick says." She shrugged and gestured him over to a structure whose elongated shape resembled that of a dilapidated stable.

It must have been her house clan, the renowned makers of the trauma crafts judging from its insignia burned into the wood just above the entrance to the long, thatched domicile. They were the sole reason Warrick was prospering and he thanked them every day with contempt and revulsion. Roe entered and cringed at how cramped it was. A couple dozen Visitants made this longhouse their home judging from the straw beds present, though from the looks of it, maybe half of that number could be sheltered within comfortably.

"You all live in here? At once?"

"No. It can't hold us all at once. Some of us take turns sleeping outside—but it's okay! Really!" She was growing defensive, and Roe grew more uncomfortable because of it. At the time, most of its inhabitants were outside except for her parents who invited them in.

"I feel embarrassed to say this, but I don't know your names," he said standing before them.

"We didn't give you them for a reason, boy," the man said sternly. The mother was upset at his terse greeting and insisted he apologize at once. It took him great effort to do so, as he made it sound like the word was far too heavy to leave his lips when he mumbled, "Sorry".

Animosity lingered in the air between the two races of Pinnacle, but somehow the delicate civility seemed to remain so long as certain topics weren't broached.

"Father, it's okay. He knows. I'm Delphine Of-Great-Duress, not Little Hex the Tenth."

"WHAT?!" he erupted, the word punctuated by the close quarters of the stall they were in.

Immediately, the towering man scolded her, but she stood her ground and stared up at the form who was three Delphines taller, explaining what happened in the forest and why she had to divulge the precious information.

"The name is Nox Maker-Of-Duress," her father said satisfied with his daughter's reasoning. "This is Myrna Of-Great-Duress. I trust that, like our daughter, you will keep our names safe," he grunted, allowing himself to sit cross-legged on a bundle of straw by a low table.

The house clan, Duress, adopted that name as their entire lives seemed to revolve around struggle and hardship. Delphine's birth was of no exception, hence her name, implying "born under duress". She was born with particular difficulty in the dirt underneath the very thatched roof sheltering Roe, without a soul to help. This revelation brought light to the nature of their bizarre monikers. Females carried the same name as their mothers, boys inherited their fathers. Though related in blood, the names were unique to the race, united together only by a house name, a theme to tie their bonds closer.

With her eyes closed as if in great pain, Delphine spoke.

"Humans still think we have to rely on them…that they must give us the charity of being named things that mean nothing to us. We give our names like that of those that came before us, describing the events surrounding our birth, so that we may never forget the life given to us and its difficulties."

Roe had to ask why secrecy was so important, a question he could no longer stifle regardless if it was taboo.

"We know more than what the humans think we do. We act stupid, naive. When your people found our ancestors, they told us we had no sense of being…no sense of the self. We were 'breathing lumps of clay'. The original grayclan had no idea where they came from. Was it a result of the Fog destroying their minds? No one seems to know. Confined somewhere in their being was the scraps of dangerous knowledge, one knowing that Pinnacle wasn't their true home. Humans claimed they walked as ghosts out there, aimless with the only purpose of escaping it before they succumbed to exhaustion. That is until a human had stumbled upon the Visitants. They knew nothing, barely knew how to speak simple words, barely could chew food, drink water without choking on it, or think for themselves. Our forefathers were reared as children all over again," Nox whispered savagely.

The grayclan man was beginning to waver, cracking his knuckles through clenched fists reliving these humiliations. Roe could tell that the story weighed heavily on his conscious, though parallels began to form between their muddled history and that of humanity's past. The history of the Visitants wasn't one full of triumph or dignity, there was no sense in prolonging their unease. The boy wanted to change the subject quickly, but Myrna continued instead.

"The Priority of that time decreed that we would be sheltered within the borders in exchange for our labor, so we could pay off our debt to the city and help in any way we know to stave off the Fog's advances or even destroy it."

Unfortunately, he learned, the story didn't improve upon its grim tone. Resources were stretched thin already. Every commodity was carefully measured among the regents in each quarter, that was one of the first lessons youngsters were taught in the Academy. The younger generations didn't know how different the world was before the Visitants arrived, but Roe could only look around for a bit to see the citizens didn't lose their share of food provisions or textiles. In fact, only a smaller amount of the surplus was divided amongst the grayclan to subsist from. Looking at their cracked earthenware plates, he saw that the portions were meager which would explain Warrick's comments about their sickly and weak states.

"Let me talk to the Priority. He is a caring man and would be appalled to know the conditions you're living in."

"No!" cried Myrna. "If he or anyone else found out we were openly complaining about their... 'hospitality', it would only cause more hostility."

"Boy, who do you think introduced these policies in the enclave? *Your* leader. The Priority knows of our plight. Besides, what kind of name is that for a leader?" Nox asked with his plump nose turned up.

"He is the most important person in the world, our leader. The Priority is tasked to lead us through the dark times, even if the devil calls and the Fog finally comes for us. His life is the top priority any human can have, even ahead of family. We give him that title to remind us of that."

Roe understood the man's reservations about humans but felt some reserved anger toward his kind as well. The humans didn't ignore their helpless state. Although things were tough for them, Roe refused to let them hold Deglin accountable for something another leader had decided on a long ago. Regents could always muddle the decision-making process if they happened to disagree with a minute phrasing of a law on the cusp of passing.

For generations, Pinnacle sheltered these creatures when they didn't need to. If the creatures of the Fog wanted to pursue the grayclan inside of it, they certainly would try to cross over and attack Pinnacle too. But the incident in the forest allowed Roe to theorize they couldn't survive an assault without bringing the Fog with them. Even so, the Visitants placed a target on the city with their presence alone!

Nox pressed on, making little effort to hide his disdain for Roe's presence.

"Look boy, the selfless things you did for my child say you have a good heart, but we have reason to be forlorn. Every day we wake up knowing we aren't wanted here, and every night we know we go to sleep beneath an angered sky, in a foreign world that will succumb to it one day. We sleep under roofs we know were meant for beasts who walked around in their own filth.

"Each day these thoughts make it harder to carry on, but we do because we want to pay back our debt and find a home for us. I do believe that our debt has been settled. The announcement of grayclan leaving during your celebration is nearing. I take comfort in hearing some of our house will be freed from this servitude."

Roe noticed that Delphine had encircled both eyes with black dye much like Myrna was doing.

"What's wrong?"

"We haven't a home, so we are in mourning," Myrna replied somberly to the ritual.

He didn't bother offering to talk to Deglin again, but Roe had planned to do so regardless of how they felt. Surely both sides could agree that compromise was possible.

In the meantime, he was warned not to be seen around the enclave unless it was dark out. Any human willing to visit the enclave without any political reason or official summons was highly suspect. Delphine's parents were very subtle about it but told him something that could be interpreted as not overstaying his welcome. Roe took heed and had Delphine walk with him out.

Turning to her, Roe found an ashamed expression roll across her face. She fell in wordlessly beside him, her head hanging low. She was wringing her hands and fingers together and hummed to herself woefully.

"Nothing will change, we must earn our safe passage, we must work for it," she whispered.

At the thatched entrance they came through, Roe stopped and turned to her, "Things will be okay, you'll see."

"When you say that, is that just a lie to make me feel better?" Again, he tried to reassure her, but she interrupted. "Promise me, if you do talk to the Priority, you'll help us…help us find a home. We can't stay here, Roe. We have to chance the Fog. We have to."

"That's suicide!"

"Who knows if that is the truth? Who knows what the truth is for anything? Your people seem happy just to sit around and gobble up everything or steal from each other to try and avoid what they need to face. What kind of living is that? Even if what you say is true Roe it's come down to this: face a quick death out there or a slow one here. And there's only one way to find out truly. We have to try and at least die on our own terms. Promise me you'll make things better."

Her eyes grew heavy with tears, but she didn't allow any to fall. "I promise."

She smiled slowly, and the life slowly returned to form in her radiant golden eyes.

"Well...you made a promise to me. Now it's my turn," she said sniffling. "I can't wait for *your* time, Roe. You'll be such a welcome sight to see in that neat black uniform."

Her lithe form slowly vanished in the dusk of night. He turned on his heel to do the same until her disembodied voice met his ears from beyond the enclave.

"I want to be able to dance, whether it's on polished stone of the Hardscape, the dirt of the enclave or the soil beyond this place. I want to dance...without fear. Can he give that to me?"

He stopped in stride to let those words sink in.

While they had made promises to each other, Roe feared that hers would be much easier to keep than his. Her family wished to be left alone with their problems, but she seemed adamant that he'd fix them. What was he to do? None of it mattered if inaction were to set the course; if Roe wanted to do something, he needed to do it before the Night of Safe Passage when everything was decided.

There was very little time to make things right and he had very little clout to work with. Roe wasn't ready to be an advocate and certainly wasn't ready to make an enemy. Yet, somehow, down in his gut, a sense of foreboding told him he would be making one in due time.

CHAPTER SEVEN

THE GENTLE CHILD

"In regard to the anonymous ethicist's treatise, I cannot help but adamantly disagree with this man's (or woman's) incessant fearmongering. All of this meandering collection of words is nothing more than questioning for the sake of questioning. Rabblerousing nothing more. But that alone is dangerous enough to be taken seriously."

- EXCERPT FROM AUGUSTINE DEGLIN'S ARTICLE
ENTITLED: IS PINNACLE ASLEEP? : A REBUTTAL

The library in Deglin's study was something wonderful to behold whether it be through the eyes of a scribe or even a shady grifter. The cavernous room seemed to house as many books as the Learner's Guild of Pinnacle itself. It consisted of twenty regimented rows of two-story shelves flanking a handsome hearth standing before a pair of cozy chairs facing it. On one wall ran a neat row of paintings, landscapes mostly. On the other, portraits of prior leaders and their families.

Above the fireplace, hung the Deglin Family portrait, one gift that each appointed Priority received. The meticulously hand-drawn portrait was commissioned to contain the family the Priority wanted to include. From some of the other sketches seen in the past, as many as thirty people were drawn to such life-like detail. In Deglin's case, there were only two others included: his late wife, Saffron, and Berl. Cycles after her death, Roe's adoption was finalized. It was then the Priority had the portrait redrawn so that Roe would fit in the picture seamlessly. Because there was no Saffron to redraw, the drafter had to retrace the original and carefully place his new son in the scene uninterrupted.

Roe strolled up and down the shelves, his eyes gorging on the feast before them, admiring the embossed titles and time-worn bindings. Such titles like The Fog of War and Other Intrigues, Bellows at Dawn: An Imbecilic Guide to Blazebeast Rearing were but a few of many titles he only wished he had the time to read.

Over on a large desk, there were stacks of papers and articles from the Learner's Guild, mostly topics Roe was unfamiliar with. But cruel reality set in knowing he wasn't there to admire the collection. His stepfather was late to the meeting he had arranged so that Roe may try and reason with him. Thumbing through Blood and Gems: Your Guide to the Trauma Crafts…Among Other Things Painful was all he could do to steel his nerves. But this book was no good, it only reminded him of Delphine. The Visitant's problem could wait for the time being. One pressing issue needed to be solved as his ceremony was fast approaching.

Roe was reticent with fear.

Sadly, I've reached my limit of disappointment today…

The man's words still echoed in his mind and Roe was convinced he'd be furious at him for trying to argue against the creed. After talking with Delphine, more pressure was added on him, so feelings of uncertainty had taken root in his mind concerning this ascent in rank. While he waited, Roe decided he would fix his attention and gaze at the collection of literature Deglin had gathered throughout his life to ease his mind.

Thumbing through stacks of paper, he found articles on anything ranging from blazebeast training methodologies to diagrams attempting to understand Visitant physiology. Among all of that, Roe managed to find one particular article of great interest, due in part to the wax seal pressed at the bottom of the article. It had a striking resemblance to the symbol of the trauma crafts quarter, an open-palmed gauntlet suspending a flame.

It was a strange article indeed, which gave him more cause to read it.

THE LEARNER'S GUILD OF PINNACLE
IS PINNACLE ASLEEP?
A BRIEF COMMENTARY

Imagine a world where its citizens tip-toe the streets of delight, basking under artificial lights. It is also a world that sows fear and panic in the hearts of man. They celebrate the moments they know life still flows through a solitary valley and wait to be smothered to death by toxic air and jagged claws. Such a world exists, a world where problems spawn from both the prominent and disreputable alike. Can you guess what city this description resembles? If you said Pinnacle, you are at least not a captive to delusion.

Man is a slave to the world around them. He is but a lowly prisoner to the mountains that encircle so high, an indentured servant to the plains he toils in, and a coward to the mists that bear down on him. In this world, very few have observed that there exists a great answer that lies in wait for man to discover. It is elusive, yet ubiquitous in nature. It is like a mind killer. Hypothesis: If one can find the patterns, and meaning, it will usher in a new era and sweep away the troubles of life. The poor beings hidden in the sea of perilous mists that Pinnacle dares to call the Fog of War must find this answer if they wish to save themselves.

The first step is to recognize any seeker of the Answer as an appropriate candidate to initiate the act of seeking. Reader, respond to the following:

1. Are you of an inquisitive mind?

2. Do you seek comfort in the bliss of ignorance? (If yes, read no further.)

3. Will you be ready to withstand the truth in all its forms, including truths that are disturbing, cold, and callous?

If you've read this far, one can assume you are a candidate as a seeker for the Answer. It is no easy undertaking. It will be an arduous walk down the path which is cloaked in illusions and a path choked by your enemies that will take any measure to brand you as the enemy. It is not for the weak-minded, but for those that are ready to awaken, to truly see the world. More meditations are necessary to finish the groundwork for this unnamed philosophy. The world has offered us a riddle to be solved, knowledge to be gained. It is we who must wake up and see it. The Heretic's Dictum might be the place to start.

There was no author's signature on the page, only that symbol. From the looks of the parchment, it was read and used significantly as there were faded tea-colored stains speckled all around its surface, uneven creases and the ink was smudged in the corner, that sort of thing. This work had to be by the same scholar he had heard so much about. The very notion that someone was developing a new kind of way to see the world was intriguing enough, but the boy always bore an affinity to such strange and unusual occurrences.

To his left, he looked at a large platter with brown and clear glass bottles filled with various tonics, ales, and beers. One in particular that caught his eye was labeled White Effervescence. Holding the paper in one hand, he lifted the cap of this bottle and deeply inhaled the dry, bitter scent encased within.

Immediately, he pictured his youth. What a nightmare it was. A particularly vivid one he could not shake away with time. His father had lost him in a crowd, and he was whisked away by a she-vagrant. This event was not imagined; rather it was something lost in his mind where a nightmare melded with a long-passed memory. Determining which was which proved to be a difficult task as the days marched onward.

The woman had asked him his name, but he was reluctant to say anything. Finally, she sat him on her lap and he felt more comfortable.

"R-Roland," he whispered.

"Ahh. Roland. You don't look like you're enjoying yourself, sweetie." He shook his head and rubbed the tears away from his reddened eyes.

"I have something to fix that. No one should feel sad. This stuff takes away the pain…makes life fun again! Trust me," she said winking. The smell was still in his nose as Roe imagined drinking from the tankard he was given that night…

"Interesting article, isn't it?"

Deglin's voice surprised Roe, who whipped around and elbowed the large glass of tonic to the floor. Roe was horrified at the sight and immediately apologized several times over the shards on the rug.

"Quite alright! I caught you off guard, but may I ask what you were doing with that bottle?"

Roe lied and said he had grown curious of the smell, how highly the older soldiers had spoken of the brand, but deep down he wanted to drink it, so he could remember that night his father lost him during the Night of Safe Passage celebration.

While picking up the article he said, "And this, it caught my eye. What is it exactly?"

The Priority smiled, "It's a rather interesting piece of writing that was proposed to a small contingency of scholars, including myself, long ago. It's merely a philosophy of sorts—a proposed way of living."

"What does it mean?"

Deglin paused, staring blankly at it before resuming his regal countenance.

"Existential gibberish. Highly theoretical existential gibberish, merely for academic purposes, with little practical use for any of us," he replied, gently seizing the paper from Roe and setting it aside.

Then he offered his son a seat and a drink, from one of the bottles he was eyeing. Knowing he was far too young to partake, Deglin made him promise to keep it a secret. Taking a sip, Roe immediately winced in the very same manner he did upon his first drink with that vagrant. Only this time, he swallowed the entire mouthful like he thought a man was supposed to.

Deglin sighed, "I take it you didn't come here to discuss philosophy and partake in underage drinking." It wasn't a question, more of an unshakable declarative. "I know what you want to say."

Roe immediately dropped the pretense of a friendly chat, tip-toeing around the uncomfortable showdown approaching.

"I don't know if I can really accept that life you want for me. I didn't even get a choice. I like having…not having a status. I like not being placed into a position where I can make enemies."

Deglin placed a hand on his shoulder again.

"I know what is best for you, but I won't make you do this. Just know one thing, son, everyone must make a choice. The world doesn't allow for its people to be bystanders, to embark upon a life of neutrality. It has an uncanny way of making you choose whether you realize it or not. The day will come when you must take a side and prepare yourself…"

"For what?"

"To make enemies in the same manner you make friends. It happens to all of us, any path in life you choose means a step closer to producing enemies."

"I don't understand."

"A man can choose to be a banker, and a beggar on the streets will hate him for having what he doesn't have—money. A woman may choose to be a guard and hate the thief for choosing such a dishonorable life and for making her job difficult. A man may choose to be a Priority and be hated by elderly regents for being powerful yet, so young…"

Deglin took a long drink clearly perturbed by the pressure Warrick and the others have been placing on him. The talk ran rampant in the barracks so this was hardly a secret to Roe who could only watch the man stare blankly at the fire crackling near the threshold.

"Do you really think one can make an enemy so easily?" Roe asked.

"As easy as breathing. Everyone chooses a side in life. The important thing is when you make your choice be certain it's the right one. Be certain the choice is what you want."

"The only thing I know for certain is that I don't want to disappoint you."

Deglin slowly sunk back into his chair. It had become habitual for him to do this as a means of feigning contemplation. Unbeknownst to Roe, it was a sign of victory achieved in battles of words. Roe's loyalty was a fault but Deglin felt warm that at least it was his now.

"And now, you're beginning to understand my words," he said bridging his fingers together.

Looking invigorated, Deglin stood up to give him a strong embrace—something he might suspect Roe had been deprived of thanks in part to his abrasive father.

After the exchange, Roe committed himself both to his stepfather and to the House of Sentinels. An elated Deglin exclaimed he should ready himself for the ceremony. He was in such an uncharacteristically gleeful state that Roe himself thought the man had reverted to the state of an excited boy ready for a chance at dueling for the first time.

As Deglin left to get himself ready, Roe told him one more lie, "I'm just going to go rest up a bit myself."

Going to rest for Roe was often just his way of saying, "Don't bother me." For now, he had different plans. He grabbed for the peculiar article from the stack and shoved it down his trousers. With his glass half-filled in one hand, he snatched the bottle with the remaining drink in the other and walked briskly to his room. Closing the door behind him with a chair propped up against it, he walked over to the curtains and drew them shut.

The room had succumbed to darkness again. As he sat in the chair, he felt the uncomfortable edges of the wadded-up paper pressing against his skin. Pulling it out and smoothing it over the desk, Roe took another drink wishing he wasn't alone. He wished Tessa was there, to be inducted beside him. Just then, a bizarre but familiar feeling gripped him.

It was as though his mind was working on several thoughts at once, longing to carry on a conversation with someone while trying to remember his history teacher's name. Although he appreciated the solitude devoid of any human contact, at times, he did long for someone he could trust like himself, someone bearing enough grace to see him as a flawed person, but also one still of value. This was a thought his mind frequently wrestled with and one that never failed to make his brain feel uncharacteristically sore.

A distinctive pressure accompanied by a faint heat in the back of his head slowly came to life. His eyes began to feel weighty, like stones sliding about his skull.

There was a hollow voice in the room that spoke, "Aspiring to be a vagabond so young? Don't want to be staggerin' at your own ceremony. Besides, it ain't good for ya."

"I've been told being dead isn't good for you either and yet you seem to be getting by."

"Who says I'm dead?"

"Look like a ghost to me… you here to give me a lecture? Cuz I pashed school aarready. Know wat I mean?"

The alcohol was already taking its effect on his novice body.

"Vagabond is no profession. Besides, I'm here because you're alone, you know better."

Roe swayed in his seat a bit to see the glowing blue visage of what looked like a boy standing next to the bed. The eerie sight never revealed his name to Roe since it made its first appearance sometime after Armin's disappearance. He came to call it the Gentle Child and so that is what it answered to.

However, Roe also met a reddened specter he referred to as the Rough Child. Both appeared and left at scattered times Roe could never predict. At first, he grew scared of the visions, but with time tolerated them as inescapable. Their ethereal nature had led him to believe they were spirits from children that died in the barracks and left it at that.

"I *don't* need the…*hic*…company," Roe grunted. "I've done fine…*hic*…sho far."

"Then allow me ask you something. When the sound of dawn beckons you awake, why do you still seek isolation?"

Roe only sniffed more of the tonic, failing to field a response.

"Your silence says more than any fib you would've told me."

"I guess – *hic* – sho."

"You can't be too happy about your life if you keep ignoring that question."

"You can't be too bright – *hic* – if you think my answer's gonna change," Roe retorted.

"I'm only trying to help, whether you believe it or not!"

"No-o-o-o-o kidding!" Roe's tongue felt bloated and sloppy in its work. His limbs seemed to misbehave too, as he tipped over the remaining bit of liquor on the floor while shifting in weight. He giggled and loudly shushed at the shattered glass to be quieter next time.

Suddenly, Ophelia's muffled voice was heard calling and a great ruckus at his door followed.

As usual, Roe insisted Gentle Child leave who in turn bowed with servitude.

Roe shooed him away as if he hadn't heard it and felt the bitter saliva fill his mouth as his breathing hastened and stomach heaved. The pressure in his head vanished, but great bouts of nausea took its place. He was sweating, but it felt chilled like a spray from a mountain stream. As he began to heave and belch, he looked at himself in the mirror and oddly admired how wonderful his white armor looked against the gilded tendrils stitched within. He also determined that it was a perfect place to vomit.

Before he did, he had enough time to gaze at the stern expressions of Ophelia and Deglin staring him down. Then he heaved all over himself.

CHAPTER EIGHT

THE ROUGH CHILD

"I saw him or it again. The mean one. Why does it bother me? Why can't it go haunt someone else? I can't be the only one who sees them. But what if I am? Am I crazy? What's wrong with me?"

- EXCERPT FROM ROLAND DEGLIN'S JOURNAL

Sitting on the bed didn't give Roe the comfort it once had. Normally he welcomed its site, finding it to be his true home. Though his stomach felt better, the noxious feeling had vanished, but a headache took its place. The taste of acid lingered on his breath.

He was embarrassed to have the two people he revered the most see him like that, but at least his stepfather forgave him. Ophelia, however, wasn't satisfied until Roe had learned something from his experience with liquor. She forced him to clean up everything that was soiled with vomit while being near nakedness for everyone to see as they walked by. She didn't want him to get any fresh clothes dirty if he decided to get sick again. His old and only partially white uniform sat in a useless pile on the floor.

Sitting there, he began to wonder how many people attended functions like tonight, hoping his ceremony would be a small affair. When someone was promoted as a sentinel, the settlement guards weren't required to attend, so he knew his brethren probably wouldn't bother. If it were his choice, Roe wouldn't have a ceremony at all.

"Ophelia?" he shouted. "What's the holdup?"

He heard the echoed footsteps down the hall and heard her huff, "Coming, child. Settle yourself."

She nudged open the door with her hip and came in with a neatly folded black uniform and placed it in his arms. Roe braced his arms thinking the outfit to be very weighty, but then found it to be extraordinarily light for something that was called "armor".

This led him to discover why Ophelia didn't have much difficulty carrying it like pressed laundry.

"As I said earlier, if you're late, I'll be the one to hear 'bout it. Now, git! I trust you don't need help dressing yourself?"

"No."

He gave her a lame smile despite it being feigned. Otherwise, she wouldn't leave him knowing something was wrong, and he didn't want her to be late. Ophelia's reputation with Deglin was contingent on Roe's punctuality after all. She smiled back and checked her tightly woven hair with her hands as she left.

Roe stared down at the uniform in his hands. In addition to how breathable it was, its texture felt quite alluring. Smooth and supple, the black color was as lively as the old white uniform, but he gravitated toward its matte finish.

Sliding on the cuirass, he discovered it was tailored down to a near-perfect fit. The rest of the collection gave him comfort knowing he could maneuver unhindered. Though there were two remaining articles on the bed that were foreign as they weren't like his former uniform. The first was the cloak that latched to the cuirass. Nothing about the cape seemed extraordinary so he moved on to the last bit. Some type of bespoke mask but proved too difficult to determine how it was to be worn given the gravity of the fast-approaching ceremony. Feeling the prickling nerves cause his fingers to fumble over themselves trying to fasten it, Roe didn't bother putting it on as he felt mostly prepared.

The main atrium was where he found Ophelia, the Priority, and the regents dressed in their finest garments. Roe wasn't jealous because he looked down at his own garb to quell that envy. He had to admit, the armor made him feel...positively intimidating.

Peeking out the door, he tried to see how many people had gathered so that he may prepare for the potential horde of eyes dissecting his quivering form.

Deglin looked over to him, "Aah Roe, you look positively daunting, debonair!"

"Thank you, sir." He stepped closer and whispered fondling the hood, "I feel stupid for asking, but what do I do with this?"

Whispering back, he winked, "Don't worry. I shall handle it."

"Good. Where's Berl? I haven't seen him since he left the gate with you."

"He's lined up with the others on the Hardscape. Don't worry he won't miss this I can assure you."

The ceremony itself was intended to overlook the Fog of War in the city's amphitheater. The Priority would enter first followed by the regents and their respective flag bearers. House Sentinels would line up to form an aisle for the procession. Deglin would make his introduction followed by the music.

"And that's your cue to walk up the aisle with the other candidate," he finished with an air of befuddlement.

Roe couldn't help but make his puzzlement known to everyone as he turned, brow furrowed, to Deglin. There had been no mention of another. He wasn't going to be the sole center of attention.

"Yes, I forgot to mention there is another young man joining as well, cutting a bit close for comfort but the more able-bodied soldiers to set an example for the others all the better I say." Deglin paused taking a hard, long look in the direction of Warrick though Roe was unsure what it was all about. "Strangely, it turns out he was eagerly waiting for a nomination. He should be here shortly, I hope…"

It didn't take the other initiate long to arrive, his presence made as he stormed down the stairs with a scowl on his face and muttering unmistakable profanities under his breath. His blond hair wasn't styled like everyone else's. A broad jawline and heavy features made him very brutish as if one couldn't tell from his temperament alone. He was straightening out his cloak in a stuffy manner and acted exceptionally fussy for a lowborn commoner. Roe rolled his eyes.

Quite a charmer, this one, he thought.

The face was familiar, and his attitude was unbearable, Ivan Fern. Roe considered himself quite unfortunate to know the brat from an earlier apprenticeship they were forced to share during their school days.

"Mister Fern, we've been waiting for you," said the Priority impatiently.

"My apologies, sir! That housemaid is incompetent. It was her fault! Clearly, she's getting far too old and manage to slow my preparations. I wanted everything to go well today, but..."

"-Fine, fine! I'm sure Ophelia's trying her best. She has had a busy day and it's quite unusual for her to be this lax. I'll have a talk with her."

Really need someone to dress you?! You mean to say, you haven't grown past thumb-sucking?

Ivan had never been one to take a liking to Roe, mostly because he wouldn't relent to his temper or back down to his bullish threats as most would. Their feud started far before his most recent huffing and puffing down those stairs. He was assured of one thing; his dislike for Ivan was quite justified and he would be closely watched just to see what exactly this chafe is up to.

"Even I managed to get my cloak on right," Roe whispered headily.

Ivan retorted, "And just whose ass d'ya kiss to get here? Wasn't Daddy's, I hope. Figured you too scared to sniff at any glory."

Despite having its characteristic vulgarity, this particular comment took Roe off guard with its uncanny and precise jab toward nepotism. Roe's eyes narrowed.

What exactly does he know?

Deglin shot them both a glance, "Something wrong you two?"

Roe shook his head slowly though feeling a bit of alarm internally.

"Alright let me have your masks. I'll put them on you when I tell you to kneel. Now, wait here. Come everyone, let's usher in our newest members," Deglin exclaimed.

A gradual hush came over the assembly. He gave a processional walk down the aisle between rows of sentinels. The nine banner carriers accompanying their respective regents followed. Represented were the trauma crafts, industrial services, husbandry, commerce, senate, food production, armament and military, healing disciplines, and pedagogy.

As the two boys stood there waiting, Roe heard the grandiose exaltation of the orchestra immediately cut the silence as the bigwigs entered. It formed from boisterous horns waking anyone who dared to sleep at the time and the singing of stringed violins. The interplay of deep-toned horns propelling the sweet strings caused the hair on Roe's neck to stand. He shivered a little bit at how wonderful and magnetic the moment was.

Cheering and applause ensued. Much to his dismay, Roe realized the hall was crowded with people eager to see their new guardians.

"All those eyes," he groaned to himself. Unfortunately, Ivan heard this and bullied his way into an unwelcomed conversation.

"Great, isn't it? All those people will know who we are, huh, as if they don't already! Naturally, they know me, but you, they only know as the Priority's fake son. His second chance at not having another screw-up."

By now, he still wasn't sure if Ivan was just horrible at making conversation or if he really was that much of a jerk. Either way, the remark made Roe form a fist at his side. The next errant comment might unleash it.

"I suppose." The awkwardness of silence was getting to him, so Roe tried to make an effort. "What are you in for?"

"What?"

"What did you do to earn your nomination?" Roe was starting to regret asking that question knowing the noxious tide of boasting that would spew from his trap.

"Apparently, Regent Warrick thought my thorough patrols and my devotion to protocol made me a superior candidate." Ivan not even trying to look the least bit modest wore a wide grin throughout the talk.

"Suppose they were bound to scrape the bottom of the barrel sooner or later," Roe sneered, then saw what he thought was Ivan patting a pouch on the side of his belt.

"What's-"

"Look alive," Ivan snapped.

There was a magnificent white carpet trimmed with gold that suddenly unfurled at their feet. As they made their way past the entrance of the amphitheater, menacing horns blared down upon them as they were introduced by a loud booming voice.

The crowd showered them with flowers, adorations, and brightly colored scarves, tossed by the young women in hopes of having Roe or Ivan catch one. Roe resisted as he would look around and then whip his head to the stage ahead. His nerves were gripping him so much that it took a tremendous amount of concentration to not trip over himself. While on his right, Ivan was cheering back at the crowd, waving, and pumping his fist in the air.

Seeing this revulsion proved fortuitous for saw Delphine jumping up and down wildly cheering beyond. Breaking his nervous character Roe waved back to her; the act calming him a bit. Despite that, he could still feel his breath quicken with his heartbeat.

As the two approached the portion of the carpet where the sentinels stood, the fearsome group whipped out their black blades and raised them high in the air with their right arm and their left arm over their hearts. It was an impressive sight to see them perform the action in near-perfect unison.

The candidates stood just before the podium where Priority Deglin was standing behind. He gestured for them to halt while trying to calm the roaring cheers beating down at them. The guards then marched up the aisle lining the edge of the Hardscape in a semi-circle. They turned to face the ominous silence of the Fog on the horizon. With Captain Raleigh leading the formation, their blades shifted and took aim, jutting out to meet the swirling and shifting void beyond. All the figures were masked and indistinguishable, but the captain's uniform had Pinnacle's heraldry, a depiction of a white flame on his cloak. He also had a special cowl fashioned for him that made him look very formidable as if he weren't already.

With the audience at his full attention, Deglin spoke:

"Good people of Pinnacle, it brings me great pleasure to welcome you all in helping us recognize the accomplishments of these fine young men standing before us, Ivan Fern and Roland Deglin.

"Mr. Fern has shown us his dedication toward not only his duties as Settlement Guard, but also in showing tremendous potential as a leader in the protection of our city, our small, dying world.

"Vigilance and perseverance are Ivan's forte. He has unwavering commitment to upholding the laws of Pinnacle that are enforced with our best interests in mind. His recommendation by Regent Warrick has earned him enough acknowledgments to be considered for this arduous position."

Deglin paused for the applause, then continued.

"Roland Deglin has given the city newfound confidence in Pinnacle's youth. He had made a name for himself within the Visitant's Forest in rescuing and safely returning a valued member of our city's Visitant community. This fine exhibition of selflessness makes him an exceptional candidate for induction into the assembly of the House of Sentinels.

"I couldn't possibly allow such a gallant act go unnoticed. I know with certainty, that I would be disappointing everyone if I let this exceptional young man wriggle through the nets. An earnest and heartfelt discussion were all that was needed to show him that this is his rightful place in our world."

Once he announced the candidates, Deglin gave the regents a chance to decline Ivan's nomination, a process only candidates recommended by the Priority were exempt from. One could see Warrick shift uneasily in his seat as he gazed down the row with contemptuous eyes. But no one spoke out against Ivan and both candidates had secured their placement.

Deglin then turned to address the Fog of War like an enemy before battle:

"We secure ourselves in knowing that these young men will be joining the rest of our men and women of the House of Sentinels to help protect our lives, our world, and our existence from the forces that seek to bear down and collapse on us. We will take comfort in knowing on that horrible day when the lamps fail, these fine examples of humanity will be there to protect not only us but our friends who took refuge in our world to escape the perils of the Fog—with its violent and deceptive nihility—to the very last soul."

With palms raised toward the murky heavens, he spoke rapturously to the crowd:

"Pinnacle, take comfort…"

"We take comfort in our own."

"Pinnacle, when death comes for us…"

"We'll meet it with a blade."

"Pinnacle, embrace our grayclan…"

"We embrace them as our own."

"Pinnacle, reject a life beneath a fractured sky."

"We'll cull any who crave it."

"Would both candidates kneel, please?"

As he approached, the two enigmatic cowls were revealed once more. He hooded Ivan first, then Roe. The whole piece was positioned over his head, resting on top of the shoulders. It was hoisted up the neck with the front finding its place across the bridge of his nose. Then he brought the hood over his head to cover the rest of the scalp.

"Let these masks remind you, that naught but your eyes are visible, of which you must rely on more than anything else. You must be vigilant, so let the mask's presence remind you of your duty to us all. You are now members of the House of Sentinels. Would everyone please help me welcome them?"

Turning around, Roe saw everyone in the amphitheater standing with applause. It was at this time that he finally felt proud having everyone show how much he meant to Pinnacle. He was also glad that he was essentially concealed by the uniform, hidden within another dark, safe place.

The gradual blue smears the lamps emitted above forced the lingering audience back to their homes soon after. The night was arriving and with it came the large menacing silhouettes that were tucked away within.

It was these nightly occurrences that drove the faint of heart to slam their doors shut. Even the seasoned sentinel could grow wary staring at the large objects floating around the valley. Perhaps it was the sheer size…or maybe it was just fear of the unknown, but most people were convinced that the shapes within the Fog were the malevolent beasts vehemently trying to break through the protection the pinnacles provided. Some floated high above the buildings on the ceiling of the mist, while some danced wildly about in the rolling hills. Arms outstretched and tentacles flopping about with strange filaments fluttering in a wild fashion. They were the collective known as the shadowforms.

Despite their occasional presence, a few tempered souls still lingered about the anterior portion of the Hardscape. Roe wanted to stay longer as there were still well-wishers desiring to congratulate him. He found that Tessa had managed to pry herself from the demands of the commissary to attend, though this didn't surprise him knowing Berl's presence gave her more incentive to come, or so he thought.

She gave her friend a warm hug.

"Congratulations Roe! Now Berl can't lord his position over your head. You're equal."

"That and he might shut up about it for a change. Tess, glad you could make it. I wasn't surprised that you came since Berl was in the ceremony and all," Roe grinned, seeing if she would take his bate.

She playfully smacked him with the back of her hand. "Will you stop? I didn't show up just to see him play with a sharp object. I came to see my friend."

Roe blushed.

Berl meanwhile came from behind to grab ahold of her. Ivan the Ego followed. He followed and jumped on the back of Berl who lost his balance. Fortunately for Tessa, Ivan didn't drag her down with them.

"Ivan! Are you out of your mind? You just got promoted to the highest-ranking guard and here you are prancing about knocking people down like the dumb-sod you are," she cried, trying not to fall over their tangled bodies.

Berl, who was helping Ivan up laughed. "Ease up, Tess. It's all in good fun. He didn't mean any harm."

Ivan began prodding her breastbone with an accusatory finger, "Yeah, Tess! Why don't you listen to your better half? It was clear that I was the most qualified candidate in the entire Pinnacle Guard. It was only a matter of time before a regent or Captain Raleigh realized how talented I am."

The sentinel came away looking slightly disappointed when his errant finger failed to prod something more substantial on her chest.

Her eyes flared, ready to start a fight. She stepped up to him, locking eyes with his clenched jaw. "Fern, go stroke your ego somewhere else! Berl may fall head-over-heels for you, but I know for sure Captain Raleigh isn't one who cares for arrogance. He can smell it on you and will make your life miserable."

"S'at right? Don't think you know what you're talking about, not something new coming from an Emlan-"

"-Wipe the smirk off your face because I know Raleigh will personally see to it that you do. Ask my brother. He did his time and service to the House of Sentinels and saw what the captain's capable of first-hand."

"There's a reason he's no longer with the House like everyone else, probably because he couldn't cut it. He doesn't have the talent, whether with the sword, trauma glove, or a fist like I do."

The snide comment was his chance he had to walk away unscathed. Making short work of the situation, she found a way to strike and took it like a starving predator on the prowl would. As Ivan chuckled and turned to leave, Tessa gazed mischievously at the hem of his cloak fluttering on the stone walk and stomped on it. The garb tore off his shoulders with an awful rip and fell to the floor leaving Berl and Roe laughing hysterically.

She smiled shaking her head at the tattered pile at her feet, "Tsk, Tsk! Ivan, not a good start to your career. You said your swordplay is good, but tell me, how's your cross-stitch?"

He snarled and gave her a dirty look to suggest the matter wasn't over. Then he proceeded to shoot his glare at Roe as he stuffed the cloak under his arm. Once Ivan was sure they knew he was thoroughly angry, he stormed off into the barracks. It was indeed a welcome sight to start the night off.

Berl, Ivan, and Roe had been given the night off because of the forthcoming dinner with the Priority. Ivan and Roe for being newly initiated, but Berl was pardoned because he was the leader's son, the kind of special treatment Roe continued to stress over. Ivan found an invitation too, but his run-in with Tessa made his appearance seem doubtful.

"Oh, Tessa, you lasted as long as you could without humiliating him," Berl smiled wryly, placing his hands on her shoulders. "I wish you would have backed off him a bit."

"Hmph. He deserved every bit of it and I was just getting started. You don't see Roe rubbing his accomplishment in my face! His ego needed a little readjusting. In my humble opinion, his parents should have done a little skin-to-skin rearing. He makes the rest of you look awful."

"He's smug but let me ask you something. If you were in danger, would you rather have a sentinel who's arrogant or one that is timid and meek?" Berl asked.

Roe wouldn't have admitted it for the sake of unity, but Berl did have a point.

She sighed. "I know what you're saying, but he just rubs me the wrong way, especially when it comes to insulting my family. I don't care if it was your father doing it! At any rate, I have to run to the commissary to help lock up…I might be late."

"What? You can't be late!"

"I really have to go." She pecked him on the forehead and hurried off down the stairs leading from the Hardscape.

"We better get ready, too. Don't suppose we have a lame excuse to be late like her. I heard some of the regents will be there and they're fussy old farts when it comes to that stuff." Berl paused seeing Roe's new attire, "By the way, I'm glad you're one of us now. I have someone who will have my back when I need help. Until death, my brother…"

"…I've got your back," Roe finished.

Berl smiled down at his blade as he made for the dining room, "Best put this away! It looks like I'm ready to shank someone huh?"

As Roe slowly walked to the Hardscape's balustrade and laid his elbows on it, he looked down toward the city settling in for the night. Picking a pink blossom off a nearby tree, he admired its fleeting beauty. Then he fixed his gaze to nothing in particular if only to think how quickly things have changed for him, in many ways for the better, without reason at all it seemed.

Despite the grave times that lay ahead, he found the warm but unfamiliar semblance of belonging. A family to belong to was what he wanted all along, an unwavering friendship or two would be nice as well. Why were they so hard to find? The newly appointed sentinel wondered if that was a common problem to have or if it was just his misfortune to struggle with feeling alone. Except, there were still instances where he tried to convince himself he didn't need love. Though deep down, he coveted the thought of knowing the comfort of its wonderful embrace one day. He felt it from Deglin, the friendship from Tessa, Berl, and an ornery beast with an insatiable appetite. A newfound friendship formed with Delphine and he still had his confidant, Ophelia, to joke around with.

"I don't want to lose them, Pinnacle," he said to the city as if it were listening.

Suddenly, his brain felt the weight of exhaustion as though it was starting to strain from reading several texts at once while trying to listen to a conversation whispered in his ear. Overwhelming feelings of loneliness, fear, and anger welled within him, but he could find no clear source for their cause.

At that moment, trickles of red light wafted around him and gathered in a glowing column tucked in a shadowy corner. Roe's heart sank at the sight of the red light glowing against the buildings in front of him. He turned to see the column morph into the Rough Child, the other apparition in his life.

"Why does *that* blossom bother to bloom knowing it will shrivel and turn ugly one day?" Rough Child asked.

"It has the chance to grow and live, not everyone's fate is horrible."

"A blossom's fate is always the same, just like a man's no matter the life lived. Look at the lives of those close to you, that mist-sucker, your brother, your father, your…mother would all know how horrible life is in this world. And what of the maid? I know for certain that misery has been her companion for far too long…"

"Some nerve you have to show up and kick me to the dirt after I've finally stood back up."

The form began to flicker a bit like freshly stoked coals.

"Did life in the gutter teach you nothing? These people are not your friends. They are your competition for survival. That's what this is all about. That's how you've managed to live. No one owes you anything, and you don't own them either. Did Ophelia come to your rescue? No. She let you suffer and fix things yourself."

"Shut up…" Roe whispered.

"…her husband died violently…soldiers have beaten her… age has rendered her…useless…but you've heard this before…"

"Shut up."

"Your Gentle Child asks you his all-important question with each visit. Now, I must ask you mine: What kind of a world allows for the righteous and caring to fester in never-ending hardship, while the wicked and cruel prosper?

"You claim the blossom grows and flourishes but behold! Look at the tree when it sheds its leaves and dies. What remains? The thorns! Thorns, wicked and cruel like the people of this dying world. After all, is it any wonder that your scholars wear such helpless looks as you are being slowly suffocated?"

"STOP! PLEASE!"

"They'll leave you one day, Roe after they've seen your shame. If your real family left you so quickly, what makes you think this manufactured one will stay for you? Like everyone else, you... have...no...purpose."

The voice laughed and pulsed brighter with each chuckle. Roe tried denying the bright visage, but with each passing moment, his words began to resonate...becoming more valid as the seconds passed.

"I-I have purpose," Roe whispered lamely, brushing at a tear rolling down his face. The Rough Child's words felt so true he half-wished he had silenced his own feeble defense and simply gave in to the thought. It was so easy, so natural to want to succumb to what he always feared was the truth.

The being snickered. "Sounds like I'm not the one you're trying to convince. You'll see, one day soon they'll slowly abandon you... until you're all alone. Now go! Don't want dinner to get cold."

All alone...all alone...

The voice echoed with a cynical chuckle as the light quickly dissipated into the twilight until the boy stood in the darkness. Somewhere deeply buried in his mind, the disturbing thought crept in. As Rough Child said, Roe came to realize his own flesh and blood left him, so this new one was bound to do the same.

It only made sense.

The blossom sat in his hand and he thought what a shame it was to see such a beautiful thing wilt and die. It was something he never could get used to. It reminded him of the way his mother had been ridiculed by Cyrus in his younger days. He likened it to Ophelia being crushed by the weight of work unfulfilled or Delphine's true self, being subdued by the city's rules.

Looking for counsel, he asked it woefully as his gaze turned toward the ominous hills filled with hidden beasts, "Why does a good thing like you even bother to be?"

He crushed the blossom with his grip and let it sink, like his hope, into the darkness below.

"Why do you bother to be?"

The hours passed far too quickly. With a blink of an eye, the seconds coalesced into heaps of minutes. He hadn't meant to sleep that long, and the Ugly One cursed himself for getting too cozy in the cellar beneath the charred threshold.

Tobias' rest was pivotal—both in developing into what was to be a promising young man and in utilizing his talents of manifestation for the mission—but still, *someone* had to be held accountable for their precious timeline.

The Night of Safe Passage was creeping nearer, and he knew they had fallen behind schedule.

The sudden boom of some god-awful orchestral calamity and the roar of hollowed cheers nearby had torn him violently from sleep moments earlier. Fortunately, he found the boy had been startled too; the Ugly One didn't have the heart to wake the weary-looking child who adorably rubbed his eyes so that it could melt even the most hardened of hearts.

Having peered through the slit of the trapdoor's opening, both were shocked to find the streets appearing to be deserted. The only commotion came from high above in the amphitheater which was glowing with lights of some type of spectacle.

They were due for some luck. This proved to be of great benefit in traversing the rest of the city relatively unabated which was the man's first concern. The next would be the difficult task of infiltrating the barracks for the most crucial aspects of the plan. Though this did little to discourage them.

As they began their climb up the hundreds of steps leading to the Hardscape, they commenced performing their rehearsed personas of tutor and pupil moving swiftly past marching guards.

Having moved closer to the glow of the amphitheater that stood proudly before them, Tobias stopped in his tracks plagued with curiosity.

Roland Deglin has given the city newfound confidence in Pinnacle's youth. He had made a name for himself within the Visitant's Forest...

"That's him, idn't it?" The boy gasped. "The one we're after? Roland Deg-"

"Quiet, Tobias!" The man said, alarmed with the breach of discretion. "You're interrupting your lesson. Now, as the text states, the development of Pinnacle had once hinged on being solely that of an agrarian economy..."

The Ugly One continued the rouse as they walked past two guards who relaxed from their suspicious gazes to retreat back to the coronation and gaze from whatever their vantage would allow.

"Sorry," the boy squeaked when they nestled near a small courtyard, still void of passersby. "It's just exciting, that's all."

Grumbling some sort of indignation at the narrow escape, the Ugly One spotted their approach. Just above them on a ledge stood a sturdy wooden lattice that became ensnared by tendrils and carpeted with lush ovular leaves.

"I am sure I don't need to remind you, that you are not to blurt out our intentions to break in, do I?" The man shot him a reproachful glance. "Now let's get going while these dregs are distracted."

Steeling himself, the Ugly One ran, planting his foot up the wall gripping his fingers on the terrace above. Having pulled himself up, he reached for the boy who attempted the same feet, less gracefully before being hoisted by his breeches to the same spot. From there, they shimmied onto a small ledge, that led to another placing them directly in front of the lattice.

As they did, Tobias gazed down to find his knees were trembling uncontrollably, but also caught sight of the one that must have been called Roland. The man saw and could only guess at the barrage of questions biting in his tiny mind. Why was he so special? What has all the fuss about him over? The boy was too busy studying the figure below—who in turn was busy admiring something in his hands—to notice he bumped into his companion's off-centered body causing him to teeter sideways momentarily.

Before he could quietly reprimand the boy, again, the Ugly One saw who he was staring at and in spite of himself did the same.

"Is that him? Roland?" Tobias whispered, shimmying to the next terrace.

"Mmhmm," the man nodded slowly.

It's been cycles...

"Watch it!" The boy's dainty fingers manage to snare the man by his sleeve in time for him to realize the ledge had dropped off leaving one foot dangling.

"So—you've proven yourself useful...for once," he said with a smile.

"More than once," Tobias corrected.

It took them one more ledge to climb before they reached the open window, allowing them to stalk the quiet corridor of the barracks.

Quickly, they stole down its path until they happened upon the bedroom they sought.

Gently closing the door behind them, the Ugly One gestured for the boy to unpack the equipment needed. As if being caught inside a room known to have held an important moment of history, the man walked about the sparsely arranged fixtures: a bed with tightly dressed sheets, a large stitched mat, and a writing desk with nothing kept on it.

"Roe," he whispered. "Still surviving I see."

"You sure this is the place?" Tobias asked, barring the door closed with a chair.

One of the drawers of the desk was pulled open to find a crumpled letter addressed to Roe. The man felt strange. But what was it? Sadness? Guilt? Fear? He did not know. It was a similar feeling he experienced when he learned of his mother's tragic passing. And what became of his father? To this day he still did not know...

"Yes," he said abruptly. "Do you have my gloves?"

The boy quickly reached in his bag and lugged out the heavy pair of trauma gloves.

"Right—let's get to it and keep a look out, Tobes! We're as good as dead if we're caught...no—don't cry! Look, I'm a man—they'll hang me, but you're just a lad...you they'll probably just spank for a bit."

Chapter Nine

The Jagged Letters

"I saw someone die today. We burned him, for being seditious. A heretic. But what does that mean? Are you born one? Are they just made? Could they be anyone that simply needs to be swept out of the way? That's the scary part. Horrors like what I saw tonight almost make me wish the Fog would just come and end it all." –

– Extract from a sentinel's diary

Although Roe had entered the Priority's personal dining hall countless times before, he still found it arranged in a manner that didn't befit the station of a powerful man like Deglin. But perhaps he had been taken in by too many fairy stories with kings and their piles of gold they had a propensity to lay upon in a secretive room at night. Here, the dining hall was clean and spacious but had an understated look that didn't fit someone who was tasked to save the last shreds of humanity. There were no elaborate statues or handfuls of servants standing at attention behind every seat at the table. His first chance at setting foot inside long ago had given Roe expectations of everything to be encrusted with valuable metals and encrusted with precious stones.

The most alluring part of the room, for most guests, was the exquisitely crafted wooden table resting at its center. The intricate carvings running down the legs and along the edges of the long table made it a masterpiece in its own right. The wistful look of the rolling lines, representing the wind, ran along its length, while interlocking tendrils from vines and the trickling of rain spiraled down the leg supports.

The tabletop was smoothed, polished, and glossy; capable of accommodating ten guests properly but one seat always remained empty at the end. This seat was constantly reserved for Saffron, even though she could no longer fill it. The rest was to be filled by the remaining eight guests.

Small placards served to arrange the seating: Berl, Tessa, Regent Warrick, and Regent Silas would line Deglin's left, while Ophelia, Captain Raleigh, Regent Magda, and Roe would sit on his right. The regents in attendance were Deglin's most trusted advisors. Silas managed the military and armament sector while Magda was the head of the legislative house. Ophelia had taken the place of Ivan who presumably, due to an earlier run-in with Tessa, decided not to make an appearance.

Everyone had arrived and exchanged pleasantries except for Tessa, who had yet to show up. Although the demanding etiquette of the high-stationed guests dictated she wasn't considered late, it didn't seem to matter for her date who was busy nervously spying through the window looking for her whereabouts. The guests were all about to sit when she came huffing in, trying to fix the few strands of black hair that was no doubt kicked up from a brisk run that began at the commissary. Her hair was still braided in the back, and she wasn't in her formal attire.

To her date's dismay, she was still wearing the black scuffed apron that she just remembered to take off upon his sharpened glare. Even so, she looked wonderful in Roe's eyes despite the formal occasion. Berl bit at his lip and shook his head when he pulled out her chair brusquely. She didn't acknowledge him.

Deglin beamed at her, "My dear, Miss Emlan, tell me, while you were walking up the boulevard, did you happen to see Ivan Fern anywhere by chance?"

Both Berl and Roe looked at her with eager eyes knowing the story behind the absence.

"I did happen to see him gathering, oh, what was it?" she thought insincerely for a moment shifting in her seat. "Some thread, a spool or two, and a small sleeve of needles between his lips. You know, I *think* he secretly fancies the life of a seamstress," her shocked expression fooled everyone at the table except her friends who were trembling with snickers.

Surrounding the entire perimeter of the room were, plants and flowers emitting pungent and sweet-smelling fragrances throughout the chamber. This aroma mixed beautifully with the savory smell of meats and cooked vegetables from the kitchen a room over.

Tessa ran her fingertips across the surface of the wood and continued, "What a beautiful table you have, Mr. Deglin. I've never seen such carvings before, and the surface itself is so well kept. I feel simply awful eating off such a work of art."

"Thank you, Tessa. This table was a gift to my beloved and myself after being sworn in. I knew this table was something she would love. Every time I eat here, I can see Saffron's face reflecting off the polished wood." He looked down and stroked the table's surface gently as if it were her cheek.

Dinner was satisfying enough and seemed quick to Roe, because of the engaging conversations that transpired during its course. The final one was raising a topic he had preferred to stay out of but staying away from attention wasn't something he was capable of lately. It had come time for Berl to regale the eager audience about his adventure with Roe and Little Hex. The others tried to pry into the reasoning behind his decision to comb the forest in the first place.

"It was just a hunch, I suppose. Kids like mischief. The forest is big and allows for mischief." Roe tried his best to cover for the hallucination he had of his mother. Then, again, Delphine's description of the woman who appeared to her sounded like the same woman who had visited him before.

But why? Why would she lure Delphine out there?

"Roe?"

He aroused and observed Deglin and the others looking at him with anticipation.

"How was your time spent with the girl?"

"Hmm? Del-Little Hex? Oh, she's nice. Quite adventurous, but then again what kid isn't? She just let it get the best of her."

"What she did was cost me production!" Warrick slapped his hand on the table and a collection of groans ensued.

"Damn it, Warrick, not this again. Clearly, no harm was done here, and yet you continue to act to the contrary. Why can't you be satisfied? What will it take?" Deglin asked.

His strained voice let the others know that he was growing tired of listening to complaints. It had seemed this wasn't the first instance.

"I want you to take action on the situation!" Warrick barked. "Show her and the rest of those heathens out there that such actions are not to be tolerated. Her clan's just as guilty. Heed my words—they're raising her rogue."

"What would you have me do? A public flogging on the Hardscape? Shackle her to a boulder in the Fog? Let those creatures rip her apart? She's just a child."

"Sir, they aren't heathens. I know I haven't spent as much time with them as you or the others have, but Little Hex and her family seem to be honest people," Roe said.

"Don't call them 'people'! You've seen how they leech off us, how they make it harder for the rest of us to survive on the crops we've grown and the land we live off. I've been around them long enough to know that they're a burden, they don't work right."

Warrick's face grew flushed, sweat was beading on his brow. His balding gray wisps were kicked up with the sharp motions thrown by his passionate rant.

"Now, I'm not as learn-ed as you prissy folks are, but maybe, just maybe it's because you've been workin' 'em beyond what they're capable of, old man," Raleigh said, his eyes were piercing around the snifter pressed to his lips. He knocked back his drink without care and propped up his black boots against Warrick's chair.

"Nonsense. It's not just the ones working in my quarter. Silas can tell you they are no good beyond a few hours making armor and the like." As he finished, Silas could be seen nodding in a matter that would make a true sycophant envious.

"Well, what about food?" Roe asked. "Suppose a human doesn't get enough food, they grow weak and can't function well. Visitants would be no different, right?"

"If you haven't noticed, we have our own mouths to feed. We give them what we can spare, which isn't much."

"From your parties I've been to, that doesn't seem to trouble you much." The captain produced a rare smile, clearly relishing every moment of watching Warrick squirm in his vain attempts at shoring up a defense for himself.

"I guess you can expect to be looking in on them from the streets from now on!"

"Oooh! Big loss," the captain laughed to himself.

Roe was amused at how easy the captain made it look to annoy the grumpy old man. Raleigh had a crafty grin on his face as he began to accidentally kick Warrick's chair repeatedly throughout dinner. Roe brought his hands to his face under the pretense of using his napkin, stifling a laugh.

Warrick must have noticed this and decided to focus his efforts elsewhere. "I am curious as to why you're acting as advocate for them so suddenly?"

"I just want to."

Remembering what Nox said made him only partially honest. From their expressions, he could tell how the dinner guests all felt about the Visitants simply by their facial expressions.

The conversation was fueled further by the other regents chiming in the same sentiment as their colleague. Ever since the day the Visitants escaped the Fog, they had been stranded within Pinnacle's borders. Everyone knew it. Their actions conveyed that of sluggish and vapid beings. But Delphine and the younger ones hadn't been showing the same symptoms, yet.

Roe hadn't counted on her staying long, as the next group of grayclan departures was about ready to be announced within days. If debts outstanding were removed, or when they grew ill beyond means of using resources excessively, humans would help them try and flee for some haven beyond with rations for the journey. That is what they've done for as long as he could remember.

"Sir, why do they all stay? I mean why wait for them to get ill and suffer as they do?" There was a potent reluctance in Roe's voice.

"We've speculated the wicked beings in the Fog had pursued them to the borders of our world. They sought refuge here with the help of some of our own, but many perished in the escape. The demons the boys encountered in the forest aren't easy to fool and certainly will not stop the pursuit of us either.

"Our only protection is the pinnacle lamps and even they are slowly failing us. If we let them all go at once without any course of subterfuge, we would lead them to slaughter. We *must* be competent after all." Deglin sounded as if he was mounting a defense rather than a simple explanation.

Seeing her friend look shamefully down at his lap, Tessa chimed in. "I was wondering the same thing. We know the story of how Pinnacle came to be, but that predates their arrival. It seems a waste to not share our history of generosity to the young ones."

"Please, there's no one else left in the world to know of our generosity. Besides, Pinnacle's youth should be taught how to acclimate to their own demise than for undue compassion," Silas snapped.

"No harm done," Ophelia interjected. "They're just curious. To withhold our history is a travesty, in my 'umble opinion, which may not count for much. But what's the point in takin' pride in our small world if our kids won't share the same sentiment and continue it when we pass on?"

Deglin found himself nodding slowly, his hands folded beneath his chin. Even though Ophelia was merely a servant with no political merit, her opinions, in Deglin's eyes were invaluable as her perspective gave him a lens he normally couldn't see through. This common truth agitated the regents, which in turn made the rest of the guests happy. It undermined their authority and opinions while making Deglin look even more capable as a leader. Roe had been given many opportunities to see the inner workings of politics since being adopted, but he never appreciated them until now. Her words made the Priority have an idea so vulgar the regents spewed their wine onto the tables where they formed small puddles.

"What do you intend on doing?" Magda asked. Her cigarette from the black holder cradled in her fingertips slipped onto the table as she looked like a cornered animal pleading with the other regents for rescue. Their widened eyes echoed this sentiment.

"I intend on telling the story behind the Night of Safe Passage. It's our most heralded event, most people are only aware that we celebrate the day we opened our lands to our guests. They don't realize our true altruism is in allowing them an honest valiant attempt to find their true home. Perhaps, even, find a way to where they can successfully navigate it and give us insight to how we can possibly beat those fiends for the last time."

Roe thought of Delphine's words at the enclave. *I want to dance...without shame. Can he give that to me?*

"I think we should let them attend," he blurted. "And not be servants, be guests. They should dance, sing, and mingle with us. It might be seen as an outstretched hand of peace to the Visitants."

Questions began flying around. The regents questioned Roe's motive. The youth questioned the regent's protests and the captain incessantly questioned Warrick's manhood. As always, Deglin managed to allay their concerns for the moment and redirected the conversation letting everyone know how late it had taken them to finish it.

As Warrick wearily gazed out the window, the rest followed suit. The mist in the distance reflected a deeper purple. Night was fully upon them.

"If you'll excuse me, I must get some sleep. I shall see to it that no one runs off from their duties. Not just today, not just tomorrow. Never. It was a pleasure as always, my Priority." Warrick whipped around and walked out mumbling Ivan's name over to himself.

The other regents filed out, congratulating Roe as they left. Everyone else in the room was relieved to see their departure, especially Raleigh. He swiped Warrick's half-finished drink and gulped it once, looking sullenly at the doorway as if Warrick were standing in it. With a forceful belch, he pointed to the boys.

"I'll see you two early in the mornin'. I want all sentinels to meet with me in the training yard. Roe, plan on gettin' there first. I have some things to go over with you before the rest show," he said.

"What? Why?" Berl cried.

"We are deciding security detail for the Night of Safe Passage. We're planning something different than what's been done before. A competition tomorrow between the guards that patrol during the day and the night sentinels to determine who can partake in the Night's festivities," Deglin smiled.

"What happens to the group that loses?" Roe asked. He grew nervous at the thought, but he looked over at Ophelia, and the enthusiastic smile she gave him bolstered some courage and even some pent-up curiosity.

"Losers work. They'll take the winning group's shift and work that too," the captain smiled. "There a problem?"

"Sounds cruel to me," Berl huffed. "Why don't we just work our own shifts? I don't mind working during the party."

"No," the captain scoffed. "Sounds like you're afraid to test your mettle? What you need to do is take after your friend and make your daddy proud. Cowardice might be swept under the rug in the Pinnacle Guard, but not in *my* sentinels."

Raleigh knew how to jilt Berl, and it seemed to be turning into a twisted habit. When Roe looked over at him, he was standing firm with his legs rigid, trying to hide the fact they were shaking. His hands were tense and balled into a fist. He didn't make eye contact, just focusing on a point on the wall behind the person he was speaking with. Bloody hell, it was textbook fear for Berl.

Then Raleigh walked out wagging his finger in the air, "Not in *my* sentinels!"

The Priority placed a hand on his shoulder whispering, "Don't embarrass me, son, please."

Ophelia and Tessa both had excused themselves following the captain. Roe was about ready to leave with them until Deglin pulled him aside as well. Over his shoulder, he saw Berl feverishly scratching his head, another nervous habit of his. The fingers were working feverishly until they realized it had not gone unnoticed. So Berl quickly waved them a goodnight, clearly embarrassed.

Now, Roe was alone with his hero.

"Before you leave, I wanted to talk to you. I hope you understand how proud I am of you and Berl," Deglin said.

Guessing where the conversation was leading, Roe was determined to quell it immediately.

"I'll be fine, sir."

"I know *you* will be. It's... Berl." Deglin glanced over at the entry to ensure they were alone, his voice brought to a hushed sound. "He'll have to show that he's capable of handling anything. There can be no signs of weakness. None! I'm afraid he's been coddled too much, and that placing him with the sentinels was a mistake. I'm ashamed to say he embarrassed me at times. The

Regency will be merciless if he fails. Please, look out for him. But he mustn't know this exchange took place, understand?!"

Roe nodded slowly, looking positively flummoxed at what was divulged to him, something more suited for his most trusted advisor.

"Promise me?!"

Roe nodded with urgency this time, somewhat scared at this unfamiliar man staring wide-eyed and unfolding right in front of him.

Quickly, his demeanor changed so drastically as if he had not just confided a long-held confession. The Priority then retrieved a sheathed blade that rested on a nearby stand before he left for his chambers. With a smirk, he motioned for him to grab it from his grip. On the hilt, were Roe's new initials R.D.

"I look forward to seeing you partake in the Night's festivities… when you win tomorrow," he winked and left the room with his hands folded behind him and head uplifted proudly in his typical procession.

Outside the lamps were emitting their usual vibrant blue swath of light toward the darkness. They reflected off the Fog and revealed the large shadows creeping about. The imposing shadowforms were fast at work.

"Not tonight, you devils." The blade hissed from his sheath as he walked out to face them. With each swipe, each parry at the foes, made him think incessantly, *Give me the strength of a soldier!* It may have been a false sense of security, but Roe fervently thought with his stepfather in charge, the lamps couldn't fail. He would figure out a way to beat the Fog!

He skipped up the stairs of the barracks, two at a time, back to his room. Finally, returning to a place where he could feel completely at ease, his only true home: his plush bed. There he could ruminate about how good things were going. But he also thought about the puzzling events that plagued the day, the very same he knew would deter any sleep.

Many thoughts reminded him his world wasn't perfect. The thought of dealing with Ivan Fern, the sight of his mother who apparently led Delphine straight into danger, and the talk he had with Deglin. He placed all hope for answers to be found in a good night's rest.

However, his bedroom door was left ajar, not to his liking, but the bed was made, its pristine look made him think of his friend and how her attendance at the dinner made him so happy.

Closing the door to his room caused him to walk in complete darkness. He hadn't bumped into anything, so no one played any funny tricks on him by rearranging anything within. About to undress, Roe encountered the peculiar scent of scorched wood.

He couldn't see any flames in the dark nor out his window which was sealed tight, but the smell was getting stronger toward the door. As he approached it, he could see the faint glow of burn markings pressed into the wood that was still warm to the touch. When he closed his eyes, the shaped letters glowed momentarily behind his eyelids, echoes from the faint glow.

Berl? he thought idiotically, *no couldn't be, he was at dinner. And why would he do such a thing?*

He fumbled in the dark to light a candle. When he managed to light it, a step back revealed black, jagged letters. It was a message in the dark that read:

Prepare for the ascent

CHAPTER TEN

A LESSON IN TRAUMA

"I hate to confess it, but when I'm at my wit's end with the commissary, I sometimes walk over to the training yard to see Raleigh tear through his sentinels. I hear the swearing. I see the flames they have to dodge from those gloves. I imagine the foes in the Fog they will have to face one day. Makes me feel better knowing I have only snobs and rich folk to deal with."

- EXCERPT FROM TESSA EMLAN'S DIARY

The smoky tendrils dissipated slowly as Roe sat on the floor studying the etched door. This phantom message had him guessing wildly until the most obvious answer finally hit him…

"Ivan… wasn't at dinner… and apparently… had somewhere he needed to be!" he whispered fiercely.

His suspicions were leading him astray as he had lacked tangible proof it was Ivan other than a grudge, but until there was evidence suggesting otherwise, he had to be the culprit. Motivations for recent events suggested he had a perfect opportunity to strike. Why not now?

When the burned writing on the door had cooled, he stood up from the cold floor that caused his legs to protest with chilled aches. It was time to fulfill his urge to trace the scorched imprints, though he knew it wasn't going to do him any good solving the matter. He also was certain sleep wouldn't come knowing someone crept into his room and violated a part of it.

Roe thought himself a wimp for it but ruled the only logical action he could take at the moment was to barricade the window and door to his room with his bedroom furniture. With whatever time that remained to him following this task, he would desperately need for sleep.

At last! Roe thought, wiping his brow.

The job was done. He was sealed in. But now his head began to throb, his eyes burning with each blink. Finally, as he laid himself down, Roe closed his eyes for only a moment, but the moment stretched into several hours.

He awoke to the creaking noise of wood being bent. Someone was attempting to open the door. The stool placed in front of it barring entry was giving way in slow heaves. He had slept in his uniform, which wasn't comfortable, but it allowed him to quickly unsheathe his newly acquired blade.

Immediately, he readied himself for the culprit's return. As the twang of metal came out, he crept slowly behind the door as his heartbeat hastened. Ready to fling the chair back and strike, he paused as a familiar voice stopped him before he brought his blade upon them.

"Whelp, what's wrong with your door?" Ophelia's voice blared through the door.

His own palm struck his forehead for his stupidity, realizing how close he was to hurting her. Quickly, he sheathed his weapon and threw it back toward the bed, pulling the chair away into the shadows.

Her voice still stifled behind the thick door cried pleadingly, "Please tell me you're ready?"

The door opened enough for the maid to see his cheeks squeeze between the small space between it and the doorframe. She was standing there and gave him a sigh of relief seeing his uniform on.

"Oh, thank goodness. Can't see why the Priority makes me get you up like this. Always on time, you are."

"You know me," Roe forced a chuckle. Little did she know his punctual behavior was purely accidental this morning as he was awoken by her. She then glanced over his shoulder and her eyebrows furrowed.

"Suppose I do, but I can't, for the life of me, know why your desk is pinned against the window with your bed. How are you to know if it's morn'?"

His eyes closed slowly as he was convinced she'd found him out. His body began to shake and stammer toward the makeshift barricade. As he fumbled to get the small desk back on its four legs, the maid began to unpin the boots wedged behind the door.

"No! Ophelia! I'll get them. You have more important things to do than dress me!" Her hand immediately pressed against her chest. Walking briskly toward the smashed boots he gave her an awkward smile.

"Are you alright? Need me to tell the captain you're ill?"

"No! I'm alright—fine more like it. I'm just nervous that's all! It's a meeting with the captain after all. I mean scare-ey!"

She walked briskly over to shoo him out the door, "He's gonna be worse if you're late. Now git!"

Ophelia usually was never this eager to get him to leave unless it meant serious business, and an angered captain was serious enough to escalate the present danger to that of having to deal with one of the shadowforms the way she pushed him out the door. Clearly, this meant there wasn't much time left to reach the yard before the captain did. To make a good impression, he would have to beat him to the punch and that meant no time to chance a stop for breakfast or his morning ritual.

Behind the barracks sat the largest drilling square left in existence—a walled enclosure whose brick walls were pockmarked with charred shapes from mock battles of the past. It was here that those initiated in the House sparred and trained with the vast array of weaponry. The area was a large, squared dirt yard surrounded by the walls that resembled an old fort on the frontier. In the middle of it was a tall lookout post. Sometimes men were stationed there during these drills hurling spears or shooting projectiles at the sentinels down below.

But the true might of Raleigh's army came ironically from the powerful and daunting trauma crafts that the loathsome Regent Warrick was developing for the pending doomsday. Row wondered if the captain ever came to this realization, that his gravitas was bolstered in part by a man he was all too eager to express his hatred for.

The wild possibilities that the Visitants could create seemed endless in his mind having seen previous concept models during exhibitions held each Night of Safe Passage celebration. Really, the only craft that had been fully tested and commissioned for use was the trauma gloves, though the weapons were nothing foreign to him. True, he didn't have a lot of experience with these weapons in close-quarter combat or practiced his aim using it as a projectile weapon being a former Settlement Guard, but every sentinel received one so his time would come soon enough.

In the past, Berl had let him look at his pair behind closed doors. It was a criminal offense for anyone to be in possession of any trauma craft unless he had the papers to supply. Such documents were only issued to sentinels, craftsmen, or any high-ranking official but this didn't stop Berl's devil-may-care nature from getting the better of him.

The yard before him was barren, the dirt had been raked recently forming small, regimented rows up and down the square to make it look more like a field to sow than a place for tactical practice. It was just Roe, the dirt, and the sparring mannequins that lined its perimeter.

"No one else here," he grinned to himself, "I'm in good company."

On the perimeter of the yard was a quaint little bench he chose to sit and wait. During that time, he realized how different everything appeared in the yard since his promotion. The space looked much larger and the evidence of many cycles worth of field maneuvers was plentiful. He even turned his hands over and under, gazing down at the new uniform hugging his body to see this was truly happening, for better or worse.

The Pinnacle Guard weren't expected to do a whole lot, having unfairly been viewed as glorified peacekeepers in the eyes of their superiors. Sentinels were called in whenever serious trouble had made a presence. The white-clad men rarely used the yard, because it seemed to see most of its time occupied with Raleigh's group performing drills and situational primers.

"Ready, Sham?"

Roe shifted a bit to see the captain standing there with a latched case, with no change in his stern facade. The young man started looking around, thinking the man surely had to be talking to someone else.

His brows drew together quickly realizing this hadn't been the case.

"What did you say?"

"Are…you…ready…Sham? Thought I was clear being's how it's just you and me. Would you like me to talk slower or dumber for you?"

"Why call me that?"

"It's what you are. I can confidently say you shouldn't be wearin' that." He gestured menacingly right at Roe's chest. "So, that's your name. Sham, meanin' I think you're a downright fraud."

"Well, I hate the name," Roe muttered.

Raleigh looked inquisitively placing one leg on the bench, "Well, would 'Peepants' be more to your liking? Wait—my apologies—come to think of it, that one is reserved for your stepbrother already. Be grateful I didn't pick somethin' worse. Now, shut your gob because I have to give ya this before the others get here. You need to practice and be ready."

"For what?"

Roe's patience for Raleigh was waning already. He knew he was being treated like a child. That he wasn't ready for what was in the box even though there was an inkling of what it contained.

Oh, how he wanted to yell at his superior to get on with it, but it would be revisiting that awkward moment Berl had earlier in the barracks. If it was repeated at least Roe was alone when the captain proceeded to humiliate him.

Raleigh thumped the black case on the bench beside Roe and flipped up the latch, nudging it toward him. Roe opened the lid nonchalantly to shake off any childish excitement he may have been showing, his way of being defiant.

In the looming maw of darkness within, he could make out the silhouette of the weapons. He probed it delicately with but one finger as if it were a disgusting thing. When the sensation of polished, cool metal met his skin, his eyes were drawn closed as he began to picture the splendor of the instruments. Splendor hurriedly melded to meet up with unrestrained anticipation wrapping his fingers around the objects. The brilliance of touching smooth, polished, strong metal, the supple cloth between the plates of the contraptions was within his grasp, it was something he couldn't quite explain to Berl if he wanted to. His eyes opened with enthusiasm likened to the way Ophelia flung open the curtains to a promising new day.

They were his: a pair of trauma gloves. The most wondrous magic he could think of.

"Yep. I figured you knew already on account of Peepants lettin' you brandish his pair like a toy. Nearly burned down the barracks if I remember right."

Looking at the gloves, Roe feigned apathy waiting to launch his own attack. "You saw that, huh? My you're a quick one! What gave it away? Was it the smoke coming from the room? Or was it the dozens of people screaming 'fire'?" He didn't care if he set the captain off. His frustration was mounting, and he knew one of them was bound to start a fight.

Roe immediately felt compelled to throw in one last barb thinking of his humiliated friend, "Captain, how did the Learner's Guild let a mastermind like you slip through their hands?"

Raleigh vaulted the bench and grabbed Roe by the shoulders in no time flat. If not for the tight grip the captain's hardened fingers had on the leather cross straps of Roe's chest, he'd have been tasting dirt by now.

"Do – not – mess – with – me!" he barked, punctuating each word with fury. "I am well within my right to kick you out into the street if I want. Do you thing you can survive another go all by your lonesome out there? Or will you need your idol to rescue you again? If you want me to kick your ass all the way to the city gate, you've only to ask."

It was nearly an exact repetition of his encounter with Berl back in the atrium. The only difference was Raleigh's victim wasn't incapacitated by fear. Roe's eyes met his and he felt truly little fear, even though he knew a hard punch might be coming. Was it stupidity or bravery? The lines seemed to blur far too often to tell until the end result was had.

"I'll settle when you do," Roe said coolly in spite of himself.

The captain lifted his captive up suddenly and let gravity do his dirty work sending the newly minted sentinel falling to the ground ruining the superbly raked ruts in the dirt. The taste of the dust he inhaled when he landed made him cough a bit. Grunting, he proceeded to stand up quickly as if nothing happened, brushing himself off when the captain turned away for a moment to appraise the yard's setup.

"What do I need to practice with? These?"

"They are weapons, after all," Raleigh grunted, tugging one onto his arm grimacing only slightly. "The most effective and lethal devices our guard has'ta offer. As a Son of Pinnacle, a sentinel, you'll need to become deadly with 'em. Otherwise, you will fail everyone. I know you don't care for me, but Pinnacle and the Priority…they mean something to you, don't they?

"So, do me a favor. Shut it, listen up, and put 'em on. If you remember your stint from Junior Deglin, you'll feel some pain in your arm when you slide 'em on. It's how you know they're anchored proper."

Roe hesitated at first but started with the right hand. The gloves themselves were heavier than he remembered and were difficult to anchor onto his hand. He tugged at the tight, protective mesh until it rested midway up his forearm then looked at his palm with the contraption on. Each digit had the small circular grooves that he remembered. The center of the palm cradled the carved glyph that gave the glove its fatal quality. It was dull orange right now, not very ornate. Small almost undetectable black specs were suspended within.

When he had succeeded with the first, Roe grabbed the sleeve on his forearm and gave it a good tug. From what he remembered, the user had to tug at the gloves to secure the hand in place and then prepare to feel a prick that caught the virgin wearer off guard. He felt the puncture in the forearm, which startled him, but gradually the pain dissipated to nothing soon enough. The gemstone in the center lit up and emitted a low hum. The procedure was repeated with the other piece until the pair became a part of him.

"Don't do anythin' 'til I tell you to. Keep your hands at the ready. Now, look here. No, not like that you idiot! Stand ready. Feet shoulder width. Now flare your fingers out." He demonstrated this simply enough with his palms facing the ground and his fingers flared out. The captain's scuffed boots were staggered apart giving him a solid foundation for support. Roe soon mimicked without needing another reprimand and stood with the captain as they faced down a pair of unsuspecting mannequins who were not formidable in the least, but they would suffice for a novice.

"See these targets? Destroy 'em," he gestured at the motionless foes.

Raleigh's stance shifted, and his right fist closed. A glow punched through his fingers, and Roe heard him grunt heaving his right arm at the target. Powerful energy issued forth and met its target which shattered in a hail of splintered wood and flames smoldering in the dirt. The captain's lips curled up just so at the beautiful sight.

"Alright, Sham, pick your dominant hand and I'll walk you through it."

The captain explained further. As the user closed the hand, he would feel resistance against the fingers. The stones in the finger pads were composed of the same gem as the large glyph in the palm. When in proximity to each other, they grew unstable and agitated. Because of this agitated state, energy was created. Keeping the hand closed built its power and if it were too great, accuracy would drop upon being unleashed, or the user could be fatally hurt from the discharge. Another reason strict ownership was paramount. Roe could now appreciate how easily they could have been killed that day brandishing them the way they did.

"This gemstone is peculiar," Raleigh smiled curiously at his armored palm. "It's a parasite, really, but it was discovered that this property also formed a relationship with the holder. It draws energy from the blood it sucks outta ya, which keeps it from growing brittle, but the holder can wield it as a weapon. But if you let it take too much from you..." he allowed his finger to violently drag across his throat to finish his dire warning.

"How will I know when to let go?"

"Suppose I need a simple answer for an idiot like you: when it starts to burn your hand. When you feel you have your target, throw your hand forward as if you're throwing any object. Use any gesture that allows you to hit the target."

Raleigh gestured again with his head, so the boy could start making his own destruction. His nerves were getting the best of him feeling as though everyone in Pinnacle had managed to find hiding places nearby just to snigger at how awful this was going to be. It was only just the two of them, but the man in tow had a nasty reputation for being overbearing. If his strikes weren't perfect, he was sure to feel the wrath that would ensue.

With his right foot out, Roe imagined clutching a miniaturized version of the captain in his hand and felt his fingers quiver. Vibrations formed that tickled at first, but he could feel the heat swell and the power he wielded within his fist tried to pry his fingers apart. He felt hot and flushed. The lids of his eyes closed with fatigue. His forearm was tingling, and his mind was racing with so many thoughts at once.

"Sham! Let go!"

Roe yelped in pain and flicked the flare down and out toward the dirt. The force knocked both backward, careening over the benches. Roe buried his face in the dirt as well as his hand. His palm was smoldering as was Raleigh's mood.

"Seems like things haven't changed. I give you clear instructions to prevent any screw-ups, but it looks like you're becomin' more like Peepants, incompetent and useless flesh! Outta just throw you out to the shadowforms as bait."

Roe stood up and readied himself to charge at him. Raleigh pressed out his left hand to halt him. "Don't start what you can't finish. You have one more chance, or you're out."

They both dusted themselves off and went back to the front of the bench. Raleigh had the authority vested to render the boy jobless with another miscue. The thought of Raleigh's anger didn't terrify him; it was Deglin's disappointment, Berl's unknown fate.

This time the burning sensation came too quickly. Roe flung with all his might, but it sailed far from the target. He tried with the left but couldn't tolerate the severe vibrations. As such, the accuracy was even worse than the prior attempt.

With frustration, the captain shook his head woefully, "We're done."

"I'm not!"

"I don't believe you."

Raleigh was laughing; becoming more condescending and boorish. How Roe hated him at that moment. If he was going to throw Roe out, ruin his life and what he worked for to escape the city's vile underworld well, he wasn't going to make it easy for Raleigh.

He stood there, gearing up another flame in his tender right hand. "Hey, Captain!" he barked like a commander giving the order on the frontline as flames left his fingertips. Roe felt deep, immense regret the moment his fingers loosened.

The flare was within a few paces from the captain, but he whipped around and made a deflection with an undulating barrier emitted from his right glove. Sparks flew and danced around him, his focus squarely on his opponent.

The captain grinned fiendishly, "I still don't believe you!"

Raleigh flung one back at his attacker who stumbled back unprepared for it. Instinctively, Roe held his thumb over the palm pressing against the glyph and the remaining flared out. The same barrier emitted from his hand, traveled through his fingertips creating the temporary ward. With a crackle, the force was great enough to send him sliding against the dirt dragging his feet, fighting to stay upright. Roe responded with a second, then a third flare. The latter he held onto the longest, making it by far the largest he had produced.

"You want to throw me out? I'll give you hell before you do!" Roe couldn't believe what he was saying. Those words weren't like him but feeling such a fierce power at his fingertips…there was something about challenging Raleigh that had sent a primal urge of competition through his body.

"You best quit now! You're just like Peepants, a loser!"

Raleigh easily blocked with his left, then swatted another with his right. The last flare fizzled away against the ward in one hand just as the captain unleashed a sidearm throw at his quarry with the other. Roe lost sight of Raleigh's projectile, as he was in awe at the captain's brute skill. The flare scooted along the ground; its path was far too unpredictable to deflect so Roe was forced to roll out of the way.

The thought sickened him as he lay on the ground gasping for air, but Roe was convinced he wasn't going to leave this fight alive. He attacked his superior officer and was going to die soon because of it, whether by the captain's hand or an executioner's for the attempted assault.

The captain was clearly ready for more but saw his opponent's feeble repose; smoke was rising from the gloves. Blood trickled down his hands as Roe peeled the heavy metal off. The heavy things were more dangerous than he had thought. The heat was overburdening; the ground beneath him seemed to heave up and down like it too was drawing in deep, heavy breaths. His vision began to blur.

Raleigh stalked closer.

Roe tore his eyes from the imposing shadow creeping toward him. He clutched the ground, squeezing the dirt between his fingers. He had to prepare for the pain and the dreadful senses that accompanied a death by fire. No screaming. No crying. He only wanted to think of a pleasant thought before he departed from this world, riding Chief was what came to mind.

Instead, something stiff prodded Roe, who cracked an eye open to find a bare hand being offered to him instead of a fiery fist. Raleigh had already latched his gloves onto his belt in an act of armistice. He wasn't happy or upset, although it appeared that he was trying to contain a smile given the unusual strain around his mouth.

"Up you go," he said holding out his rough, sweaty palm.

"I tried to hurt you. If you're gonna finish me off, let's get it over with," Roe mumbled.

"Don't be stupid. That's what I wanted from you. For as long as I've known you, I never saw that fire inside you that showed me you care. You were actually content with bein' a Settlement Guard. You're a sentinel, not some piss-ant like *them*. And in time, I hope you can earn your real name back. Go rest up a bit, I've got more in store."

Roe made for the bench when the captain said haughtily over his shoulder, "Besides, Sham, you couldn't hurt me if I was bed-ridden."

Whether or not that was true didn't matter to him, because Roe was glad he didn't hurt anyone and was proud of defending himself to the captain of all foes.

When the other sentinels finally arrived, Roe found there to be much less than he expected. There were more Pinnacle Guards by far, but their skill paled in comparison to a member of the House. Were there large numbers a commentary about the Guard's expendability?

The group found themselves gathering around the captain, who was explaining the details of why they were gathered. Many slapped hands, grunted, and showed off other so-called masculine displays of approval when Raleigh declared a tactics competition was going to be held. Most, but not all of the women were reserved if their relaxed stances had anything to say about it. The captain briskly explained how the winner was to be determined.

Four guards from the night patrol would face four from the dawn patrol in the training yard to represent their respective sides. The task was to incinerate four of the opponent's "civilians" they were protecting before their own civilians caught fire, without crossing the center line. The teams were also given the approval to dispatch each other in the process. Of course, Raleigh made them all use a smaller carved glyph which emitted a weaker flare.

"It'll still burn clothes, skin, hair, but in armor, you'll just feel nice and toasty," he said.

Once a guard had caught fire, he, or she would be disqualified. Of course, the captain wouldn't stand to be a simple bystander knowing he was able to hone in on each of his soldiers' particular weaknesses, so he boasted he too would be in on the action. From the tall lookout post in the center of the training yard, Raleigh would perch and hurl flames indiscriminately at everyone below.

Many volunteered for the competition, but those new to the House were unaware that this wasn't Raleigh's style. He wanted to expose the weakest and the most inexperienced guards first making Berl and Roe prime targets for selection. Chosen alongside them was one older woman with a scar on her cheek and a husky man twice the size of Roe. He carried intimidation in his eyes, much as Berl did. This was not going to bode well Roe thought sizing up what was across from them.

Their opponents appeared better-skilled if their cunning matched the confidence they demonstrated. Two of them had cocky smiles on their faces, one woman egging them on, and a young man who was the most daring of all pointing at each one of his opponents, as if issuing an execution by firing squad. He had short blond hair and that broad, loathsome scowl, Ivan.

Priority Deglin had quietly arrived, standing in the entryway watching everyone with narrowed eyes, but paid particular attention to Roe, appraising every move he made from the looks of it. The grim almost pleading expression he gave his stepson was a look that spoke of a promise he had better make good on.

Roe couldn't fail, but he also knew they were severely outmatched and couldn't carry his pitiful team of greenhorns by himself.

The two groups lined up, each sentinel protecting his denizen. Roe took his place next to Berl and nudged him for a bit of encouragement he sorely needed. Before the captain took his place atop the outpost, he issued a warning to Roe's group most likely to undermine their confidence even further. From their demeanor, the three didn't expect to walk out of the battle without being set on fire.

"...And I don't want anything to happen to your pretty haircuts!" Raleigh shouted.

The soldiers were ordered to hood themselves. Nearby, several more guards were standing idle with pails of water ready to douse the unfortunate. Soon, another man took position in the tower as well, Regent Silas. In addition to overseeing the military district of Pinnacle, the man helped coordinate military tactics with Captain Raleigh.

Silas introduced himself to everyone by saying in a churlish way, "I'm here to help the captain burn you alive, I'm afraid."

On an otherwise calm morning, the firefight started with a whistle.

Raleigh kicked things off by launching a flare down toward the night guards. Roe pushed an unsuspecting Berl out of the way, deflecting it. The flare was more powerful than anything Roe felt as it sent him to the ground. The burly man was shuffling indecisively back and forth, while the scarred woman got hit immediately. Screaming helplessly, she nearly tripped over Roe flailing her arms about. She was quickly doused with water and dragged away.

To his disappointment, Roe saw one of the civilians had already been torched. He gathered himself and slid back to block the flames barreling at another friendly mannequin, deflecting it just enough to skew its trajectory over the top wall, fizzling out against Aurascape's stone structure.

Gathering a flare in both hands, Roe sent the right at an approaching guard and followed it up with a left that sailed toward his legs. The man ducked the first, but the follow-up struck him on target. He fell to the dirt, frantically trying to pat down the flames biting at his leg.

Instantly, the burly man hit a mannequin, which evened the score in hits. Above, the two men were launching flares on both sides, taking advantage of any mistakes the sentinels were making—whether it was turned backs or tunnel vision.

Raleigh eyed Roe for a moment but quickly shifted to a complacent Berl with a grin on his face. Before the captain could send something his way, Roe beat him to the punch. The aggressor had no choice, but to move on the defensive showering the canopy with sparks. Recognizing the opportunity, Berl managed to hit another target and run back to the safety of the group. This left three civilians for the nights, two for the days.

Smoke billowed across the scorched arena, causing the act of breathing to become difficult. For a while, the action stalled, but Raleigh and Silas forced their captives to move. Doubling their efforts, the two attacked with both hands and tried to burn both sides' targets too. This maneuver took everyone off guard, resulting in one lost civilian for both sides.

The score whittled down: two to one.

Ivan lunged out from the smoke, kicked up some dirt into the burly man's face, and hit him square in the chest with a flare. Amidst the crackling fire and the man's screams, Roe could hear Ivan laugh callously. Then he slowly formed a flare that he held up near his head and sent it passively, as if teasing him, toward an unguarded civilian. An enraged Roe vaulted over the burly man writhing on the ground to begin his attack on Ivan. It was brought with such a ruthless ferocity one could only have for a hated foe.

Roe went right, left, and right, with flares and dodged two of Ivan's while rolling out to deflect the final one he threw. Roe imagined the stupid smile Ivan had hidden behind his mask and desperately wanted to wipe it off his face with a victory.

The stepbrothers then ganged up on a sentinel that was busy deflecting and sent him out, doused with a bucket full of water. But soon enough, the sentinels' own weapons became their enemy as everyone was staggering from the energy spent.

Raleigh prepped an attack toward Berl, but he didn't need to send him out that way. The sentinel collapsed suddenly in a manner that pointed to heat exhaustion. Roe desperately tried to wave his arms for a cease in the action, but Raleigh ignored the plea. The boy was dragged off with some whoops and hollers heard in the background at the site. The fierce competition had culled the weak.

Roe was now alone.

There was one civilian to guard on both sides and now he was outnumbered. His sluggish limbs made Roe contemplate submission, ready to let the last civilians burn until he saw Ivan's shrouded form through the smoke and shove one of his comrades toward the back to protect the remaining target. The man then took a direct hit from above as he stumbled from the push. The rivals were left. Everyone paused, and the cheering guards grew quiet with awe at the spectacle before them. Among the flames, the two figures eyed each other and were revving up the final blitz.

Ivan drew an index finger across his throat as fiery energy churned within his palm.

"C'mon, Fern! Burn me!" Roe roared.

Left - right - left. Ivan launched his barrage first.

Roe geared up, shuffling to his right to block the next flame. Back...forth they fired, blocking, and dodging. Roe backpedaled, deflecting while protecting the two civilians that flanked him.

His ears met a deafening roar. An explosion cut through him as he was sent violently to the ground. He yelled, fighting the air, quivering with shock. Roe began to taste blood.

Chapter Eleven

The Killer Made of Air

"I no longer fear death for I've been made a witness to the
horrors capable of Man."

- Taken from Saffron Deglin's diary

A trickle of blood slowly rolled down Roe's cheek, coming to rest on the crease of his lips. The thick smoke pelting his face burned his nose. The sentinel gasped once more trying to escape its grip on him. The flare that had just stuck was large, far too large for one of the participants. It came from high above in the post from Raleigh. He was favoring Roe as a target—there could be no other explanation.

Gritting his teeth, from pain and rage, Roe struggled to his feet and sent a large flare to punch at a support beam setting the wooden outpost alight. The men atop were forced to vacate quickly before the teetering lumber collapsed with a smoldering wave of soot and ash. The silhouette of the enemy was barely visible through the undulating air; Ivan had taken cover. Roe had to act, ready to be taunted as a loser or loved as the winner.

He simply had enough.

With one last flare forming in his sore palm, Roe vaulted up a fallen support beam, flames licking at his feet with each step. Ivan saw him and tried his best to stop him forcefully. With each step, Roe could feel bursts of hot air zooming closer to his body. Roe leaped from the toppled pillar and side-armed a flame over Ivan's head while contorting his body enough to avoid Raleigh's attack. He hit the ground tumbling into the legs of some of the onlookers.

And soon, the groans and cheers rang in. The question that gripped Roe was: who were they coming from?

Looking over awkwardly at his lone civilian with disgust, Roe could only count three smoldering piles of wood. Over his shoulder, he saw a flame light the hem of the mannequin's ragged shirt. The fire's slow course consumed the lopsided wooden man until it fell off the pike like tender meat on a spit. His head rested back on the ground.

Peeling off his gloves, Roe buried his hands into the cool, sandy topsoil. The puncture sites on his forearms were reddened and tender. The world was spinning beneath him. The ground seemed to break, heaving up and down with each breath he drew again. Hands hoisted him skyward. The night crew cheered his name and found a new best friend, while the rest found a new name to curse.

When the hero was just about done receiving accolades from his new friends and jeers from his opponents, he opened his eyes wider to see Raleigh giving him a subtle congratulatory nod before walking away to dispense orders for the losing side. Deglin was more vocal about his approval, but only after everyone had left the scene.

"My, oh my! That was *phe*-nomenal! Raleigh had told me he was going to pit the odds against you, but still, you emerged victorious! People will be talking about this for quite a while!"

"Thank you, sir. Where's Berl? Is… he okay?"

"He's fine. I saw you try to help him while defending yourself. That was very selfless of you."

Roe was cautiously appraising the area to ensure no one was eavesdropping.

"Well…I just wanted to keep my promise."

Deglin only nodded, quizzically still wearing a look of worry on his face. Roe wondered if this was just the first of numerous occasions where Berl would have to be saved, and the Priority must have known this as well. Deglin issued a pat on the back before allowing Roe to leave for some respite.

Time ticked by. As each minute wilted away, it seemed to do so faster than the one preceding it. Ruminating to himself quietly, the Ugly One suspected this was the natural course it took when a future event was heavily anticipated.

Making short work of carving out the message in the target's room hours earlier, the man once more found himself and his ward back in their hiding space beneath the trapdoor of the charred hearth. The jagged black teeth of the support beams were still present along the perimeter of the foundation. To see the ruins in seemingly the same state, after being set alight those many cycles ago, led him to wonder…why?

Perhaps, he thought, *after the assault on the supposed heretics inside, people had not deigned it feasible to rebuild on such a tainted foundation. Yes, the place is probably riddled with such ridiculous superstitions that no one would dare purchase the rights to it. Even the houses near it are vacant. Course—had it not been for that rat, Warrick, and that cowardly prick, Deglin, the house would still stand. Perhaps, my life—would be different. No! It would be different…my parents, perhaps—hell—they would be alive still!*

Tobias grumbled in his sleep from the makeshift bed hidden in the murk of the cellar. The man must have accidentally prodded him during his internal chastisement. He scooted close to hug the grimy wall so as to not repeat that error. In doing so, his body discovered most of the space had been rendered uninhabitable due to a collapse that cut off most of the cellar's square footage.

He squinted at the small form in the corner who stirred once more.

"You awake, boy?" he whispered.

"Hmm? S'it time, Ar-I mean, you old harlot's brood?" he asked sleepily.

The Ugly One chuckled at the innocent voice of a child who couldn't be more than nine years old saying such a vulgar thing. His voice certainly pricked his spirits considering the gravity of their next task. Though he was about to take it upon himself to deviate from its course. His mind was already made up, but he couldn't tell Tobias how exactly.

He did feel quite…*ugly* having purposely and quite unnecessarily drilled the image of Tobias' wisp-like manifestation into him over and over until the boy was on the brink of passing out from the blood loss.

As he lovingly forced another noxious bottle of that foul liquid into Tobias before he drifted off for rest, the Ugly One whispered pleadingly, "forgive me, little one, please forgive me."

"I shall return, Tobias. Rest well," the man said ascending the ladder to check if it was safe to crawl through the trapdoor.

"Wake me…when we get there…" Tobias said softly, before turning over in his covers.

Walking as discreetly as possible through the busy streets, the man sighed a breath of relief that his plan actually worked. True, Tobias was the one designated to conjure any manifestation if possible, but this next step was something he had to do himself. Tobias had shown him what details to consistently picture in his mind and the best hiding place to meditate from.

This was a wisp-form though. Nothing of a wisp was that detailed and thus served a great purpose in its simplicity to summon with this wicked thing. The parasitic bracelet was then anchored on his forearm, and the man grimaced from the sudden prick of pain that followed. Up the steps of the Hardscape…almost there.

His heart gave a sickening thud with each step as he nestled in a crevice that overlooked most of the paths leading from the Hardscape.

Warrick planted the Heretic's Dictum in the house and tipped off the authorities. I saw him slip it in my mother's recipe book one night he visited Father. That book was where they found it. And Deglin did nothing to stop the burning...

The Ugly One repeated those facts over and over until he arrived at the conclusion that he could not relent. No. He would not relent. Not now.

Before he sat and began his meditation that would clear his mind to that of an empty black sheath of canvas, the man said a simple statement.

"Warrick *must* die."

Roe had surpassed his expectations the moment he found himself clinging to the doorway of his room given how exhausted he felt coupled with the painful aches that coursed through his frame with each footfall laid on the hard flagstones. Without any regard for the prospect of falling on his blade or something blunt from his outfit, Roe collapsed in his bed ready for his fatigued mind to take him just about anywhere if it meant sleep was involved.

Footfalls echoed in the corridor and he groaned throwing a pillow at the doorway not realizing who dared to disturb his precious rest.

Dodging the pillow as he entered, Berl shouted, "I think you might need that, don't you?"

Roe feebly rolled over and groaned once more and he found his eyelids barely capable of propping themselves up. "Oh, that was awful. Glad to see you didn't get torched."

"Can't get torched when you fake passing out."

"Who's saying that?'" Roe asked sitting up, his protective brotherly instincts flaring away from the lulled feeling his mind had been slowly gathering.

"It's nothin' really, but I overheard some of the guards that lost their wager. They said it was pretty convenient that I managed to be taken away without being set on fire, unlike everyone else. They suspected I was getting coddled."

"It was hot out there! Our blood was being wasted on the stupid thing. It was sure convenient for them that they didn't say anything when I was around. They're just sore. You handled your own and your father's...happy enough," Roe grimaced kicking his boots off.

"What were you and Father talking about anyway? I was a bit messed after they dragged me off, so I could have imagined it."

Roe felt a bit of warmth course through his cheeks, "He just wanted... to congratulate us. We were at a disadvantage, thanks to Raleigh's lousy choice of teams."

"That's all he said? Y-you aren't lying to me, are you?"

Roe moaned again, sat up, and shook his head annoyed by the question and eager to deflect it.

"Forget it," Berl said shortly. "Sorry, I just get so worried sometimes, knowing he expects a lot outta me, and I know that I am not living up to his standards, but he wants me desperately to live up to him! And..." Roe could see Berl feverishly scratching his head wildly up and down watching loosened hair strands wave side to side as they wafted to the floor.

"Stop! You're gonna go bald doing that," Roe swatted at the hand that was rooted in Berl's scalp. "Listen! You hung in there with me today. You did your fair share. You helped me rescue Delphine, and you have Tessa to call your own. If you ask me, you are doing well for yourself."

Berl nodded lamely, clearly not seeing the same things as his more confident counterpart did.

Before any other subconscious fear could be uplifted to reality, he thought it best to leave and rest up himself.

"I'll stop bothering you," he said weakly. "We still have work tonight and I can't afford to miss it."

Roe issued a wave at him without looking and his lids closed. It took only a matter of seconds until he was beyond the awareness of his room, but still far from the ethereal dreamscape. Surrounded in nothing but the dark canvas of his eyelids, he heard the familiar moaning enter his mind with just a subtle echo that slowly grew louder until it pounded its way into his mind like a horrible reality.

The scene for his nightmare had been set.

A noticeably young Roland flinched when his father scooped him out of bed. The man's grip was strong, his stout fingers dug into the boy's slender arms thwarting any chance to wriggle free. Being violently snatched out through the bedroom door, his mother clawed at the arms of his captor before being flung aside like a soiled shirt. He was rushed onto a broken path that was tucked away behind the thatched hovel. Looking over a broad shoulder, he saw her silhouette through the glass disappear briskly.

The burly arms of his father and the cool night air caused him to yawn. He tried to rest his head on the thick neck of the man, but his face was pushed away. Roe was scolded for the act.

From an alcove in a dirty alley of the city, a man fell from a stoop with a tankard in his hands. The child fell with the man onto his hands and knees. With no time to check for cuts or scrapes, the boy was hoisted by the scruff of his shirt and lifted to a seat under a concealed stoop. His father vanished.

A woman suddenly hoisted a flagon in his small hands. The cold metal stung his fingers. He looked within it and found the percolations tickling his nose. The woman's mouth moved as if speaking, but no words issued from them. Roe shrank in his seat as she began rhythmically stroking his hair like a pet. She winked while he touched the rim with his lips to sip at the bitterness swirling within. As if dissatisfied, she wrapped her grimy fingers around his throat with one hand and forced more beer into his small mouth with the other. An eruption of pain caused him to sputter. A wave of fire crashed down his throat as he continued to cough. The remainder was spewed upon the pavement.

The boy whimpered when he fell to the ground the second time. On his hands and knees, he crawled. Intractable fingers out of nowhere clawed at the soles of his bare feet. He kicked to get away. Looking up to see the streets of Pinnacle, he saw them begin to heave up and down like ripples; the buildings mimicked the motion of birds bobbing in a vessel's wake. The shrieks and hollers of the jovial people around him turned ethereal and frightful. The crescendo grew louder and echoed as if conjured at the mouth of a cave. It was a party of dancing and decadence that engulfed the streets around him.

With a dirty hand, Roe felt the ledge of a stair and found a wall of them built to the murky mists above. He frantically scampered up to escape the ghouls, the masked citizens shrieking at him from below. Roe ascended to meet the sky that burned bright with a color of violence, with yellow tendrils cut across it like cracked glass. Then bursts of fire fell from above and pummeled the masses in the streets below him.

The world grew dimmer and his vision blurred. The bitter taste of saliva in his mouth was growing and the boy dropped to his stomach. The sweat rolling down his cheeks ran cold when he rolled onto his back, feeble.

The earth beneath him was spinning, so he pressed his body against it as if he had the power to stop it. A horrific scream once again filled his ears. He looked wildly about expecting to see a new form of terror and saw nothing at first, but the screams tore in his head still.

Pale blue swathes bathed the area and covered him until a crippled arm, stringy and raw, reached down from a grate in the canopy he sought shelter under. He screamed once until the rotten flesh slid across his mouth to caress it shut and his body went limp.

Falling out of bed, Roe awakened to find himself already screaming.

Ivan had dallied in the drilling square after most of the others consigned to their fates had grumbled off the challenge that happened hours earlier. He fired off countless flares at the same spot of the blackened wall before becoming lightheaded again.

Though a mannequin would have been a more appropriate representation of Roe's body—compared to just using his waning imagination to fill the blank space—Ivan recognized there would not be enough mannequins to tear apart that would allow him to recover from his loss to the Priority's fake son.

One last spin to the left and a heavily thrown fireball with his right punched the same blackened spot signifying this would have to suffice. His brow was thick with sweat as he made for the barracks to change out of his sodden uniform.

Earlier, as he walked past the daily board of patrols marked out by colored pins scattered strategically amidst the detailed map of Pinnacle, Ivan had noticed the large scribe stationed next to the thick log book of assignments he had pilfered earlier. It seemingly looked a bit thinner, but who would notice a few pages gone. This manuscript logged all guard activity within the past rolling one hundred and eighty days. The fact that it included records of every individual's assignment had been an unforeseeable advantage that only occurred to him after recalling the bulge of coins that lay tucked away in his quarters.

"A mere transaction of business," he said to himself.

His days at the Academy did serve a purpose after all. The regent had given him an ample start for his work in unraveling the corrupt rule of Deglin and his associates. Ivan in turn greased this scribe's palms into misplacing certain documents that announced Berl Deglin's lapse in coordinated drills and numerous mundane patrol assignments a child could perform without fear of injury or danger. Such a transaction had been timed properly, during which everyone had still been in the throes of the pending mock battle in the drilling square.

Having stripped himself of the now putrid-smelling armor he threw carelessly on his, otherwise, clean bedsheets in his quarters, Ivan glanced at the sheets and said to himself, "Least it will remind that maid of what a *real* man smells like."

Then he rummaged through his footlocker to ensure the pages of the log were still safely tucked away.

After collecting them, and dressing back into civilian clothes, Ivan set off to meet the regent at the preordained meeting spot behind the jail on the other side of the Hardscape's vast arcade.

This was only the beginning, he thought to himself. Learning what he could from Warrick—a great many things concerning deceit and subterfuge—would become invaluable in his ascent to the top. It would not stop with Deglin. It would only *begin* with him.

After Warrick's succession to the Office of the Priority, Ivan would then focus his attention on the old man, whom Ivan knew enough to be too focused on the pomp of finally obtaining what was supposedly his right. Warrick's victory would be Ivan's, but first thing's first...

Warrick's pocket was markedly lighter after the transaction and it felt simply wrong to him, like the gritty skin of a mist-sucker. Despite undergoing numerous exchanges of currency for any good or service rendered, Warrick hated prying himself from coin he thought was so difficult to come by—what with everyone in town trying to beset him with financial ruin. At least this loss came with a better investment than more coin, it meant more power.

After the Fern boy slipped him the incriminating evidence of Deglin's misappropriation of a sentinel, Warrick couldn't help but feel a bit shocked. He was half-expecting evidence that could only count as hearsay or something even less tangible than the whereabouts of his son's patrol.

The smug little wretch did ask for more money this time around. Learning a little too fast for his own good. I might have to cut him off if he begins to wise up...

This particular eve before the Night of Safe Passage celebration was promising to be one of the best in recent memory. The regent preferred plodding down the secluded, far-flung walkway that gradually lowered itself to the city proper, rather than taking the hundreds of stairs that the architects of Pinnacle were inept enough to have built from the Hardscape.

The beautiful foliage and abundant trees peppered the silvery light of the lamps' glow onto the deserted path, or what Warrick thought was deserted. A small fiery-haired girl was sitting on a nearby bench, grabbing the leafy fronds of a fern.

Her strands of hair peculiarly fluttered about her face, like that of an impending windstorm.

A windstorm? Warrick thought. *There's no such thing. Just like sorcery only existing in stories...what the-*

The girl issued a blood-curdling scream before staggering away and disappearing into the dense undergrowth. Warrick whipped around and saw nothing at first. Without realizing it, his breath hastened and there was a dull pang in his chest.

"Who's there?" he barked. "Guards! This is Regent Rufus Warrick and I need immediate attention!"

But no guards came. The only movement was the flittering leaves in the tree branches above. Once more he called before panic truly gripped him. His unanswered plea forced him to abandon his destination and briskly trot up the path to safety. In the corner of his eye, he thought he saw a man, but hollow in appearance.

Warrick felt the sheer force of a wall suddenly slam into his back, then shooting pain crushed his face. The force caused his teeth to smash together. He realized in a daze, that the might he collided with was the knobby brick wall of a nearby building.

As blood trickled through the grooves in the stone path, Warrick looked up blankly to the footsteps of a ghost. Not because it possessed the immaterial or translucent form like he saw moments earlier, but because he saw someone he thought was *supposed* to be dead. As the man stared down at his broken victim, Warrick could plainly see a murderous glint in his eyes embossed by a fire kindling in his gloved palm.

"The greatest beast is Man, Warrick," he said with a deadly whisper. "Your mere existence bears testament to the Heretic's Dictum. You may not remember my family you destroyed because of it, but I swear to any god in existence, that you *will* remember mine you ugly rotten harlot's brood!"

Warrick voiced the one thought that gripped his mind, "Not like this! I don't—"

A blinding fiery light clouded his sight; a brutal heat crushed through the temple of his head until…nothing.

Looking around frantically, Roe saw nothing had changed, even the peculiar scent of smoke-stained clothes lingered. A casual gaze out the window over-looking the practice yard let him know it was still a wreck from the competition.

Smoldering wood and clothing were everywhere, not to mention the destroyed outpost. On one section of the brick wall was a fresh amount of scorch marks. Roe wondered who made them. The sight caused him to liken the sentinels to simple children with fire, wielding a power they had taken for granted.

Once more, he looked out the window, this time to take notice the churning sky was almost starting to turn ghostly pale light.

Night was arriving.

Frisking himself for his weapons at his belt to ensure he hadn't left them, Roe trotted down several flights to the main landing where he found it to be choked with soldiers caught up with the change of shift. He strode over to the wall that posted assigned duties for the night where he was to be stationed near the schoolhouse. The posting was within the district that housed libraries and the buildings of pedagogy.

My first shift as a sentinel, he thought. It sent chills of anticipation down his spine though it had just dawned on him he hadn't had time for nerves to overtake him with the unknown station of his position.

As he fumbled to latch his bootstraps, he took notice of how he was slowly being deserted. Looking around the hall, people had been leaving the area quickly. Word had spread through the drone of frantic scraps of conversation that a murder had occurred just outside the Hardscape. Though Roe was stunned at the boldness of such an act, eventually his curiosity got the better of him and he too decided to join the crush of people placing themselves in the investigation.

Outside, near an intersection of Carriage Lane and another darkened thoroughfare, stood a ring of onlookers. Roe hurried down the long flight and helped the other guards clear the area of gawkers who tried to disturb the scene. He could barely make out the symbol on the dead man's robe, which wore the armored glove, the palm raised up kindling a flame.

Trauma crafts.

It didn't take a master sleuth to know it was…

"Regent Warrick!" a woman shrieked from the crowd of gawkers.

The man's face was near unrecognizable as half of it had been burned; tissue was bleeding and blistering, all the way up to the hairline. Trapped air within had escaped his chest when he was turned to supine. The faint gasp that escaped his chest cavity completed the gruesome experience. A few women fainted from it. The acrid scent of seared flesh and hair wafting in the air forced many to cover their mouths or step back.

The captain squinted his green eyes and gritted his teeth, studying the body before he slowly covered it with a blanket from a nearby stand. It wasn't long before many of the bystanders could be heard shouting slurs and insults in the direction of the enclave. Many were already convinced it was the Visitants' doing despite the lack of soundproof evidence. Typical.

A man shouted, "It was *those* damned mist-suckers. They wanted to get rid of 'im. Look! Look at the burn marks, the impact near the head. Trauma gloves!"

"Could have been a sentinel," replied Raleigh with raised eyebrows.

"You dare accuse one of yours so willingly?" he asked.

The captain stood from his hunched position over the body and slowly trudged over to meet the man's wavering confidence.

"No, but you have no proof it was grayclan, just as I have no proof it was one of my own. Point is, I wouldn't go throwin' an accusation I couldn't back up, or I'd look pretty damn stupid like you right now."

This did nothing to quell the chants of harsh pejoratives made in the name of the Visitants. With makeshift weapons, the angry horde marched down Carriage Lane with plans to attack the enclave. Raleigh dispatched guards to protect the perimeter and keep the Visitants on notice about the incoming danger.

Roe saw a sentinel in the crowd hitting people and throwing one to the ground, trying to make an arrest. The mob tried to push their way with brute force but were no match for the conditioning of the guards. A couple of bodies rested in the streets, untouched, unmoving. Its site caused Roe's hand to slide over the hilt of his blade, just waiting for someone to rush him. But fortunately, that wouldn't come to pass.

Priority Deglin came bursting through the heavy door of the barracks, accompanied by the sound of cacophonous horns, signaling his entrance. He stood atop the protruding ledge cropped directly over the river above them.

"Silence!"

Deglin's voice was that of thunder as it echoed among the buildings below them. Roe had never heard him sound so fierce. The crowd halted and slowly turned around. He began to lecture the whole lot of them as he descended the steps.

"Everyone! We're already investigating, but your actions right now hinder our abilities to solve this egregious crime. Don't try to avenge Warrick by acting this way. Did anyone see what happened? Anyone?"

A small hand raised, buried deep within the bodies and limbs of the crowd. A girl was pushed forward, and she shied closer to the man. She had fiery-red hair with gentle blue eyes that were enveloped in tears. Deglin lowered himself to meet her gaze and gathered saccharine words to use for her. She was staring off, not making eye contact.

She saw it alright, that violation. Roe thought. *But how much?*

Deglin turned her away from the crowd, making her stare at the river, and sat alongside her. After a few moments, Deglin caressed her for a moment and had a guard escort her away to a family member nearby.

Roe walked over to where the body lay pretending to examine the scene, but really spying on Deglin's conversation with the captain. A peculiar object rested on the street near the corpse, surprisingly left untouched.

"What do you make of it, Captain? She said a man made of air attacked him and left him here. She can't be telling the truth...could she?"

"Unlikely she's lyin', as bizarre as her story is. Others have been questioned, but no other eyewitnesses. Judging from her description, it's not native—not from the valley anyway. Pinnacle has no cloaking capabilities that magic or science can explain. And look at this"—he nudged at the device on the ground with the toe of his boot— "no guild or manufacturer in Pinnacle has been working on somethin' like this."

Raleigh fondled the object for a moment, studying its handle and trigger mechanism like that of a crossbow, but the rest must have been foreign to him despite his expertise in weaponry. The puzzled look on his face was irrefutable at any rate. He unceremoniously placed it in a lockbox brought by a fellow sentinel and instructed him to have an armorer and a military scholar examine it.

"There's no precedent for this, Captain," Deglin whispered gravely. "I must meet with the regents, something needs be done. I've calmed the citizens for now, but they're going to want action. I know what we must do but this must be clandestine..."

By that time, civil unrest was non-existent for the moment, but for how long? Tension still hung thick in the air and Warrick was beloved by so many. This was obvious. His death wouldn't go unheeded, and all Roe could think about was Delphine. He knew her kind wouldn't be safe for long.

Roe ran back inside the main entry of the barracks to sign his name in the log book and prepare to meet the guard he was to relieve. The arched gate of pedagogy was his destination.

As Pinnacle's expansion grew in its nascency, district walls were created to consolidate similar operations for the ease of civil functions. Each district gate possessed small alcoves on either side that were built so that light never found their interior. Even during the day with the golden lamplight, a guard could see fine outwardly from within, yet no one could see inside. They provided good vantage points, but these nooks weren't restricted to simply district gates. They were littered throughout the general architecture of the cityscape.

Roe pulled on his mask and hood to hide his identity. After all, this guard he was about to meet was his "shift enemy" as Roe came to liken it. He didn't want the man to know he was the one who was going to make him work agonizingly long hours for the celebration. No one was visible when he arrived at the gate, but he waited a little while. Finally, he heard footsteps and saw the sentinel emerge from the darkness. Roe could only tell from the slight wrinkles around his eyes that he was an older man. They exchanged awkward pleasantries and he reported off. His disparaging comments about some boy named Roe Deglin followed.

"Gotta say," he said rubbing his stubbled chin, "I'm pretty upset at that smug fake-son of Deglin's. You know? What's his name...hmm..."

"Roe?"

"Yeah! That's the name! Burns my hide to hear it too!"

It was inevitable, but Roe's innards squirmed a bit allowing the scathing remarks to go unchecked.

"I tell yeh, that kid, got lucky. Now I have to explain to my wife that I gotta work *all*...day...and *all*...night. Gotta give him credit, I had no idea that little runt had so much guts. Deglin's real kid on the other hand, well, I feel bad for the Priority. I know the man won't admit this, but uh...I think the guy likes his adopted son loads better."

Roe stood rooted to his spot, "How do you figure?"

"It's how he acts and how he talks about him when he's not around. Word is he's been spending all his time repairing that kid's appearance as a sentinel, somethin' that needn't be done *if* he was right for the job. Any little slip-ups coming from the leader or his family should arise – well – people ain't forgivin'. Whatever he's plannin' on doin' with Warrick's death, it best be soon. That was the one man Deglin didn't want to die."

"Why? The captain's important too. After Deglin, he's one of the most powerful men in town."

"Raleigh has military power, sure, but Warrick has power with the citizens. The trauma crafts are the magic that makes those folks we protect believe we have a fightin' chance when hell breaks loose. They're the true rulers despite what any regent tells yeh. Why do you think Deglin was so hasty tryin' to calm them? If he loses them, he loses this city—the world.

"I gotta get some sleep. Thanks to Deglin's other runt, I have an angry wife to deal with. A little tip? Don't get married," he chuckled, "but seriously. It's encouraged to move from one alcove to another within the district, it keeps criminals guessin'. The more crooks you catch, the better you look."

The boy was left standing in the dull glow of the lamps. How he was tempted to say, "Roe sends his regards" knowing he would be the one to indulge in a celebration soon.

The guard may have imparted good advice, but he never mentioned how boring the assignment was. "Who would steal a textbook?" he muttered under his breath as he strolled passed the glazed glass of the library near the Academy's grounds.

Recollections of the days he lugged around stacks of used books taller than he was to lectures made him shudder. He was sure that any kind of crime committed wouldn't be among textbooks, academies, and archives. People desired the expensive clothes and vices opulent folks would covet, the kinds of lavish things many would kill to get their hands on if their deaths were imminent and needed a taste of wealth before snuffing it. Roe acknowledged he really wasn't in a place to complain though. He fared better in the past few days than most of the guards had in weeks. It was nice because this job gave him precious time to think.

Hopping from one alcove to another afforded him his solitude once more. Because of this, he welcomed the job. But as hours passed by with nothing out of the ordinary, he began to wonder where the cries for help were now. He was ready to make himself useful but heard nothing resembling trouble.

"Free money," he shrugged.

Hours later, he happened upon a remarkable view perched over the pedagogy district's center plaza. From here, Roe sat and overlooked the city, even stealing a glance down at his feet dangling over the streets below and at the partygoers gliding across ballroom floors in the distance. Despite Warrick's death, there was still cause for celebration to be found on another day still alive.

Roe caught onto one steady tune that had a wonderful cadence. He found himself tapping his hands on his thighs as if he were at the party enjoying the scene and playing music for the guests.

Ruh – puh – pum – ruh – puh – pum, the booming instruments seemed to say.

Then he looked in the distance beyond the rooftops to see the shadowforms at it again.

With narrowed eyes, he whispered, "What are you?"

"They're *big* baddies!"

The sudden voice caught him off guard so much that he nearly fell off the edge of the building. Fortunately, he had a hand resting on the ledge that braced him. He nonchalantly placed a hand on his blade and turned around slowly in case of danger. It had to be a rogue sneaking up on him at this time of night.

His racing heart began to calm when he saw it was only his friend with the shimmering skin and the golden eyes glowing in the dark.

"Delphine!" he whispered. "What're you doing out here?"

"How do you know my name? I haven't told you a thing," she gasped. "Can you read minds?!"

"It's me, Roe."

He had to take his mask and hood off for her to finally embrace him, then sat beside him. He didn't have the heart to send her home though he had her slink into the shadows with him as a precaution.

"So…what are you up to?" she asked, settling in.

"Working, I guess." Looking around as if he'd done his job he said, "Yep, looks like everything's good here."

"I just found out that my boss, Warrick, died. Sounded horrible, especially since no one knows what killed him. It wasn't grayclan though," she added quickly.

"What do you think will happen?"

She looked away, "Know how a chosen few who've paid their debt to Pinnacle get to travel through the Fog beyond? Well… guards came to the enclave and called out names. Tonight, some are going and tomorrow more will be leaving. Some of my house clan will be going tomorrow." She paused for a moment then said awkwardly, "I will be. A few gathered their meager savings and paid my debt, so I can go with my parents and get away from this place. I wanted to come tell you on the chance I don't get to see you. You're the first friend I made outside the enclave. Humans don't like us."

"I'm sure some-"

"-None do. I've been told it's because I'm repulsive," she said bluntly.

"You don't think that, do you?"

"I do… because it's how we are. To us we look okay, but to you, we're repulsive. That's how it's been since we came here and there must be some truth to it otherwise, why say such a thing? At least I don't look too repulsive to you since you're still talking to me. Right?"

There on his face stuck a disgusted look, but she continued.

"There are enough of workers in the trauma crafts to replace us, so the city won't take a huge loss from us leaving."

Roe then asked her how the regents decided when a particular grayclan had paid their debt.

"Depends on the work we do. Warrick said it was based on how hard we worked and how valuable we were to the city. Every mist-sucker gets paid, but most of it goes back to the city as a part of our debt. Each of us has debt as soon as we're born. Some can give their money to another so that they are able to leave sooner."

"How much does each grayclan owe?"

"Don't know," she said scratching the back of her neck. "Must be a lot if most are old when they are given permission to leave."

Music echoed once more in the surrounding estates and manors which grew louder as the night went on. More laughter and shrill squeaks resonated, and the good people below were more than drunk on spirits, it was lust and all things lavish from the sound of things.

At one point, the twosome stopped and gazed up at the tower looming above them. Eyes were on the sky, as it was beautifully ugly, haunting even. Aurascape began to glow and chimes rang out, signaling the group's successful passage into the ominous mists, risking a chance at discovering a new untainted home existing somewhere beyond…hopefully. The chimes could be barely heard through the carefree music. As quickly as they rang in, the chimes ceased. The parties continued below.

Ruh – puh – pum – ruh – puh – pum

As if addressing her departing brethren in person the girl whispered, "Find us a home."

Roe entertained Delphine about the Story of Pinnacle, how the city was allegedly created, and how mysteriously the Fog arrived. He told her of the dangerous words that survived so many years since their conception long ago, the time of ancient humans that suggested they brought the doom creeping upon them. He spoke of the same words that were banned from being spoken of or replicated in print, the Heretic's Dictum.

When she asked about the world beyond, he shared with her what was passed on to Pinnacle's youth. When all children of Pinnacle went to the Academy, they were told how the world used to be, how they had a sun to wake them and moons to lull them to sleep, the stars to count and arrange into shapes with their fingers pointing at them. But that was long ago before the world grew angry at the inhabitants living on it and decided to swallow them into an unforgiving death. No one possessed the knowledge as to why it happened, but many thought it was simply the world's way of saying it was humanity's time to die.

They shifted from this grim conversation to work, Pinnacle's architecture, and finally rested upon the uncomfortable subject of family.

Family. A subject Roe cared to avoid.

He told her how much he hated talking about them and seeing any vestige of them. This allowed him to rethink his hypocrisy in reading Armin's letter daily.

"I miss the fighting," Roe said composedly. "I miss the crying and the utter misery my family had. I miss the sleepless nights staring at the ceiling, letting overbearing shouts I heard beneath the floorboards try to lull me to sleep."

"Why? That sounds awful!"

"Because I still had them. I still had someone."

The girl's head cocked to the side, eyebrows furrowed.

"I knew they loved me and my brother. They loved each other—at least I convinced myself of it. Despite all the bad...I still... *felt* I had a family. Those fights, those sleepless nights reminded me of what I had. Least then...I wasn't alone."

"I think I understand...in a very weird way. I'm sorry for you, but at least you have your friend, Berl, and that girl Tessa. And me." She smiled turning away. Roe then smiled at the discovery he made; even grayclan blushed when given sufficient cause.

Their conversation had steered him away from the time. It was dawning. The lamps were changing. He needed to be at the post near the gate for shift change!

To his pleasant surprise, Delphine left without any objections, moving silently in the shadows of the building spires, support beams, and awnings.

At the gate, Roe wasn't so lucky with anonymity this time. The guard recognized him and went on a tirade, although Roe wasn't paying attention. Of course, there was the occasional nod, and saying innocuous things as the man threw wild gestures about. After growing tired of the one-way conversation, Roe interjected and walked away without making eye contact. He didn't care if he had been rude, for he had the whole day to do whatever he wanted and then have the whole night to enjoy the festivities.

When he arrived outside his bedroom door, he stopped for a moment. That did mean…Delphine…

The thought of not having her in his life made him have that same empty feeling he had felt before.

"Well Roe, at least you can say goodbye this time," he said looking woefully down at his feet.

Closing the door to his room, he sat down on the bed ready for sleep. But there existed an intriguing discovery that prevented his relaxation, however. He realized with frustration that a visitor paid him a visit once more. But was it the same one?

On the door, right below the original black etchings was another cryptic message meant for his eyes only. The words gave him the same uneasy feeling as if he were being watched. Tracing the letters in the dark led him to picture the words clearly in his mind:

Music hides the guilt

CHAPTER TWELVE

THE NIGHT OF SAFE PASSAGE

"Celebrating life by indulging in debauchery, misconduct, and alcohol is the Night of Safe Passage. It's what everyone lives for, quite literally. The lamps could fail anytime, and the intellectuals say the magical barrier hits its weakest frequency of the cycle around this festivity. Kids are told that if they have any desire to do something regrettable, the Night is the best time for it. You could wake up dead tomorrow and no one would speak of your foolery."

- EXTRACT FROM THE FOG OF WAR
AND OTHER INTRIGUES

"What happened here?" Berl gasped.

Despite making every attempt at maintaining secrecy, Roe could no longer withstand the worst of these occurrences. The burden was far too much to bear alone, and he was becoming quite frightened at the thought of intruders coming and going seemingly at their own discretion. He had to tell someone but struggled mightily with the decision. Berl was the one person he could trust—for now.

At first, Roe wouldn't let any suspicions he harbored worry him, but as soon as he tried to sleep, his mind began to race once more. Guilty faces of suspects pulsed in and out. The images burned on the door were burned in his mind and the intrusion it left behind was something more permanent.

With his mouth agape, Berl's head could be seen darting between Roe and the door, until this act grew tiresome and was quickly nixed.

"Would you stop? I didn't do it. How could I? It looks like someone lit their finger on fire and jammed it into the wood. Do my fingers look like withered candlewicks to you? Whoever did it made sure I wasn't here to catch them. First time it happened when we were at dinner the other night. This one looked like it was done during my patrol last night."

"Why don't you come out and say something? Father can look into it."

"No! Just give me time. I want to see if I can catch this guy myself. If it happens again, I'll say something, okay?"

"Why not now?"

Indeed, it was a valid question. Roe did not reply to this aloud but internally reasoned that dragging the authorities into this would only shed more unwanted attention toward the buried secrets of the Deglin family. The lies, the nepotism, were all there. This was bound to only point to more reason to pry into their lives. Roe simply refused to be tangled in any sort of agenda that would undermine the family's capabilities.

"So," Berl said with his back turned, "do you think Ivan did it out of revenge?"

"It did cross my mind. Though I think Tessa would be his primary victim right now, and as far as I know she hasn't told you of any mysterious messages burned onto her door. Look," he said gesturing to the inviting party forming in the streets below, "drop this for now and let's go out for some fun. We both could use it."

Berl slapped him on the back with approval upon hearing these wise words.

Any guards granted the night off were still required to suit up with weapons to keep up customary appearances, as well as to help should the need arise. The sentinels had always been ordered to maintain a professional and courteous demeanor regardless of their circumstances.

Roe grinned when Berl reminded him of the proper etiquette and replied, "I think they made that rule especially for you, my friend. Best pay attention."

"From what I've heard"—Berl glimpsed over his shoulder this time, for safety— "Captain Raleigh drinks like a pig from a trough, I'll hardly be noticed."

As they stepped out from the barracks, the Hardscape was already bustling with crowds of people dressed up in the best clothes they could afford or obtain through other, less dignified means.

Golden lamps were strung from the top of Aurascape and sprawled out like dew drops clinging to an elaborate web. Throughout the Hardscape, mirror-plated lamps held aloft by entrapped gasses, dangled brightly above the partygoers, occasionally spurting a shower of silver-coated flakes upon them.

The youth could be seen keeping busy in makeshift boats holding races down the winding river, trying to tip each other over or spin their competitors' woven boats in torrents of dizzying circles. The sight always was a joy for Roe to see, as he wondered what it was like to be a carefree kid again. When the only problems for a child were making it through another day of class or finding a friend to explore the sewers with. His problems were more focused on surviving without parents or keeping his dwindling family intact. Those rickety boats had an ironic effect he had not realized until now; their presence made him feel at ease, but they made it hard to forget why he sought refuge through their sight.

From the amphitheater nestled at the base of the craggy peaks to the enclave in the far south, Pinnacle was bustling with music and jubilation. The amphitheater resounded, filled with music. Had the musicians of the orchestra pictured anything in their mind to inspire their creativity, it must have been the image of a heavily-disciplined battalion of soldiers. The music was slow and fierce, but with great passion. The pebbles on the ground of the dance platforms quivered with heavy vibrations of drums being pounded to the rhythm of a march. The stringed melodies that were laced underneath felt like a sweet innocence amidst the proud crescendo of authoritarian horns.

Women were twirling, men were shuffling and then there were their faces. Many of which were hidden by vexing masks, preventing any onlooker from knowing the identity of its holder. Some boasted exaggerated fake smiles, while most chose to have elicited motifs each sinful, seductive, and dark. They bore dangerous looks and flaunted gaudy shapes that sent shivers down Roe's spine as their heads weaved in wild sways as if in a trance.

Deglin had encouraged everyone to conceal their identity this cycle so that revelers would be forced to mingle and be cordial to strangers. The idea was to elicit comradery among partygoers as they tried to meet their desired matches. It seemed to be working given the wanton displays of enthusiasm toward perfect strangers hard at work.

"They must be running low on the good stuff looking at this lot," Roe mumbled to Berl pressing through the curtains of bodies.

Tessa was already waiting for the Deglin brothers in front of the barracks where a few grayclan were performing for everyone. The area was choked with onlookers and they were forced to wait to meet her for the time being.

Roe decided to use this as a reason to part from the crowd and look at the different exhibits being displayed by the various guilds competing for grants and continued research from the state.

A man in a puffy tunic and small oval spectacles declared in succession, "everyone to me…everyone to me," plucked a small walnut-sized orb from a metal cauldron and flung it at a sparring dummy. The orb struck—*thump*—and stuck to its shield now giving the spot an appearance of melting wax. The dummy's arm then shattered where the orb had stuck. People gasped at first but gave raves to the man representing the Pinnacle Learner's Guild, Deglin's old firm.

Beyond him, was a woman handing out pamphlets that Roe took with great interest.

Behold! Another sensational prototype from the Trauma Crafts, as made possible by the irreplaceable Regent Rufus Warrick, may he rest in peace.

Introducing the Gale Glyph. Much like its predecessor, the Flare, this invaluable creation fits inside the trauma glove to force a burst of energy at an opponent to stagger them or disarm them of their weapon.

Enlist in the revered House of Sentinels and try it first-hand. Remember, Pinnacle needs you come doomsday!

This exhibit drew the largest crowd Roe could remember seeing and the very reason his progress through the arcade has been stuffed. A sentinel was standing with his blade drawn at Captain Raleigh who was standing ready, gloves already dawned. In his palm was a luminescent hewn stone, the Gale. The sentinel charged. Raleigh's fingers flared out and sent the man flat against the padded wall behind him.

The spectacle caused Roe to look completely dumbfounded at this new magic. He rubbed his eyes to ensure they were still functional, then felt his pair of trauma gloves clipped to his belt. Looking at them with childlike wonder, he pondered to himself when the Gale would become standard issue for him.

Tucked away, another exhibition took place upon a raised makeshift stage. Curious people surrounded the gray-skinned beings who, at first, stood huddled together kneeling and hunched over. Everything about them was still. With some reassurance from a few others in the crowd, Roe included, they received enough encouragement to dance in front of the humans for the first time on paved stone.

Three slender women rose effortlessly from the stone, spinning upward as if they were souls on ascension to paradise. All three had white cropped hair, shortened to that of a man's. Their loose-sleeved clothing wrapped and twirled elegantly through the air, with arms contorting and bending in such a fashion that it made the lengthy white sleeves flutter like wings, mere extensions of the body. The performers were wearing trauma gloves though these models were more discreet than the sentinels possessed. Yet these women had turned a weapon, the Gale, into something equally stunning.

Forcing their hands to the ground, they pushed off the stone walkway forcing their bodies skyward again. Spinning and twirling, they assembled into formation allowing their bodies to commence into a dizzying whirl. The look was so beautiful as if they were delicate flowers caught in an eddy. There were no smiles on their faces, just serene concentration. A slow descent back to the ground signaled the end of their performance.

They bowed graciously and moved to embrace each other with grateful smiles of victory. It was a momentous accomplishment indeed. Roe was exhilarated to see that their efforts did not go unnoticed and he whistled excitedly for them. These creatures were so talented, and yet many in Pinnacle had chosen to ignore how they have enriched their lives.

One such sentiment came from a woman whipping a scarf around her neck as she spoke to her date, "What vulgarity. I certainly hope this was a one-time only variety. The scum's so eager for *our* praise...I hope the Priority has the graciousness for us refined folk to send them all off on their way for the last time."

When they were finished watching, the crowds dispersed enough to allow Tessa to squeeze through. She chose a dress that most would consider plain than pretty. Her hair was not styled in any fancy way like the other women, she wore it loose over her shoulders—a look sure to spark Berl's ire, Roe worried.

And sure enough, he found Berl to be unforgiving of her choice in style as they gesticulated angrily to each other amidst the crowd. Already forcing himself to enjoy the celebration despite his room being vandalized, Roe sped over to the couple to break them up casually as if he had no idea they had been squabbling.

"Tessa, I'm glad you got away from work! You look great. Really great!"

She hid her anger for a moment and smiled. "Thanks. I'm glad someone has the eyes to notice." Hers meanwhile burned fiercely when she glared back at her date.

Roe chuckled rather awkwardly, "We should get a move on if we're going to get a good spot for the benediction, or before one of you murders the other."

Slowly, they made their way down the stairs near the river where people were gathering. The Priority was already seated above on the Hardscape next to the other regents. An empty chair where Warrick would have been sitting reminded everyone of the recent tragedy.

Since it was impossible to have enough seats for everybody on the thoroughfare, people took advantage of anything that could support their weight if their legs weren't capable. Roe imagined that if one looked from the top of Aurascape, it would be impossible to see the stonework of the streets with everyone flooding in to hear his speech. Barrels, ledges, window sills, balconies, rooftops, signs, shoulders, tree limbs, and many more things were used as supports. Those that couldn't get creative were forced to stand.

The three were fortunate enough to find a spot among a few other sentinels on a balcony near the platform where the Priority would be talking. A chime, loud and boisterous, rang out and the commotion of the party ceased. With the silence, Roe closed his eyes and felt the vibrations pulsate through his body. The neck on his hair prickled. The feeling rippled down his arms. Deglin stood up with a subtle smile and approached the platform, his figure stood tall, trying to match the giant tower behind him. The lamp above was glowing, but its light clearly flickered with feebleness. Then he spoke:

"Good people, I welcome you to another night dedicated to life, another Night of Safe Passage. This night we mark the occasion where a few of our refugee Visitants find their way safely through the Fog of War, back to their proper homes that their ancestors sought so long ago to find.

"Their ancestors took shelter in our city, adrift from their course, and we provided them security. Our ancestors gave them security, they gave us knowledge. The shadowforms pursued them with abhorrence; we protected them with fellowship. The shadowforms lashed at them with claws, so we provided a shield. This evening acknowledges the reciprocity that both races have benefited from since that fateful day.

"We now celebrate for our friends and family who could not live to see this day. I say this now more than ever, amid the untimely death of our beloved Regent Warrick. But we can take solace in the many contributions he made to Pinnacle, in its defense and preservation. It is with a heavy heart that I say his death has been established as a crime, a murder most heinous and puzzling.

"As we look above, the lamps flicker, growing weaker. They struggle to subdue the advancement of the Fog and its dark sycophants that try to stop our hearts, cease our breaths, and extinguish our existence. It seems a rogue managed to pierce the Fog and attack our brave Warrick, taking advantage of the Pinnacle lamps' growing feebleness. Some of our selfless friends agreed to leave early and draw their attention away from the city. I ask that you all show your respect and support for these brave Visitants, both adult and child, who will be risking their lives for us…

"Pinnacle, take comfort…"

"We take comfort in our own."

"Pinnacle, when death comes for us…"

"We'll meet it with a blade."

"Pinnacle, embrace our grayclan…"

"We embrace them as our own."

"Pinnacle, reject a life beneath a fractured sky."

"We'll quell any who crave it."

"I thank you and please enjoy the night's festivities, my friends. With all the recent hardships, I ask of you one thing, when the music plays, forget your troubles; when the laughter begins, allay your fears."

The words of his speech made some cry and bury their faces within shoulders and hands. Fortunate given the recent circumstances, many seemed satisfied with his decision to force more Visitants to leave than what was expected. This act was unprecedented, and the tension was still present, for some people thought Warrick's death was preventable, had it not been for letting the grayclan seek refuge in the first place.

The crowd dispersed; the music played. The revelers seemed too eager to forget and all was well again. The food was some of the best the city could provide for the cycle. The many spreads looked tangy and delectable, good for the slices of breads and platters of vegetables. Roe decided that his morning toast would be better, so he abused the usage of his trauma gloves, making toast with them. With practiced hands, he conjured just a feeble glow to brown both sides to his liking. The crisp loaf melted in his mouth tantalizingly.

An inebriated Regent Silas staggered forth to greet him and wished to impart his congratulations on the feat witnessed at the training yards. Unlike Warrick, Silas' tendencies pointed more to the pragmatic side of the authority spectrum and away from irritable mannerisms making him far less loathsome to socialize with.

Without any regard for his searing hands, Roe placed his palm on the regent's thick ceremonial coat when he grabbed the boy's shoulders in an unexpected embrace. Silas turned to grab a drink off a nearby table and Roe saw the fingers of smoke wafting from the fabric. In an effort to prevent another dead regent, Roe gripped Silas with a hug of his own, fiercely swatting him on the back feigning his appreciation of the adulations just received. The regent gave him an awkward smile and a raised eyebrow as he disappeared into the crowds.

Roe peeled the gloves off and clipped them to his belt, swearing he would never abuse their power to cook food at his whim, although he knew this would realistically last only a few days hence.

In the distance, he could make out the heads of dancers bopping up and down in circles. Many were having such a time trying to dance, but Roe was one exception. Instead, he thought he'd try being a spectator yet again and watch the others be foolish.

The dancing gradually became more elaborate and forced the journeymen to file out, as the experienced dancers were eager to impress anyone they could. Suddenly, Roe felt a soft hand grabbing him to dance.

"What say you, Roe? Indulge an old woman?" Ophelia grinned.

"Um…you know, I can't. I'm no good," he said taking a wayward look away from the dance floor.

But he soon discovered something desperate in her eyes that told him she needed it. The look conjured the same rotten feeling Roe had looking at Chief confined inside his paddock. From this vantage, the barracks was another captive force, one not so easily escapable for the housemaid.

Knowing this, he mustered a smile up at her and beamed, "I'd love to, I only hope I don't make us look lousy."

"Nonsense," she said grabbing his arm with renewed vigor. "You could dance like a corpse and I'd still enjoy this!"

They danced slowly matching the tempo of the violins' humming. His cheeks were warming up nicely with each turn they took. But when he heard her laugh with such zeal, the intimidation coming from the gazes of onlookers felt nonexistent. For the first time, he felt comfortable dancing. The look of her awakened eyes darting about, taking in the scenery more than made up for Roe's missteps in the choreography.

Over her shoulder, however, a sentinel sitting on a bench caught his eye. His mask was lowered. The expression on his face informed Roe of how much he was despised right now. Most disturbingly, however, was the sight of his blade slowly dragging its edge across his throat as he glared back at the dancer.

Ivan.

Looking concerned at first, Roe realized who he was with and gave his partner a smile to quell his fear and divert any worry.

Shouting above the music he sputtered, "I-I hope I'm doing okay. I don't get to dance often."

"You're doin' marvelous…a natural like my husband. Every cycle we would dance until our feet ached. Every night, before bed we would share a dance together, no accompaniment, just his humming. You remind me of him, you know?"

"Do I look like him?"

"No but you have his character. You have a kind heart like him n' bravery beyond knowin'."

The musicians wrung out the final chords as the patrons on the floor bowed at the showers of applause made for their efforts. As Roe gave an embarrassed, shallow bow, he could feel his cheek ready to burst from the blood filling them. However, seeing the maid's face light up was enough for him to feel such joy for her.

The music transitioned to a faster tempo, signaling their exit. Ophelia thanked him for the dance to which he responded, "Let me know if you care for another," although he had secretly hoped she'd forget the offer.

On his way off the floor, Roe had noticed something peculiar jerking back and forth among the throng of dancers and found an unmistakably inexperienced soldier, who had forgotten to secure the scabbard from his belt. It quivered back and forth like a minnow's tail and struck the backside of an older, patrician-looking woman who gasped, "Mary, I think someone just...*spanked* me!"

Unfortunately, the wonderfully entertaining sight wasn't enough for Roe to stem the provocation awaiting him from another encounter with Ivan Fern. With some difficulty, he approached a bench where Tessa and Berl were sitting. Ivan had jostled himself between them gossiping, no doubt to Berl, as Tessa scooted away to talk with some acquaintances. Visualizing the disturbing spectacle that was brandished at him during the dance, Roe became shameful that he felt threatened enough to stroke his blade to ensure he knew its exact placement if the occasion should arise.

Ivan laughed. "Hey, Roe! You gettin' sweet with the old maid, huh?"

Inside Roe was waiting to unleash the first fist of many to come, but he knew he'd be severely reprimanded for the act.

"How's work going? Looks as though you won't get the chance to get sweet with anyone tonight." His comment caught Tessa's ears, which compelled her to laugh as she looked over her shoulder giving Roe a look of approval. "Ophelia simply asked for a dance, and I'm not a stuck-up turd like you. She deserves fun like everyone else."

He refused to let Ivan have the satisfaction of seeing him angry, so he stalked away through the dancers, holding his tongue as best as he could with Tessa in tow.

"I'm relieved to know that I'm not the only one that can put him in his place," she said admirably. "Your wit is coming along."

"Didn't know I was being evaluated."

"Consider it a surprise inspection then."

"I'll never understand why Berl finds him amusing," Roe said reluctantly. It only took moments before he recognized the stark, sobering truth.

Berl wasn't accustomed to friendship, but neither was Roe. The difference was Roe's lack of friends resulted from a carefully and purposefully planned introverted existence that he yearned to achieve. Intrigue, gossip, and fervent whispers went hand in hand with status. And so status is what he avoided like sewer gas. Being the victim of rampant rumors wasn't helpful for Berl, who was desperate to find friends in any place he could. This made his recent arguments with Tessa seem more troublesome.

It took him a little while to ask her, but Roe finally found an opening and took it.

"Are you and him…okay?"

She nodded slowly, "Why do you ask?"

"Well…I saw you fighting on two separate occasions now."

She gave a heavy sigh, signaling an unwanted topic she didn't want to broach. Roe was about to relent when she changed her mind almost on the spot.

"He obviously doesn't like my appearance. He constantly hounds me over what I wear and how I don't act. That night at dinner? I was late because of work. Tonight, I didn't want to wear anything frilly. It's simply not my taste and he's ashamed of it! I love him, Roe, but he makes the act seem more of a chore than a desire. I seem to be simply a means of showing off his growing influence over people so long as I can maintain the ruse he wants people to see. But it's all about who you know, right?"

"I think he wants to impress his dad, show what caliber he can be. He's pressured to live up to impossibly high standards—"

"—In Berl's mind perhaps," she said crossly. "His dad hasn't lost confidence in him. It's all in his head."

"I…believe his father may…differ on that statement." Roe looked away suddenly wishing he had kept his stupid mouth shut. Her expression changed to that of an interrogator.

"You know something! Tell me! And don't you dare lie to me because you are horrible at it."

Roe stammered trying to recover. Fortunately for him, the subject in question was on his way over. She saw this as well and turned quickly back to Roe.

"This talk never happened"—she leaned in to whisper—"but it will be continued later when I deem it safe!" she added quickly.

Berl's return was a welcomed one in that he didn't have his usual accomplice at his heels for a change. The threesome strolled the thoroughfare, escorting Tessa home as she was due to open the commissary in the morning. It was going to be a hard day to catch up after a long night of celebration and determining the post-celebration inventory, tallying surplus and deficits was no small feat.

Not realizing how late it had been, Roe grew worried that he would miss seeing Delphine off. Berl asked him where it was he had to be so urgently.

"I'm going to see the Visitants off."

"Why? You aren't responsible for the escort, are you?"

"I made a promise to Delphine. I told her I would say good-bye before she left," Roe said, somewhat defiant.

Berl roared with laughter.

"Roe! Come on. She's grayclan! Since they've been here, their presence has caused Pinnacle nothing but trouble. They constantly get sick, their behavior repulses everyone around them, and their existence in this city causes trouble with other workers struggling to make a living by having to compete with them. Need me to continue?"

"That is not fair!" Tessa interjected. "They had no choice. They were pursued in the Fog and *we* discovered them, *we* took them in. Would you have really turned them away knowing it might have led to their death? Sure, they may be taking some of our jobs, but their contributions to our safety and weaponry have been invaluable."

They stopped as they reached the stoop of her building.

"Regardless," Roe said hugging Tessa, "I'm going see her. I don't care what anyone says. Good night, you two." They issued the same and Tessa closed the door to her flat above the commissary, with Berl right on her trail.

Her muffled voice could be heard saying, "Uh…you know you aren't staying the night, right?"

This caused Roe to chuckle, imagining Berl's disappointed face after his advances were shot down.

Heading back toward the party alone, Roe buried his hands deep in his pockets, with his gloves securely clipped on the belt, grazing his thighs with each step. He stumbled mid-step as his path was abruptly cut off by the advancement of a child in a medic's mask with a satchel slapping against his buttocks. A caretaker by official profession, though most called them puppeteers due in part to the strung-up clientele they had to tend to.

Roe had known one once growing up in the streets. Somehow, he got the idea it might have been a viable way to roof himself over petty theft as many parents of the last generations would refuse their children to undergo such training in a vile vocation. But Deglin's summons came calling before Roe could determine if working with corpses was indeed a talent he possessed.

"Forgive this poor wretch, sir," the little figure said, though the small voice had been altered by the respirator. "Many stiffs to care for."

"My apologies," Roe replied listlessly, watching the boy unlock one of those hideous glass coffins to attend to the fresh corpse within. It was that of a gaunt young woman posing with a wilting bouquet of flowers. The morbid site renewed his ruminations over the bizarre occurrences recently. His mind was a mosaic of foreboding echoes.

The mysterious resurrection of my mother...leading Delphine into danger. Then there's Regent Warrick's murder. And the thing that attacked him was said to be otherworldly. And that peculiar object of which no one seems to know its identity.

Something more troubling was the Priority's unprecedented decision to send off more grayclan. If this was a response to the heated fervor of their mere presence in Pinnacle, why not send them all and be done with it? Their life expectancy wouldn't be considerably higher within the magical barrier considering many citizens wanted to burn their enclave to the ground.

Something's not right...

Roe hadn't realized he'd spoken most of his rumination aloud, loud enough for party goers in the vicinity to hear. Some bystanders looked at him cockeyed and laughed, but there was no time for him to debate the soundness of his mind. A sentinel came rushing toward him.

Huffing and straining up the stairs, she stopped and bent over to catch her breath, with a hand stretched out to him. The other was resting on her knee.

"Are you okay?" he asked. She nodded and was trying to talk, but her breathing was coming so fast.

"No time! Roe...need...you...right away. Little Hex and her family aren't leaving. The girl said she wasn't going unless you were there to say goodbye. Please help us. The Priority will be furious if they miss the reception of the crowd. Timing is everything now!"

Sparing her the effort, he told her he would run on ahead. There was no need for her to hurry as she sat on her haunches, looking at the ground.

At the tattered longhouses, he could see that it was bustling, an expected site. The Visitants that were leaving carried only what they could and offered to the rest of the other house clans. There were fourteen, including two other children; this cohort was the biggest to leave since Roe could remember. This cycle was different for him though. In the past, he hadn't gotten attached to anyone within their ranks, but his heroics in the forest changed that.

Delphine came bounding toward him. Nox and Myrna were with her now and exchanged pleasantries with him. They were dressed in matching black robes like the others. Perhaps it was to fool the shrieks who dressed similarly?

Roe was going to be escorting them with a handful of other guards up the Barred Ascent, where they would leave Aurascape on a retractable platform, an old installation originally meant for a quick egress by leadership if the situation called for it.

The time for the long walk toward the tower had come, the place where their new freedom and danger would begin. Roe looked at her and she stared back. They were both so happy to be together, but the togetherness was fleeting. The farewells were near. His eyes teared up thinking of the dangers the poor people would surely encounter. Children would be facing those shrieks. Did they know what they would encounter? Did they care? Delphine was just another person leaving his life; it was something he should have been used to.

Up ahead, the crowds lined the streets, but Roe didn't hear the cheers he had hoped for. Some people clapped, but the sound was hushed by condescending remarks. Anger flooded his mind, knowing Delphine's cohort was about to risk their lives drawing off attention from the city.

The convoy's pace quickened, but Delphine was falling behind. Her parents had stopped to wait for her, but the guard at the top of the stairs near the mouth of the tower was growing impatient.

"Come on, come on. Don't dally!" he shouted. "Your window for escape is narrowing. The shadowforms will only be occupied for so long!" Loud flashbangs were echoing down upon them, more noise to use a disturbance for the awful creatures.

Delphine stopped and began frisking herself. Her eyes widened and ran the other way. Myrna called out to her, but Roe tried to assure her he would get Delphine moving.

"We'll be in the main chamber up the stairs. Get her there now," the guard shouted. The rest vanished within the darkness of the entryway.

"Delphine!" Roe shouted. "We have to go. Don't let them leave without you!"

He grabbed her by the arm, as she crouched on the stone path. Roe knelt next to her, a sense of urgency was pummeling his innards. Another flashbang erupted in the sky above them, causing him to jump and curse under his breath.

"Roe, I'm scared," she frowned. "I can't. I can't do this."

"Don't be afraid. You aren't alone in this. When you're with those that love you, you can handle anything." Those words reflected a similar sentiment of his mother, so caring and genuine.

She cried a little but looked up and smiled gently. "I'll miss you, Roe. Look here. I made this for you. I dropped it when we started moving so fast...something to remember me by."

She placed a pouch tied off at the top in his hand. No matter what it was, he was glad she cared enough to give it to him. It could have been a rock or blazebeast dung for all he knew but it didn't matter right now. They remained silent and just embraced despite the commotion around them.

Nox had been one of the last to disappear through the oblique archway, his love, Myrna, closing fast behind him. He could catch her echoed pleas to the soldiers to wait for their daughter.

Despite the growing tension and frenzied barks of the black-clad soldiers demanding they hurry, Nox purposely slowed his movements, feigning weakness to stay closer to his love. He wouldn't leave his child behind either, but there was something about the surreal strength a mother could summon when her child was threatened—a power Nox realized he sorely lacked. Myrna wouldn't budge, her resolve was stronger than anything he had seen.

"C'mon, you gray-skinned wench," a guard roared at her. He began pulling her by the arms like taking a stubborn beast of burden by the reigns. Before he could march to help her, arms seized Nox from behind.

Myrna broke free and attempted to run toward the archway, back to her daughter. Another guard grabbed her from behind and she struggled, kicking the air as she was hoisted up.

Something's foul! Nox thought, spinning around to confront the officer.

"Unhand her!" Nox roared. "Our daughter's still out there… what are you doing?!" The murky foyer didn't allow him to see the full brunt of the horror, only that Myrna's head jerked back suddenly, and she gurgled a cry before going limp.

"Myrna!" he screamed, sending an elbow to the jaw of the guard flanking him. Another approached but was dispatched by a kick to his abdomen. Behind him, echoed screams crashed down the hallway toward him. It was only a second in delay before Nox regained focus, but all too late.

He spun around. Into the darkness, Nox swung his fist and met only air. Another bloody sob from his beloved rang out, this time somewhere farther in the tower's belly, making him more disoriented with his surroundings. He screamed again and felt a sudden, blunt force between his shoulders that emitted a fresh crack of bone. The Visitant fell to his knees first, something he didn't feel immediately as they crashed against the hard, stone floor.

Before he could utter a warning for his daughter, or a prayer for his people, Nox only saw a flash of white flash and saw no more…

"…this one's stirring a bit…glad we snared him first…."

His head throbbed horribly as Nox instinctively tried to rub it but found he could no longer move his hands. Screams were still percolating in his mind, but this time they sounded feeble and helpless. He tried to open his eyes but found his lids grew heavy and so too his head.

Slowly opening his eyes, he found his arms shackled behind him to an ornate pillar that possessed a protuberant ridge that pressed against his aching back, flaring his chest out. Upon seeing his shoulders stretched abnormally taught behind him, he immediately felt the fresh burning throb radiating from them.

A high-pitched squeal somewhere outside his periphery brought the disturbing reality that the human brutality did not fall short on children. His skin grew chilled. Nox steeled whatever courage he could to scan the room in hopes that his daughter had not been caught but couldn't clearly see enough tortured bodies to verify her whereabouts.

Only until a smaller built soldier was thrust forward to interrogate Myrna, did Nox find the smallest trace of relief—or was it hope?—amidst the torrent of horror he was witnessing.

"Consider this your initiation, Fern, you stupid bootlick," one of the officers said to the boy who walked hesitantly toward the trembling woman.

"W-where's the other one," the soldier identified as Fern said uncertainly. The officer next to him knocked him aside and grabbed Myrna's throat issuing the question, this time with force.

Myrna lifted her trembling face overcome with numerous strands of blood-stained hair and spat as capably as she could.

Nox cursed aloud as the black-clad figure's hand raked across her face as her head swayed slowly.

With defiant eyes, she slowly raised her head one more time to utter with such rage, "You should be proud. How brave of you to strike a fettered, *angry* mother..."

The men chuckled to one another as they vanished somewhere in the depths of the chamber as Nox fought in vain against the thick chains. Loud ballroom music, like that he remembered from the festivities earlier tonight, flooded the chamber.

The many candle brackets that bathed the cavernous chamber in a dull light were extinguished by an abrupt billowy sensation he never felt before, brushing against his skin.

He frantically threw glances all about the hollow until his gaze landed on her, finally resigning himself to the inevitability of their horrible fate. His limbs hung lamely.

"Myrna, I am your husband always," he screamed through the graceful crescendo, unable to control his tears.

"And, I am your wife always," she cried.

"And our daughter still lives for us," he said defiantly. "She will live and fight on!"

A bright white light filled the room and deathly silence reigned in the chamber. There was only peace.

Chimes rang out again. It was a haunting noise. A premonition before the blue glow visible from the previous night flashed once more. Delphine looked at Roe and nodded determinedly knowing what she had to do. Then the music in the distance began to play loudly and slowly.

Ruh – puh – pum – ruh – puh – pum

They ran with all their might up the spiraling steps to the tower entrance. Reaching the archway near the top, Roe frantically searched for the main chamber. It was hard to find anything, as he had never been allowed to set foot in Aurascape before, but he heard the echoes of chanting further in its bowels. That must be where they needed to be! The music outside made it hard to determine the words, but they provided him with enough guidance to follow a murky corridor until…

There they are!

At the front of the room was the family, the family Roe was going to reunite—but something was wrong. There were chains and weapons drawn. Screams and tearful pleas echoed toward the two. A moment passed; Roe gasped as numbness radiated through his body.

Hooded figures at the distal portion of the room whipped around in their direction. As soon as Delphine rounded the corner, he immediately grabbed her mouth. She screamed, but it was muffled by his hand, as well as the rumble that filled the room. He felt the warmth of her tears rolling down and over his fingers. The room filled with the bright flashing light suddenly, the same light they saw the night before, the same light that witnessed many cycles past, and to the same music he was mesmerized by.

Roe briefly caught the sight, his lips trembling. Grabbing Delphine with one arm and the other one still over her mouth, he shimmied to the shadows beneath a sprawling set of stairs leading to the landing above. The light vanished, and the loud, horrific sound had been extinguished by the music outside. Even though they were in danger, he stole a glance to see what had happened, and why he had kept Delphine from meeting her family.

In the back, tucked away, was a beast, a hardened primitive face, fixed with a wide grin and violent, glowing eyes. It was retreating into a recess of the room, dragging against the floor. The chamber itself grew dark again. The beast fled.

On the floor laid desiccated corpses strewn about. Their tattered arms strung to chains hanging from stone pillars bore the appearance of marionettes strewn about from a child's tantrum. One chain didn't have a captive, a slave. It dangled naked and without purpose, he knew was meant for the one known as Little Hex the Tenth.

Two robed figures in black lay next to each other; their arms restricted, and their hands imprisoned, denied the right to embrace. Voices from hooded men at the front of the room appeared and they were calling for the missing grayclan girl and the guard that was with her. They were being pursued on this night meant to celebrate life, this Night of Safe Passage.

Roe lacked the courage to tell the girl that her parents were dead and that she was supposed to be among them.

Chapter Thirteen

The Hillock

"You shan't find a more fiercely loyal creature than that of the blazebeast, but therein this admirable trait lies the beautifully tragic crux of it all. When rider and creature do manage a bond, they become indivisible. When its rider passes, it has been documented that the blazebeast will keep watch by its master's grave often times until it expires too."

- Extract from Bellows at Dawn: An Imbecilic
Guide to Blazebeast Rearing

"What's wrong with-?!" Delphine screamed.

Roe clamped her mouth shut once again. Her arms were flailing violently, and her muffled screams still carried across the expansive chamber. She struggled her best to wrest herself free, but Roe had to restrain her to the point of hurting her as she squealed beneath his shifting weight. The fight was hard, and she struck him a few times, but still, Roe somehow held on.

For only a moment, he nearly let her go to save himself. If she wanted to hit him, she could go and get killed like a foolish child, but then Ophelia's words entered his mind of how well she thought of him. If his hands hadn't been occupied, he would have hit himself for even thinking a second of his cruel intent.

The darkness in the rear of the chamber could shelter them for only so long. Assessing the situation, Roe knew he had to keep her quiet and act fast. Any guard worth his badge would kill them on sight. The approaching footfalls and creaking of leather boots interrupted his thoughts. Roe pressed against the wall, harder this time as if it could budge and give them an inch more of cover to hide within. The doorway out was just beyond the two pairs of legs now standing ahead of them.

"Where's the other guy?" the first voice said. "He's supposed to bring that little mist-sucker here. How in the hell are we going to replicate this again? It's too late. Party's almost over."

"Look," said the second, "the depletion already occurred, didn't it? When we find the girl, we just kill her. And no one needs to know any different."

Delphine whimpered.

"What about the guard gettin' her? He's missing. And what about the Priority? If he finds out what happened…"

"Deglin's ain't gonna find out! As long as she doesn't show up alive to expose us, we're fine. If that sentinel does, we'll turn 'em in for treason. I think it's fairly obvious the mist-sucker's with him." replied the first.

Deglin doesn't know these people were killed? Roe thought.

"Yeah…but we don't have a clue who he is."

"No," the voice said quizzically, "but Una does. She went to fetch him, 'member? Let's go find her but have someone guard the stairs below just in case."

Their footsteps disappeared. The only thing that could be heard was Delphine's whimpers. Roe tried to console her, but all he could do was insist upon their escape.

"Don't move. I'm gonna get you outta here," he whispered.

Tip-toeing over to the withered bodies, he found them to be hanging only by wrinkled, paper-thin skin and brittle ligaments. Delphine's parents hung silently attempting to embrace each other. Their dulled eyes remained open. The gold and gray coloring were glossy and faded. Roe delicately closed them and attempted to bring their hands as close as their fetters allowed. While doing this, he quickly but gently removed the outer garments of her mother and left the bodies to their fate.

Unexpectedly, Delphine tore out from her hiding place. Overcome with anger she rushed up and began to strike the sentinel. Roe caught her hands gently and slowly pushed her away all the while tearing her vision away from the corpses.

"*You* knew!" Delphine hissed. "*You*…knew, didn't you?! You're just like the lot of 'em. You lie and send us to die! That's what you humans have been doing to us…all this time! Is that why the Fog bears on us, as punishment for your sins?! You hate us so much, th-that your ch-charity is somehow a burden!"

His body tingled with the stinging harshness of her words.

"I promise you, Delphine, I had n-no idea this w-was going to happen. No one knew! That's why they must have been doing th-this in the tower. Had I known, why would I risk my job—my *life*—to steal you from harm?"

He stared down at the robe dangling in his hands rubbing it. It took a while to coax Delphine into wearing it. Her face was blank, while her eyes were already gathering a reddened and puffy appearance. Roe had to dress her as if she were an infant, in the same robes her mother died in, tugging her limbs into place. She felt them and pressed a sleeve to her face as a small child would. The robe was dragging behind her and gathering dirt—something clearly not tailored for her. It was the type of thing the guards would be looking for, something suspicious. He began to frantically cut it down to make it fit her form properly.

Then, looking through a window, Roe saw the people below still dancing to the accompaniment of the orchestra and the faraway moans of a crying girl.

Ruh – puh – pum – ruh – puh – pum the music continued unabated.

They went on enjoying the night as if nothing happened. With the gentle cadence of music, their lives were but a fantasy laden in cloth, a wonderful lie. To make the illusion complete, they wore masks of paper, ceramic, and ignorance.

The stairs leading down from Aurascape were unoccupied except for the summoned guard who had positioned himself haphazardly at the base. His attention was clearly on the splendor he could not partake in.

Without hesitation, Roe sent a flare down striking a cart, and hid for a moment. Soon enough, guards were busy trying to extinguish the cart as he hustled Delphine down the steps to grab a mask from a nearby street cart, placing it over her face and concealing her hair with its cowl.

Streams of tears were falling beneath the gold mask that bore crafted forlorn eyes. Her hand was slithering about in his grip and formed an abrasive pain that caused Roe to soften his grip. It was only for a moment, but that was all that she needed. He looked through the crowd and saw nothing but swarms of people.

Delphine had vanished but only just.

Soon a small swath had been cut in the crowd moving in the other direction. There in the crowd of smiles and spirits, a small black-clad figure walked purposefully through the dancers toward a guard staggering in place, drooling over his tankard. He saw her. Delphine's fists clenched, her teeth bared, brandishing them like an angry animal. Seamlessly, a shiv emerged from her clenched fingers. Roe tried following, fighting against the crowd's current.

His shoulders grazed against people who were laughing and kissing one another. Their masks were making him feel disoriented, the more he tried to track the hooded girl's path. As he slowly neared her, his torso felt the caress of hungry hands groping him. Another brazen set of fingers moved up his chest dragging sensually across his shoulder.

A woman forced his hand on her breast.

"Touch me," she cooed. "Touch me where it pleases you most."

Another tried to grab him by the arm, in such a manner that begged him to stay. He scampered away distraught, instinctively whispering, "I'm just a *boy*. God...I'm just a *boy*."

The sentinel gripped the girl by the shoulders, begging her to stop. He dug his fingers into the balled-up knot of her hand and briskly unrolled them until he heard the clanking of the shiv hitting the ground. As they proceeded down the street, the crowds thinned.

To maintain that safety, Roe felt it best to place all his trust in Tessa. She had no ill will to the grayclan and little love for the guard, it was his best chance for now. He had to risk it.

The front door heaved slightly with each fist Roe sent to it, all the while wondering if she had already fallen asleep. Because it was so quiet, coupled with their status as fugitives, the noise seemed ear-shattering in the vacant street. The knocks grew more urgent. For a moment, he thought about breaking through as he heard the terrifying voices of people approaching. In his fearful state, Roe was certain they were guards. The shadows on the pavement crept closer as his knocks hastened until Tessa finally opened the front door looking confused.

"Roe?! What is it? Do you realize how late it is? Do you realize I have work? Who's that with you?" she asked peering over his shoulder at the hooded figure.

The expression on his face had been dire enough to inform Tessa something was terribly wrong, so she sheltered them before the voices reached the flat. Creeping through the window drapes, he saw only rowdy people on their way home.

"Are you alone?! Is anyone here?"

"Berl's stupid body is here, trying his best to ignore me sleeping. What is going on? You're scaring me."

"Tess, something's happened! I'm so scared right now I can barely talk! I-I don't know what to do. I'm more worried for her though," he whispered making a gesture toward the still clothed figure in the corner. Delphine was sitting on the floor with her head buried in her lap.

"Its Delphine, we need shelter, but you have to promise not to tell anyone! Not even Berl—no—*especially* not Berl!"

He went on to explain what he had seen and how they ended up on her stoop in the late hours of the night.

"Roe…what are you saying? This can't be true…it can't be. Does Deglin know?" she asked looking a shade paler than before.

Roe shook his head.

"Can we hide here?"

"What? No. If you don't want Berl to know, she can't stay here. He's here practically every day and he'll know something's up if I ask him to stop coming by."

She thought for a moment then said affirmatively, "Tampson. Go to Tampson's. It's perfect! He has a place in the forest not marked by any map they'll have. She'll be safe there. He doesn't care for the guard, remember?"

"Do you know the way?"

"Yes, but it's difficult to get to. You won't find it without me," she said putting her work boots on. She then held Delphine's hand and tried soothing her as they tip-toed out onto the dim street. As she closed the door softly, Tessa cautiously looked up at the dark pane of glass of the room where Berl must have been sleeping.

Roe didn't want to risk taking the blazebeasts as they were surefire to make a raucous, but they'd get to the hideout faster. Time was something they didn't have, so they chose the risk and took the noisemakers.

At the pens, the beasts were all asleep and so too, it seemed, the guard monitoring the mazework of paddocks. An empty bottle of scotch and a table reeking of alcohol stood in front of the man who had propped his chair against a wall. The beasts, however, were easy to disturb.

Their large tails were swaying rhythmically against the dirt, back and forth. Roe found himself delicately stepping and hopping over the swaying flesh being ever so careful not to kick any dirt into their great nostrils. Chief was resting near the gate where Roe whispered his name. The beast's eyes flashed open and jumped up to his feet alarmed. A scatter of bellows echoed nearby in response.

Roe shushed him when he started to vocalize eagerly, but the only true remedy for this was his freedom.

"If you shut up," Roe hissed. "I'll take you for a nice little jaunt to the woods! But…only…if…you…shut…up!"

Roe was growing tired of the antics, but Chief at least understood what a ride meant. He contained the noise as well as a blazebeast could. Any rider would know it would be like asking a bird to stop chirping or a fish to stop swimming. It was inborn.

Tessa grabbed Haddy and they rode off with Delphine sitting flaccidly in front of Tessa. With her condition, Roe didn't trust the girl would keep herself safe.

With tensions biting at him, Roe finally caught a glimpse at the forest slowly crawling into view, forcing them to slow the beasts to avoid hitting the trees. Chief was agile, but not nearly enough to be charging through thick timber that laid ahead of them. The part of the forest where Tampson lived was not the same place where Berl and Roe had met Delphine, so Tessa was forced to take point.

Wading through the swaying stalks of grass, the three approached a broad hillock. Had it not been for Tessa, they would have missed the darkened, earthy entry at the base of it. A large tree grew at its front, its enormous roots had uplifted the shaft of the tree away from the ground. And underneath it was the hollowed-out space, dark but large enough for a person to walk under.

Roe glanced over his shoulder, listening for any signs of a pursuer. There was no noise, nor visible evidence of intruders. He followed the two girls inside and quickly shut the disguised door behind him. Immediately their nostrils were greeted with the musty scent of earth and tree roots. The ground lowered gradually into a dugout beneath the earth. Tampson's living area was surprisingly spacious as Roe began inspecting the craftsmanship wondering if it was all Tampson's doing.

The chamber itself was supported by wooden buttresses that reinforced the mesh of tree roots to support the walls. It was a single living area, but everything necessary was there. Tampson himself was sitting by a fireplace he fashioned from stone and turf which vented upward through the roof to the outside; another shaft supplied the room with fresh air as well.

"Never in the day," he said sternly, turning to his unannounced guests. Tessa and Roe looked as if they had made a notable intrusion.

Tessa glanced all around wondering what he meant until she saw him staring at the glow in front of him. "You mean the fire?" she asked.

Her brother nodded.

"The fire, the smoke, the entrance. They aren't to be used during the day. If you want to stay hidden, stop announcing your existence," he said sagely with his back turned away still.

"Makes sense but why live out here?" Roe asked though Tampson didn't respond immediately.

"It's a place to hide, a place to forget," Delphine said lamely. She took off her mask and unhooded herself. Roe had nearly forgotten that she was still in the clothes her mother died in.

"Clever, young lady. You can say that I have two homes. There is one where people can find me if I want them to and one where I don't. This place happens to be the latter." He frowned. "I see trouble on your faces and I wonder what you saw tonight?"

No one answered at first until Roe grew tired of waiting and said he had to go find someone if the girl was to remain safe. Both he and Tessa left, but her brother promised to watch over his guest.

Outside, Roe felt a sudden urge to cry, but simple tears weren't going to make him feel better. He wanted to stay brave for the girl, for everyone that was helping him, and brave for himself of what he may have to do to survive.

Tessa sat him down and asked what happened. Again, he tried telling her, with the idea she wouldn't believe anything he said, but somehow, she did. Somehow, despite the outlandish descriptions he supplied, her trust in Roe didn't wane.

"How can you believe such a story, Tess?"

"We're friends, you big idiot"—she grinned, wiping away a tear—"besides, you remember what I said at the celebration? I know when you're lying, because you are hopelessly bad at it—but not only that, I can see it on your face. Something's changed in you. And look at Delphine. Something happened tonight. You don't need to know the mannerisms of a Visitant to know when they're upset. They cry like we do. They lose like we do."

"Am I a bad person? I...I helped kill them by not knowing Tess! I led her parents! And Delphine, I thought about giving her up..." he looked away.

She fiercely cupped his chin with her fingers, "But you didn't! You could have easily given her up and have been called a hero for your compliance and no one would have known any different.

"Well, except me."

"Listen to me, I can't make the feelings you have go away, but I'll help you make things right. Just be strong for her. That's what she needs from all of us right now."

He sighed.

"I need to make for Pinnacle and figure out where this Una is. She knows who I am and knows that I was last seen with Delphine. I'm scared to think of what I might have to do to save that girl. I just hope it doesn't come to that," he shuddered heading toward Chief.

So many questions had raced through his mind at that moment. Who could he trust? Berl? The captain? Ophelia? Could he go to the Priority? His mind reeled at the dilemma and the problems he would have to confront.

It was obvious that Roe needed to reach Una before the guards did. He realized that if the woman didn't cooperate, he had to ensure she wouldn't speak out about him. If she understood the plight of the grayclan, she might do so, but if she were fiercely loyal to the captain and Pinnacle, he would have to prepare himself to kill her to save Delphine.

Take a life to preserve one. Roe began his trek back to Pinnacle with the prospect of murder on his mind.

CHAPTER FOURTEEN

DEADLY KNOWLEDGE

"Only the innocent die in here."

- ALLEYWAY GRAFFITI OBSERVED IN PINNACLE

The Ugly One cursed savagely under his breath, as he left the safety of the cellar. The countless hordes of drunk folk enamored by the grand spectacle of celebration—or horrible farce of it—as he thought, made his skulking about easier. But their ignorance wasn't the excuse for his vulgarity. Ill tidings were rising quicker by the hour.

Tobias had taken ill and hadn't realized it until his symptoms manifested more bluntly. His brow beaded with sweat. Plagued with a low-grade fever, that was steadily climbing. He had no form of antipyretic to give him, and when he looked over the boy's body, his wrist glistened an angry shade of red. A scant amount of green pus was seeping out of the swollen puncture site.

An infection...

He knew each time the bracelet was affixed to the skin, Tobias was risking a blood or skin malady, but the gravity of the moment—the thought of Warrick's presence and avenging his family, overcame his rationality.

You didn't bother to check and see if he was using a disinfectant before each use, damn you, Armin.

With what precious water they had, Armin made a cold compress and wedged the torn scraps of cloth under his armpits, and stripped the boy to his undergarment. The moldy, decrepit crates in the cellar proved to be of some use, however. Within a brown bottle, he found trace amounts of spirit left inside and applied it to the site. The boy shrieked briskly before returning to sleep, a good sign Armin thought.

Despite having to worry about being a proper nurse, the mission had to continue as well. The ghostly, pale glow from the tower was visible even from their hideout, and despite knowing the fate of those poor creatures, he was aware there was nothing he could do for them now. Their sacrifice would not be in vain, he said to himself in a poorly convincing fashion. As he walked by, he noticed some men who were much too busy gawking at their comrade vomiting in an alleyway to notice Armin's deftly hands steal a bottle of their whiskey. He glanced at its label and placed it in his satchel.

This reminded him of another problem, his satchel was able to accommodate the large container. He noticed the disappearance of his pistol shortly after he scampered away from the Hardscape. After thoroughly frisking himself, he realized with fervent anger when it must have fallen out.

"Warrick...even in death you infuriate me with your meddling," he muttered to himself, he shoved his hands into his pockets.

Though as he watched the discovery of the old regent's body— and the weapon—from afar, Armin suspected this, perhaps might be a good thing. The single-shot pistol was something foreign and might stoke the fire of curiosity more than a supernaturally inspired attack.

Someone would have to shift focus to what is beyond this place, he had thought, as it was locked away.

On top of that, the pistol had grown old and its use to him had waned with each time it misfired. But there was still the boy...

Tobias needed medical attention, that was clear. And despite it being who knows how many cycles since he was last seen, Armin still risked compromising the mission at the chance of being recognized if he presented the boy to a healer or physician. No, he would call for help—Tobias deserved better—but the Fog needed to be addressed first. To do that, he had one more message to scribe according to his mental itinerary.

To set the events in motion, he quickly mounted the ivy-covered lattice of the barracks and began his climb to the window ledge. Only once did a nearby skulking figure give him pause. Torchlights flickered from a nearby alleyway briefly illuminating the area. This figure must have visualized his danger drawing closer because he quickly fled the entrance of the barracks down a narrow dirt path cut away from the normal paved streets.

"A sentinel…why are you in such a hurry? Couldn't be him… could it?" Armin wondered descending back down.

But the sentinel passed directly below Armin giving him a perfect view to verify it was truly *him* before wisely dawning his hood once more.

"Where do you think you're going in such a hurry?"

Before he could change his mind, Armin hopped down from the final ledge onto the Hardscape carefully following the rogue in the dark.

As Roe filed out of the barracks, he was amazed at his newfound luck. It was quiet and empty inside, allowing his index finger to frantically scan the night guards' posting list to find the woman that carried Delphine's life in her hands. It seemed everyone was either asleep, working, or desperately trying to keep the night alive. That only meant guards were about, and torchlights could be seen coming his way. But Roe ran into another stroke of luck; the district Sentinel Una Otho was responsible for was adjacent to the barracks, a couple of blocks away, if that. Her knowledge was deadly, and he had a horrible feeling that no matter what she decided, the encounter was going to end badly but people in Pinnacle were never renowned for their optimism.

Sticking to the guttered trenches he had quickly familiarized himself with from his previous life, Roe passed vagrants with smirks he could barely make out in the night. Some were talking to themselves, others disturbed from their sleep by his huffing and his boots clapping on the ground.

The statue above the gate was rising above the rooftops, with a venerable stone woman looking down on everyone. Her face was lit up by the torches resting at her feet. The expression on the stone visage had always made him wonder why she looked so scornful. Roe had guessed the people that worked within had ties with Aurascape, the government, and his stepfather. They were of a higher status, a perceived better breed of human perhaps.

Ensuring his face was covered, Roe proceeded onward while slipping his weapons onto his hands. No one was at the gate, but he remembered the alcoves that had served him so well and approached them one by one whispering, "Una". He heard a response at the third alcove and spoke into it.

She slowly stepped out.

"Who sent you?" Una asked.

"The captain,' Roe lied quickly. His sense of urgency allowed for the mental lapse. He failed to create a plausible excuse before the meeting. "Some guards have been reported off their posts. Have any been here bothering you? He was thinking of it as a random inspection, I didn't see anybody when I arrived but ...I was just asking—for him of course."

If this were Tessa, she'd have caught him after the first sentence. Roe could only hope she couldn't notice his giveaway. Her eyes narrowed a bit, he was losing her alright.

"Doesn't sound like him. He would have sent someone under secrecy to observe first, but you came right out and asked. That's not the captain's way, he's not as stupid as you suggest. What do you want, really?"

Roe's fears gripped his body. In his mind, he could picture himself standing over her lifeless corpse. Was he foreseeing the aftermath of this exchange? He was losing control of his mind as it was clouded with awful thoughts again. He was anxious, fearful, and worst of all, panicking.

His right palm vibrated gently as the heat in his hands grew, approaching the moment to strike.

She looked at him terrified. Her eyes widened, and her right arm was slowly reaching to draw her blade with Roe begging her to stop. The tension in his hand ceased.

Finally, he revealed himself to her. Her eyes widened. Yes, she knew who she was talking to. It was Roe, the one she ran after before the ceremony and the one who stayed behind with the missing girl. The fugitive.

"Roe…they're looking for you. For the mist-sucker too. What have you done with her?"

"Please, listen. You have to promise me to…"

Suddenly, her body contorted as it was flung back into a wall while her blood speckled Roe's face. Una's body left a downward crimson streak against the white plaster until her body rested on the ground with a bolt lodged deep into her chest. With what energy that hadn't left her from the attack, she began sobbing weakly. A dark pool was forming under her. As he knelt beside her, Roe could feel the warmth of it wick into the mesh fabric surrounding his kneecaps. He screamed for help and shot a flare skyward with one hand while compressing the wound with the other.

"Aaaah! Take it out!" Una screamed, after seeing the bolt. "Please! Roe, I won't tell anyone, I promise—just please take it out. I don't want to die."

She tried reaching for the bolt and he stopped her hand briskly and held it firmly in place resting on the shaft.

"No! You'll bleed out. Just relax and help will get here." Her breathing became rattled and labored. Blood stirred from within. Each breath sent her further from the living and each time she gargled more.

Finally, the frantic noises of people could be heard as Roe continued crying out, more desperate and angrier this time. Their torch lights illuminated the area revealing the sheen of blood surrounding both sentinels. As they started asking him all at once, Roe became lost to them all. He told them in fragments what happened until his eyes caught a strange shroud from the rooftops beyond them.

The torchlights hit it enough for him to see reflective orbs, almost like eyes. They blinked at him and then the figure fled. Roe thought his emotional state was making him delirious, but his suspicions were justified when he heard a thumping sound strike off a barrel and saw hay being flung in the air. The scattered footsteps grew softer until they vanished entirely.

Numerous people gathered around the drifting body before them. Roe could hear coughs and crying which told him Una was still lingering. Aid was there trying to stop the bleeding, but he feared the wound was much too aggressive. His sweat ran cold when he heard whispers of his name and murder being mentioned in the same breath.

They're onto you, Roe. The wicked disembodied cackling of the Rough Child returned, enveloping his mind.

Roe shook his head in a desperate attempt to hush them. His erratic behavior would get him implicated certainly. The struggle to keep his mind quiet allowed the Priority and Captain Raleigh to arrive unnoticed by him. Together, they stood with an imperious gaze, as the boy's fate rested with a dying woman.

Shushing erupted from the crowd as the gurgles and sputters of a dying voice could be heard.

"I…can't…I…can't…", it said.

One voice encouraged her to hang while another dared to say she'd recover. Roe's eyes opened wider. He developed a sick feeling in his stomach again when he heard Deglin whisper to her, "Who did this? Roe… did…did *he* do this to you?"

Roe stepped back and felt the presence of a body seize his shoulders, preventing any further retreat. Amidst the steady quivering of her pain-ridden face, Una made a distinctive side-to-side motion, very slowly, until it rested on the pavement permanently.

She's gone. She's dead! Roe thought, looking utterly horrified.

"What are you worried for? You're off the hook!" the Rough Child's voice spoke internally. *"Her not so much! I'd say she's more on the hook judging by all that bleeding!"*

"STOP IT! SHUT UP!"

Roe fell to his knees pressing his palms to his ears before looking around to find the crowd staring and judging him. Though unknown to him, Roe suspected their thoughts harbored awful words and accusations, though who could blame given what little they had seen.

With a face that bore more disgust than embarrassment, Raleigh's rough hands grabbed under his arms, hoisting Roe to his feet. After ensuring he was able to stand on his own, the captain brushed into his young sentinel as he stormed away. A sudden movement caught his eye and he saw a white sheet flutter down to rest over Una's body.

She was now covered, and the cleanup began. Guards pushed civilians back home as blood was slowly soaked up from the pavement. The only thing left was to send her body to a soon-to-be grieving family.

Desperate to leave the area as soon as he could, Roe dallied only a moment to see if anyone would step forward to shackle him. No one laid their hands on him or accused him of a crime. So as soon as he deemed it safe, he briskly walked home. The dried blood meshed to his legs scattered as he stared at his feet in contemplation.

He rubbed his hands through his hair dreading what the Priority must be thinking with another unexplained murder. For a moment, he thought about trying to explain himself to Raleigh, but it seemed the Priority wanted to speak with Roe first.

Deglin was pursuing him with a stretched-out hand. His voice grew laden with concern, like the expression he carried on his face. Wiping his hands which were still stained red, he ordered Roe to walk with him back home quickly. They weren't alone, as Regent Magda was there to report back to the barracks, a common practice when a murder occurred in their quarter.

Deglin wiped his brow. "Boy, what happened? Why is there a dead sentinel in my city? Two unexplained murders in two days and I've nothing to tell the people! Why were you even there, Roland?"

Roe didn't bother to look at him. He was careful of what he said with a regent nearby and he had absolutely no trust in their ilk.

"I was simply looking to talk to Una, sir, nothing else. We spoke earlier during the party. Things were quiet. I didn't see any harm in it."

It was predictable that Deglin would prod for more information.

"What happened?!" Deglin asked again grabbing his arm with force this time. Roe stopped in front of Aurascape with a scowl on his face this time.

"Would you believe me if I told you? I doubt that very much, sir."

"Roe, you act as if I'll treat you like you're feebleminded."

"And what if I am?!" Roe snapped. "What would you think of me then?"

"I'll believe you, trust me. Tell me what you know so that I can remedy these problems before they get worse. You do trust me, don't you?"

"I...do. The problem is that I feel like I can't trust my own eyes," Roe turned away. "What's wrong with me? Am I really losing it? Is it this city that's doing it?"

Deglin's eyebrows furrowed and his head tilted slightly. The more they talked, the more it became clear Roe couldn't tell him the real reason he had to confront Una—not with Magda still listening at least. Instead, Roe told him only what little he saw to appease his curiosity. More time was needed to figure out his stepfather's intentions.

"What I mean to say is...it's what I *didn't* see. That bolt in her, someone behind me shot it at her. I didn't see who. There were torches about. Beyond their flickers, I could only see a black figure in the shadows on the rooftop across the alley, and then I heard footsteps fleeing. The noise died before I could pursue."

Deglin didn't answer immediately but assured Roe that he believed his observations. The words helped him feel a bit calmer. When asked if he could speak to the captain, Deglin replied that it wasn't a good idea. Raleigh was busy trying to solve the crime and Roe's recent actions at Una's deathbed had...

"Disgusted him a bit," Deglin said, grimacing. "I can only hope that the fleeing Visitants found safe passage tonight."

It saddened Roe to know Deglin's preoccupation with mending his family's name had blinded him from knowing about the atrocity in Aurascape. The thought choked him up inside. Brief images of light, the rumbling floor, and the emaciated corpses holding each other draped in chains were the only images he could think of. They would echo in his head and when darkness set in his eyes, the falling tears beneath Delphine's mask would provide the backdrop to what little rest he could snatch.

"Get some sleep, boy," the Priority said woefully.

In all his time living with the man, Roe came to know Deglin well enough to see behind his mask of optimism. He was utterly, desperately troubled. He thought it was an unsettling sight to see a leader as strong and composed as he was, rendered helpless and distressed. No one was immune to fear it seemed.

Roe waved feebly to the man, who turned to usher Regent Magda in the other direction. He decided to return to bed, with the hope that a proper moment to speak to Deglin alone would eventually present itself.

By now, Roe had expectations of what to find in his room and sure enough, he smelled something familiar, smoke. He gasped as a hissing noise resonated against the wood from within. The culprit was just beyond the door and had nowhere to go, except for a high fall to his death out the window.

I've got you now, Ivan!

Roe heaved his way through the door as the distinct sound of a thud came from within. Making a demand to surrender shouted into the darkness, but heard nothing. Roe grabbed his blade to encourage the figure to move and swung the weapon wildly. More shuffling came and then something smacked against his desk. Roe swung outward to attack. He couldn't see what he hit with his fist, but it felt like flesh and bone. As soon he made contact, he tried to latch onto his foe.

A white flash hit his eyes and pain smashed Roe to the floor. He kicked wildly trying to halt the escape, but he barely touched anything in the process. The door flung open, and he saw a man retreat before his footsteps grew into silence.

Roe lay on the floor in the dark with the candlelight of the hall creating a small column of light across his body. The physical pain across his face reminded him of how much life he witnessed being taken away tonight. Una's death and the grayclan's lost lives hit him worse than the blow to his head. The injustice of the bodies lying there, exposed...

The thought disturbed him knowing someone had silenced Una permanently for him. Or was it? Whether or not it was an intentional plot or if she was just a random victim was unknown. Roe was still on the floor when he heard more footsteps coming, half-expecting to see the captain's disgusted features. Berl's face appeared instead and was looking around until he saw Roe's legs on the floor.

"R-Roe? What happened?" he asked as he lit a candle.

Roe rubbed his eyes, "Something attacked me in here. I couldn't see who, but he was...just help me up."

Sitting on the bed, he asked where Berl was to keep up the appearance that he had not just been prowling outside Tessa's with a fugitive.

Berl sat next to him looking disappointed, "Tessa's. I had the intent of sleeping there but...she wouldn't have any of it. I dozed off for a while thinking she wouldn't be that heartless to wake me but... apparently, she is."

"*She* woke you up?" Roe said slightly alarmed.

"Yeah, I heard the door close after I fell asleep and saw her leave. Don't know where she went but she left with someone. It was too dark to tell who. I went back to sleep and next thing I know she's telling me to leave."

"Sorry to hear that."

"Tell me again, what just happened? I smell something burning. Did you check your wooden stationery?" he grinned.

Roe shook his head.

"Can't wait to see what tonight's message is!"

A candle wasn't necessary. The two could see the fresh red glow of heat in the dark. The messages were getting fresher and each time, Roe got closer to finding the culprit. The message stood unfinished:

Seek The Dustman For hel

"It's not finished, Roe."

"I see that, but the Dustman? The Dustman's a myth. It's used to scare the pants off kids wanting to become rule breakers."

Berl agreed.

"Why go through the trouble of sneaking in a place that houses numerous guards and risk getting caught just to write that? None of this makes sense," Roe groaned, sitting on the bed. "Do you know anything about him?

"There's the inflated version kids tell each other, and the less colorful version adults pass along. Kids are told the Dustman's a demon that is enslaved in the vast burial catacombs that run beneath the city. Anybody that decides to disobey the law was punished by being locked down there with it. It hunts what's given to it for sport.

"There is also the part I heard from my father and few of the regents. He was once a mortal man but has been kept alive and horribly disfigured through magic as a punishment for trying to destroy Pinnacle."

Berl had mentioned that the adult version was much more plausible.

"Do we know anybody that's old enough to remember the true version?" Roe asked.

"Someone we could trust?" Berl added.

"Someone who won't think we're completely nutty?"

They looked at each other for a moment and chorused, "Ophelia".

Chapter Fifteen

Shades of Wrong

"I told this new kid, Johnny to lay off the makeup. I gave him practice on a newly deadened book lady they strung up in a case last week. I told him she's to look like she's alive and reading and not like one of the working ladies at Annica's. Was a bit funny to see his face go red like that."

- JOURNAL FRAGMENT FROM A CARETAKER

The more thought he put into the idea, the more reluctant Roe was to ask Ophelia for help. The idea itself was completely absurd and she would probably pity him for accepting such a ludicrous story. A story told as nothing more than a cautionary warning to errant youth who were naïve enough to believe in a demon-man that still lived hidden beneath the city. And speaking of things hidden, he wondered how long his own secret would remain intact.

Delphine was safe for the time being. Roe trusted Tessa who in turn had trust in her brother and by extension, so did Roe. His next worry was revolving around silencing Una. Unfortunately, her silence was more permanent than he had intended, causing one to wonder if the result would have been any different had the murderer not interfered.

The next puzzle would be figuring out who, or what, the vandal was and what the phantom messages meant. He thought the only way to find out was to stake out in his closet and catch the person in the act. Doing so, however, proved to be impractical and a bit ridiculous as time was working against him.

By default, Roe thought about the Dustman. Did the beast really know something? There was one way to find out, and the boys were spying on her, their heads leaning over the balustrade from the landing above. The old woman was eating alone at a table on the main level of the barracks. The area was dimly lit as many candles had been snuffed out for the night. Only a small chandelier illuminated her slight form.

In its faint orange circumference, they could see her leaning woefully on her elbows at the table, picking at the food and nibbling occasionally. Ophelia would never admit it to any living soul, but her days laden with particularly frustrating and strenuous tasks had been increasing lately if her limping gait was any indication. Roe could read her mood like a book by observing the condition of her plait.

Tonight, her hair lacked orderliness, to say the least, as many strands were clearly out of their usual arrangement as if kicked up from a brisk run. A few locks dangled against her cheeks from both sides. It was common knowledge in the barracks that only when she was in her room would she dare let her hair drop. This lapse in her personally sanctioned protocol was indeed a rarity. But tonight, was different for many reasons.

The boys crept down the stairs softly, but it was Roe who intentionally made some noise as to not startle her.

"Hello, O. It's Roe. I have Berl with me." Her face remained unchanged; it was focused down on her plate.

"What are you two doing up? I'd have thought you'd be asleep on your night off. Are you looking for your father?" she asked nonchalantly.

"No, actually we were looking for you. There's something we want to ask you, something we thought you might be able to help us with."

She waited without speaking as they sat down edging closer to her, so they could speak softly. Berl began to nudge Roe to ask since he was more intent on finding out.

"Ophelia…we were sort of wondering if you knew anything about the Dustman," Roe blurted out.

"Have you been getting visitors in the dark, Roe?" she asked without looking up.

Both sat looking nonplussed at her unforeseen response.

"D-Did you see the back of my door, O?" Roe asked rubbing the back of his neck, still unsure of what to make of the situation.

"I was young and a liar once too you know. When a child has something to hide, people with even some sense can pick up on it. That day I startled you and saw your furniture scattered 'bout, I had only to wonder what you were hidin'. You know you can trust me boy, but your secret won't stay hidden."

She paused and closed her eyes as if taking in barely perceptible words meant for her ears only.

"Can't you feel it?" Her eyes slowly opened, her gaze fixed on their scared features. "Something foreboding's comin' this way. Somethin's going to happen that will change the course of this city. It feels something awful like the last time…the last time Pinnacle fought itself. Phantom signs in the dark and unexplained killings are very ominous things. Young Deglin?" she said in an uncharacteristically stern voice. "Where does your loyalty lie? Your father or Roe?"

"Both. I wouldn't willfully betray either one. I trust them, and I hope they trust me," he replied wondering why it had to be a choice.

"I hope that's true. If anyone else that is loyal to the Priority finds those markings, they'll suspect something terrible of you, Roland," she said turning back to him. "Given the recent events revolving around you, that is."

Berl insisted that his father would never convict Roe under false pretense. Perhaps it was the experience of dealing with Deglin for far more cycles than Berl had been alive, but the maid looked quite skeptical and did not bother to hide such dissent. Ophelia was only able to offer her hopes that he was right, but she, of course, had known the man much longer. She acted as though she knew something about Deglin the two of them didn't.

"I'll help you two find the Dustman, who is quite real, I'm afraid. More creature than man but, the title's still apt. It's unknown if that 'orrible ditty the kids sing down the storm drains is true or not, but he does creep beneath our feet, in the catacombs that sprawl under us."

Curiously, Ophelia grew reluctant to say more. When asked about the origins of the Dustman, she grew sad. Instead, she had them tell her what they knew, and they gave their wild versions.

She chuckled, softly wiping a tear from her eye.

The story she told happened long ago. A man had tried to incite rebellion in Pinnacle as he was unhappy with the conditions of the city as many lived poor and in squalor. Because of this, he poisoned the minds of the citizens with radical ideas of destroying the pinnacle lamps to allow the Fog of War to engulf the city. This radical deemed the action necessary—the best course to rectify Pinnacle's problems. His rationale had much to do with the Heretic's Dictum.

"That would explain why it was banned then," Berl shrugged. "Never told us that part in school."

"Why would they? It's nothin' but dangerous knowledge to them," she replied.

Ophelia studied their faces before continuing, all the while her eyes would shift to the dark corners of the hall and to the entryways. Clearly, this was secretive information that had to have some hint of truth to it.

The man was charismatic not unlike Augustine Deglin and swayed many to his cause. Soon, a revolution erupted, and a great battle was fought for control of the city. It was known as the Freedom Rift, or the Suicide of Pinnacle, depending on which side told the story.

"Many orphans were created the night Pinnacle fought itself," Ophelia continued leaning closer over the table. "The uprising was quelled as you well know. Thanks in part to your father, Berl, peace returned. The leader of the revolution was tried and many of his followers punished. In exchange for his comrades' lives, the man took the blame entirely. He convinced the court that he had seduced his followers with tempting offers they couldn't possibly refuse—the promise of a better life. And given the current circumstances you see we're resigned to, who could blame 'em?"

She pressed on to say the man was punished not with death, but with life extended unnaturally, forced to live in the catacombs and to hunt for any other dissidents thrown his way. He was denied any possessions that would let him feel the slightest bit human, not even the owner of his true name. The creature didn't possess much memory of his past, those who he loved, or those who loved him in his isolation. People described him as a bent and twisted creature that grew wild in the dank murk.

"Do you know who he is...er...was?" Roe asked, barely containing his passion.

She thought for a moment only to shake her head with absolution and told the boys about a metal grate by the ministry building. They would know of the place because of the neglected trees behind it. The overgrowth and foliage would show them its location.

"As I mentioned," she said, "the kids like to gather there and tease the poor man, shouting that awful song down those halls below. They paint those 'orrible faces of the man on the rocks. I wish they would leave him be...I...wish people would forget him but I suppose the regents don't want people to forget. At any rate, you'd both best get going, but listen! Don't tell him your name if he asks for it; it will only serve to make him angry. He lost his long ago and it only reminds him of that misery."

"How do you know this?" Roe asked, his eyes narrowing slowly.

"I met him once," she recounted effortlessly, "near a sewer grate by the street. It was dark, and he asked me to talk with him awhile. He sounded oh so lonesome down there. I couldn't see him, but I could hear his voice echoing from deep within. But the conversation stopped being so civil when I told him my name. It filled him with some sort of madness. Oh my, I shudder just thinking of the loud terror. I was just thankful to be up on the streets. Now shoo! Go on! Before I decide to stop you."

The boys walked away leaving Ophelia at the table alone in the flickering, dim light. Berl didn't bother turning around, but Roe couldn't help himself feeling something was off. Ophelia buried her face in her hands, her shoulder heaving in the dying candlelight. He didn't know if it was due to her day being so trying or because she felt bad for the creature they were going to see.

"Why do you think she insists on addressing the thing as a man like that?" Berl asked.

"Well, he was a man once after all. Maybe he still is. Maybe the song is a bit made up for the shock. He could be just a prisoner down there, fed by guards in isolation."

"Then why not just put him in the prison where someone can keep an eye on him?"

"His notoriety," Roe answered with ease. "If he was as charismatic as Ophelia said, what do you think he could accomplish with a prison full of criminals with nothing to lose?"

Berl nodded in agreement and turned to find Roe cowling himself again.

"What are you doing that for?"

"I don't want us to be spotted trying to break and enter down there. Assuming he's real and the Dustman escapes and we're seen in the area, I don't think your father and the regents will go easy on us. I suggest you be smart for once and do the same."

Berl wanted to argue but, for the umpteenth time in his life, found it easier to simply obey.

It didn't take them long to find the ministry building with its brazen gothic façade. At its feet stood a few old and beautiful mausoleums that rose above scattered gravestones. It was a fearful place at night, although in the daytime it was known to be just as forlorn.

A few minutes passed, but with the light from a lantern Roe grabbed from a nearby post, they found the menacing thorn bushes they were seeking. The bushes were sheltered by mangled trees and flanked by boulders, that nestled against the mountainside. A pinnacle lamp stood high above them, rising tall upon the apex of the mountain. The boulders at the grate revealed crudely painted whitewash faces equipped with sharp teeth and glowing eyes. Sharp teeth. After all, the Dustman couldn't possibly be a monster without them.

"Do you think he really looks like that, Roe?"

"I hope not," he whispered darkly, soaking in the grim reality of their task.

Nearby, was a simple message scrawled out with what looked like a thick worn-out brush. It was simple but startling in its brevity.

"HE AWAITS," it read.

Berl was convinced that they were going to get caught. Roe waved him off, dismissing his fear as, "stupid". He even took the time to remind him that he was supposed to be skilled at being stealthy, rebuking him for being unsure of his abilities when he finally had an opportunity to make good use of them for a change.

To make him feel a bit more comfortable and lighthearted, Roe had decided to make a wager with him. If he could speak with the Dustman and leave without anybody finding out, Roe would win. Berl, of course, thought they would get caught.

"I was thinking," he said pacing in front of the grate, "let's just go tell Father what has been happening in your room. He could have someone stake outside the door as a lookout."

"I don't want to get him involved, I've told you this," Roe hissed, his annoyance palpable. "He's dealing with enough as it is. Look, if we don't get any answers from this Dustman we can talk to him. Deal?"

"Deal. But you don't expect me to go down there, do you?!"

Again, Roe shook his head, saying he wanted Berl to wait outside hidden in case he needed help.

"Look at it this way," Roe grinned, "the good news for you is if I don't show up by morning, it means I probably died, and you win the bet. The bad news is I won't be around to give you the money!"

"That's not funny!"

"Really? I thought you would have gone for that sort of humor at a time like this. I'm not sure what to think anymore, reality is really broken," Roe grinned.

"Shut it and go before I change my mind," Berl grimaced.

Drawing in a deep breath, Roe reached down to yank the heavy metal grate from the hole. Slowly, he descended the rickety ladder into the dark depths, already imagining something horrific waiting to claw at his legs.

What would the truth be? Would he find the man, the demon, or anything at all? Either way, he was determined to find out. As he placed the grate down with a heavy thud on the grassy lawn, he could hear what sounded like faint laughter echoing up at him. He shuddered a bit and lowered himself further into the darkening maw of the graveyard.

Carried on the dead air floating up to meet them, a raspy, ancient voice warned, "Go back whence ye came from, boy… nothing but death shall find you here…"

The Priority stood fixated on the family portrait hanging over the fireplace, one arm bracing himself against the stone hearth. It was one of his heavily relied upon distractions—or was it intended to have been a means for meaningful introspection? He had forgotten exactly the purpose of his ritual given the recent events.

Staring up at Berl giving an unjustifiably strong smile gave Deglin a disturbing amount of humiliation as the figure stood positioned behind his father's powerful presence. He mused and suspected it was a horrible forewarning of things to come, that the Priority himself would be needlessly spending countless hours protecting his son from the harsh reality of Pinnacle and the enemies he oafishly made along the way.

Saffron looked quite patrician to the casual observer, perched on a regal bench with his wife. But the grip she held the day of the portrait's commission spoke of her true feelings. Her polished fingernails dug deeply into his palms. She hated him, plain and simple. Well, his feelings for her were nothing short of mutual. The very minute he was ridden of her, he associated with what a freed prisoner must experience the moment their debt was paid. He followed the trail of the portrait to its final piece.

Roland. This boy was supposed to be his victory. An acquisition he thought of as nothing short of brilliance. Adopting the troubled youth who found his temporary home in a different spot of Pinnacle each night. The same boy who, after experiencing a volatile family life plagued with a disgruntled brother and emotionally disturbed parents, was viewed as an Elder—now synonymous with the description of miscreant.

And the timing of the adoption was impeccable. The man experienced a seer of guilt flooding his guts... thinking the adoption had been anything but general goodwill. Deep down, it was another ugly truth. This boy's love was authentic, but could Deglin say the same in return?

But he has potential. I did him a kindness... not simply from the adoption but the events leading up to it...The people saw it as nothing short of selfless to take on such a burden. I was helping you, Roland. This was meant to be reciprocity.

But he conceded that at least the boy proved to be loyal and bold when the occasion deemed it necessary. His appointment to the House of Sentinels was therefore justified. Wasn't it? This logically, he thought, was to be the next appropriate move.

It wasn't supposed to be like this. But now ever since his promotion, Roe has been acting the same way Saffron had when she betrayed me. Same reluctance to speak, same trembling voice. He's hiding something and wouldn't it then, be the case, that you cannot domesticate an Elder out from their miscreant nature?

He shuddered at the thought but refused himself a chance at failure again. This time he would act.

Someone from behind cleared their throat and Deglin suspected it was intentional. He grew lost in thought the moment he summoned Ophelia who had been acting rather sullen lately. Deglin turned around to see her trying to secure her hair back in a formal manner.

"Ophelia, I do apologize for disrupting your dinner, but I have one pressing thing to ask you," he said walking a circle around his pair of chairs. A test needed to be conducted before he could act, and he made himself its proctor.

"How was the festival, did you enjoy yourself?"

"Yes," she said simply, "you could say I benefited from it. I got to speak to some of the old barracks servants and did a fair amount of d-"

"-Excellent, excellent," Deglin cut her off abruptly with a slash from his arm through the air. "Spend any time with Roland tonight?"

Ophelia shuffled a bit in her stance, a long pause was easy to make sense of. A child could tell she was struggling to find a proper fabrication. The truth did not take this long to recall, but a believable story was something that required enough thought and skill to be properly formulated. Of this much Deglin knew all too well when dealing with those conniving regents.

"No," the woman stated firmly. "I've haven't seen him all night."

Deglin sighed and felt a cold lump drop into his belly.

So that's how it is to be? Very well, let it begin.

"Just my curiosity is all," he said aloud. "Our young Roland's been quite busy...I just wanted to ensure he had a chance to rest."

"Of course, sir. If that will be all I should go and get some too," she said ambling for the door.

"Before you do, will you fetch Captain Raleigh for me?" He asked jovially with his hands folded behind his back. There was a wry smile on his face.

"At once, sir." Ophelia did not smile back as she left.

Raleigh had been notified, though it was difficult to discern his reaction to Ophelia's news. He didn't bother to mention why she sounded so distraught. The maid did her best to hide the overcoming grief that would soon issue from her behind closed doors. She had unintentionally sicked the guards on her precious Roland.

She waited far too long to reply, this was her error. When Deglin spoke to her there was something peculiar about his tone, a subtle, but menacingly interrogative note buried within the benign friendliness of it. Like poison lurking within the simmering soup. She recognized him using it numerous times before.

But what could she have done? She chastised herself as she walked briskly into her room, slamming the door shut. She lied and thought it might just pass his head. After all, it was an exceptionally busy festival, he might not have seen them dancing and talking. It was possible he was far too distracted with the ceremony and Warrick's death. But if she had told the truth, what would be the ramification for Roe? For herself? Had he seen her speak to him about the markings on his door?

She quietly curled up on her bed thinking of the worst possible scenarios. The decisions in life were enveloped in a harsh reality where it often involved divining the ramifications of a choice where the only distinguishing characteristics were shades of evil. It was far too often the reality of the world where choice is thought to be bisected between right and wrong. No, more times than not it was determining wrong from the slightly lesser wrong. Oftentimes, the cruelty of it all is realizing that no choice is truly the correct one.

"You poor old fool," she sobbed coming to the awful conclusion, "there was no right answer. No good, just shades of wrong."

CHAPTER SIXTEEN

A DEAL WITH A DEMON

"I snuffed all the lights out except a candle I was lurking over.
I told those little brats that if they didn't behave, I'd tether
them to a sewer grate and have the Dustman come and drag
them into the depths where no one would hear them scream
as he tore them open. They scampered to bed, worked like
a charm. Perhaps too well, one seemed to have wet
themselves in the retreat."

- JOURNAL EXTRACT FROM PINNACLE CITIZEN
CONCERNING THE DUSTMAN LEGEND

THe air had quickly turned foul below the surface causing Roe to cough in dreadful heaves. With each step taken away from Berl, the surface, and safety itself, had become sour and tinted with the stench of decay. It was near-total darkness here, except for the silvery-blue light filtering down from the precious opening to safety that was slowly disappearing from his sight. He looked for a while circling in his footsteps searching for any light in the distance. It took a while for his eyes to adjust to the murk, but he could finally see the faint orange glow of fire beyond. With his hands stretched out in front, he dragged his feet along the dirt path taking caution for the uneven ground.

Edging closer to the source, he noticed the intolerable amount of noise he was making. The light was his focus, but he knew he wouldn't make it far if the catacombs reeked of danger. The rustling of his boots and the quivering of the metal on his belt made him easy to find. The decision to come down here was looking more foolish by the minute.

Roe could only see more glowing white images crudely painted on the rocks. Everywhere he looked a white face was watching the young sentinel. When he cocked his head slightly, the images were as fleeting as his imagined childhood ideas of what the Dustman would look like. They turned out to be figments of his fear-ridden mind for as crept closer to inspect them, he discovered there was nothing but grime covering the walls.

It grew silent except for the hollow noise of air flowing through tunnels that gradually became cramped as he found himself forcing deeper into the earth's belly. The one he chose was tall enough so that he could stand, but the strands of his hair brushed against the ceiling, and his shoulders drug against the walls. Feeling their cold, hardened embrace about his shoulders, it felt as if it was getting tighter and more restrictive. Roe squeezed forward wondering if he was going to become stuck and unable to dislodge himself, or worse, wondering if the walls were closing in.

Pressing onward, he was relieved to see the area opened into a recessed room filled with linen-clad lumps placed upon shelves cut into the rock walls. He shivered as he gazed at the destitute deathbeds, of those that couldn't afford a memorial or a grandiose mausoleum on the surface…or those hideous glass caskets.

Standing there a moment allowed his overactive mind to suggest the corpses could spring to life at any moment. He imagined them tearing through the burlap with their bony fingers and scattered groans all the while gnashing at him. Roe coughed and moved over to the wall, toward more crudely painted faces looking at him. Reaching out this time, he was able to feel the smooth touch of whitewash.

These are real, he thought.

If he was to find the Dustman, he had to follow the dreadful paintings and since his path became viewable again, he could tread with a bit more care than before.

At each corner, he stopped, peaking both ways and placing a hand on his blade only to find nothing. No noise and no sight of anything for that matter. His boredom had finally gotten the best of him as he was becoming more careless in maintaining secrecy. He hadn't seen any sign of the Dustman's existence, except for the crudely drawn paintings of a monster on the walls which he concluded must be one big ruse. It seemed the only to be afraid of was the wild shadows being cast in the dim glow of the faraway chamber.

"Stupid," Roe sighed. "Just a stupid joke and you fell for it."

But as time wore on, Roe felt as though his mind was playing tricks on him. The more time he spent searching, the more certain he saw eyes watching him. Every few steps that he took, something clung to the shadows following him in the dark fringes. Each time he turned to confront his pursuer, they vanished like the white pictures he imagined on the walls back at the entrance.

To keep his mind off chilling thoughts, Roe hummed to himself. The song he chose was the only one he could think of at the moment, though grossly inappropriate considering the dire situation he was in. It was the Dustman's song.

After all this time, he couldn't believe he still remembered the words. But how could he really forget? True, it had been so long since he gathered with the kids of his youth to sing the song down the sewer's grates. They were brave enough to sing it, why shouldn't a sentinel?

It went:

In the darkened halls where the dead men sleep;
In the hallowed earth where the spiders creep.
When you meet the creature, set the place alight;
Hide the demon, show the man. Keep him in your sight.
The Dustman walks among the dead;
The Dustman creeps, and reeks of dread.
Speak your words and tell no one;
As darkness falls, you'd better run.
When twilight sets, his eyes turn red;
Escape his grip or you'll be dead.
The Dustman seeks you in the ground and hunts you, hunts you,
down...down...down!

In his time spent with the other wayward kids on the streets, Roe learned the simple rules of the game. That when the song ended, some lucky individual was given the great distinguishment of jumping out of the bushes near the grate and grabbing unaware children from behind that were new to the story. Roe was ashamed to remember he had been one of Armin's victims in their youth, but he got even by scaring others when their time had come.

By the time Roe was old enough to brave the bushes himself Armin was already gone so the younger kids had to feel his vengeance. Although as he looked back on those times, he felt a twinge of guilt knowing he probably caused a few sleepless nights, the same ones he had experienced from the crude trick.

After a few rounds, he stopped. His stomach knotted with apprehension, as he heard something haunting, being carried on the dead air flowing toward him. The sound had smooth and velvety notes to it. It was distant, but Roe walked toward it, a male's voice. It would have soothed the sentinel, had he not been so terrified by who or what was singing it. He found himself oddly captivated by the wonderful voice but his feet grew resistant to move forward. His eyes scrutinized in all directions as he crept closer...

There!

He could hear it clearly. Something rising from the depths. A voice sang while hands clapped out the cadence.

"Dustman walks among the dead, Dustman creeps and reeks of dread..." the voice chortled.

Roe's heart was pounding faster, and his throat lurched from gulping a large lump of air.

"The Dustman seeks you in the ground and hunts you, hunts you down, Down, DOWN!"

The voice cackled once more.

"Oh no, this can't be him!" Roe whispered, urging himself forward. "It's gotta be a prank."

The room he found himself bore six torches on pillars surrounding the edges. Two were dimly lit while the others stood naked and without purpose. The singing continued in the distance as he made a grab at one. As soon as his fingers met the shaft, his hand repelled back as something with leathery flesh tried to grab him. He scampered back and yelped at the shock.

Searching all around, Roe heard rattling, like teeth chattering. Then another, and another. Deafening rattles enveloped the room. He whipped out his blade and set his feet ready for an attack. The thought that tore in his mind, as absurd as it was to call attention to given his predicament, was of Captain Raleigh's hardened look, and courageous stance. That is how he would need to act to survive this.

When he heard movement to the left, he lashed out in the dark but sliced nothing but air. Something scurried beneath his legs and another bounced off his shoulders landing behind him. One hit him so hard that it dislodged the blade from his hand. He heard the awful sound of it nestle into the soft earth.

One of the torches flickered; glowing orange embers were all that was left. Now there was but one. With no weapon in hand, he grabbed for his belt and noticed the trauma gloves. Slipping them on, he pressed his forearms in to fire up the gemstones and felt the slight prick of pain. He sent out a flare in the darkness only to see it hit the wall and fizzle. The small burst of light that followed revealed only dirt and scattered bones strewn about the sandy floor.

Something scratched at his neck and he swung a fist behind him nicking whatever little blighter was attacking. Another larger flare was released, and it lit up more bones strewn about the floor. Then he saw a rogue pair of legs scurry away. Before he could register where they went, the stinging sensation of pinching mouths at his skin sent Roe tripping to the ground and a flurry of small bodies swarmed him.

There was more than soft dirt and sand on the floor. Vile sludge and soft, fleshy tissues engulfed Roe's body as he rolled frantically to put out the nagging stings of biting mouths. The acrid scent made him choke, but he flailed his arms about to get free. The creatures were shuddering and quivering; biting at anything and anywhere they could get a hold of.

With a flare in one hand, he thought he could struggle to his feet and send them off for good with one well-placed shot, but he was tripped up only to send an errant flame down to the ground. He braced and felt the searing heat scorch the earth near his boots. The flare itself was small but he managed to hit one of the creeps. Its fiery body ran about the room wailing and crashing into others of its kind. The flaming creature's path illuminated another beast. Roe didn't wait and brought a heavy boot atop it. The squelching noise gave way to a muffled gasp of breath beneath the impetus of his foot.

As he readied another flare with both hands, something crawled up his cape and onto his neck. The thing tore at his ear and he yelled in agony. Caught by the surprise of its savagery, Roe stumbled backward into a pillar with the creature on his back. It was crushed from the impact of Roe's weight. The final torch fell from its holder and was extinguished.

"No!" Roe cried.

Stray attacks ensued with more fury as the light in the room was completely doused. In the pitch dark of the chamber, Roe clawed and punched at the air. Casting flares proved too slow and energy-consuming. But he couldn't fight them like this.

Rage took over and he yelled with all his might. He wasn't ready to die like this! No, he'd just as soon turn himself into the authorities. He clapped two flares from his hands together in frustration. The room filled with light and flames issued from his hands, hands that were fighting hard to stay rigid and strong. The power of the inferno was boring his legs and body down into the ground. His arms were numb and shook from the force.

All around he saw the tiny eyes reflecting the awe-inspiring sight of their doom. The bodies of the wicked fast creatures came into existence for a few moments. Shrieks and screams ransacked the area and the quivering bodies began to sound their retreat as the scurried frenzy in the dirt ceased. Roe fell back to the ground when the fire from his hands stopped. He yelled once more at the surge of power—the adrenaline coursing through his body—yelling to drive them off for good.

Darkness and silence returned to the room. He stood there a few moments and buried his hands in the dirt to cool them off. He fished around on the ground to find the base of the pillar, so he could prop himself up properly. His hand grazed a torch protruding against the stone and lit it with his glove.

In the blaze of light, he scoured the room looking for the blade he dropped hoping they hadn't made off with it. After he found and sheathed it, he went over to the bodies he crushed. The figure he had stepped on looked to be about as high as his shin, but it was hard to tell because of the mangled frame. It was dressed in what looked like a tattered loincloth with long gray hair, and bone-white skin both frail and thin. The face was very gaunt. There were no lips on the creature, just small, sharp baring teeth.

Roe gasped.

The laughter continued just beyond the room. He followed the long corridor leading downward toward the arch of a door. Its steps were gritty and slippery. Roe grew careless focusing on his thoughts more than the placement of his feet and slipped, sending him tumbling downward.

"Hmmph? A visitor? Seems right. I hear someone. You fell. Mind those steps. Been a while since they've been swept!"

It laughed.

Roe didn't know if the voice was addressing him or not, but he decided against speaking, first looking around to see if he could find out where it was coming from.

The singing continued.

Scanning the cavernous room—that looked more like a cavern than a prison—Roe saw two large sconces emitting a soft light on either side of a door, a crimson-stained chair resting in front of it. This metal door possessed a large barred window facing him from across the chamber. The floor of the room was simply a narrow walkway reaching out across a seemingly bottomless pit. This restricted path led up to the metal platform upon which the chair was affixed.

Nearby, there was a taut rope from which was suspended a counterweight hanging silently in the dark. Roe traced its path and found a circular tumbler that rested next to a sliding lock pressed against the door. Roe discovered it terminated at the lever pulley mechanism that locked the door on the other side of the abyss.

Above the prison door, as if crudely carved by the hand of a deranged criminal, stood an excerpt of the forbidden words of the Heretic's Dictum:

THE GREATEST BEAST IS MAN

But why these particular words? Why were they so important?

The song grew louder, the clapping frantic, almost deranged.

Roe stepped timidly onto the metal landing and the platform sunk a bit beneath his weight. He heard a huge thud behind him. The sudden noise jilted his composure. Instinctively, he jumped aside thinking he had tripped some sort of booby trap but soon found himself half-teetering looking over the depths below. Sitting on the ledge, he took a deep breath looking over his shoulder to see what awful thing he had done.

The opening had been blocked, a door with no hinges, levers, or knobs. It looked just like the prisoner's door. Roe groaned with despair knowing he had just made himself a prisoner too. There were two other slabs on either side of the one he had entered, but he needn't try to know they were sealed tight.

The creature began stirring within his cell. Bones crunched, and deep, gluttonous breaths echoed from within.

"Hmmph? You don't have to stand on the threshold of my home. Come in, come in from the cold," the raspy voice said. It was perplexing as it sounded ancient, nothing at all like his singing. And when it spoke, the voice seemed to make an inquisitive inflection, "Come now, I suspect you haven't got all night, hmmph?"

Roe stepped cautiously toward the door, though the shadows from within the cell were making the act quite difficult. He heard very cheerful humming along with the scraping sound of teeth grating greedily against bone. The bending shadows filled the room, long skinny arms were casting wildly grotesque shadows against the wall. The arms were flailing about and clapping in exaggerated motions as if caught in a dark trance.

As Roe approached the circular platform hesitantly, he stood behind the chair mounted to it, thinking somehow it would bolster his courage. He felt the chair swivel a bit on the platform as he pressed his hands against its back to stifle his fear. It was such an odd thing to note given how desperate his predicament had become.

"Please have a seat," the voice invited.

"I'd prefer to stand, thank you," Roe squeaked.

"Courtesy? In this world? Ha! How alluring! I must insist that you sit regardless. For you see I'd be a terrible host if...I...were to make a guest stand. Hmmph?"

Roe sat down on the edge of the chair which he found to be cold and hard, not wonderfully comfortable to make a guest sit in. As his weight sunk onto the seat completely, he heard another thud. His arms and legs were bound by metal clasps with such a death grip he thought his hands and feet would burst. He tried kicking out, but he had nowhere to go and his frantic movements caused the chair to lock in place.

"Is this any way to treat your guest?!" Roe yelled.

"Hmm? Assurance, lad. That my guest won't leave. You see, it's been oh so long since I've had anyone to talk to…anyone thrown down here against their will," he laughed maniacally. "I didn't want you to leave so soon."

"Why the chair?"

"Not my doing. A place for dissidents to be locked up. To be forced to sit and look upon the creature of original rebellion. When they see my eyes, they see their death forthcoming. When I'm set free, I kill my own. Think of it as a new form of execution. As such, I sometimes have an audience when I hunt. The soldiers from above."

"Then what they say about you is true."

"Hmmph? Indeed, but I fear time is vital to you, so let's not waste any more of it. After all, I assume you risked seeing me for a reason. Wouldn't want it to be a wasted trip," he cackled once more.

"That depends. Are …are you the Dustman?"

"That is what I've been told. The echoes from above tell me so. Now then, you know me lad, but I don't know you. Have a name do ya?" he asked.

"R-" His teeth latched on his tongue, catching himself. In the back of his mind, he remembered Ophelia's words. Roe fumbled in his mind to come up with something, any response but a name. The words were stuck in his throat.

"A friend!" he choked. This amused Dustman immensely.

"Excellent!" the creature acclaimed. "I was wondering when I would find one. Now, what brings you down here, lad? Hmmph?"

"It's a bit hard to explain. I was directed to you, but by who I have no idea." He felt the crushing grip of the metal clasps around his extremities and he chided the creature to let him go but his pleas went ignored.

"Thought-provoking. Yes, directed by ghosts. You want to be set free and I want your company. We both have needs, lad. The question becomes this: can you satisfy mine?"

Roe asked him what he had in mind. He would do just about anything to be freed. The pain had turned into tingling and numbness would soon follow.

"Ever enter into a compact?"

"Funny you should ask. I made a deal with a girl that I intend to follow through on. Whatever you want, I'll do it, but I'd like to get out of this chair, please?" He thought a bit more courtesy would sway the creature toward compliance.

"Will you try to escape?" he asked.

"Don't have...much of a choice, do I?" he winced from the pain, considering the pits on either side of him.

"A falsehood. You always have a choice; people simply deceive themselves into thinking otherwise. You could always leap off the ledge to escape. You would...most likely die from the impact but you...would be escaping me," he said sadly.

"No," Roe sighed, annoyed by the correction. "I don't plan on throwing myself off to my death. But I must say you're wrong on one account."

"Hmmph?"

"Th-There," he groaned with pain trying to wiggle his fingers and toes to life, "there is no choice in death."

"No, lad. Even with something as ultimate and inescapable as our own demise, a living being still has the choice to strip death of its victory over us. You can die on your feet or you can die on your knees. But I do enjoy this foray into philosophy, delving deeper into its intricacies."

Through the darkness, he could see Dustman's emaciated arms stretch suddenly through the metal bars of the door. Each hand was equipped with slender, long fingers with sharp yellow nails.

Soon, they retreated into hiding behind the door. Roe heard a metallic snap and the tethers on his chair snapped out of place and he was freed. The first thing Roe did was rub each and every place that had been strangled by the metal.

"I at least have been given enough freedom to dictate when I can release my guest...my prey." Suddenly, a gangly arm protruded between the metal bars. "A gentleman's agreement then."

Roe gingerly reached out to grab his ghoulish hand to solidify the arrangement. His grip was clammy and felt as though the firm pressure from a gentleman's shake would rend the skin from his bones. The creature coughed abruptly and one of the candles extinguished causing the already dim cell to grow dimmer. His grip tightened, and Roe found his body pressed against the cell; his face being squeezed against the bars. He could briefly trace the creature's bulging eyes in the dim light, they were tinged a murderous red that appeared to be growing more intense by the moment. His breaths became louder and animalistic. Roe tried to break free of the grip but was struck with fear.

"In...the... d-darkened halls... beneath our feet..." Dustman struggled to sing a strained version of his melody. Roe felt the grip loosen slightly against his clothes and he forced the creature's fingers against the bars.

"What are you doing? You're such an unpredictable thing! You're cordial one minute and the next you're trying to force me through a metal door...and now you sing?!" Roe threw his hands in the air and kicked the door.

The beast retreated and then a flicker of flame was brought back into the world, his room filled with light once more.

"Apologies. I like to keep my room as bright as possible, but I must spare what candles I have. You see, the darkness makes me...grow wild, something I have no hope of controlling when the room grows dark. My curse. Bright rooms, the light, control the madness, so the song goes, my curse. The singing reminds me of pleasant things, thoughts. It reminds me of what I once was," he shuttered, "though in forms of half-remembered dreams."

The conversation regarding their wager continued. Dustman explained the terms. Roe could ask him as many questions as he wanted, within an allotted time, if and only if the Dustman was given the chance to hunt him down within the catacombs afterward.

"That's sick," Roe said, repulsed.

"'The greatest beast is Man', lad. Priority Flood—the man who sentenced my imprisonment—had a bit of cruel streak harbored within. It was no secret among his circle that he enjoyed hunts and games of risk. This was but another game to pleasure himself with. So, what shall it be?"

Roe bristled at the thought but looking around he saw death seemed to be the only certainty at this point. Falling to his death in the pit, starvation, or throwing himself onto a blade, those prospects weren't enticing to him. If he was going to die, well, he was going to choose to die on his feet.

At least with the hunt, he had a chance to escape. A small one, but that was all that was afforded to him. The stipulation was he had to be bound in the chair to face the Dustman, so he couldn't get a head start. The other doors wouldn't open anyway without the Dustman's cell door to being opened by the counterweight.

The creature made another pondering noise.

"Instead of getting the guards involved—as they are far too busy finding you from what I've heard from above—I shall summon the bone keepers instead. Yes—they can… light their wee candles that will…burn the rope to the counterweights providing your time limit and compensate for the guards' absence," he laughed once more, clearly excited by his innovation. "This will abide within the terms I am bound to by those that enslaved me here. This action starts the time for questioning. When the time ends, the ropes snap…the doors open…and then…"

"And then?"

There was a hesitation, as the voice replied gloomily, "You try not to die, lad."

There was almost a trace of sadness to his voice and Roe seemed to know why. The Dustman gained pleasure by being freed from his prison and given the thrill of pursuit, but it also meant the demon within him would be released.

In the light, he could make out the creature's mangy, sparse hair hanging down to his chin. Realizing this lapse in secrecy, the demon retreated farther back in the so cell as to not be seen. Like the creatures Roe encountered in the other room, he was emaciated and pale, with bulbous eyes that reflected in the light. It took great courage for the sentinel not to gasp when he saw the unexpected glimpse.

Roe sat down once more closing his eyes as tight as he could, thinking it would steady his nerves.

"I'm ready…I think…"

Dustman started rattling a bone between the cell's bars. Soon the creatures that attacked him earlier returned, but the Dustman calmly reassured him that he was safe if he remained still. They perched themselves on the ledges bringing with them a candle that was placed under the rope. The site would normally be considered cute seeing the small hands cradle their wax so lovingly…if one could ignore their rampant desire for flesh and bones.

"Hmm? Revolting things, aren't they? Normally, the guards drive them off, but tonight is a special night indeed. One you are all too aware of. It seems you've killed three of the little blighters by the looks of it. Well done, that will buy you a bit more time, but not much, I'm afraid. Let us begin, shall we?"

The candles were lit, and Roe was bound to the chair once more. Trickles of smoke wafted lazily upwards. The hissing and crackling of the rope fibers set about terrorizing numbness in him. The chattering teeth continued, and the keepers sat there staring at their target eagerly, while some nibbled on tiny, yellow bones. He knew what they were eager to see happen. If the Dustman were successful, they'd get something other than bones to chew on, but Roe wasn't planning on that. Above all, he certainly wasn't planning on owing Berl money!

His mind was frantically sifting its contents for any semblance of a question, but the pressure he was under merely caused him to panic and fidget. The only one he could think of to get rolling was, "What are you? A man? A demon?"

"Hmmph? Depends on who you ask. The children say demon, the adults say man. I, for one, prefer to be dynamic, ever-changing. The mystique is attractive and keeps me from growing forgotten. I…I don't want to be forgotten. It doesn't matter, as those that have witnessed me firsthand weren't able to escape to reveal anything. My identity remains hidden in songs and cautionary tales…"

"I've been getting hidden messages in my room. Who's been sending them? One told me to seek you out!"

Roe heard nothing for a moment and he tried squirming against his fetters. To his periphery, part of the rope was glowing, and strands began to kick up from the rest. He asked the question again, pleadingly this time.

Dustman theorized what each one meant. The first two revolved around the Night of Safe Passage, the first was more obvious than the second. The ascent, as the message said, seemed to refer to Roe's ascent up Aurascape to discover the murderous ceremony the guards had mentioned. The guilt he referred to was that of the people of Pinnacle. They danced, laughed, and indulged in vice, thinking only of themselves, the problems they wanted to forget. They were too busy to know the true meaning behind the celebration. The patterns suggested being that of guidance.

"I saved one of the Visitants from the ceremony. She's safe for now, but I can't hide her for long. If I don't do something, they'll find her and kill her!"

"Quite a problem you brought on yourself! Suppose that's the lot of the righteous within the confines of Pinnacle," he laughed.

"They were innocent though! They had no-"

"-No! Innocence doesn't exist in this world," the Dustman said fiercely. "It is an illusion made by those whose fault is too heavy to bear and so choose the path of denial. It is all an illusion! Everyone has a role to play. Everyone has their role! This innocence you speak of is as intangible and foolhardy as the Priority's hope for everlasting protection from the Fog-"

"-What?! What's wrong with that?"

"-If protection means sacrificing lives—humans or grayclan— no one should live. Where are the scales to say your human life has more value than theirs?" Their exchange grew heated, fueled by a desire to arrive at a common truth by any wanton needs.

Roe couldn't argue against that line of reasoning except that he knew destroying the pinnacles meant certain death. Something wasn't right. He pressed on, asking about the words etched above his door.

"Those words are outlawed because they elicit something every person of power dread from their subordinates: skepticism. To question!" the Dustman wrung the bars in a fit of frustrating rage. "THAT THERE CAN EXIST SOMETHING MORE THAN THAT OF WHICH YOU AND I CAN SEE OR HEAR! WAKE UP! YOU'RE ALL ASLEEP! WAKE UP!"

Roe gasped. "It's *you*! You're h-him! The man who wrote that paper of Pinnacle being asleep!"

"I've only one regret." Even when asked about family or friends, Dustman's answer remained the same. Roe wanted to know what this was, but he was running out of time. The rope was fraying. The chattering grew louder. He figured he had only one question left and it had to be worthwhile.

"What should I do then?"

"Do what I couldn't do, lad. If you want to save that girl… to save everyone…you must first wake up. You must become… an illusion killer."

"But…the Fog of War?! How? I don't understand!"

But it was too late. Roe's pleas succumbed to the Dustman's wild singing that had been roused up. After one round of the ditty, Roe shifted his legs and discovered the platform could swivel again. The lock had reset after he was released the first time. This could prove valuable, but he'd have to time it right…

By the time the second round started, the lights had been blown out by the bone keepers to speed the wild transformation. The haunting words from the demon's singing nearly caused Roe to yell in despair, for the fiend was singing of demise, singing to make his quarry scared. He had to ready himself for what he had to do.

Survive, survive for Delphine. Live to see her live.

The Dustman managed to tell Roe one thing more before everything turned to hell.

"I enjoyed our talk. And lad—whatever happens… I am very glad to have met you truly."

Sweat rolled down Roe's cheek, he could no longer hide the terror surging through him. The boy's strident, panicked breathing grew faster, *hih-huh*, in and out of his mouth as if he were suffocating. The involuntary spasms gripped his chest. As if on its own volition, his mind was screaming, panicking.

This can't be real...none of it! You're asleep Roe! Wake up!

In the dark, Roe balled his fist and screamed a desperate command to himself, "WAKE UP!"

The rope snapped.

The doors crunched open and he forced his bindings open with all four limbs at once. As he tried swiveling around, the chair jammed, and Roe was thrown off. The blood-curdling roar to his right filled the room. The chattering against the walls intensified. The only thing guiding his flight down the ramp to the doors was that faint glow where he had come from.

The sounds of panting and growling grew faster and closer. A cold and bony grip seized his shoulder. Nearing the three doors, he stumbled to the ground. The ghoul on his back tumbled over careening against the wall. The demon occupied the center exit, trying to gain composure. Roe rolled out of the way and took the left door, sliding down an incline. The chattering bone keepers were scampering across the walls, pelting him with their bodies, trying to knock him down.

At the end of the corridor, he met no stairs, only a gradual slope upwards, covered in sand and grit. He frantically clawed and kicked his hands and knees upward. Not making progress, he found himself sliding down again toward certain death. His legs felt like rubber as the murderous panting from behind drew closer. Old tree roots suspended out from the walls to graze his face as he peered over his shoulder. He grabbed one with desperation, but it snapped immediately under his weight. He tried for another bracing his right leg against the wall which allowed him to shimmy up.

The Dustman's hardened fingers sank into his leg and pulled him painfully down. His other leg lashed out at the hand, but it held on with a death grip. Roe kicked out hard, this time further back striking the creature's face. The grip eased, and he used this moment to move his leg upward to gain a better grip, shimmying more until he reached level ground. He looked down only to find a tangled mass of hair and bulbous eyes glowing fiery red staring up at him. Thick saliva squeezed through the grimy teeth looking at his escaped prey.

Finding his composure, Roe discovered he was back in the part of the catacombs possessing the coffins and monuments, things that looked more familiar to him. A path laid before him and went up a set of stairs to a door that eventually led back to the ministry building.

Before he closed the door, Roe heard the muffled shout of the Dustman, "Kill you some other time, lad!"

The ear-deafening roars from below did not cease.

Roe propped himself against the door for a moment then slid down, pressing his back against it. He felt a pang of nausea grip him and with it, the burn of vomit attempting to bubble its way up his throat. His body wretched, the bile began to force its way up until slow, deep breaths suppressed the urge to be sick.

No sounds were coming from behind the door, but he could find no way to lock it or hold it closed except with his weight. After allowing a few more moments of silence to pass, he deemed it was safe enough to get up and leave.

Being in a smaller room with a lack of adequate airflow made Roe realize he had collected many bad odors from his excursion. Breathing through his mouth proved to be even worse.

Outside, Berl was found intently gazing down the hole his friend had vanished into, so he didn't hear Roe's approach at first. When Berl heard his name called, he ran over from his hiding spot and gave his friend a big hug.

The moment they embraced, he shoved Roe away and made exaggerated sniffing motions with his nose. A volley of questions ensued the most intrusive being how he came to smell like a decaying animal. Instead, Roe staggered away from him with a blank look. He had gleaned information from a creature of fable and somehow lived to tell. Those questions could wait.

"Did we get caught?" Roe asked vacantly.

Berl replied, "Damn, yeh smell like death!" he laughed pinching his nose.

Given the recent time with the grim company of the catacombs and almost ending up dead himself, the comment was errant, indeed.

To fully demonstrate his irritation, Roe grabbed some slop lingering on his shoulder and smeared it atop Berl's head.

"I wouldn't dream of depriving you of the lovely scent. Now, did we get caught?" Roe asked haughtily.

"No, but-"

"-Guess I won then."

Chapter Seventeen

Tears of a Sentinel

"My sis told me the Priority had made his choice of who he was going to adopt. That Roe Elder of all people! Biggest heretic alive since his idiot brother killed himself. Still makes me angry to know I wasn't the one despite having a real family. I hope one day I get a chance to prove my worth and show Deglin he was wrong to choose that oddity."

— Extract from Ivan Fern's journal

"Captain?"

"Out with it, meat," Raleigh grunted, his back turned away.

The sentinel awkwardly shifted his weight before reciting the orders he had just been given.

"Your orders, Captain, are to expand patrols to locate the grayclan girl known as Little Hex the Tenth to the…mercantile district…the commissary?" he said incredulously.

Raleigh turned, abruptly cracking the knuckles in his left hand, "That is an affirmative, Private. The Priority received intelligence the girl was being kept somewhere in the vicinity and wants the area combed—thoroughly. Is that clear?! If you find the order absurd—please reach in your trousers and tell me if you can find your stones—that way I can start looking for the next harlot's brood petite enough to fit in your uniform!"

"Yes, sir—I mean no, sir. I-I've got the stones, I can assure you. It wo-won't be a p-problem," he said scampering out the door.

In normal times, the sight of a subordinate squirming would have brought immense pleasure…but times were different. Tonight, was different. Only an hour earlier did he find himself in the unfortunate but predictable situation of being summoned by Deglin once more.

At least the summons was worth the energy of prying himself out of bed and gathering his uniform. The moment took on a sensational bent when he heard the news of a grayclan girl supposedly held hostage by a sentinel. But usually what turned out to be scandalous news ended up having some sort of crime attached to it. This is where he came in.

To top it all off the man had suspected his son—the *one* worth his salt—Roe, who was currently unaccounted for.

"Sham, the hell have you gotten yourself into," Raleigh muttered leaning over the balustrade of the Hardscape.

Despite the occasional whooping and hollering reverberating down below, remnants from the celebration, there was something eerie hanging in the air. A deafening calm, like a foreboding silence before the fray, staged battalions of armies facing one another down before the blood was let. He had read much about battle in excerpts of ancient tomes that survived from the time of his ancestors before the Fog. All this knowledge was wasted, spent staring at the same oblique murk, never given the chance to show if he truly was formidable as most saw him to be. Sadly, through the trenches of all of the hard-fought battles, were those only won and lost inside his own head pitting himself against his own reflection. Cold comforts, they were.

No true combat. No physical war. Was tonight some-how, different?

It felt like it did during the Freedom Rift—his only true taste of war as a meager Pinnacle Guard. It was due to his heroics for Pinnacle that he helped quell the rebel forces and he began his path toward the most feared soldier the city had known. Feared and hated—they went hand-in-hand like newlyweds.

Ever since the day the Freedom Rift ended, he had grown loathsome toward himself, but Captain Raleigh did not know why or had not come to terms with it. The drink always made it easy to suppress the awful truths. It was clear though, doing the right thing often meant a higher chance of mortality. But a small insurrection in the streets was pale in comparison to the stratagem that was war.

From the books in his room, he had learned about the old days: Moving artillery and soldiers to various theatres stretching across the occupied lands, protecting supply lines, executing a pincer formation—that was real war. But that was also freedom. Freedom from the Fog…even if it meant death by that wretched abyss. Those same military texts explained that the phenomenon, *fog of war*, was meant to signify uncertainty in military tactics, uncertainty of the enemy forces, lands, and capabilities. The name was apt. Same could be said of its literal form sprawling across the earth waiting to do everyone in and finish the job it was created for. War too was known as a realm of uncertainty, of this much he knew.

Uncertainty. Fear. Hatred.

Raleigh pushed off the balustrade hard and walked toward a dead marionette in a nearby glass coffin, to appraise its grotesque form.

He paced around it speaking to himself, "If I snuff it one day peacefully serving Pinnacle…is this how I will be remembered? A gross perversion of death? We're brought up to not fear death by seein' it as nothing more than forever sleep. Instead, we become trapped, suffocatin' in a glass box. Or, can I die like an honorable soldier would, in battle? Free."

Before he left the study, Priority Deglin had given Raleigh an ultimatum the moment he showed any resistance toward the man's plan born of paranoia.

"Round up Miss Emlan and her brother. Bring them to the keep for interrogation—verbal and physical means, if necessary," Raleigh remembered him saying. "Let us see if Roland's loyalty comes around on his own before we do anything drastic. You will do this, or I can easily have you tried for sedition. It's only a simple matter of planting the evidence in your footlocker for my soldiers to find once I give them the order."

Again, Raleigh looked toward the horizon seeing the horrid silhouettes fluttering within. He felt anger, he felt helpless, but worst of all he felt like he was suffocating. It made his skin crawl, his teeth itch, and the joints in his fingers stiffen and twitch. He could feel the will to live, leaving him.

"Bring me war and I shall be set free...by death or something else entirely. But will you do it this time, Captain? Do you have the stones to die in battle? A fog of war grips the battlefield. Gather more intel, then strike."

He called out to a sentinel hurrying his way out of the barracks. The young lad stood at attention but with an annoyed look about him.

"Your name, Sentinel?" Raleigh barked.

"Fern, Ivan Fern, sir," he said, militarily. Raleigh quickly recalled the name as being one of the new initiates alongside Sham.

"Fern, your orders are to help me find Tessa Emlan, and her brother, Tampson. You may use force if you must, but bring them to the keep for questioning, understand?"

The young sentinel saluted and said, "Yes, sir! I will find them all and bring them to you at once, sir!" Then Ivan began his sycophantic trot down the stairs to the city proper to begin.

The captain then gave a hard glare back to the window of Deglin's study addressing the night and his opponent, "I've made my choice, sir. Let us do what must be done and take to the battlefield."

Something in Pinnacle changed during the time Roe had spent underneath it. He couldn't figure what it was precisely, but things felt off. The misty ceiling above and the air were the same, but the city was harboring an awful disquiet. Berl took notice of an unusually regimented increase in guard activity.

Many more were out marching door to door, of which many had been forced open; the guards gave no notice and hardly any time for the residents to respond to the fists pounding against the wooden doors, breaking the silence of the still twilight. The site gripped Berl instantly.

"R-Roe? They aren't looking for us, are they?"

"Doubt it, they have no reason to yet."

Saying this may have allayed Berl's fears, but it didn't settle a lick of Roe's problems. They were looking for *her*, he knew it. He was only somewhat relieved as it appeared most of the force had been dedicated to searching Pinnacle itself, not the outlying forest and villages—something he thought quite peculiar. Given the number of buildings to check, it would take them a while to find her, but they would eventually.

After all, the world was choked down to a small patch of land, or was it? More and more did he begin to suspect something amiss but even if he was almost certain he thought of death. He has once played with the idea of ending it all thinking there surely was a better life thereafter, somewhere beyond the perpetual despair of this one. The problem was there was always that small kernel of doubt, of fear, that he'd be wrong. Often times, the kernel formed into a mountain.

Roe sat down frustrated, knowing he had no plan or courage left to act on. Dustman said if he wanted to save her, Roe would have to destroy the lamps' barrier, a problematic solution seeing's how everyone would die—or so everyone said. Even if he did try and somehow got caught, Roe would have to attempt to escape the Dustman again, but certainly, the state would ensure it would be a surefire execution rather than a contest of chance.

And even if the scholars were wrong about the barriers, the Fog, and the circumstances mixed in between, how was he supposed to go about destroying it all by himself? How would he even know how to destroy those towers? The only clarity he could find at the moment was that Delphine had a right to live and he intended to see she did.

"Berl, let's get outta here," Roe insisted, as he disguised himself once more though Berl saw on point to it.

Walking back home, they saw many broken doors with the guards questioning half-naked people in the streets. Some were being taken away in the direction of the prison. Roe recognized the banker that had exchanged currencies, being taken away with his hands bound, perhaps because of suspicion and further questioning. What would be his fate? Could it be torture or something with a bit more finality?

Back in the barracks, they found the main hall overcrowded with voices and bodies. The interplay of the white-clad Pinnacle Guard and the black figures of the House of Sentinels made everything chaotic.

Demands were made to many by Captain Raleigh and Augustine Deglin. The Priority himself was trying to calm the angry guards, but it was unsuccessful. It took the captain's deep and harsh shouting to silence everyone. The boys noticed his hand resting on the hilt of his blade during the exchange.

"Ladies and gentlemen, we have a situation on our hands," he yelled irritably. "The Priority's law of the land, and I suggest you listen to him or you'll start trouble with me. You'll form pairs and patrol the entire valley. When I mean the entire valley, I don't mean just the street corner or the nearby tavern, I mean from house to house, lamp to lamp.

"We have a missing grayclan girl on our hands and she needs to be found. Anyone who sees her needs to bring her back to

Aurascape, no questions asked. Your pairings on the wall, look for your name and find your partner. You don't like it, turn in your uniform, and start looking for another job! You're soldiers of the Defiant City. Act like it!"

Although most looked reluctant to follow the orders, none were bold enough to challenge him, either out of fear of Raleigh's wrath or the fear of being stripped of job and home. Slowly, they trickled outside to meet the twilight and begin the search. Roe somehow lost Berl in the process of staying upright amidst the crush of shifting bodies going in complete disorder. Their cause would have been noble but only Roe knew that combing the city would only be a waste of their time.

Time was wasting for him too. He had to do it. No more hesitation. He had to trust the Dustman, destroying the lamps, and replicating a rebellion was going to be his fate.

That there can exist something more than that of which you and I can see or hear! Wake up!

Somehow, someway the words sounded correct, but he found no reasoning as to why. It felt as though he harbored the answer but needed the words of another to ignite the way, to reveal the true nature of the world. Roe nodded to himself for encouragement.

But he had to escape first and tried sifting through bodies moving in every direction toward the door. The hearty musculature of the captain stopped him in his tracks.

"Going somewhere, Sham?" he asked with a wry smile.

"Sir, please, there's something I have to do…It's important!"

"No. You see…patrolling the barracks is where you need to be."

"But…"

Raleigh's green eyes narrowed in a conniving fashion, darting his head back and forth as if searching for someone in the crowd. He walked away briefly only to return with a sentinel between the strong grip of his hands. "Look who I found! It's your best chum, Ivan! He'll make it all better, don't worry!"

Roe's eyes narrowed. The captain maneuvered Ivan toward him until the both of them smiled as though they had just uncovered a dirty secret of his.

"Fern, now that I found Sham, have you had any luck with finding the others?" Raleigh queried.

Others? Roe thought.

"Yes, sir. I found one—she put a helluva fight to get her here though. We'll find the other, don't worry," Ivan said sycophantically before turning to his left, "Hey, Sham! Looks like we're going on a hunt! Maybe we'll be the ones to find the little mist-sucker!"

"Why so eager, Fern? That keen to have the honor of tasting the captain's boot first?" Roe's fury rose another notch. As much as he disliked the moniker Raleigh gave him, Roe sheltered some respect for the man.

"Do you really think she'd be hiding under our noses?" Roe asked, with great restraint. "That's a bold assumption. With the number of guards going in and out, I doubt she'd make it in here unnoticed."

Even though they weren't close to her hiding place, Roe was still anxious about room-to-room searches. There would be no plausible way to explain the carvings that would be found on the backside of his door without the truth being involved with the story.

"You've got nothing to hide—least I don't think you do. Besides, we can't take any chances," Raleigh replied. Fern echoed him with pride.

Roe cocked his head defiantly toward Ivan.

"After you're done with his, you want to have a go at my boots, Fern?" he said coolly.

At least he got a rise out of the captain from that remark. He never considered himself the type of person that sought pleasure by tearing anyone down, but Fern had become the exception.

"You'd best get going, Sham. Maybe you two can start gettin' to know each other on a more intimate level when you're searchin' through each other's things."

Not bloody likely, Roe thought as he turned away.

Before he could attempt to lose Ivan, Roe saw someone motioning at him. He looked different…almost predatory.

"What's going on?" Deglin asked abruptly. "Where have you and Berl been all night?"

Roe shot him a confused look to perhaps deflect his suspicions, but he wasn't falling for it. Deglin had noticed their rooms were empty. From the sound of it, he was still oblivious to what Roe was hiding but felt obligated to remind the boy of how he was taken off the street, pushed above the common rabble. How he sheltered him, provided the best Pinnacle could offer, treating him like a son from his own blood.

"You wouldn't lie to me would you, Roland?" Deglin asked conceitedly. "After all, that I have done for you? You would be so casual to hurt me so?"

Roe had been ready and willing to tell him the truth but instinctively, something told him to lie. To lie. He didn't say anything; the boy just sighed and looked away feeling a harsh penetrating gaze bore into his back. Perhaps Delphine was onto something when she said she didn't trust the man. Even if her life were at stake, Roe couldn't bring himself to lie to this man. He cared for him and was afraid that Deglin's love for him was waning.

"Please…please sir, I have to go," Roe stammered. "Ivan's waiting for me. We have to find this girl."

Walking away the Priority said zealously, "You had better not be lying to me!" Roe knew that it was all but uncovered. Deglin just needed proof and he was going to find it eventually.

Purposely leaving without Ivan, Roe hurried up to the next landing. But soon after Ivan's drawling calls met his ears soon after; demanding he wait. Rolling his eyes, Roe waited impatiently at the top.

"Where do we start?" Roe asked. Ivan gave no answer at first but was itching his neck clearly not in the moment.

"Why don't we start with *your* room?"

"How'd I figure you'd say that? Instead of trying to annoy me, we start at one end of the hall and work our way down systematically? Let's put that small brain of yours to use for once and think."

"Like the captain said, you don't have anything to hide so why not start with you? Look, I tell you what, I'll cut you some slack and we'll search the old maid's room first. Then we can move on to yours? Otherwise, I can turn you in for insubordination. Now move it, Sham!"

Ophelia's room was one of the most secluded, as it was nestled near the Priority's chambers, adjacent to his prized carved table in the dining hall. The door was closed; the crack between it and the floor was black. Roe begged Ivan not to disturb her and to move on to his room, but he wouldn't listen. A fist pounded on the door and a demand rang out that it be opened immediately.

"This is an inspection by order of Priority Augustine Deglin. Open the door or you will be arrested for insubordination."

Roe snapped at him.

"Ivan, you have no cause to be arresting anyone for insubordination. Besides, she's probably asleep, you idiot!" His face flushed with heat as the brute's behavior continued. His glance shrank to the floor when he saw the door creak open and Ophelia blocking the entrance looking rattled.

"Roe? Ivan? What's going on? Why all the yellin'?" she blared, briskly closing her robe with one while trying to fix her hair with the other.

Roe couldn't look at her. He hated himself for just being there, for being associated with Ivan and disturbing her in such an awful manner. Ivan again demanded that she let them search her quarters for the missing girl. She obliged and tried to provide light for the two.

Her room, like the rest of the barracks, was well above reproach. Not a thing out of place or a stray article on the floor. That all changed when Ivan stormed in.

The closet was flung open and clothes were strewn about the room, bookshelves scooted out from against the wall sending books falling to the floor. Ophelia fell into a fit of tears at the scene of disorder. Roe yelled at him to stop, but Ivan seemed hell-bent on proving himself to someone.

"I was told you were hiding something, and I demand to know what it is!" he hissed backing her against the wall. "I-I am not hidin' anything. I've got nothin' to tell you. Roland, what are you boys doing to me?" she cried.

Roe wanted to tear himself away, to flee to his room and bury himself in the dark away for as long as he lived. He was losing her, and he was losing Delphine with each passing moment. The outlandish idea of simply walking out, to forego the life he once knew was becoming more enticing as it was inevitable. He began to tremble, utterly terrified that something awful was about to happen, and no matter what he chose only the degree of horror would be changed. For an instance, he gazed out her blackened window, reminded of what this was all about. Now he felt reckless wanting it all to end, ready to march to the nearest pinnacle and start his suicide mission until he heard a horrific sound that pinned him to the spot.

Ophelia screamed in agony as Ivan tried twisting her arm behind her back in a violent manner of submission. All the while, he was trying to rationalize himself, justifying his sycophantic zeal and why he felt the need to hurt a tired old woman.

"Berl told me," he grunted against her resistance, "she was hiding something damn important about the mist-sucker. I'm arresting her, Sham. Don't try and stop me, or you're next!"

One more tug, one more pull, and she was brought to her knees grimacing. Inside, Roe was struggling to find composure. Agony filled his body as if that were his arm being bent. The maid fought valiantly trying to free herself, but Ivan resisted her movements. Roe knew what he was seeing yet he stood nailed to the spot. His hands raked through his hair trying to lamely explain to himself that he was dreaming. It could only be a dream! His parents' death, Armin's abandonment, the Fog, all of it! It had to be! Nothing felt true anymore!

Wake up! You're asleep!

Roe flung himself at Ivan with such a fury he hadn't known in all his life, striking him in the jaw without thought. An icy chill crept down his spine knowing what he had started.

Ivan fell backward.

"You're finished! I should have burned you back when I had the chance!"

Roe ordered Ophelia to run for help, but Ivan slammed the door shut and dove for her. Roe caught him first, tackling him onto the bed. His hands slipped from their grip on Ivan's writhing wrists. The maid shrieked at the cold and terrifying twang of a blade briskly unsheathing.

Desperately, he tried to find Ivan's arms but felt a blunt pain against his chest as he crumbled onto the floor. He laid there gasping on the floor, the impact winding him. On the bed, Ivan rolled onto his knees with rage glimmering in his eyes. His blade was held eagerly looking to taste blood upon its virgin metal. He leaped from the bed. Roe rolled as sparks rose from the floor where the blade had struck. Again, Ivan swung, but Roe couldn't dodge this one so quickly after his maneuver. He braced for the sharp agony, but it never came. Ophelia soared onto his shoulders, allowing Roe precious seconds to stand before she was quickly flung against the bed like a soiled shirt.

Echoing from his cavernous mind, he heard the cackling Rough Child chide him, "Cut him down!"

Roe immediately whipped out his blade. His initials on the hilt were palpable in his tight, sweaty grip. Ivan swung, but Roe was quicker.

With his body plunging full force at him, Roe stumbled on the tousled thick rug and his arm met resistance. The weight of Ivan's body smashed on top of him, his head smacking against the cold stone. There was a tough struggle marked with a hard gritty, sickening sound of bone.

Lying from underneath, Roe looked up at Ivan whose lips were contorting, his eyes fluttering quickly. Tears began to form in his reddened, panicked eyes. Crimson streaks writhed through his teeth from a deep grimace of pain. Ivan let out a whimper and simply groaned "Roe?" as if in disbelief of what he had done.

The sentinel's eyes didn't move after that, though they were looking at him as if to make sure his attacker would never forget this moment. The hilt of the blade was sticking into Roe's abdomen making it hard to breathe, so he pushed Ivan off, his body tumbling limply to the floor. The carved white initials "R.D." were now pink and were staring callously back at Roe, as they stuck out of Ivan's chest.

Roe looked over the lifeless body near the door and then over to Ophelia. He tried to revive him by shaking him and calling his name frantically. Barely seventeen, just a boy—like Roe—he was dead.

A searing cold swept through Roe's body and his fingers began to tingle, prickle. His vision began to blur at its fringes. This time Roe could no longer hold against the strength of his tears. He cried for him, for Ophelia, Delphine, his parents, Armin, and anyone who would have to see any horror in their life. He understood their pain.

"O? O-Ophelia?!" was all he could say. He was shaking uncontrollably and sobbing with disgust, he kept calling her name hoping it would take away the shock. She slowly knelt on the floor and placed a hand on his face.

"Ophelia? I… didn't m-mean to. I-I didn't mean any of this. I didn't want to come here, but I wo-would have been arrested an-and what have I done? What have I done?!"

She held him in her embrace and stroked the back of his head shooshing him like a child. He was no longer a sentinel or a soldier. He was a child crying in the arms of an adult who was trying to shield him from the cruel reality around them.

Looking over from her shoulder, Roe stole a glance at the body that no longer was Ivan Fern. He was gone. Now there was just a corpse, a pale lump of clay that was stiffening by the minute. He wondered what Ivan was experiencing right now, much like Una. What were they seeing? Were they feeling? Were they somewhere else moving, thinking, loving, hating? Anything at all?

"What am I going to do?" Roe coughed amidst his tears. "I had no choice…he was hurting you. I-I'm done for, Ophelia! I'm done for. But I have to know… I need you to tell me I'm not doing the wrong thing. Tell me the truth!"

From there he divulged why the valley was embroiled in panic, and why everyone was being questioned. Why the girl was missing. He hid her from harm and now everyone in Pinnacle was paying for it. From one simple act, Pinnacle was slowly dying from the inside like a deep-seated disease manifesting to the surface. Roe didn't care if she was going to betray his trust, too many secrets weighed upon any mind and his had become over-encumbered.

The entire time she remained the same, looking as caring as ever. When it was all said, Ophelia told him in a hushed voice that he had done the right thing. In fact, Roe would have made his real father proud if he were alive.

"This isn't something new, is it?" he asked.

She looked down and shook her head slowly. He was told that seeking out the Dustman was the best thing he could have done. What he saw tonight was exactly the reason the man acted as he did so many years ago. Tonight, Roe was about to replicate his path.

"I just hope...that you don't fail the way he did. He told you what you needed to know. What has happened with Delphine cannot be undone now. We have to follow through this time; we have to destroy the barrier...destroy this evil infesting everyone's minds. Even if we all must die," she said with an air of fear in her voice.

Clearly, the idea weighed heavily on her. She had lived through one crisis already, the Freedom Rift, and Roe was about to replicate it once again. Ophelia was ready to become a rebel judging from the way she steeled her body.

"But how? I don't know where to begin. We can't do it by ourselves."

"Yes, but we don't have to. I..." she couldn't finish her thought.

A thud at the door, someone was taking the bedroom door to such a fervent task. Their eyes bulged looking at each other in horror. She hopped up and stepped delicately over a pool of blood forming toward the door. Roe grabbed a bed sheet throwing it over the corpse though he didn't bother to drag the body farther into the darkness without risking the noise. He had to rely on Ophelia's words, not his blade.

The voice at the door was crude and loud.

"Is Roland Deglin in there? The Priority is looking for him immediately. You're required to come in for questioning too, Ophelia…I am sorry. If you refuse, I am to arrest you immediately, so please don't give me a reason to, miss."

She was cooperative and nodded through the cracked door, but she didn't allow any part of the room to be visible.

"I don't know where he is, sir, but I'll tell him as soon as I see him, just give me a moment in private please. I need to dress, you know, my delicates 'n all."

The voice outside said he would wait in the hall so she wouldn't attempt an escape. Ophelia closed the door as calmly as her nerves would allow. In spite of the dimly lit room, she was visibly upset.

"Ophelia, I need to turn myself-"

"No!" she whispered fiercely as if scolding him for cursing in public. "No matter what happens, I will *never* give you up, boy! Do you hear me?! I *won't*!"

She fiercely kissed his forehead and Roe's skin crawled knowing something bad was going to happen. The next time he saw his hero, his stepfather, disappointment was going to be the least of Roe's problems.

The housemaid opened the door and peaked down both corridors, signaling for Roe to leave the room quickly. He padded across the hall and hid out of sight in the entryway of another room. She came out and walked toward the dining hall. Roe opened and then closed the door behind him, walking out with her. The guard saw him and told him what he already knew.

Without acknowledging him, Roe followed Ophelia who had already disappeared around the corner.

It was amazing to see the drastic change in the ambiance within Priority Deglin's dining room compared to the night they all had dinner together as one. The area was well lit but was very unwelcoming indeed. The plants were hunched from neglect. No tantalizing aroma filled the air. The only thing elegant and welcoming was the dining table. But even the guests seated at it were not very welcoming. Some were frightened and some solemn, but each had a guard flanking them with a blade drawn.

Sitting in distress were Berl, Tessa, and Ophelia. The captain was sitting in front of them all, thumping the table metrically with his fingers. They turned to look up as Roe entered the room. Deglin was clever, for he gathered the people that were the closest to Roe and pitted them against each other to get to him. Someone was bound to slip. They were fearful. The lot of them had good cause, for interrogation was imminent.

Chapter Eighteen

Roland Unwanted

"As your newly appointed leader, I have nothing but the brightest hope for Pinnacle's continued future, and I shall help guide you all to be as defiant as this city is. If you cannot place trust in yourselves, you may then at least place your trust only in me."

-- Written account taken from Augustine Deglin's appointment speech

rmin saw the drastic change in the firmament the moment he broke free of the crumbling shaft. It felt as though he was reborn into a different world. A miraculous image rendered from the sight of fluffy clouds scudding across an endless blue and a horizon that expanded into an infinity of colors and shapes rather than a foggy maw ready to envelop the world. It was a marvel the cramped and dilapidated tunnel within the cellar had stayed intact long enough for him to extract Tobias to safety. It was this tunnel he discovered accidentally the day he wrote his suicide note—the same tunnel he and the boy used to enter that hellish abyss once more.

He turned to look at the slender hole he pried himself from and wondered if its collapse was imminent. Twice did he inadvertently snap the rotting wooden buttresses in his task of pulling Tobias through the cramped space using only a thick set of blankets and rope made into a crude stretcher. If that tunnel were to collapse, the mission would essentially fail, and those peoples' fates would remain as prisoners. There would be no one to prod them further toward discovery.

But the boy's fever was growing fierce and the reddened rash that issued from the puncture site on his wrist climbed up to reach his elbow. His companion only stirred by a jarring movement, otherwise laid in his britches drenched in sweat.

Don't die, Tobias. You're far too young...for death...for this mission... too young to be the fierce force of magic they try to mold you into. This is no life for you.

Armin gave his bracelet, tucked away in the satchel hanging against his waist, such a disgusted scowl.

Such an unnatural thing and look what it's done to poor Tobias. But you are to blame for that, Armin. You forced him to make that manifestation over and over just to tire him. To protect him. But from what? From the unnecessary act of murdering Warrick. It was a pure deviation from the plan, you know this and can fess up to it. And now, you take another deviation as help has been called to extract the boy. To save him from yourself!

There was a gentle humming in the distance coming west over the craggy mountain that stood menacingly between him and his goal. Or was it a mountain? He could reach out and feel the dusty earth that rested on its rocky slopes. Still, he wondered what part of it was real and the other a clever and elaborate illusion.

Waiting for the source of the humming to come into view, Armin sat resting near the tunnel's opening, readjusting the formerly cool, washcloths tucked between Tobias' armpits. His thoughts turned toward the stone mass towering above him.

This was the source of those disturbances to the fleet's airships. The confounded mountain reacted strangely to the testing made by the scientists and those blasted glass orbs of theirs. Had it not been for me telling them where it was that I emerged from, the search for those fabled complex illusions would fail to move beyond that of a fairy-tale such as Pinnacle...

His thoughts were jarred back to reality as the humming grew close enough to cause the ground to vibrate where the airship was making its final approach. Despite his current state of concern for Tobias, Armin couldn't help but revel in the technological marvel of the apparatus even after countless voyages within the clouds above.

It was likened to sailing, the ship's body like that of an old frigate he saw a drawing of back in the days of tutelage in Pinnacle.

Though lacking sails, the ship's power was derived from an energy he had yet to get a grasp on when it was explained to him. Didn't matter now—they were here, and Tobias would be taken care of.

As several uniformed individuals began to disembark from the ship, Armin waved his arms frantically gesturing to the still figure on the thick blankets. The tallest was standing with a harried-looking man frantically scrawling as he looked about wildly. Armin didn't have to guess that this was a field scribe documenting every observation, scent, sound, and action associated with the work of a Dispeller—those tasked to rid the world of illusions.

"His status?" a young medic asked Armin as she flung a satchel down next to the still figure.

"Unrelenting fever the past several hours now...I suspect an infection from those wretched bracelets they made him wear. Why they make children—"

"Dispeller Elder," she said curtly, not taking her eyes from the boy, "I suggest you bite your tongue. He's here. Yes...*him.*"

Armin quickly looked over her shoulder and watched the tall man approach at a brisk pace. He had a bald plait and was dressed in a handsome military overcoat; Armin sighed to himself at the unexpected sight of his superior, Head Dispeller Farley Agathon.

As he rose to his feet, the medic grabbed Armin's arm and warned, "If you plan to have a row with him, you best meet him halfway before he trudges over here. I've no intention of playing mediator with a critically ill boy to manage. Let me work."

"Then work," Armin said curtly, jogging out to meet the imposing figure.

"Dispeller Elder," the bald man said stopping abruptly, stroking his well-developed jaw. Armin saluted quickly and gestured over his shoulder.

"Head Dispeller, Tobias' sick. We need to get him extracted. He's—"

"Fallen ill, yes it wasn't difficult to discern the panic in your phonetograph's transmission. You didn't bloody lose that too, did you?"

The question was anticipated knowing the contraption was considered invaluable to the operation and quickly whisked out the device that appeared to be nothing more than an ordinary wooden box. There was a latch on the side that opened to reveal its clock-work innards: a thin sheet of metal, something resembling a series of metal coils wrapping into a small conical opening, and a set of parallel running threaded rods.

The Head Dispeller showed a great sense of relief at its site. Then he fixed his attention to the craggy peak ahead, studying it carefully.

"So, this is it?" he asked in awe. "Mount Bullrush is the *complex illusion*? All this time in our recorded history? This is it?"

"Yes, but what of Tobias? He's quite sick. Looks like he starting to show septicemia, it must be!"

"I had no idea your limited time spent within has made you competent at giving medical diagnoses, Dispeller," Agathon said looking at the black mouth of the escape tunnel. "Clearly, it did nothing to repair your gross disregard for orders. Killing a man, in cold blood. Your report was quite disturbing indeed, but your candor was certainly a relief if not expected."

"If you knew Warrick, what heinous things that man was capable of, you'd know there was nothing cold about it, sir," Armin said, straining his voice to be calmer. "Righteous perhaps."

"That is for the Patriarch Convent to decide, not you. You murdered him," the Head Dispeller said. "Such a crime, in our nation, bears a similar penalty."

"He was wicked."

"That characterization will be determined after we render this illusion down to nothing and we are able to thoroughly investigate. That is beside the point, I should have you-"

"But *you* won't, sir, respectfully. Because only I possess the necessary information and wherewithal to ensure we save those people in there! My actions have spurred a burgeoning skepticism! If only you could see it! It is only a matter of time before revolt! Upheaval! But I must get back in there and ensure it happens," Armin said making for the opening.

"Very well, Dispeller, but I am sending my forces through with you."

With his arms already pulling himself halfway inside, Armin's voice echoed back, "I advise against that, sir. This tunnel is the only entry in and from the looks of it, has one more trip in it before collapsing, and I don't want anyone bumbling around in the dark jeopardizing the mission."

"Bold as brass, that one," the Head Dispeller said to himself before turning to the black maw in the ground. "Very well, the crew of the *Morningstar* will be placed on standby then, when it begins to dissolve. And when it does, justice will be waiting for you, Mister Elder," he yelled warningly.

Armin's voice crawled up to meet him, "Look on the light side of things, sir. If this tunnel collapses down on me, you won't have to worry about ensuring justice finding me at all…"

There was an unnerving disquiet in the dining room.

Clearly, a secret was wedged from privacy, but Roe had no idea who it was, or to what extent. A simple poor choice of words could be enough to kill them all for what little he knew. The captives were sitting in a row, the interrogation had already commenced. One by one in front of everyone, Raleigh started asking questions about Little Hex.

Tessa was first, then Ophelia. Both denied knowledge of anything, but Roe was never worried about them. In the corner, Deglin grew frustrated and impatient at the lack of results, his weight shifted frequently until this became wearisome. He strode alongside each person sitting, casting an appraising look at them until he pounded his fist onto the table, breaking the disquiet.

"May I remind you of how good your lives are thanks to me? Be grateful for the lives you've been given. Be grateful I am dedicated to keeping you all safe from the Fog! Be grateful that you don't live beneath a fractured sky! The world would collapse on us if not for me!"

Still, no one spoke. Berl's interrogation was next and Deglin began it by treating him with the utmost dignity. Unfortunately, the others had not received equity in this regard but Roe's thoughts finally gained footing. The man was playing to his son's sensitive side; he wanted to play the loving father to manipulate him, a tactic that seemed to be used before. Deglin knew his son would fold easily under the weight of overwhelming guilt.

"Berl, son," Priority Deglin said seizing his shoulder, "I've done my best to ensure peace and prosperity for the citizens while trying to appease our Visitant guests. This balance of course, is no easy task. Why would you want to jeopardize what I've done, what...*you've* done to help keep this peace? I know that somebody in this room is lying, keeping secrets that endanger us all. It was secrets that killed your mother, did you know that?"

Berl shifted his gaze down along the table, staring blankly, searching for guidance from within. Roe, meanwhile, had no hope that he would play the role of a best friend and lie to his father. He found himself digging his fingernails painfully into his palms waiting for the inevitable.

And to everyone's surprise, he said nothing.

"No? We'll see about that. I can't give you special treatment. You will be punished like the rest."

Berl's leg was shaking rapidly and he was anxiously scratching his scalp again. Moving on, Deglin walked behind the rest, slowly inspecting them with scorn.

Roe startled at the tensioned hands clapping on his shoulders. Deglin gave them both a good painful squeeze.

"I've been good to you, haven't I? I didn't have to adopt you, to take you in as my own. What happened to your family was a tragedy, but inconsequential to my family. Some might even say that Pinnacle had benefited from it. I will give you one last chance; tell me what you know about the missing girl."

Roe waited for a moment, drew in a deep, labored breath, and braced himself for what he had to do. Inexplicably, a dangling noose swung dolefully behind the curtain of his eyelids.

"I don't know anything, sir."

Deglin removed his hands briskly and started to walk around the table drawing a calculating smile across his face.

"I am…very disappointed with you, Roe. I've come to a bold theory. You see, I think you know more than you are letting on. I have this overwhelming sense of certainty that you know her exact location. Why would I have such feelings you might ask? Well, it appears my own son's loyalty lies with his father as it should be."

Berl had done well with the interrogation or at least he thought. Thinking for a moment allowed Roe to look deeper and realize Berl wouldn't betray his trust with the present company in the same room. He had already told his father. There could be no other explanation. Deglin was only giving everyone a chance to fess up and seek mercy. The issue was exactly what Ophelia was worried about. She somehow knew Berl couldn't appease both sides.

"I know of the secret visits you've been receiving, and I know that you and Berl were looking for a certain entity tonight. I know because that *thing* was found running loose in the catacombs. I have had to dedicate valuable resources to try and lock him back up! Remarkable that you escaped though. You're the first, to my knowledge."

"Must be an Elder trait—too stubborn to die."

"You were always too bold for your own good. Why couldn't you be more compliant like Berl?"

Roe gazed fiercely down the table at Berl who looked blankly at the floor.

"Well, what can I say? I learned something about your son, my so-called 'brother' tonight."

Deglin raked his hand across Roe's face, causing many at the table to flinch.

"He is a loyal son! Unlike you, he obeys me and even when he deceives me, he ends up telling me the truth of his own volition. He seeks peace while you seek chaos. Berl is the same reason I have your friends here tonight," he smiled fiendishly.

"Berl, what did you do?" cried Tessa.

His figure didn't stir, but his lips mumbled, "The window to Tessa's flat was cracked open. I-I heard her directing Roe to her brother's. I don't know why." Tears began to bead on the wooden surface below his face.

Berl lied. He lied.

This entire time, it was Berl fooling everyone, making Roe believe his loyalty could extend beyond his father. When Deglin questioned his son about why they went to Tampson's hideout, Berl seemed unaware and only offered more silence.

Suddenly, there was a demand made to speak out of turn. A guard from behind pointed to the door across the room. Ophelia's room. Something dark was seeping from beneath the door. It flowed through the grooves of stone running carving their way through the floor making small canals and rivulets of crimson.

Deglin motioned for a guard to investigate with him as they left the room. Roe tilted his head toward Ophelia who was still sitting, tall and proud as if she were staring down her executioner, accepting the cords of rope around her neck. She gripped his hand under the table and sat in silence. Captain Raleigh never left his spot in the corner as he studied each of them throughout. Moments later, Deglin returned.

At once, Roe saw a blade at his side, the same one that he forgot to remove from Ivan's body. Roe squeezed Ophelia's hand so hard he thought he was going to break it. The Priority slammed it into the polished wood of his beloved table for everyone to see. It was rooted in place to stand on its own with blood running down its edge. A small collection of red began clotting in the cracked wood. The letters "R" and "D" on the handle were still stained pink.

A pained expression swept across Deglin's face.

"I realized you and Ivan didn't get along, but to murder him? What are you some kind of monster?!"

The Greatest Beast is Man...

The words never sounded truer.

Looking at the rest of his captives, Deglin questioned why they claimed allegiance to him as if their brains were addled. Then he rounded his blame on Ophelia, which was something Roe wouldn't stand for, even if Deglin was the most powerful man in the world. He pushed away from the table, pointing an accusatory finger at the Priority. A cool metal edge was caressing his throat.

"Is that how you respond to someone saving a life of a citizen you claim to care about?" Roe yelled. "*Your* so-called sentinel was harassing her to the point of nearly breaking her arm. He attacked us. She's the victim of an extremist you created! You ignore the problems of your city guard and hide behind the captain to fix Pinnacle's problems. Why do you think the citizens are angry? What have you done to ease their fears other than maintain their dependency on you? What reason have you given them to keep their doors unlocked at night? I hear the cries that go unheeded. I've seen the squalor the Visitants live in and the empty stomachs that crawl to work! Do not preach about the good life you've given us! Otherwise, people might think your standard's a bit low."

Roe stood there staring him down, realizing he could be killed by a flick of a wrist, with just a command, but he continued.

"I lied to you about the girl. Do you even know what they've been doing to those poor creatures you claim to be saving? When a Visitant asks why their friend disappeared, you don't offer the truth to them. Your guilt, along with the citizens is... buried in the music."

Deglin's eyes widened at the sudden revelation.

"It was you! *You* kidnapped the girl."

Roe nodded defiantly.

"Where is she?"

"My memories gone fuzzy."

"I will have you killed if you disobey me," Deglin hissed.

"I guess you're gonna have to kill me. It appears as though you're rather good at sending people to their deaths, sir, knowingly or not."

"Roland, I am so ashamed to have taken you into my home, ashamed that you bear my name. You are no longer Roland Deglin. Henceforth, the annals of history will simply know you as Roland Unwanted, a heretic. I sentence you to be executed at once!"

Gasps and protests filled the air. Roe was grabbed from behind, the grip of the guards sent sharp pains through the bones of his arms as they were wrenched behind his back.

Roe was ready to die, if only because he knew he couldn't be alive to allow Delphine to be murdered, for harm to come to Tessa or Ophelia. He had to die if that were to happen. When he was being forced out of the room, one objection came from an unexpected source.

"Sir!" Raleigh pleaded, "All due respect, his crimes are grave, but it'd be a waste to kill him now if we can't find the girl. I urge you to reconsider. We'll execute him—no question—but he may have information. The Dustman did cycles ago, with a little physical persuasion, gave us what we needed. Give me some time with him. I'm sure I can beat the information out of him."

Indeed, the man looked serious. This was no ploy. Roe gave him the same disgusted look that he gave Deglin. Then spat saliva across the captain's face.

Roe was an enemy to Pinnacle now, an enemy to the two most powerful men, the Priority and Captain Raleigh. He wasn't allowed a chance to say goodbye or to thank the people that helped him try to save a life. He didn't get to see their faces in hopes that they'd bring him comfort before his death. There was no chance to hug and tell Ophelia how much she meant to him. No chance to embrace Tessa and tell her he'd never allow her to feel alone.

Roe Unwanted was off to prison, treading the path of the demon that incited the original rebellion long ago.

CHAPTER NINETEEN

THE PATH TO REBELLION

"Though it may be grossly unpopular and difficult to do, one must take the time to acknowledge the Visitant incursion on Pinnacle—for without them—the trauma crafts would have ceased to be, and we would be rendered to mere fledgling children wielding sharpened sticks."

— EXCERPT FROM BLOOD AND GEMS: YOUR GUIDE TO THE TRAUMA CRAFTS...AMONG OTHER THINGS PAINFUL

A careful and final look back at the interrogation allowed Roe to conclude he had finally accepted his fate of dying. If he had a chance to revisit it, there wouldn't be a thing he would change. As the demon had said, even with death as the only ultimatum, a choice was still present and he would choose to die on his feet. He had prepared himself in every way he thought possible. But how could one really prepare for something like this?

LEAVING BEHIND FAMILY WASN'T AN ISSUE FOR HE HAD NONE. The few friends he had gave him a parting gift of loyalty and support. Finally, there was the rugged life he had lived in his short existence that didn't seem to have a chance for improvement. If secretive mass killings, deceit, and apathy were the things that compromised "the good life" as Deglin proclaimed it to be, Roe had refused to be any part of it. He was ready to move on to the place of nothingness he knew was awaiting him. He was ready to move on from the searing slag-hot agony…

Cold sweat was trickling down his back from his sweat-matted brown hair. He was trembling terribly. There was no amount of preparation to help Roe ready himself for what happened before his imprisonment. Though his legs were jarred against the corner of the cell in an uncomfortable fashion, he refused to move. The searing pain from his arms beckoned him to remain still at all costs. Looking down at each forearm, he could see the dark blotches of drainage seeping through the wrappings he had fashioned from soiled pieces of garb found in the corner of the cell. He had yet to look beneath the filthy bandages to discover what they were hiding…

His detainment had only been but a few hours, but he was already growing impatient and restless. He wanted out, even if that meant calling the hangman. The air smelled similar to that of the catacombs, which wasn't surprising to him; the cell was putrid, filled with ragged and soiled clothes and who knows what else. There was shouting in the background, cursing and slurs volleyed at the guards. Repetitive clanking and whimpers were growing.

He felt lowly and abandoned, but the latter was a more familiar and less unwelcoming friend. He wondered if this was what the Dustman felt when he had been locked up. He wondered if the creature had anything to miss anymore. At least he had those nasty bone keepers to keep him company.

Roe didn't even have his uniform to take comfort in. He was stripped of his weapons and uniform prior to his torture. All he had on were tattered brown clothes like the ones he saw emitting the horrendous odor on the floor. It was cold and nowhere felt comfortable to sleep. When would Raleigh come for him? Sitting and waiting there made Roe think about the long path that led him astray and who helped get him there, Berl.

There was no anger anymore; it didn't soothe his pains cursing Berl or wishing terrible things upon him, but he was still reeling over telling him anything. It would have been far better if Roe had taken the burden of a secret on by himself. His stepbrother was always so timid and docile, too much to be the son of a leader. His passive nature was how the two met several cycles earlier.

At that time, every child of Pinnacle was required to take an apprenticeship in each quarter of the city while attending the Academy. It was an effort to instill work ethic and skills in the children, starting at an early age.

After the rotations were finished, the children were assigned to work within the quarter in which they excelled. It was Pinnacle that picked the jobs, the citizens had no choice in the matter.

But when the Visitants came, their obligation to the city took priority over the youth and Pinnacle stopped the apprenticeship so the Visitants would have the jobs.

The extra time allowed for mischief, naturally, to arise in any child. Luckily, Tessa and Roe even in their nascent times were inseparable. They would take turns sneaking away from their respective assignments to see each other. Often, they would find a quiet little nook to nap or talk about how they'd find adventures in the Fog and beyond.

But on one seemingly ordinary day, while they were busy avoiding classes at the Academy, Roe and Tessa heard a commotion from their perch. Down below, kids were knocking papers out of Berl's hands and shoving him back and forth, looking like a burlap bag being tossed about. He wasn't sure why he was the victim so often, but an older Roe had suspected it was just because of who his father was. The terrible part was on this particular occasion, Deglin was watching, studying the entire thing from afar, and did nothing to help. Could he protect himself? Could he show his father that he was strong?

No, he couldn't.

Berl wouldn't fight back or defend himself the way Roe would have. He pleaded with them, but of course, children would never rescind so quickly. They always enjoyed seeing their victims squirm; they liked to see them cry. Berl did both and it thrilled the agitators to no end. They laughed and howled and made sure he was thoroughly shamed and humiliated. The biggest of the group grabbed his hair, pulling him to his feet while Berl's small hands listlessly grabbed at them to pry himself free.

After the boy was on his knees crying once more making a ruckus, Roe and Tessa, along with her trusty sling, managed to scare them off. Talking with the boy helped them get to know the son of Deglin better and realize that he wasn't some bombastic or self-righteous snob they had pinned him for, but quite the opposite. His fragile personality made him more likable in Roe's eyes. The friendship propagated, and after getting to really know Berl and his varying shades of vulnerability, Roe cherished him all the more.

But how times have changed.

Roe finally steeled himself and looked down, making a startling cry at what he saw, what he remembered, and what he suddenly felt. His mouth was trembling in horror.

Deglin had chosen the letters carefully for his victim, each worse than the last. Fourteen in total, eight on the left and six on the right. Not only did the Priority make sure Roe wouldn't forget who he was…but also that the citizens would never forget after watching his corpse hang from the Hardscape.

On his left forearm, UNWANTED was burned in place, while his right bore the Deglin name with a savage slash through it.

Before the branding commenced, Roe did his best not to squirm. Despite an inborn desire to plead for mercy, Roe's teeth latched onto his tongue to prevent this. He only demanded the Priority do two things, to perform the torture himself and to look him in the eyes as he did so.

"Who do you take me for?" Deglin scoffed, appraising the fierce glow in front of him. "I shall savor this more than it shall pain you, heretic."

Fortunately, there was no memory of what happened thereafter. Only his arms told part of the story and that was sufficient. His thoughts shifted to the morning where it all changed, the market. Among the crates of produce, where he saw the phantom he missed, his mother. For Roe, the feeling that brought his attention to her was the same one he felt sitting there in that cell. He gazed up and allowed his eyes to adjust but saw no one.

Shaking his head as he looked back down, he grabbed one of the smooth cold bars and rubbed his hands up and down on it, then another. The cool trace made him refreshed in such a hot and stifling building. But there was something he didn't expect to touch, a hand, that stopped his comfort. He startled and saw... *her*. Sure enough, his mother was back. Not in white though, she changed to the colors of mourning.

"You're back?"

She nodded, kneeling by the rusty bars. She appeared to want nothing more than to gaze at Roe.

"Why did you leave me again? The market? You came to me and left," he said hopelessly. "I was finally getting along okay without you and Father and Armin! I had forgotten what abandonment felt like and now you're helping me learn it all over again." He had no intention of making amends with her. She was developing a knack for hurting him.

"I had to," she said gently. "You simply don't understand what's going on right now, precious."

He narrowed his eyes.

"You've *never* called me that before," he said, knowing the pet name was new to him. There was a slip up in her façade and he found this very peculiar.

"It's not important, Roland! Listen to me!"

He tapped the bars of the cell with his hand. "I've got all the time in the world—er I would except your son's a criminal. I'm gonna die soon."

"Oh, what little you know. So far, you've done what's needed to be done. We couldn't be more thrilled with the results," she smiled.

"I killed someone!"

"Yes...a deviation, but given the circumstances, it was inevitable. Don't linger on it."

He asked who the "we" she mentioned entailed, but Roe came to a startling conclusion before she could answer.

"It's you!" he pointed, forgetting the searing pain the motion would cause. "You've been writing the messages."

She nodded.

"Why?"

"To guide you. To allow yourself to awaken."

The metallic sounds of a grate being unlocked echoed down at them. She backed away.

"Leaving again?" Roe said with false disappointment. "Not surprised, you're quite good at it. But I need to ask: Why did you lure the girl into danger? Why did you start all of this?"

The words were soft, but he barely heard her say, "To set you free."

She then disappeared back into the unlit recess of the jail.

Someone was coming, and the banter of two voices grew louder. Tessa and another guard appeared by his cell. He stood up to meet her, amazed she was allowed to be there.

"How did you-"

"-I...was let off," she said evasively, peering at the guard behind her and choosing her words carefully, "mostly in part of my relationship with Berl more than anything. Ophelia...the others...I'm not so sure."

She looked at Roe's arms and shuddered before continuing with a quiver in her voice.

"I'm so sorry about what happened to you. I despised Ivan, but I wouldn't wish that on anyone. Ophelia told me the whole thing after they took you away," she said looking down. She had a long brown cape on with loose-fitted clothing. Over her shoulder, the guard kept his vigilance.

She continued.

"He was nice enough to allow me a visit with you, though I'm surprised the Priority allowed even a supervised visit," she gave a heavy sigh. "Before the captain comes, Roe...there's been something I wanted to tell you—Berl was weak."

"Weak? What are-"

"What he did was cowardly to see, that he not even look you in the eyes as he sold you out. But you, you're brave and strong. I guess it's taken me a while to notice it," she said in an unusually sensual voice.

Roe was nonplussed and gave her a confused look. With her index finger, she begged him to edge closer to the bars. He hesitated but ultimately obeyed.

"I must be dead," he whispered to himself.

"I need to give you something before I go," Tessa said, leaning in with vivacious eyes and a sweetened smile meeting his lips.

The cold metal of the bars pressing against his cheeks, and the warmth of her lips were all he could feel. His arms didn't burn agonizingly, and he knew not of anger or resentment. He thought of her and then immediately of Berl, which caused him to pull back. He tried to warn of Berl's disapproval, but she hushed him with a finger to his lips.

With her face still away from the guard, Tessa shot Roe a positively annoyed look followed by an overstated wink. Roe issued a wry smile, cottoning onto the act.

"That was...nice...Tess. I've been waiting for that since...a while," Roe said bashfully.

Rolling her eyes at his horrible improvisation, she continued her seduction and touched lips with him again. This time, he noticed how fragrant she smelled. The spice, the saccharine notes emanating from her soft cheeks; everything felt warm inside his body. She whipped around dramatically to the guard who found himself gawking.

"Do you mind?" Tessa shouted. "I won't get to see him *ever* again and you stand there ogling? You want a free show, s'at it? They don't show the good stuff out at Annica's Inn?!"

Her harsh tone startled him. He fidgeted with his hands and fumbled in his steps, but soon stumbled away standing at the fringe of the corridor. She whispered for him to reach around toward the back of her thighs.

Roe blushed terribly, "Tessa, I don't think-"

"Just do it, you big clod," she whispered. Then spoke up to allow the guard to bear witness, "Now's not the time to be bashful, my love."

The guard edged away out of sight, chortling to himself.

It wasn't that she wanted the touch specifically, but what was latched to the belt under the cape, his trauma gloves.

"How did you-"

"Meet me at the ministry building," she whispered making toward the exit. "Guard, I'm ready to leave this wretched place. I can't stand to see him like this. I need to leave."

Roe quickly secreted the weapons as they passed by her inconsolable act returned as though it was going to be last time she'd see her beloved. He waited a little while for the silence to be uninterrupted and then went to work on the door trying to melt the lock enough to force it open. Several attempts went by and with each, he nudged against the door to feel the resistance. Once more, he forced the door open, louder than he had wanted, but was freed.

He heard the frantic footfalls approach and hid behind a couple of barrels across from the cell. The guard realized his fault and scampered away to alert the others with barks and shouts. Sneaking out wasn't as hard as escaping Aurascape. Most of the guards were still canvassing the valley for Delphine, so the usual number garrisoned at the prison was not there to halt his escape.

Upon his arrival at the all too familiar courtyard of the ministry building, he saw the cityscape deserted. Nothing was stirring; it was an eerie feeling. Whispers of his name led him to a trail that traveled out to the hills behind the squat building. Tessa was subtly waving her hand, crouching on a nearby hillside sprawling in undergrowth. This vantage gave a great view over the buildings near the Hardscape where a line was forming in front of the tower.

With good fortune, Roe was able to scale down the embankment just outside the jail. The guards in the distance could be heard shouting threats and directing people to stay in line nearby. On his hand and knees, Roe slowly crawled up to meet her.

"Might I say you are about as romantic as a rugburn," she huffed.

"Tess? What's going on? What's with the line?"

"Roe, while you were locked up, the Priority's been growing paranoid about Delphine. He's rounding people up and interrogating them-"

"-But none of them know anything! Only a handful of us do-"

"Exactly! He's losing it, losing control of the city. Warrick's murder—that sentinel Una—now Ivan's death has them filled with insecurity. Hasn't been this many high-profile murders under any Priority in such a short time. All of this lumped in with the missing grayclan girl has made him look horrible as a leader. To instill fear in his people must be his last resort," she said sagely.

Roe asked her about the fate of the others and discovered Berl was forced to "hide for safety", as Deglin put it. Tessa feared that this wasn't the case. Ophelia had been stolen out of Pinnacle to the hideout where Delphine was which was utterly farfetched for him to fully comprehend.

"I find that hard to believe. No way Deglin let you all go willy-nilly!"

She shook her head.

"Because he didn't. You see," Tessa bit her lip, "we had a bit of help from someone…unexpected. In fact, that's how I got a hold of your trauma gloves."

When he asked who the new ally was, he didn't expect to find out in the way he did. Strong, callused hands gripped his shoulders in the same manner as the one he felt in the training yard…

No, it couldn't be!

An icy feeling hit him, as he looked at her in horror. Roe didn't have to turn around to know who it was but did so to distance himself from the unforgiving presence.

In the gentle glow of the silvery blue lamps, Captain Raleigh's stern, green eyes and a short crop of gray hair gave Roe cause to fear for his life. Raleigh was smiling like a fiend.

"Sham. Looks like we got work to do."

Chapter Twenty

The Assault

"In spite of a glowing commendation from myself to the Regency, the Pinnacle Guardsman known as Brevin Raleigh has unexpectedly declined appointment as a sentinel. His quick thinking led to a premature ending to the Heretics' rebellion. The Suicide of Pinnacle has been prevented. I shall have to invoke the Decree of Valor to be sure I have his loyalty."

-- Fragmented passage from
Priority Flood's journal

"What do you know?!" Priority Deglin roared at the figure standing before him. "Tell me or I'll beat it out of you!"

I don't recognize you, Sentinel. Where's my son? What have you done with him? the beleaguered man thought savagely as the quivering figure took another step back, only to have two more sentinels hold him still.

"Tell me where they are, and you won't be harmed—you know more than you let on, boy! I've lost one son tonight, I won't lose another," yelled Deglin.

"I-I don't know anything…" the sentinel whispered, wiping away a tear from his eye before it could cascade downward.

With a sickening grimace across his face, the Priority ordered him restrained, and crossed the room quickly to strike him across the face.

"Tell me *everything,* damn you!"

The guard squealed at the shock of the pain brushing across his cheek. "I don't know! I don't know! Please! Stop-" he screamed.

Deglin struck him across the other side and flicked his hand away, reeling from the pain. It had been cycles since he ever had to exercise the use of his own hands to threaten anyone let alone strike them. The power of his office had made the act obsolete. Why do it yourself when you had others so willing? This occasion was different. He could feel his grasp slipping, and needed to ensure his fingers still worked.

The sentinel's face was already showing blotchy contusions on both cheeks. A few more strikes and the guard buckled under the shock of the attack. The guards strained trying to keep him from tumbling to the chamber floor.

I don't recognize you? Where's my son?

"What is the matter with you? Have you no stones? Fight back, damn you! Fight! Fight!" Deglin spat at his boots and strode over to render one more slap across the boy's face. This time, his captors let go allowing him to fall to the floor and cower at their feet.

Ahh...it makes sense now. There's my son, Berl Deglin. The utter coward.

"Listen to me," Deglin hissed at the cowering black-clad mass, "if you truly know nothing else of the heretic's plans, then you are of no use to me as a soldier or a son."

"What d-do you wa-want from me, Papa?" Berl cried, trying to get up to his hands and knees. "I'll do anything—anything!"

"Of course, you will. I have power over you as both your father and your ruler," Priority Deglin said imperiously. "Show me your worth and listen carefully..."

The imposing visage of Raleigh gave Roe the same sense of revulsion he had when Una was struck with the bolt. He grew lightheaded at the thought of seeing the captain after his erstwhile threat to beat a confession out of Roe.

"Tessa, you trying to get me killed?!" Roe shouted. "Deglin put you up-?"

She shushed him urgently. The captain covered his mouth and yanked him hard down to the ground. The guards on the Hardscape gazed in their direction and Roe couldn't help but bury his head in the dirt, embarrassed.

"Slap me with Warrick's soiled britches if I ever seen a stupider clod!" the captain whispered savagely. "*Now* listen, I hate to disappoint this little victim fantasy you've been havin', but I'm not the villain here. We're after Deglin. You're a wanted man now, but as it stands so are we." He looked away allowing the words to finally sink in. Across his visage was an unmistakable look of puzzlement.

"What's going on?"

"Simple. Deglin knew you were hiding something and couldn't find you, so he rounded everyone close to you in an attempt to squeeze for the information. Suppose he hadn't intended on gettin' the information so easily…" Raleigh muttered.

Roe immediately knew whom he was referring to but allowed Raleigh to finish.

"…and since I escorted the prisoners away from prison rather than to it, well—you can work over how I am now aligned in this fight."

"Why? Not that I'm complaining, but…"

"We stand for the same thing, Sham. I heard about what you saw tonight. You weren't supposed to see it, but…you've lived so that you can spread the word of this tragedy. We can't talk here. If your goal is to save the girl, we gotta follow through on your plan. No going back."

"You don't mean…"

The captain nodded and brought his finger across his throat and pointed to Aurascape.

Roe interjected, "Wait! What do you mean by *my* plan? I thought we were in this together?"

"You didn't know? I had no qualms with allying myself to you as I had heard you had roughed out a master plan," he said with a tone devoid of sincerity. "*You* set things in motion when you saved Little Hex. The only way to really do that is to break down the Priority's power. Destroying the lamps is the best way to do that, but Deglin still has many allies in the guard, allegiances even I can't break."

In addition to his gift of allegiance to the cause, Raleigh also had another…gift of sorts to give. In his possession was Roe's sentinel uniform with the blood of Una and Ivan still on it, the same slop from the catacombs too.

"Gee, if this were an unmarked gift at my birthday party, I'd bet all my money *this* was from you. Couldn't even try and wash-" As the captain shot him his typical death stare, Roe took a lesson from Berl's many run-ins and corrected himself. "Thank you, Captain."

His blade was also returned to him, this cleaned off at least. Given the circumstances, Roe didn't bother being upset about the uniform being so dirty. It was better protection than the prisoner's tunic, something he could change out of at a moment's notice. The exchange ended when Tessa supplied his brands with a fresh set of untainted bandages.

"It'll still hurt something fierce, but at least it will stave off any infection at least until we can get you to a physician…assuming we make it out of this one," Tessa said applying the dressing despite her trembling fingers.

"Oh, and Sham?"

"Yeah?" Roe turned eagerly, wondering what the next gift would be only to find Raleigh's warm spit splatter across his smiling face.

"Just a little payback to ensure no hard feelings." Even the disgusting act couldn't keep Roe from maintaining his smirk if only for a little.

Tessa broke the lighthearted mood, insisting they head out immediately. Something was going on down below and the guards were on the move. The three stuck to the perimeter of Pinnacle initially. As they edged toward the front entrance to the south, they cut through a small, deserted neighborhood to save time.

Following the river out, nothing in the environment was different, except the unaccounted smell of something musty and metallic, a very faint scent that lingered but grew in potency over time. They tarried for a moment seeing no one was in pursuit to investigate the oddity. Roe stepped toward the river where it grew the strongest. The moist air carried the scent to him. Looking down, he saw the river was tinged with red, slowly growing darker.

"Blood," said the captain, clearly disgusted.

What followed the blood was a ragged shape of a body floating in the current. A few more bobbing silhouettes followed. No one said anything, but they all stood there watching them float down and out of sight.

"Resistance was their crime," the captain said grimly.

Of course, Roe thought, they'd deny questioning since they didn't know anything. The fact the people were being treated in such a manner as they did, suggested this was the case and showed Deglin's tightening grip on the city. The Priority had no reason to kill them unless they meant trouble.

Turning around to look at the city lit up against the twilight in such a vibrant and festive manner made Roe realize if he ever returned to it, he would probably be just another corpse caught in the current. Seeing the dead bodies turned their brisk walk into something much more urgent.

Tessa led the way as they plunged farther into the tree line of Visitant's Forest. At first, Roe thought Raleigh had no idea where it was, but soon the captain deemed Tessa too slow and trudged ahead of her, disappearing for a moment. When the two reached Tampson's best-kept secret, Raleigh was there accessing the door already.

The dugout was not terribly roomy to begin with, but it could hold the six fugitives with a little room to spare. Greetings and hugs were exchanged when the three arrived. The greeting to Roe was a firm handshake from Tampson and Ophelia's welcoming embrace.

"Do you think Deglin's spotted the dagger you planted in his back?" Tampson asked.

"If he knows you and Ophelia are gone, I'd say so. If not, he'll know soon enough. Can imagine the ugly look on his face when he finds out," Raleigh chortled.

Everyone was so caught up in the unexpected reunion, they had nearly forgotten about the reason they had been gathered in secrecy. Delphine, the lonely Visitant girl was sitting in front of the roaring fire, not paying attention to anything in the world around her. She just sat in front of the metal grate, motionless.

"She's been like that since you left, Roe," Tampson whispered. "I can't get her to do anything. She just says 'no' when I offer her *anything*."

Had she simply given up and not cared to even feel rage? Roe didn't know what to say to her, nothing anybody could say would ever be enough to console her. Was silence the answer? Roe didn't think so. When his parents died, Tessa approached him simply to talk without having any magical words to say. Nothing she said helped him wholly overcome the loss, but knowing comfort was near had been a good enough start.

Approaching her slowly, he sat down beside her facing the fire. Roe cleared his throat to issue a greeting. Again, she said nothing.

"Delphine...I...just wanted to let you know we're-"

"-Did you know?" she cut him off. "Did you know?!"

Roe shook his head quickly.

"Honestly, I had no idea that...that's really what was happening. I wasn't even supposed to be there, but the guards said you wanted me to be there to see you off. Remember, I just became a sentinel! They're only allowed in Aurascape." He shook his head knowing time was running short. "Doesn't matter. Not now. We're all here for you. We're going to make this right, not just for the ones we lost tonight or in the cycles past, *everyone*."

She grabbed an ember that was flung from the fire and rolled it around between her fingers. A foul smell emitted from her coarse skin.

"This doesn't hurt. It's nothing. Compared to what I've felt tonight…this feels like a tickle. It distracts me just enough until it grows cold and then I begin to remember why my eyes hurt from crying. You plan to make things, right? Then prove it," she said defiantly.

He stood up quickly and said with affirmation, "I will".

The others had already gathered at the table when he approached. They looked upon him as if they couldn't talk or move without him saying so.

"What do we do, Captain?" Roe said at once.

"Dunno," Raleigh shrugged nonchalantly biting at one of his fingernails.

"You must be joking! You're the Captain of Pinnacle! You are the commander, the tactician! How do you not know?!" Roe took great effort to lower his voice as he quickly glanced over his shoulder to see that the girl had remained stationary. Here's hoping he had been quiet enough.

"A couple things, Sham. First, I'm not the Captain of Pinnacle anymore. I gave up my position when I decided to help you and second, this is your operation. You're the leader of this fight. So, lead us!"

Roe ran his hands through his hair and allowed his body to collapse into the chair from the weighty burden that had just been placed upon him. He felt both frustrated and tethered to the guidance of the Dustman's words…

That there can exist something more than that of which you and I can see or hear! You're asleep…wake up…

It couldn't be, he thought. But what could exist beyond the Fog? Peril? Death? Roe was convinced Deglin's sheer determination to keep the pinnacle's barrier intact was of utmost importance. Of this he was sure. Another point was the fierce determination to snuff out heretics and anyone associated with their supposed dogma.

But why? What did they point to?

Dustman had alluded to the significance of these words. This simple collection of words was somehow a threat to those in power. Finally, one gross supposition was that Deglin's reputation was tightly interwoven with this idea of keeping everyone dependent and grateful for his efforts of holding the Fog at bay. But what if that meant—no, it couldn't be...

There was no going back now.

"Okay. This is going to sound insane—probably is—but I'm afraid our only course is... to destroy the magical barrier," Roe said bracing for the indignations approaching.

"We'll all die. They're for our protection! I want to save Delphine, but is there no other way?" Tessa pleaded.

"I don't see any! It's the six of us against all the guards and sentinels that Pinnacle can muster. If we're caught, well, at this point, a premature death would be our fate regardless. Deglin made that clear when he decided to try and execute me. But thanks to you, Tessa, I am not rotting in that cell. Ouch!"

Roe felt a swift pang of pain in his shin from Raleigh's boot. He, of course, forgot to acknowledge if it weren't for the captain, she wouldn't have been able to see him in the first place. Raleigh then proceeded to correct Roe's overestimation of their lack in number.

"We're not that outnumbered, not entirely at least," he said inquisitively. "Most of the guards show their loyalty to Deglin, true, but I've gained some allies that respect my command over his. They're seasoned veterans I served with during the previous revolt. Sham's right though. We need to destroy those lamps."

"All of them?" scoffed Tampson. "We don't have the time or the manpower to do that, old man! We don't even know how."

"You don't become the Captain of Pinnacle without knowing how to think in a crisis. We'll figure it out when we get there, relax will ya?"

"Pfft," Tampson replied. "I'll have whatever your having."

A case was made about the shrieks, the shadowforms, and the other beasts that lurked in the gray haze. Suddenly a thought sparked and bolstered a flame of confidence inside Roe; perhaps they could help make the plan work. He slammed his hands on the table with excitement and asked the captain when his men were coming.

"En route," the captain assured him.

"Okay. We move on the lamp standing behind us. It's the closest and would provide us with some protection when we need it. We take it and destroy it. Just the one, nothing more should be necessary if what I'm thinking is right anyhow. Tampson and the captain are coming with me. Tessa you stay here with Ophelia."

Tessa rejected this idea immediately, but Roe luckily had anticipated this and explained to her that he needed a fighter to stay behind and protect the other two should the need arise. When he phrased it in a way that involved her potentially hurting some good-for-nothing, he knew she would come around to the idea. It was but another case of Tess and Roe knowing each other too well.

Through the tangles and fronds, the three followed the glowing blue of the pinnacle lamp they were to attack. Except for Aurascape, Roe had never been up close to the structure in the wilderness before. There was never a need. Because the pinnacles provided the primary source of protection, most of the problems the city would face resided within the city itself. As a result, the towers weren't guarded with a lot of force. Roe had hoped the Priority wouldn't anticipate their move and be proven wrong. Since his escape from jail, he was sure Deglin learned of Raleigh's defection by now. They needed to hurry.

The hill from the habitable side was a gentle slope up while the other side seemed to have a sudden drop into oblivion. As they made the ascent, they had to stop for a moment as they saw a rider astride a blazebeast dashing from the tower. The creature's spikes were emphasized in the light of the lamp. From the look of it, they were heading back to Pinnacle with great haste. When he realized it was only a solo rider, Raleigh motioned them to continue upward.

Roe stopped short and watched the others sneaking their way up ahead. He checked himself, both his weapons and his emotions. He frisked for the trauma gloves and his blade to ensure they hadn't been forgotten, but he knew he was just stalling. He wasn't ready to kill again. Raleigh must have sensed his absence and hurried back to meet him.

"You ready for this?" he asked sternly. "This could get rough in a hurry, violent even. Ivan…didn't give you the chance to prepare for that, did he?"

Roe shook his head looking down.

"I know what we might have to do, but I just hope it doesn't come to that."

"Agreed, but you understand this could be goodbye kid —for good."

Death he meant; it was plain as day though the captain did tiptoe around the subject in an almost protective manner. But that wasn't Roe's focal at the moment. In a manner of minutes, he could be dead. The tussle with Ivan felt different because it was so sudden. But this…readying to kill or preparing for the grim finality of death felt so much worse when given time to think and allow all the horrible possibilities to flood a soldier's head and dull his bravery. What was going to happen in that tower?

"Sham! Snap out of it. Don't wimp out on me now," he beckoned toward a well-hidden Tampson waiting for their approach.

"I will! I mean I'm not backing out, I'm just not ready to kill more. Too many have died already," Roe replied, trying to harden his cracking voice.

"Unfortunately, more will die before the night's over. Don't show fear. These are sentinels after all."

The captain saw the boy's eyebrows instinctively raise from the stark truth. Raleigh sighed, trying his best not to show his frustration. His brawny fingers pinched the bridge of his nose looking as though he was rapt with the difficulty to choose his words carefully.

"Look, just let me do the talking, maybe we can take it without force. They may not know that I'm a traitor and we could get lucky. Just be ready."

Roe nodded and followed him up. As they drew closer, he realized how much smaller the other pinnacles were compared to Aurascape. Nearing its base, the placid humming began to emit from their target. He also noticed his vision was beginning to blur at its fringes again, his breathing became shallow, and pulling in air felt tiresome and burdened as if he was back in the Fog.

"Strength of a soldier, please…strength of a soldier," he whispered his prayer under his breath.

The threesome stood bathed in a blue tinge; the glow intensified, through the stone archway leading inside. Tampson was told to wait outside the entrance, as he wasn't dressed appropriately for the ruse. Roe's eyes wandered and found him reading a crossbow that was equipped to fire as many as five bolts at once or rapid-fire, depending on the size and speed of the target he tangled with. This seemed to instill some confidence in their plan, but Raleigh didn't give Roe any more time to prepare. He simply followed and clenched his fists.

Inside the structure, was a bare stone chamber with the only roof being a canopy that stretched upward to meet the conical apex. A spiral staircase led to this canopy where the lamp itself was sheltered. To his amazement, Roe saw the orb hovering and spinning slowly held aloft by a blue column of trickling light that shot straight down before it met a stone statue, whose arms were stretched high above as if readying itself to catch it. The room had five guards, all sentinels. Two were stationed at the top looking at the orb while three idly sat at a table playing a card game. Roe flanked the captain by a few steps and walked over to meet them.

The sentinels stood straight up at attention for Raleigh who said confidently, "At ease, gentleman. I'm here on inspection. Report."

"Sir, nothing out of the ordinary here. However, I'm worried about what's going on at Aurascape," one said. The captain asked him about his concern. The word had come to him that many of the guards were being dispatched to the forest and combing through it for a secret location. The search in Pinnacle had been fruitless.

"I was uninformed of this. Who told you?"

"Don't you know, sir? A sentinel came by a moment ago and gave us word from Priority Deglin. Come to think of it, it was his boy."

Roe whispered impulsively, "Berl".

They all looked at him nodding. It was him they saw leaving. He wasn't hiding, but actively trying to stop the cause. His best friend was single-handedly trying to sabotage the rebellion. Roe dolefully gazed over to the captain and saw the anger building in his once expressionless face. He was grinding his teeth and the bones in his hands cracked.

"Why are they searching there?!" Raleigh demanded.

It was Delphine! Of this, Roe was gravely sure. Berl somehow knew of Tampson's hideout. But how? Roe's best guess was that Berl had in fact seen Tessa leaving with someone but couldn't tell who.

"The grayclan girl sir, th-they think she may be there along with the defectors," the guard faltered.

"I need you to take your men and go find them; it's alarming to waste such a resource to find a fabled location in the tangled growth of wilderness out there. You're better off finding them in the villages or Pinnacle! How dare that man command *my* sentinels behind my back?!" Raleigh yelled rather convincingly.

Roe was hoping that the captain's fierce voice would intimidate the guards, but these were sentinels of course, not the typical rabble of Pinnacle Guard.

It didn't work.

"Sir, our orders from the Priority himself were to keep vigil here and not leave under any circumstances. His word trumps yours, sir," the other added respectfully.

They were running out of time, and Roe grunted with impatience. The captain heard this and didn't hesitate. With furrowed eyebrows and an alarming sound of his blade hissing out of its scabbard, Raleigh gave the guards one last chance to live. Roe felt his body grow numb at what was unfolding.

Raleigh sighed as if bracing for what was to come.

"Son," he said, with the air of a caring father, "you'd best leave now while you still can."

The sentinel gasped, stepping back, his eyes widened. "Sir? W-what are you doing?"

The bravest of the three brushed himself to the front and unsheathed his blade informing the defectors, as guards of Pinnacle, they were sworn to obey the Priority over the captain, under penalty of death. The captain pushed Roe backward and swung with precision at the timid, youthful guard, cutting his wrist and disarming him on the spot. Raleigh used his leg to sweep him skillfully to the ground. The young man hit his head and lay there motionless, still breathing.

The other two unsheathed their weapons, one struck Raleigh in the head with the pommel while the other blade was angling into his gut. Roe, without his conscious will, let loose his blade and lunged forward to meet it. The harsh resistance made his arm recoil and his hand sting from the impact. Then he felt the man's kick to his stomach, which sent him falling to his face.

Captain Raleigh signaled for Tampson to rush in. Almost immediately, small streaks of blood shot out like red plumes from the foes' chests as they fell. Roe looked up to find Raleigh already charging up the stairs amidst the destructive flares raining down at them. He tried sheltering himself against the statue, but the force of the magic was shaking its foundation, causing it to shift awkwardly. Tampson tried providing cover for the captain from below.

Roe heard coughing coming from somewhere behind him. The timid sentinel, who looked no older than he, was regaining consciousness. Roe groaned at the sight. He wasn't ready to finish him off, but could he if must? Standing over the figure, he regretfully slipped his gloves on and started a flare in his hand. The heat was building and swirling in his palm. He was ready to spike it down, ready to snuff out this life at his mercy, but then something happened. His victim's eyes opened, and Roe stared into the brown depths of life. In them, he saw Ivan's eyes, his fear when his blade had rested in his chest.

"No," he whispered savagely.

He grimaced as the pain he felt from the intense force in his hand was smothered with the pressure of his palm. Thick smoke trickled through his fingers. Kneeling, Roe held his captive's arms behind his back.

"P-please, I don't want to die," the young man cried trying to scurry away.

"You won't. Don't resist and we won't hurt you. We have to destroy this lamp and we aren't leaving until we do." Roe was pleasantly surprised at his composure. Notwithstanding, the sentinel squirmed at the words, but Roe held on tighter. Somewhere above near the canopy, the captain was showing signs of fatigue, but he was still holding his own against the two virile men. Roe pushed himself up ordering Tampson to guard their captive and flung out his blade running up the spiral flight frantically until they leveled out to a platform wrapping around the beacon itself.

The men had been at it trading blows without any leverage gained, but the new blood added to the skirmish changed the odds enough. With his right arm, Roe thrust his blade at the exposed back of a sentinel who deftly deflected. Drawing the attention off Raleigh as long as he could, Roe knew his comrade could finish the job on even footing given the proper time. But when Roe heard a loud groan and the clatter of a sword falling, he feared the worst. To his relief, the captain finished a downward slash on his opponent who fell to his stomach. Raleigh's blood-flecked face sneered, ready for the straggler.

Those few seconds caused Roe to lose focus, who barely managed to see the blade coming at his torso ready to run him through. With a pivot, he sucked in his belly, narrowly missing the blade's path. But the sentinel swung upward striking Roe with his fists wrapped about the hilt. Roe fell to the ground, his vision fluttering in violent waves.

Raleigh seized the man from behind and pinned him against the wall.

"I have a bit of problem," he began, fingers tightened around his quarry's scruff. "This tower must be destroyed, and I'm in need of some inspiration. Please, inspire me and I'll make your death quick!" he demanded.

The guard laughed and spat rapturously in his face.

"Thanks. I think I've found it right here," Raleigh snorted.

With a surge of Gale from his left hand, he slammed the guard's back against the beacon causing a large flash of light to pulse from it. The hum turned into a waning buzz as the body fell through the space between it and the platform. His screams echoed downward growing fainter until it was silenced by a thud. The orb however swayed in the air, back and forth, in wider and more erratic arcs.

Captain Raleigh gave a throaty roar to evacuate.

Roe barreled down the stairs trying not to look at the calamity unfolding above. Raleigh was hot on his tail, urging him to go faster. There was a loud cracking sound from the orb that finally dislodged from its suspension. Bouncing against the hardened walls, they were pelted with the stinging rocks showering down upon them. The orb was giving chase, trying to plunge its massive force upon them before they could reach safety.

Down below, Tampson pushed himself off his captive and saw the closer his companions got, the larger the debris became. Bricks and cart-sized boulders were falling, some smashing into the table below sending playing cards fluttering about like leaves.

The orb pummeled through the statue whose arms were still extended upward trying to brace the fall. Instead, its arms crumbled. The large figure began to teeter toward the door just as Raleigh and Roe reached the main level.

The four figures had made it to their feet on the main level but were far from safety as they would soon discover. The foundation beneath them lurched and nearly threw them off balance as they ran out the door not waiting to see if the statue would remain in its stance.

Nearing the edge of the hill, the ear-shattering explosion behind them pommeled the serenity of the night as the statue's head punched through the wall. The momentum of the hill's slope carried their legs to almost unnatural speeds as they dodged their way down the slope blindly placing each foot without knowing if a root or rock was going to spell their doom. Loud crashes reverberated around them, as the debris punched through trees and careened into one another.

The dirt shifted beneath Roe's feet as he saw a large oak falling ahead, causing him to slide back to avoid it. He stretched out one hand to the ground to balance himself but slammed into the hardened wood striking his chest against its trunk. The noise from behind him was ominous as it grew in intensity. He looked back to find the quarried stone was not stopping. His legs felt bogged down and rendered flaccid at the surrealistic doom approaching.

Roe clawed on top of the tree and soared off as soon as he could find his feet. The world was spinning with his arms and legs fluttering limply about.

Finally, his face met the cooling touch of something. What it was exactly he did not know; for everything was quiet, and he couldn't see. The world became silent. His sight of the forest surrendered to a gradual cascade of darkness. What was to come next?

Chapter Twenty-one

The Battle of Visitant's Forest

"As for the shadowed beasts in that wretched oblivion, we can only speculate what lurks within. There have been no eyewitness accounts to date as anyone who has entered has not ever returned. The shadowforms are our only glimpse of what fate awaits us. From there on, it's purely up to our wild and fearful imaginations."

- Passage taken from The Fog of War and Other Intrigues

S hrouded in a world that was devoid of everything, even the senses, the only thing that felt native to Roe was fear. He was too frightened to move, too scared he would feel immense pain, or worse, realize he couldn't feel at all. He wondered if he was even breathing. Was he dead? Was this the beginning throes of death? Would he drift on in an endless void of darkness, or would he meet the ghosts of the countless dead? Maybe he'd meet his father again and Armin as well.

Roe waited motionlessly, but nothing happened. From deep within the recesses of this nothingness, he heard his name crescendo from seemingly nowhere. The echo shook Roe, shaking him back to where he needed to be. It grew closer and louder, light filtered inward. Green eyes were surveying him. Beyond them, the sky looked dreadful.

"Am I dead?" Roe grumbled.

"Not yet. If we stay any longer, that may change," Raleigh warned.

"Tampson? Where's Tampson?!" Roe shot up from his back. Raleigh pointed over to his left where he was found sitting on the ground reloading bolts into his crossbow. Roe rested his head back down with relief and asked about the other younger guard whose life he had spared.

"Didn't make it. Body's over there," Tampson said darkly. "Wouldn't venture to look though. Nasty sight."

Roe had mixed feelings. Though he felt utterly sick for the guard that died, he also felt relief wash over him that he had been spared from doing the deed entirely.

Tampson lent Roe his arm and hoisted him up to get a better look at the sky. The red broken streaks were faint, but their intensity and color grew with time just like he remembered from the first Freedom Rift. The ceiling was growing sluggish with large reddened cracks crawling toward the horizon. The mist wasn't swirling and shifting as it once had.

"A fractured sky," Roe said, awed by the enormous breadth above. The stories he had heard were true. "It looks angry at us... like we've done something terrible."

"Maybe we did, or maybe it's just a ruse," Raleigh said.

"What do you mean?"

"We're old enough to remember what happened the last time we saw this. If it continues, it could mean the end. I'm not convinced. Shortly after the revolt, the sky healed itself just like that, as if nothing happened. It didn't collapse and fall on us; the Fog didn't advance on us and the Priority was at peace again. It was too neat of an end for a catastrophe. I think it's a scare tactic to keep us obedient and terrified."

"And what if it's not?" Roe managed to ask, unsure if he wanted to know the potential grim truth.

"Well, that would make me wrong, Sham, and I'm never wrong," he said unfurling an uncharacteristic smile. Roe shook his head at the unfettered egotism displayed but was glad the captain was alive even if he still despised the boy. Roe's nickname stuck so, it appeared he still hadn't earned his real name back.

"Where were you on that day?" Roe asked eagerly. He could tell the men weren't eager to divulge, but Roe was feeding off the rush of a near-death event and wanted to be bold for a change.

"I was in the jail when it happened, that's where my assignment was and had been until I rose up to become captain. Nothing glamorous," the captain said plainly.

Tampson grunted as he locked another bolt into place, "I was a guard, a sentinel at that point…in the barracks…I think-"

A shiver went down Roe's back when a grotesque whooping escaped the Fog. The shrieks. He had heard their cries before, but this time was different. Destroying the lamp was causing the Fog to seep inward and where the mist went, the shrieks and other abominations would surely follow.

"Oh no," Roe whispered.

"You sure this plan of yours will work?" Raleigh asked.

"You sure the fractured sky is just a ruse?" Roe retorted back. "We better get moving, they'll be on us soon and we need to time this right. They're coming for the girls an-"

"-Things would be better if Peepants hadn't sabotaged us," the captain sneered.

"I see that! I'm not so sure what's going on, Captain, but I don't think Berl's hurting us by his own free will."

Raleigh waved his hands dismissing any excuses for Berl, "I didn't see no one on that mount holdin' a blade to his neck!"

Sensing danger, Raleigh then darted off in the direction of the hillock, with Roe and Tampson in tow. After a few minutes, the two arrived to find the captain talking to a grizzled sentinel before he plunged back into the dense undergrowth and shadows near the hillock.

"Who was that?" Roe asked.

"Reinforcements." Raleigh looked at his face and asked, "Why so worried?"

"I dunno…maybe because there's only *one* of him!" Roe whispered savagely.

The captain wagged his finger and whistled. All around them, flickering lights loomed within the darkness of the woods. Roe suspected there had to have been dozens of them.

"Do you ever get used to being wrong, Sham, or is it somthin' you have to live with?"

Judging by their flicker, they came from trauma gloves, which meant they were sentinels. Not very impressive in number, but what they lacked in numbers, they made up for in experience, tactics, and skill. Raleigh revealed most in their ranks were older than the Priority and didn't care for the youthful leader or his tightening grip on the city.

As the three entered the mound, they heard a sharp whistle cutting the air and found Tessa's sling already hissing at them. Luckily, it had been Tampson who had entered first as he anticipated his little sister's scare tactic and dodged the rock with the flick of his neck.

"Aim's a bit off," he scolded playfully.

Seeing her brother allowed Tessa to sigh with relief and relent, but she waited for the rest to enter before she allowed herself to sit.

"Well, what happened? Is it destroyed? Do we need to move on?"

"Little girl, you dare question my success?" Tampson said, with a slightly affronted smirk.

"Just asking. You came in looking like you came from a funeral."

"Made a few more funerals in the process," Raleigh said tactlessly. "But it's done."

Roe asked how the Visitant girl was, and Tessa stepped aside to reveal Ophelia on the floor with Delphine. The girl was smiling for the first time since Roe rescued her. He wanted to get the maid off that floor because he was sure her bones must be protesting horribly at her age, but the sight of her working her maternal magic on Delphine made him stay his tongue. Raleigh waited a moment before he called Ophelia to the table. The rebels all sat down and talked about the next phase.

"Turns out we only needed to destroy the one pinnacle, Tess. They act like a flood gate," Roe began miming the actions on the table as he explained. "You destroy one, the mist will seep past it like water, like a dam that's been breached."

Captain Raleigh's smile testified he understood the plan's course.

"But what of those things that you and Berl encountered, what d'ya call them? Shrieks? If the mist travels inward, they'd follow it and enough of it will be in the air to keep them alive! You're just adding more enemies into the mix, Roe!" Tampson protested.

"Besides, when we escape, where are we gonna go? Back to Pinnacle?" Tessa asked bewildered.

"Exactly," Raleigh cut in, leaning forward over the table keenly. "We all know we're outnumbered. That's why we need our newfound friends in the shrieks to help!" Their plan was met by pale, blank faces around the table.

"Hey you lot, listen! We use them as a diversion to allow us to punch through the lines of Deglin's loyalists. The distraction provided by the shrieks and the sentinels the captain secured will give us a better chance to slip by in order to head back to Pinnacle.

"Once there, we go to Aurascape and get Deglin alone to confront him. If we can get him to abandon his grip on the city, maybe we can reach an agreement..." Roe trailed off seeing the growing disgust on Raleigh's face. "You'd best prepare yourself at the near certainty that you're wrong about the Deglins. We won't have the time to pick you off the floor because you lost yourself in emotion. If that sissy is loyal to his father and his father wants all of us dead, you'd better not hesitate to snuff 'em both!"

"*If* Deglin doesn't surrender," Roe stipulated, "we will do what we have to in order to protect ourselves." He had hoped this would be enough to satisfy the man.

"That's also assuming we haven't just brought about the end of days for the scraps of mankind alive..." Tampson said gloomily.

Raleigh instructed them to wait for the fighting to begin outside in the forest. Only in the confusion of a battle, would everyone run for Aurascape.

"That means Little Hex and the old gal too," he finished.

Roe walked over to the girl and explained the plan to her in a way that would allow her to feel safe enough to approve. Her face had gained a little bit of her normal gray hue. He explained the diversion, the shrieks, and the violence that almost certainly would ensue.

"Running is all you need to think about," he said succinctly.

She understood that much, but the next part made him uncertain. In the corner on a stand, there was a lighter blade more suited for her. He didn't want her to go defenseless; they would kill her on sight.

"Delphine...take this. On the chance we get separated... if any guard tries to take you...use it. D'ya know how?" he immediately chastised himself internally knowing earlier in the night she had prepared to use a shiv on a combat-trained man.

She nodded and silently showed him on herself, dragging the blade across her neck and making a jutting motion at her chest.

Roe continued, "I promise you won't have to use it, it's just a precaution. If we do get separated, scream for me. Scream so I know where you are. These people here, are your friends. They'll protect you. We'll make it right."

It was determined the captain was going to protect Ophelia, Tampson fittingly would protect his baby sister and Roe was responsible for Delphine. They came to an agreement that under no circumstances were they to wait for anyone. They would stay only with the protector or the one being protected and meet at the arranged site in Pinnacle. It was a grim prospect, but they understood it lessened the group's chance of survival lumped together in the fray.

The candles inside were then extinguished.

In the darkness, they sat silently, occasionally rendering hugs and handshakes to one another in case the end was forthcoming.

Outside, the night became more active. The shrieks' ghastly noises were audible from somewhere behind the mound.

The loyalists' blades were heard whipping in the trees cutting down thick shrubs and annoying branches as they moved closer. Smoke was intentionally made inside the mound with wet pine needles placed on the fire to draw them closer. The fire pit was then smoldered. They sat in the dark anxiously listening.

"On my signal, we burst outta here and bolt! Don't look back," the captain whispered.

Outside, they could hear the muffled shouts of the loyalists. "Looks like we found them, but I have no idea how we can get to them. No signs of an entrance or anything."

"Well, find a way, you dolts," the leader replied urgently.

Suddenly, the stillness of the night was broken by one solitary explosion. The fighting began.

Yells and the sound of creaking trees shook the earth and roots out of place within the mound. The horrifying groans of the Fog creatures were audible even beneath the roof and all around the rebels. The mist crawled across the earth thick enough to keep the shrieks alive. The sounds of flare explosions doubled as ally rebels were on the attack now.

Amidst the dissonance of battle, Raleigh yelled "RUN!" The door burst open. Flaming trees and a reddened sky were there to greet them…

The rabble in the streets could not tear their eyes from the horror they saw streaking across the sky. The light cast from the lamps' artificial twilight changed to a dull, feeble glow; the structures themselves were slowly swallowed by the doom stalking toward the city. And it all was a pleasant sight for Armin as he marveled at what everyone else couldn't comprehend.

He did it. The little wimp did it. What'm I saying, Roe, you're the bravest of us all!

At once, Armin recalled the sight of his little brother in the jail cell through the eyes of the manifestation he had cast that allowed him a risk-free visitation. It was the first time he was even able to see Roe, in far too long. Though the moment was riddled with the pretense of magic, the Dispeller cherished the exchange and took in the blackened horror on Roe's skin.

Among his time fraternizing with the old rebels—now long since killed off—as an unruly adolescent, Armin had heard the rumors of the hidden, cruel side a scorned Augustine Deglin harbored. Seeing the awful confirmation permanently engraved on his brother's flesh was more than he could bear...

If you are unable to, brother, I'll get that harlot's brood even if it means I face Agathon and Mercy's Calling for it.

But Pinnacle was fresh in the tumults of the second rendition of the Freedom Rift. Only this time, Armin was going to ensure it meant the collapse of his kin's slavery.

Surely, the Head Dispeller would have to pardon him for Warrick's death if it meant the source of this horror was destroyed.

"But it's not," he muttered to himself as he fought against the panicked crowd running. The vantage from the Hardscape allowed him to scan the forest beyond and witness it alight from the specs of fire, the bursts of minuscule flames. The treetops fractured the gentle golden glow that grew larger from within. A wildfire.

His eyes burned with hatred as he stood at the menacing mouth of the Aurascape, whose guardians had abandoned it to wage a battle with their own brethren. His fierce hatred for Deglin carried him to the only place he knew the cowardly man would seek refuge, the depletion chamber…where it all started.

It would be there, tucked away in hiding, that Armin Elder would avenge his family. Priority Deglin would meet his fate among those he swore to protect: the innumerable voices of the Visitant men, women, and children that were permanently silenced. Waiting for clear passage to begin his ascent, Armin sat in hiding marveling at the precipice they were all fearfully looking at. They could not see all the good unfolding in the face of chaos. How could they?

They were still asleep.

Roe threw his head around to spot any pursuers or flares coming their way while trying to lead the girl through the tangle of branches and brambles. He tried to spot Aurascape's lamp through the darkness, but the bold sky dampened the tower's normally vibrant blue light. All around, tree branches were falling and splintering while billowing fires belched curls of smoke.

At nearly the same time Roe realized they were alone, so too did Delphine. He felt her prying away from him as he tried pulling her in tow.

"We have to wait for Ophelia! I'm not leaving her!" she screamed.

"No! Raleigh'll take care of her; C'mon! Keep up!"

Her feet dug into the ground. Without uttering a warning, he stopped and hoisted her over his shoulders. As he did, the air grew hotter and brighter. He turned and saw a flash of light. Throwing Delphine down, he ducked in time to hear the flare smack the tree behind him. Roe tumbled down an embankment and rolled into the bushes.

Delphine wasn't there.

Most of the battle had progressed behind him from the distant screams of men dying, but he was still afraid. He continued to call her and trot in different directions but found no sign of her, dead or alive. In the bushes behind, he heard someone approaching and he readied himself, friend or foe. The rustling grew louder as the Emlan siblings came barreling through them.

"Delphine, have you seen her? We got separated!" Roe cried.

"No! I thought she was with you!" Tessa yelled above a nearby explosion.

He struck a tree in frustration. They tried to get him moving. pulling his arms, but he refused. Tampson was tugging at Tessa's sleeve, pleading with her. Roe was going to stay in the forest to fight off anything that came his way, he promised Delphine that he would make things right.

When he heard the worst scream he could think of, he felt his heart lurch in place. It belonged to a girl. His girl. His responsibility. A single tear ran down his face as he ran toward it, a prayer tearing desperately through his mind.

Strength of a soldier...strength of a soldier...

CHAPTER TWENTY-TWO

AURASCAPE

"Aurascape. Its innards beautiful n' gaudy, a palace in its own right. But Master Deglin told me just the other day, it musn't look like a palace from the outside. It is to be stark, tall, and cold. To stamp out fear in the valley folk, and to strike fear in the Fog."

-- EXCERPT FROM OPHELIA VESTA'S DIARY

Roe's legs kept firing, with the siblings closing fast behind, all the while trying to convince himself that everything would be alright. But recent events allowed for an unrestrained imagination fraught with images of the worst type. He expected to find her gone altogether... or worse, the thought of seeing her dead, her vacant eyes staring up at the fractured sky.

In a clearing, he saw the shrouds of two beings, one big and one small. The bigger one lying on the ground with something protruding from the body. The smaller one was hunched over it. Long locks of hair were wafting gently in the newly discovered breeze, and he saw the gray-skin shimmer in the night.

"Delphine!"

This was followed by more jovial shouts he couldn't help but unleash. He slid down beside her without any regard for the corpse next to her. He hugged her, but her arms hung limp at her sides, uncaring to the reunion. She simply looked predatorial at the guard she killed. Then her gaze fixed up at her protector, her eyes glaring with unspoken unfaithfulness.

"Delphine, I'm sorry. After that flare...I had to throw you out of the way. I didn't mean for you to have to..." he said, grimacing at the body next to her.

Shocking everyone, she ripped the blade out of its resting place, blood painting her cheek. She wiped it clean and stuck it in her belt without uttering a word. Then, her head cocked to the side as a confused beast would; she studied the dead man intently. But then she crawled toward him on her hands and knees and straddled the body with her face hovering over his.

The man's eyes remained open, and she felt his still warm body, the kill was fresh after all. When the two locked eyes, she cocked her head and began to shudder. Right before her audience, she began to hum. She grabbed the man's eyelids and opened them taut, as far as the skin would allow. A small ghostly-colored aura began seeping from the man's eyes and emptying into hers. It lasted only a few seconds. When she was finished, she closed her eyes, moving her head slowly from side to side, before unceremoniously pushing off his body to face her companions. Something changed in her and she could feel it course inside.

"What…what happened to you, girl?" Tessa asked with a hand pressed to her mouth.

Delphine shrugged.

"Learning. Thrusting a sharp blade out of the body leads to more damage to the innards, bleeds more," she replied to herself, internalizing. She closed her eyes and nodded quickly mouthing words silently to herself as if readying to recite a long passage from memory.

"Yeah…but you're different somehow," Roe added.

"Not much though. The kill wasn't as fresh. I waited too long. I'll know better for next time… learning, after all" she finished tapping her head with her index finger.

"How do you know that?"

"Whispers among the clan say that these 'memory kills' are how we learn faster, grow quicker. Some of our elders have spoken about it in old tomes we have. No one could ever attempt it since killing's a crime in Pinnacle. Until now, we all thought it was myth," she said wide-eyed. "I thought now was as good a time to find out seeing's how this one was about to do to me what I had to do to him."

She brushed the leaves and pine needles off her frock and bolted through the trees without warning, calling for the rest to follow her. They looked at each other in disbelief but followed with the echoes of a battle still dominating the forest's background.

Roe occasionally stole glances over his shoulder hoping to see the missing remnants of their party as they began to disembark. But they never came. Tessa gently tapped him on the shoulder signaling it was time to go. In a forlorn manner, he sighed and whispered their names goodbye for the final time.

"In summation," Priority Deglin said bracingly, after hearing the scout's account of the battle recently unleashed, "Captain Raleigh has defected taking with him the numerous old codgers and derelicts that oppose my reign—simply because of my youth—and destroyed a pinnacle in the process. All of this, of course, happening prior to the breakout of a full-scale battle whose fires and plumes of smoke I can register from here?!"

He gestured wildly through the window of the depletion chamber, his once smoothly combed hair looked tousled in such a way that would make Ophelia cringe with embarrassment.

"And to top it all, you say you aren't finished with the battle report?" he asked, exasperated.

"N-no, sir," the subordinate said, his ashamed stare fell to his feet. "The beasts in the Fog have…well…joined the fray—attacking anything there. As it stands, the rebels have the upper-hand having flanked our forces and adding those horrors into the throes as well."

Deglin barked out his last—and for that matter, futile—commanding order to muster the Pinnacle Guard in a push to the forest. Now he could only brace himself against the festooned wall in defeat. The horizon outside was a violent smear of color seemingly undecided about how exactly it wanted to appear for doomsday. Somewhere below, he could almost hear the shattered cries of the scared populace running amuck pointing at the lamps' waning color.

He had heard of what color the lamps would take when their powerful circuit was cut but had always thought it as pointless speculation. It would be impossible to tell, he thought. No one in their right mind would desire to know what the end of Death's path looked like. What would defeat look like?

Each golden fluctuation in color from those towering structures signaled another victory in the fight for life, the fight for control and to give them the illusion of safety. That was what was passed down as your duty to Man from your predecessor, Augustine. It was the best gift a ruler could receive: subordination. Protect them from themselves. Through subordination, fear grew. Fear fostered the need for protection. You were to be that protection. It was to be your city, Augustine. Your people. They were destined to be taken into your arms and embraced, shielded from their fears. And with the doom of the Fog bearing down on us, how will you be remembered? As the man who was too kind for his own good. Too eager to dispense forgiveness...

The harsh and sobering thought stunned him. What would he do now? His defeat was nigh, but he simply would not let this be his final moments as the Priority of the Settlement of Humanity, the Defiant City.

They will come for me, the rising tide of vermin will come for me and I will be here, but not to forfeit. I will show them that Pinnacle's defiant nature was a mere projection of my sheer will. I will not give in. I will learn and start anew. I will start anew!

But that could mean only one way...a desperate final stand...

The thick, heavy lever near the alcove on the wall, remarkably stood out against the light in his vengeful, desperate eyes. A simple thrust of it and the grinding of gears would set things in motion.

As Deglin began to ascend the final set of stairs to the canopy above, he felt, for the first time in his life, the brisk caress of an invisible force against his skin. It frightened him dearly, making him hasten to the top. He thought this eerie sensation must have been what the mistsuckers felt before succumbing to the depletion chamber.

The bright and friendly decorations hanging from the towers and rooftops were overshadowed by the ominous sky and the screaming citizens beneath it. Children cried, women screamed, and buildings were robbed of their occupants.

The rebels dismounted and left their rides near the pens with the others. The thoroughfare was no longer crowded. Most of the people who had stood in a line on the stairs in front of Aurascape had dispersed, fearing the collapsing sky over the guards' knifepoints. It was such a dramatic change over the course of a day; children were playing in the now blood-tinged water of the river not so long ago.

Even though the rebels lost two of their own, the plan didn't change. It couldn't.

In the distance, the gathering mist inched closer, overtaking the scant villages and creeping to the edge of the forest, skulking its way toward the city. Around the valley, however, the Fog of War was growing weaker and thinner.

Something quite unexpected for the end of days.

The rebels kept their course. They were so busy scanning the area that Delphine managed to rid her presence of them. Yet, this time, something told Roe not to worry. He didn't know what happened to her when she killed the sentinel but landed on the supposition, that she somehow benefited from it possibly growing more dangerous because of it. Tessa had suggested she traveled back to the enclave to gather and evacuate before someone could stop them. Roe wasn't sure what was going to happen, but, at least, if the world was going to topple and engulf everyone, he wanted her to be with her clan and not among those that hated her. She was no longer his priority. Her willful disappearance from protection made this clear. And time was running short to mount a search party.

Halfway down the street, a Pinnacle Guard stepped out and pointed his sword at them. Then more white-clad figures appeared from dark entryways and around building corners to surround them. The pristine condition of their uniforms and virgin weapons made them look weak compared to the battle-weary rebels standing before them. The soldiers hollered with excitement and boasted about the rebels they've caught, flaunting the prospect of promotions they'd receive and the accolades they'd get. Those guards had only swords, not the ranged weapons, resolve, and grit the threesome had.

Roe looked at his comrades, they nodded, readying themselves. Tampson flung his crossbow out from behind his back and Tessa readied her sling by winding it up with rapid swings. Three large spiked metal shards were already in place, ready for her to unleash.

Before they could initiate combat, a deep buzzing sound punched through the air. Everyone stopped and gazed fervently skyward at the hazy ceiling above to try and understand what was happening. As it grew louder, people started to panic and hug the walls of the buildings.

The high-hanging lanterns swayed slightly on their lines, bobbing up and down. The sound's intensity quickly strengthened. Tessa, Tampson, and Roe crouched to use the distraction to their advantage and flee. It was no secret that the Pinnacle Guards were, by nature and through substandard training, skittish.

The sky above was disturbed. A swath was cut into it as a large craft abruptly appeared. It bore the general shape of a boat, except the stern and hull were bedecked with numerous circular contraptions that burned a hot blue color. On the side of it was the perplexing gilded lettering: *INF Morningstar*.

It hovered directly over Aurascape before vanishing into the mist. The force of its propulsion caused the lanterns to become dislodged from their resting place, tumbling toward the streets below. The ricocheting off spires and blunt impacts downward made the volatile oils inside explode. Their delicate casings burst into violent shards.

The people saw the explosions and scattered. Many were pushing each other, some tumbling down the tall stairs to the streets below. Some sought shelter where they could, but the lanterns supplied enough force from their fall to penetrate the roofs of the buildings. People careened out of those structures whose windows glowed from the fires within.

The rebels ran as well, but pell-mell into the chaos. Most of the lanterns were strung near Aurascape, exactly where the threesome needed to be. Through the punctuated bangs of exploding shrapnel, they jumped over flames and weaved through people to climb the stairs to reach the Hardscape.

By then, most of the lanterns had already fallen and were simply burning in puddles of viscous oil. The jail itself was alive with fire which was of no consequence to them until they heard a familiar voice pleading from within.

"Berl!" Roe yelled running for the jail but was halted by Tampson's firm grip.

"What are you doing?! He betrayed us! Nearly killed us! You really think he deserves to be saved after all of that?" he shouted over the roar of the inferno.

"Can you live with yourself if you let someone die knowing you could have saved them? There are two sides to every story, Tampson. Are you gonna help or not?"

But the question proved rhetorical as Roe didn't wait for his decision. He went in to find his friend, his brother. Shouting his name through the crackling heat, he found Berl near the back, isolated from everyone else. There weren't any other captives. No survivors of the interrogations.

In the cell, Berl was pressed against the bars trying to dislodge the door. His knuckles were white and raw from the effort.

"Berl, where's the key?"

"I…don't know!" he coughed. "I think one of the guards has it!"

"There's no one here! Do you have your trauma gloves?"

His head shook in despair. Roe took his pair out and tried desperately to break open the lock as he had before. Because of the imminent danger, he wasn't heating the lock nearly enough before urgently thrusting his weight against the door. Berl kicked at it as Roe applied his fiery hands to it until finally, it gave way with a sharp groan. The boys ran out of the jail without hesitation, fully expecting the roof to collapse at any moment.

"Where are your weapons, Berl?" Roe said, hunched over ridding his face of the smoke.

"I-I don't know. If they are here, they'd probably be in the storage chest the guards kept when they jailed someone. It's near the door."

The entrance was where he meant and fortunately, the jailer did keep a pair in there, though expectedly didn't fit Berl's adolescent hands, which meant they'd be extremely inaccurate. Still, they were better than bare hands. Outside, the siblings had called out to them within the sanctuary of the empty amphitheater. Tessa was whistling for them within its darkened foyer.

"We can't be seen out in public like this. There may not be guards now, but they wanted to kill us just a few moments ago before everything turned to hell," she whispered looking about for danger.

"Yeah, no thanks to him!" Tampson shoved Berl. Roe moved in between them, knowing Tampson's strength could flatten him to the ground.

"Roe, it's the truth! Don't hide from it. Things would have gone a lot smoother if he hadn't come along. Good men and women gone, all because *he* can't tell the difference between loyalty and doing the right thing!"

Roe inched closer to Berl and realized the discoloration of his face was not from soot and dirt. He was bruised across both cheeks and one eye that was swelling.

"What happened to you?" Roe asked, trying to touch his cheek. Berl turned away, shoving Tampson from him. Roe demanded the question this time and once more was given no response.

Berl was still seething over the recent interaction, not only of the horrible fact it was done by his father, but that he allowed it to happen at all.

Disturbed by the wounds, Roe grabbed him by the arms and yelled pleadingly, "Who hit you?!"

"My father!" Berl snapped. "Would it really matter who did this to me? The fact that it was done was bad enough! *He*...hit me because...because I wouldn't say anything. I wouldn't say where you were, so he hit me! I could've squealed but I didn't!

"After the captain left and you all disappeared, he knew you must have defected. I held out telling him where you could have gone, but then Father came in h-he...just walloped me over 'n over until I had guessed that Tampson's secret nook in the forest was where you'd be, but it was only a guess. I had no idea you would *actually* be there, Roe, honest! Where else in the valley could you have gone? He's my father...it was...hard...to lie to him. He hurt me so bad...I had no idea he could."

Roe didn't bother with the retort, having another shared bond with Berl that he was currently guarding under the bandages of his forearms, still gnawing with pain.

"But, Berl, what about the etchings I hid in my room? I told you not to say anything to your father!"

"It was a distraction. I had to fess up some information as he knew you were hiding something. I could have fessed up about seeing you leave with Tessa and the girl, yes—Roe I saw you three leave. But I didn't say a bloody thing! You didn't want Father to help so I tried to buy you some time to make things right like you wanted. We had no idea who made them and if they were even meant to be taken seriously. How was I to know he would see them as a threat?"

"What now?" Tessa asked, looking fatigued. Roe had to choose his words carefully for obvious reasons given the present company.

"Berl," he said gently "we have to stop your father. He's growing paranoid. He's having the guard execute resistors and citizens. We must convince him to stop this. Where is he?"

"What are you going to do?" Berl's eyes narrowed.

"We have to try and reason with him," he said softly.

Roe's ears grew warmer as he knew that if Deglin resisted, the three would need to kill the man to stop the madness as Raleigh had beseeched. They weren't foolish enough to tell Berl their true intentions. The inescapable problem was, how would the end play out knowing this was the most probable one?

Roe shuddered.

"Aurascape, at the top," Berl pointed. "He knew something was wrong with the lamps and went up there to see if he can stem the movement of the Fog somehow. What's wrong with the sky anyway?"

While using the Barred Ascent, Roe felt compelled to divulge what their plan had been.

"What?! You'll kill us all!" Berl had stopped in his tracks blocking further progress to the next level.

"No, your father is going to kill us all!" Tampson snapped.

Berl separated himself from the others, "Not if I can help it. He won't listen to you, but maybe I can talk to him, give me a chance. I'll make it up to you all and for those that died tonight."

"We didn't make this decision out of nothing. If your father knew about the grayclan being executed each Night of Safe Passage, he has a lot to answer for. This fractured sky was a way to get his attention. We'll give you the chance to reason with him, this is our non-violent solution," Roe said, feeling the pent-up tension building in his guts.

He hoped they weren't just telling Berl what he wanted to hear. Roe held out a faint glimmer of hope that the Priority wasn't truly unraveling and thus using any means necessary to keep his power. But Raleigh warned the young rebels to prepare for anything, even to kill. His presence was already missed, for the captain would know what to do. Hell, he'd take the initiative and burden the load they all felt.

Before he knew it, Roe found himself back in the chamber that took all those Visitant lives. Each Night of Safe Passage, the chamber made those aware, round up the hopeful creatures trying to find their home, and stole that hope as it stole their lives. Everything seemed darker and uglier from the first occurrence he saw it.

This time everything was like Deglin's dining hall at dinner. Elegant and vibrant, spacious, and serene. The flashback came to him as if it were happening again. Screams were echoing all around him and the music was alive again.

"Is...is this where it happened?" Berl asked.

"Yes," Roe muttered.

"I don't see any sign that there were killings here," Tampson said.

"You questioning what I saw, s'at it?" Roe spat. "You think I'm crazy? Think my brain got addled? *I* know what I saw. *I* know why I had to hide Delphine. I saw the glowing eyes and the crooked smile that appeared and disappeared." With each exclamation, he prodded Tampson's chest like a bully would.

He ran over to the pillars with the chains still attached. Roe was so frustrated with Tampson's doubts that he showed him what that ceremony was like. He took a chain, dropped to his knees, and hung there like he saw Nox and Myrna had. All the while explaining to them how he saw them die in front of the horrendous stone creature that stood before them outside its lair.

"Roe calm down. I believe you. I just meant that they did a quick clean-up job," Tampson said, sincerity registering in his voice.

"I did see it," Roe said feebly to himself.

As the rest approached the front where the dead bodies had been, they saw the pillars but no bodies, no signs of a struggle. The chamber was, on the surface, beautiful despite the atrocity it housed. It had an elegant ceiling with a beautifully adorned mural painting and support beams trimmed white and gold.

Then there was the beast itself, unceremoniously out in the open and obviously none too foreboding. Something was wrong. The eyes and maw didn't glow like the previous encounter. As they slowly moved toward it, a large crystalloid vessel rose from its head, hovering over it.

The flames in the brackets of the rooms flickered, slowly and then regained their size. Even with their presence, the light in the room darkened to unnatural levels repeatedly. When it darkened for the last time, Roe immediately sensed danger. With weapons drawn, they stood in the dark listening to a cold wraithlike voice and felt a shocking chilled breeze move amongst them. It touched Roe's shoulder and crawled down his back. The sprawling swaths of air wrapped themselves around each one of them, in very intimate places at times. Roe tried batting it away, but the sensation was inescapable, the task proved impossible; like he was enveloped in water but remaining dry.

Once more in the dark, the voice returned.

"Young ones?" it laughed. *"Steel yourselves children, for a demon walks amongst you."*

Chapter Twenty-three

His Right Hand

"The Path of Maleficence is the most predictable and the easiest you toil on. For it is here I will find you in your endless pursuit of wonton destruction and hatred for no other reason other than to fulfill your blackened hearts' base desires. And so it shall be that when you exhausted your supply of imaginary enemies, will you then be left to turn your malice upon each other. A fitting end, a punishment from His Right Hand."

– Unknown

Submerged in penetrating darkness, Roe grazed the shoulders of his friends as he trotted back to the safety of the group. That horrible voice made them cower toward each other like vermin cornered by a predator. In the chamber, they discovered its presence had left. But for how long?

"What was that?" Berl whispered.

"Don't know but it's not a friendly," replied Tampson.

Through some unknown power, the lights bathed the chamber and they could see again. Immediately, they fanned out across the room.

"*Can you find me now?*" the voice laughed.

"When we do, I guarantee you'll regret it!" Tampson said, gritting his teeth.

More laughing ensued, this time echoing from a different corner.

"*Arrogance? A pity. You're far too easy a foe. Why waste my time? Why disturb me now that my beloved children are unshackled?*"

The chamber went dark again, but briefly enough to allow the demon to appear without a grandiose entrance. It sat on the steps in front of the stone face. Its head was tilted down, its eyes closed, nodding its head up and down rhythmically.

"We need to find the Priority. We have to talk to him, stop him from hurting everyone," Roe said urgently.

"I am unaware of his location. He is near though." The demon winced and shook its head, eyes still shut.

"What are you doing?"

"Observing dichotomy. Watching my children kill and be killed. It's delightful and revolting. I can see them—all of them. I close my eyes and see through their many."

It opened what would be considered its eyes, revealing two dark, empty voids. The black metal staff that was twirling in the demon's wispy hands ceased abruptly. As it turned its head, the horrible eyes narrowed as they landed upon Roe.

"Your face is familiar to me."

"I don't see how. We've never met," Roe said, his throat parched from fear.

"I've seen you lost in my realm, the Fog of War, your folk mournfully call it, with a gray child. You killed two of my brood and escaped. That is how I know you, Berl and Roe. Your names echo with the memories of that day."

"We were attacked and had to defend ourselves," Berl cried.

His statement went unacknowledged. The cane whistled as it cut through the air, twirling effortlessly once more. The demon stood to walk up the stairs nonchalantly ignoring the repeated demands Roe had made to reveal its name.

"Does a moniker matter to you that much? Wouldn't it be more prudent to know my place in all of this? I am nothing more than a demon of Pinnacle, a shepherd of the people. I protect you from the forces beyond this place and in return, I feed on the gray ones they bring me, a contract. Their essence is particularly flavorsome.

"And I have you to thank for I cannot fulfill my end of the bargain and get what I am promised. You are the ones who broke the barrier. Your actions were predictable. Once you saved the gray child, you set things in motion that cannot be undone. The circuit is now cut, and I can no longer perform what I was meant to do. You have rendered me without purpose. For that, I shall simply render unto you the same fate and make that weak fool Deglin rebuild."

Berl quickly bristled at the idea his father bowed down to such a vile thing. Or had it been once…human? For one could see the fleshy tones of skin and facial features giving the entity some semblance to humanity. But smothering this flesh was a lustrous and rotten vapor, like a poisonous wisp, seemingly made of the Fog itself. It bore a shrouded cowl over its head and appendages like that of the mist. The body was cloaked in black, curling smoke that gave the appearance of a robe. Roe could see now where the glowing eyes of the shrine had come from—the demon's face, awful in appearance, but still possessing a flicker of humanity trapped somewhere therein.

Aurascape must have been a shrine dedicated to this beast. Pinnacle offered it sacrifices each Night of Safe Passage and humans obliged because it meant protection. But protection from what?

The son of Deglin shook his head slowly, "You're lying. You have no power over my father!"

"Stupid boy," it snarled. "Your father is nothing more than a servant to me. *I* am the guiding voice in his ear. His law manifests from my tongue, the same as every predecessor before him tending to the tethers of those structures man mistakenly calls…guardians. It is *I* who tell the people when to sleep and when to rise. *I* am time itself. I am the one they should worship, but every time one of you ineffectually cries for help, the Priority is too oft praised as their leader! Despair, for I am the one true leader of this realm."

Roe became more anxious as the demon's anger grew. The hue of the wisps emanating from its form was churning into a hotter color, like the pinnacle lamps burning midday.

"We just want to find the Priority and leave, okay?" Roe said calmly, his hands raised in a placating manner.

"No! I have protected him for too long. He will perish, but only after I crush you beneath my heel. Your bones will serve as portents for his future. If you wish to know the name of your demise, then I shall indulge you this one wish. I am His Right Hand, call me Carceram, the preordained antidote for maleficence. Now, oblige me this one request and challenge me in combat. Defend yourselves oh children of Pinnacle!"

Carceram strode down the steps, his visage burned like freshly stoked coals. With his quarterstaff resting atop his shoulder, he swiped the tip against the floor with a savage stroke that sent sparks dancing along his feet as its edge caught fire.

The group readied themselves for a deadly fight. Tessa still had the crossbow Tampson had given her before they escaped the forest, but instead slung it on her back and chose her deadly comfort in her trusty sling equipped with metal shards. Tampson had his own crossbow readied, while the young sentinels armed themselves with their trauma gloves. Everyone seemed to have the same idea that ranged combat would be their only chance to live.

With a crack on the floor, the demon swung out with his weapon. As his targets soon discovered, their foe's intent was not to crush them with its heavy head but to scald them with the arcs of fire sprouting from it. The impact caused a stone pillar to shatter as Berl was flung sideways from its force. Tessa unleashed a searing shard at the demon, striking his hand and causing him to wince. Tampson tried his luck shooting, but the creature was much too fast as it disappeared through a pillar of the room.

All was quiet.

The walls themselves seemed to quiver with laughter, the glass windows suddenly burst into a hail of shards raining down upon them.

"Who shall die first? The son of Deglin? No...I want him to suffer more. I think...yes, the lovely young lady. I want the boy to cry a little when I kill her first," it laughed.

"You can only hope to try," Tessa scoffed, though showing great fear in her vigilant eyes.

Roe edged closer to her as a precaution, but she shook her head backing up against the wall. He then turned his attention to the crystal vessel hovering at the front of the room. It made him wonder how a wonderous thing could encase such a hideous entity. Roe was about to reach for it when he heard the screams of Tessa. A choking mist began to engulf her, as the arms of Carceram wrapped around her neck.

She had no choice, but to drop her weapon to attempt to tear away the crushing grip on her throat. Roe was too far away to do anything effective, and she was struggling too much to use a ranged weapon.

Out of nowhere, Berl jumped on his back, trying to burn him with the energy in his hands. The fire didn't faze him; it was the mere inconvenience of Berl clawing at him that angered the creature. Tessa wriggled herself free to scurry away while Berl continued to burn the demon with his gloves.

With its torso exposed, Roe charged pell-mell with the point of his sword aimed right for the gut. Seeing his mark, Roe swung in an upward arc. The demon flung itself around forcing the blade's owner to maneuver away to avoid hitting his comrade. The force of the aborted swing sent Roe careening off balance and along the path of his foe's strike, causing him to skid across the smooth floor.

"I flick you away like pesky insects. Far too easy," it chortled.

"Ugh," Roe groaned, getting to his feet. "Cocky freak. Wait—Berl watch out-"

But the cry was too late as his figure was hurtled to the floor, the impact a horrifying sight that caused Roe to cry his name in dismay. He lay there motionless. Tessa rushed toward him, ignoring the threat still present.

The fire from the cane arced out again, this time at Tampson, narrowly escaping its path, but the crossbow in his grip was not as fortunate. He surely felt the heat of fire consuming it, as he quickly threw the weapon down, kicking it aside in frustration. Roe charged up again and flung flare after flare out toward the wisp missing both times.

"Damn it, this isn't working," he huffed. "I need to get his attention."

Roe taunted the creature to come closer, practically begging to be killed knowing it was bound to work on this arrogant fiend.

"Lost your touch? I figured the true leader of Pinnacle would have finished off some pesky children by now," Roe shouted mockingly. "Suppose that's why Deglin was placed over you! At least he in the end made people afraid and not from having an ugly mug like yours."

The creature strode toward him readying his weapon to strike Roe down but suddenly halted as he surveyed the room. His gaze suddenly fixed on Tampson who had been charging the creature from behind. The demon lifted him up in a torrent of haze that suddenly vanished down Tampson's gullet.

His body lurched and struggled a few times before casting a malevolent gaze at his sister.

"Tamps?" she cried. "What's wrong?! What are you doing? NO!" Tessa squealed, as Tampson began strangling her with his strong grip.

"Go on. Kill your friend if you so desperately long to help," the demon said in an equally mocking tone.

Roe, who had been caught up in the horror of Tessa's desperate strains, ran over without any concern for the demon and was seized off the ground.

"Here is your cry for help, your chance to play hero. Listen to her life being squeezed from her lungs. Do I not spark fear in you? What about the sounds of her death knell?"

A wave of agony crept through Roe's back, his body smacking to the cold marble. His vision began to blur, his hearing seemingly failing with it, for he registered an agonizing roar that shook the room. Forcing his eyes open, he saw the creature stagger from something that struck its head. What it was, he had no idea as it shattered into vibrant dust upon impact.

Through the distorted vision and amidst the ear-splitting screaming that still filled the area, Roe saw a figure standing at the opening of the chamber holding a stone-sized object in their hand, it glistening like crystal. He rubbed his eyes fiercely, trying to will his vision back to its acuity.

"Armin? It can't be…" Roe gasped, scampering on his hands and knees, putting great distance away from Carceram who materialized on the far end of the room.

Before the man could field a response, a figure rushed him, restraining him to the floor wresting the object from his hand. It shattered.

"Oh no," Roe whispered as he watched the possessed Tampson feverishly try to strike Armin. As the two continued their writhing tussle, the wisped being rounded back to his gnawing little annoyance.

"You dare question my power?! I have not begun to show my might." Roe didn't reply, not this time. He continued to crawl feeling hope drain from his heart. "You crawl on your belly and cower from real power!"

Roe reached for the stone-faced beast and grabbed its sharp incisor, trying to hoist himself up despite his legs protesting in an agonizing manner. Finding a place to rest in the carved mouth, he began to feel very cold. He was too weak to try and dislodge the vessel resting within its maw, as he couldn't even support his own weight.

"Hope this works," Roe gulped before addressing his foe for the last time. "You hide in the dark...like a coward. Taking the lives of...tethered women and children...the Dustman...would be ashamed...of how you hunt."

His Right Hand pointed the edge of his staff accusingly about the room.

"Words coming from such a vile thing. You—all of you—are nothing but an experiment. Your lives were brought about, not by any act of love, but by utility. You are but rats, to be used for a purpose you cannot fully comprehend. It matters not. Roe Unwanted, you will die now. I grow tired of your tongue and shall burn it from your mouth."

Roe was swaying in his seat, his fingers growing lifeless. He felt as though he could not dodge this one.

With one big swipe, the largest arc it could muster, the Pinnacle demon launched the final attack. The heat was fast approaching, and Roe could feel it begin to nip at the hairs on his face. Arching ever closer, he loosened his grip and tumbled down the steps.

The heat passed over him and he felt the shock of the force pummel the shrine. The demon shuttered madly understanding now that the burning zeal of his own rage and pride rendered his own execution. The staff clattered to the floor. The beastly carved stone face fell to ruin and the glow of the vessel within it began to fade. It rotated slowly, before surrendering to gravity. Mist gushed out in all directions, sweeping the floor like a tidal wave. Its path was unimpeded by the confines of the chamber as it cascaded through the shattered windows and many doors of the tower.

The foe was losing himself, his power leaving him along with his life force. Finally, much like the children that were created from his flesh, he started to leak black smoke from every orifice in his head, wasting away until the only thing left was his black cane resting in ash, its fire extinguished.

But Roe saw nor heard any of the demon's downfall since hitting the floor. With his body mired from injuries, he could only muster the strength to look with quiet awe as his brother, of flesh and bone, press himself from the floor, his foe unconscious. He drew a finger to his lips and slid behind a pillar, out of sight.

"A dream…all of it…must be…" he murmured as he allowed his head to rest on the cold hardened floor. He closed his eyes half-expecting the next time they opened it would prove none of the horrific past was real.

A shrill cry from somewhere in the dark recesses of his stupor, the words shambling to say his stepbrother wasn't moving, tore him back to his horrible reality.

Chapter Twenty-four

A Beginning and an End

"Good people, there is nothing to fear. And do you know why?
I am your Priority. I am your protector. I would save you, save
you from anything and everything in this world and in that
wretched opaque beyond. I will go as far as to save you all from
yourselves if that is what it will take."

- Extract From a written account of Priority
Flood's inauguration speech

"T amps, is he...dead?" Tessa cried. Tears were streaming down her battle-weary cheeks.

"No, Tess. He's still breathing, see? He took a good hit to the head. He'll be okay, you'll see," a woozy-looking Tampson said, hugging her tight.

Roe knelt beside him, tracking the shallow breaths being drawn. Despite his disloyal tongue, Roe couldn't help but fear the worst for his friend. In the eyes of his critics, Berl had redeemed himself. The vestiges of his bruised face and matted hair conveyed contrition from any prior cowardice. Roe saw the scared little boy that finally stood up to danger and paid for it, possibly with his life.

There wasn't anything to be done except finish what they started, but Roe wouldn't have to travel far. As he was pulled onto his aching feet, the Priority himself was serenely walking down the last set of stairs that led to the apex of Aurascape. Despite the turmoil of the night, he managed to look his best wearing a sleek robe that gave the appearance it had never been worn. Deglin didn't say anything and didn't acknowledge any of them, his eyes focused solely on his injured son.

"Will he be alright?" he asked, stroking Berl's hair.

"He will be, no thanks to that damn thing you kept on a leash!" Tessa cried.

"That *thing* kept us safe until you miscreants decided to burn half the city. My son's terribly wounded, and I have you to thank for corrupting him," Deglin retorted, easing himself back on his feet.

"I don't think the bruises on his face gave him much reason to remain by your side. I know what you did to him," Roe said coldly.

"It was necessary! It hurt me more than anything else I've experienced in my life, but I am a leader first and a father second. He was hiding something that threatened the continuity and security of Pinnacle. I had to find out, no matter the cost! Not that it matters now. The lamps are in disrepair, the barrier lost and now we all shall die because of it."

"The Fog of War?" Tessa gasped

"Worse," Deglin warned, staring gravely at them. "Why do you suppose the Heretic's Dictum was banned? That we were nothing but a group of power-hungry zealots? The answer to Man's demise lies in those words. The barriers you destroyed served to keep us safe."

"The barriers weren't meant to keep us safe! You just wanted total control 'no matter the cost' like you said. I assume then you knew what was happening to the Visitants all of this time?" Roe asked.

"Yes, I was aware. My intentions were for the best, for everyone. I did what benefited the greater good. I provided existence. After all, that was what Pinnacle was meant to provide. The city was designed to be an experiment where deceit was the cure for a malady that befalls our race."

"Designed by who?"

"Even I do not know. That knowledge was lost long ago. But this creation around us seemed to be designed to root out a commonality that has plagued our kind. This sought to answer the following: How would we react to a controlled environment where the rules were made for us, not by us. How would folk act if they thought the world might end tomorrow?

"Carceram was a creature created to conjure the powerful specter that kept Pinnacle shrouded. Such a feat of magic required immense power. It was supplied with souls, at first from lawbreakers and the worst of the worst. As time when on, we began to feed it souls that bore more lifeforce-"

"The grayclan," Tampson said savagely.

Deglin nodded and continued.

"A small sacrifice, but those putrid creatures enabled the righteous to live. Everyone would continue to live each Night of Safe Passage none the wiser to the machinations that went on, staying away from the curtain so to speak."

"Did you bother asking them if they wanted to die for us all?" Roe grimaced, trying to point an accusatory finger at him.

"Don't be ridiculous! No one would dare volunteer. It was the least they could do for stumbling upon the illusion and jeopardizing us all. They may have given away our location by lingering near our borders like a bunch of imbeciles! We gave them a chance to experience life and they needed to pay theirs back to us."

"What happens now? You gonna arrest us again?" Tampson said staring him down.

"If you're looking for another fight, Mr. Emlan, I must disappoint you. I have no intention of arresting you, for what am I the leader of? A broken city? To whom do I command? An army that fights itself? And what citizens to guide? You three have brought the Suicide of Pinnacle to fruition."

A tear rolled down his cheek. The disappearance of the oppressive Fog broke his efforts of any remaining stoicism.

"How could you?" Roe asked, allowing the horrible truth to sink in. "I respected you more than anyone else I knew! You were a father I could love and one I thought could love me. You let me down."

"Believe me, Roland, the feeling is quite mutual. I had considered you a son, but now I regret ever having the thought. You were the worst thing to happen to me, to Berl, and Pinnacle itself. My worst mistake. It is no wonder why you had no family when I found you. You will find out soon how grave your mistake is. You'll realize how you've become the executioner to your friends and Pinnacle. I swear by it, that one day the friends you've made will grow to hate you after what you've done here tonight."

A red glow bathed the room through the shattered windows. Deglin motioned to the lamp resting just above them. He stepped toward one of the broken windows, looking out and beyond the city.

"You see? It's already started. We're no longer hidden, no longer safe. I've failed everyone. I wasn't tough enough, ruthless. You made me soft and weak. Such a disgrace is intolerable. I know nothing of a greater pain…than failure."

"Don't make this difficult. The city can recover and so can you. You must redeem yourself and learn from your mistakes. That will take away the pain," Roe said in a desperate fashion. Despite the physical and emotional wounds, somehow, he still cared for the embattled leader.

Deglin edged closer to the window, kicking a shard of glass out of it. He gazed out into the dying twilight and shook his head slowly.

"What has anyone truly learned from tonight, but Man is its own enemy and is the malady itself. That is what the Dictum means…that is what Carceram warned of."

The greatest beast is Man… Roe thought to himself and gasped at the scandalous rationality of it, with the horrors he had witnessed all his life to bear testament to it all.

"But there was so much more that I desired to know…so much I was hidden from…what was it all for…perhaps in another life…" Deglin prattled on to himself.

He dragged his feet toward the shattered glass lying on the floor at the windowpane's edge. Roe felt an inkling of what he was doing but remained motionless thinking it wouldn't be that simple to get rid of him.

"It won't take away the pain of failure, but I know what will. Even though you have betrayed me, you can make it up to me by not telling Berl..." Deglin trailed off.

"Not telling him what?" Roe asked.

"Our secret. I tried...I tried...to be a good father. I tried to love him, truly, but I could not. I cannot love him. I tried so hard to protect my people...but...I have failed, and you have shown me my errors tonight," Deglin then turned toward the darkness of the night. "One day I shall begin again in a new world...and now...I go onward from this misery."

Through the violence and tragedy that shrouded the past few days, nothing came close to what Roe saw from Deglin after he finished speaking. The man he grew to call "Father" disappeared through the blackness of the crimpled window arch. He felt the grip of Tessa's hand on his shoulder as she wept. Roe had anticipated it, but he still lurched forward onto his knees. It alarmed him feeling the rush of tears wash over his cheeks, deeply convinced Deglin's death would have brought more solace than it did.

As she trudged through the deadlands that once were dominated by the Fog's magic, Delphine couldn't focus on the dead stalks that surrounded her people. Since the incident in the forest, she felt different but invigorated with the feeling that she was no longer defenseless. She felt stronger, fierce even. The strange and unfamiliar memories of those she did not know, however, were also present. Then there were faces that felt familiar yet vexingly could not place how she knew them.

A side effect from the memory kill. Must be.

Behind her, she could hear the cries of her people; some wept for those that had chosen to stay out of fear of the unknown confines beyond, and some mourned for the loss of their only semblance of home. One gray-skinned woman whom she had ordered to help evacuate the others was busy slowly dobbing black circles around her eyes.

When she offered the substance, Delphine pushed the dish away. Her cheeks bore black tendrils down her cheeks. Rivers of grief.

"We are in mourning, sister," the woman said appalled at the breach in custom. "For we have no home."

Delphine couldn't help but smile at that empty truth as she felt, for the first time, the sensation of wind brushing her snowy hair across her face in an annoying fashion. Then she gazed to the infinite horizon, no longer impeded by oblivion.

"No, we don't. We must still find one, but that is the thrilling part of it all. We have an honest chance at it now."

She had promised herself since the heartbreaking moment she chose to pry away from her companions—those she internally accepted as a family—that she would not look back from it. It was unintended, but the chaos provided her people with no better cover for an escape. No, to risk leaving only after a cease in hostilities would be unwise—their departure would render them with such naked exposure. There would be no chance to wait and pray for the rebels to win out the night. But she fervently prayed for their victory and for their forgiveness.

Her thoughts seemed to trace back to the motley handful of humans that risked their lives to see her people have a chance at continuing theirs, true and limitless. Most of her company had passed her as they slowly plodded over the hill into the new world waiting for them.

Delphine Of-Great-Duress turned a final and painful gaze back to look at the pillars of smoke, and the glow of gnawing fire and wondered if she would see any of her heroes again.

Roe heard it suddenly. He craned his neck and saw a pair of legs disappear up the landing above.

Reaching the stairs to investigate, he wondered what he was going to find up there and down below upon his return. Berl looked in bad shape, but there was nothing he could do until a healer arrived—if there was one still alive. With Delphine vanishing, Raleigh and Ophelia dead, Roe felt the blood of a city on his hands. He was preparing himself for death to rain down from above like the nightmare that started it all. Roe didn't want to see his friends die. For the end to come, he had to be alone for the calamity.

But something perplexing happened instead: the end didn't come. Death was nowhere to be found. Not stalking from the collapsing firmament nor bearing over the hills in a tide of churning clouds filled with gnashing monsters.

Atop the canopy that housed the lamp, he gazed up awestruck. The sky he knew ceased to be and a new one formed in its place. To the west where the city gate was, he saw a radiant black expanse stretch as far as he could see. It was dotted with small white jewels of light rendering the sight beautiful and reassuring. He suspected they must be the stars he was told of that existed so long ago. Everything looked so pristine and magnificent. Beyond, however, the scenery stopped looking so beautiful and reassuring when he turned his gaze away from the valley.

The unanswered screams in the night, the cries for help, were of the same nature that had troubled him for years. Even now they still went unheeded. Now they tried to claw their way up to him, like vermin escaping a flood. Ironically, these were pleas he couldn't allay, cries he couldn't bear to listen to. A knot formed in his gut and his knees gave way to the overwhelming weight of his mistakes and fear of the terrifying unknown.

Looking up at the night sky, the only peaceful entity he could find, Roe wondered aloud, "If Pinnacle was the experiment, then who was its designer?"

"That is what he would like to know as well."

Roe whipped around and saw Armin dressed in a bizarre overcoat, with a field bag slung over his shoulder sitting on a bench bathed in the crimson light of the defunct beacon.

"Surprised to see me, brother?" he said with a sheepish grin.

"I don't know what I'm seeing," Roe said, feeling overwhelmed. He stammered at the sight, then tore his gaze back to a world that was supposed to have been dead.

"I know that look. You cannot see things the same... when something you know to be the indisputable truth is... anything but."

It was true, Roe thought. Looking at the firmament glowing with the light of a new world, he wondered what other deceitful things lay hidden and what knowledge they were trying to conceal.

The individual that looked shockingly like his deceased brother stood up and slowly walked forward spreading his arms, "And now, Pinnacle has been awoken to the reality of the world it was sealed from. It is our job to figure out why and *we* couldn't have done it without your help, Roe."

"We?"

"Forgive me, brother," Armin said ruefully. "After all, it has been—what—numerous years, or should I say cycles now that I am back here? Dispeller Armin Elder...of the Assembly of Dispellers.

The Imperial Nation of Earth is here…after what you've done tonight, they'll want to have a word with you."

Despite the scandalous appearance of Armin and his disturbing tidings, Roe was lost to the external world. Skepticism flooded his mind and determining what was the truth—what was real— seemed to be his only guiding principle. The previous days were arduous and perilous; it felt like that of an unspoken initiation into a life he had no idea existed. His eyes widened, the hair on his neck prickled. His stomach broiled with nausea; his legs began to teeter.

I must be hearing for the first time, breathing for the first time, seeing for the first time. I must now be finally awake.

Whether wanted or not, something within his being told him that there was no going back. The Roe Deglin he once recognized was gone. What he had known his whole life to be true, wasn't. It plagued him with an ardent sense of betrayal and a thirst for vengeful inquisition.

The path was set. The fork in the road had long since passed. The end had come.

Suddenly, it became self-evident to the boy of seventeen. Roe had become an illusion killer.

The end had come and with it ushered the beginning of something far greater.

THE ILLUSION KILLER

Acknowledgements

There were a great number of conspirators and well-wishers behind this story, and all of them I owe a great deal of gratitude.

Foremost, I would like to thank my dad who was the very first reader and collaborator of this work. There were many brainstorming nights spent drinking beer and stargazing to push this story forward. A big thanks goes to my mom and brother, who were always a source of support and encouragement when times proved to be tough.

A special thanks goes out to Sharon, Skip, and the good people at Chanticleer Book Reviews for their help in putting these characters (and the author) through their paces during the scrutiny of the revisionary process.

Next, my gratitude must go to the people who gave their time and insight to improve this work, particularly Mary Waldrep, Shawn P. McDougal, Shane Allison, Rob O'Barts, and Rowan Donnelly.

Finally, a special thanks and shout out to the amazingly talented people at MiblArt for the fantastic book cover.

About the Author

J.V. Rutz is a longtime fan of the Fantasy, Science Fiction, and Historical Fiction genres. He was born, raised, and educated in the state of Wyoming. Much of the inspiration for the landscapes from the world of The Illusion Killer comes from real-life experience from his travels through his picturesque home state. Rutz now resides in the equally picturesque state of Arizona.

https://jvrwrites.wordpress.com

www.ingramcontent.com/pod-product-compliance
Lightning Source LLC
Chambersburg PA
CBHW030547180626
46816CB00005B/1435